Praise for *The Giver*

"With characters so real they feel like ~~~ ~~~ pelling storyline, this is a beautiful, special novel. I loved it and didn't want it to end!"

—Liane Moriarty, #1 *New York Times* bestselling author of *Big Little Lies*

"Moyes paints an engrossing picture of life in rural America, and it's easy to root for the enterprising librarians."

—*The New York Times Book Review*

"Epic in scope and fiercely feminist . . . an unforgettable story."

—*POPSUGAR*

"An epic journey of friendship, danger, and literacy . . . an ideal read."

—*theSkimm*

"Compelling . . . An epic feminist adventure that candidly paints a community's soul-searching with great humor, heartache, honesty, and love."

—*The Christian Science Monitor*

"[A] dramatic, sweeping story . . . As well as creating wonderful strong characters, Jojo Moyes has an incredible eye for historical detail—I really felt as though I was riding over those Kentucky mountains with those women."

—Sophie Kinsella for *Bustle*

"*The Giver of Stars* is a richly rewarding exploration of the depths of friendship, good men willing to stand up to bad and adult love. Moyes celebrates the power of reading in a terrific book that only reinforces that message."

—*USA Today*

"Bestselling author Jojo Moyes has a unique way of using her prose to make her readers feel great emotions—love, passion, sadness, and grief—and her latest novel, *The Giver of Stars*, does not disappoint." —Parade.com

"Inspired by the history of the actual Pack Horse Librarians, Moyes depicts the courage and resourcefulness of these women in loving detail. *The Giver of Stars* is a tribute not just to the brave women who brought the light of knowledge in dark times, but also to the rejuvenating bond of women's friendship." —Associated Press

"Timeless, Jojo Moyes' greatest work yet, and one of the most exquisitely-written—and absolutely compulsory—novels about women ever told."

—Lisa Taddeo, #1 *New York Times* bestselling author of *Three Women*

Praise for *Still Me*:

"Delightful." —*People*

"*Still Me* offers a warm conclusion to the *Me Before You* trilogy . . . resulting in the best entry in the trilogy yet. . . . Moyes has crafted a clear-eyed tale of self-discovery and the sacrifice required to live a life honestly in pursuit of the things you love. [It will] keep you sighing with delight to the very last page."

—*Entertainment Weekly*

"Jojo's work never fails to bring a smile to my face with her honesty, humour, and empathy about what it is to be human—[*Still Me* is] a must read!" —Emilia Clarke

"While the series may have started off as a romance, Jojo Moyes has turned Louisa Clark's story into one about learning to be, and to love, yourself."
—Bustle

Praise for <i>After You</i>:

"Jojo Moyes has a hit with <i>After You</i>."
—USA Today

"The genius of Moyes . . . [is that she] peers deftly into class issues, social mores, and complicated relationships that raise as many questions as they answer. And yet there is always resolution. It's not always easy, it's not always perfect, it's sometimes messy and not completely satisfying. But sometimes it is."
—Bobbi Dumas, NPR

"Expect tears and belly laughs from <i>Me Before You</i>'s much-anticipated sequel."
—Cosmopolitan

Praise for <i>Me Before You</i>:

"A hilarious, heartbreaking, riveting novel . . . I will stake my reputation on this book."
—Anne Lamott, People

"When I finished this novel, I didn't want to review it: I wanted to reread it. . . . An affair to remember."
—The New York Times Book Review

"An unlikely love story . . . To be devoured like candy, between tears."
—O, The Oprah Magazine

"Funny and moving but never predictable."
—USA Today (four stars)

PENGUIN BOOKS

THE SHIP OF BRIDES

Jojo Moyes is the #1 *New York Times* bestselling author of *The Giver of Stars, Still Me, Paris for One and Other Stories, After You, One Plus One, The Girl You Left Behind, Me Before You, The Last Letter from Your Lover, The Horse Dancer, Night Music, Silver Bay, The Ship of Brides,* and *The Peacock Emporium.* She lives with her husband and three children in Essex, England.

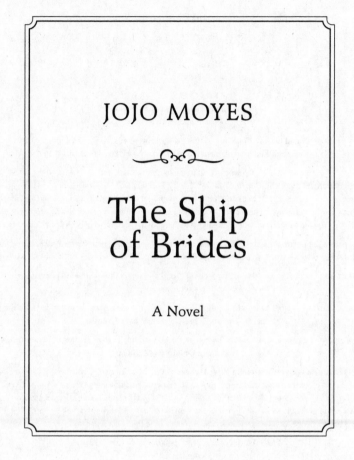

JOJO MOYES

The Ship
of Brides

A Novel

PENGUIN BOOKS

TO BETTY McKEE AND JO STAUNTON-LAMBERT,
FOR THEIR BRAVERY ON VERY DIFFERENT JOURNEYS.

PENGUIN BOOKS
An imprint of Penguin Random House LLC
penguinrandomhouse.com

First published in Great Britain by Hodder & Stoughton, a Hachette UK company, 2005
First published in the United States of America by Penguin Books 2014

Extract from the poem "The Alphabet" by war bride Ida Faulkner quoted in *Forces Sweethearts* by Joanna
Lumley reproduced with kind permission of Bloomsbury publishers and the Imperial War Museum.

Extract from *Arctic Convoys 1941–45* by Richard Woodman reproduced with kind permission of John
Murray (Publishers) Ltd.

Extracts from the *Sydney Morning Herald*, the *Daily Mail*, and the *Daily Mirror* are included with the kind
permission of the respective newspaper groups.

Extracts from the papers of Avice R. Wilson reproduced with the kind permission of her estate holders
and the Imperial War Museum.

Extracts have also been included from *Wine, Women and War* by L. Troman, published by Regency Press; *A
Special Kind of Service* by Joan Crouch, published by Alternative Publishing Cooperative Ltd (APCOL)
Australia; also extracts from *The Bulletin* (Australia) and the *Truth* (Australia): all efforts have been made to
contact the rights holders but without success. Penguin Books and the author will be happy to include
acknowledge for all extracts in future printings if the rights holders care to get in contact.

LIBRARY OF CONGRESS CATALOGING-IN-PUBLICATION DATA
Moyes, Jojo, 1969–
The ship of brides : a novel / Jojo Moyes.
pages cm
ISBN 9780143126478 (paperback)
1. War brides—Fiction. 2. World War, 1939–1945—Fiction. 3. Australia—Fiction.
4. England—Fiction. I. Title.
PR6113.O94S55 2014
823'.92—dc23
2014007440

Printed in the United States of America
13th Printing

Set in Agfa Wile Roman Std

ACKNOWLEDGMENTS

This book was a huge undertaking in terms of research, and would not have been possible without the generous help and time given by a large number of people. First thanks must go to Lt. Simon Jones, for his good-humored and endlessly patient advice regarding the finer details of life on board an aircraft carrier—and for particularly imaginative advice on how I could set my ship alight. Thanks, Si. Any mistakes are purely my own.

Thanks more widely to the Royal Navy, particularly Lt. Commander Ian McQueen, Lt. Andrew G. Linsley, and all those on board HMS *Invincible* for allowing me to spend time on board.

I'm very grateful to Neil McCart of Fan Publications for allowing me to reproduce extracts from his excellent and informative book HMS *Victorious*. And to Liam Halligan of Channel 4 News, for alerting me to Lindsay Taylor's magnificent piece of film: *Death at Gadani: The Wrecking of* Canberra.

Access to unpublished journals kept during this time has been fascinating and helped add color to a period I was born too late to experience. Thanks in this case to Margaret Stamper, for allowing me to read her husband's wonderful journal of life at sea, and reproduce a little of it, and to Peter R. Lowery for allowing me to do the same with that of his father, naval architect Richard Lowery. Thanks also to Christopher Hunt and the other staff of the Reading Room at the

Imperial War Museum, and those at the British Newspaper Library in Colindale.

Miscellaneous thanks, in no particular order, to Mum and Dad, to Sandy (Brian Sanders) for his marine knowledge and huge library of naval warfare books, Ann Miller at Arts Decoratifs, Cathy Runciman, Ruth Runciman, Julia Carmichael and the staff at Harts in Saffron Walden. Thanks to Carolyn Mays, Alex Bonham, Emma Longhurst, Hazel Orme and everyone else at Hodder and Stoughton for their continuing hard work and support. Thanks also to Sheila Crowley and Linda Shaughnessy at AP Watt.

And thanks to Charles, as ever, for love, editorial guidance, technical support, babysitting and for managing to look interested every time I told him some fascinating new fact about aircraft carriers.

But greatest love and thanks to my grandmother, Betty McKee, who, nearly sixty years ago, made this very journey with unimaginable faith and courage, and still remembered enough about it to give me the basis of this story. I hope Grandpa would have been proud.

In 1946 the Royal Navy entered the last stage of its post-war transport of war brides, those women and girls who had married British servicemen serving abroad. Most were transported on troopships, or specially commissioned liners. But on 2 July 1946 some 655 Australian war brides embarked on a unique voyage: they were sailing to meet their British husbands on HMS *Victorious*—an aircraft carrier.

More than 1100 men—and nineteen aircraft—accompanied them, on a trip that lasted almost six weeks. The youngest bride was fifteen. At least one was widowed before she reached her destination. My grandmother, Betty McKee, was one of those lucky enough to have her faith rewarded.

This fictional account, inspired by that journey, is dedicated to her, and to all those brides brave enough to trust in an unknown future on the other side of the world.

Jojo Moyes
July 2004

NB All extracts are non-fictional and refer to the experiences of war brides, or those who served on the *Victorious*.

The Ship
of Brides

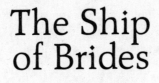

Prologue

The first time I saw her again, I felt as if I'd been hit.

I have heard that said a thousand times, but I had never until then understood its true meaning: there was a delay, in which my memory took time to connect with what my eyes were seeing, and then a physical shock that went straight through me, as if I had taken some great blow. I am not a fanciful person. I don't dress up my words. But I can say truthfully that it left me winded.

I hadn't expected ever to see her again. Not in a place like that. I had long since buried her in some mental bottom drawer. Not just her physically, but everything she had meant to me. Everything she had forced me to go through. Because I hadn't understood what she had done until time—eons—had passed. That, in myriad ways, she had been both the best and the worst thing that had ever happened to me.

But it wasn't just the shock of her physical presence. There was grief too. I suppose in my memory she existed only as she had then, all those years ago. Seeing her as she was now, surrounded by all those people, looking somehow so aged, so diminished . . . all I could think was that it was the wrong place for her. I grieved for what had once been so beautiful, magnificent, even, reduced to . . .

I don't know. Perhaps that's not quite fair. None of us lasts forever, do we? If I'm honest, seeing her like that was an unwelcome reminder of my own mortality. Of what I had been. Of what we all must become.

Whatever it was, there, in a place I had never been before, in a place I had no reason to be, I had found her again. Or perhaps she had found me.

I suppose I hadn't believed in Fate until that point. But it's hard not to, when you think how far we had both come.

Hard not to when you think that there was no way, across miles, continents, vast oceans, we were meant to see each other again.

INDIA, 2002

She had woken to the sound of bickering. Yapping, irregular, explosive, like the sound a small dog makes when it is yet to discover where the trouble is. The old woman lifted her head away from the window, rubbing the back of her neck where the air-conditioning had cast the chill deep into her bones, and tried to straighten up. In those first few blurred moments of wakefulness she was not sure where, or even who, she was. She made out a lilting harmony of voices, then gradually the words became distinct, hauling her in stages from dreamless sleep to the present.

"I'm not saying I didn't like the palaces. Or the temples. I'm just saying I've spent two weeks here and I don't feel I got close to the real India."

"What do you think I am? Virtual Sanjay?" From the front seat, his voice was gently mocking.

"You know what I mean."

"I am Indian. Ram here is Indian. Just because I spend half my life in England does not make me less Indian."

"Oh, come on, Jay, you're hardly typical."

"Typical of what?"

"I don't know. Of most of the people who live here."

The young man shook his head dismissively. "You want to be a poverty tourist."

"That's not it."

"You want to be able to go home and tell your friends about the terrible things you've seen. How they have no idea of the suffering. And all we have given you is Coca-Cola and air-conditioning."

There was laughter. The old woman squinted at her watch. It was almost half past eleven: she had been asleep almost an hour.

Her granddaughter, beside her, was leaning forward between the two front seats. "Look, I just want to see something that tells me how people really live. I mean, all the tour guides want to show you are princely abodes or shopping malls."

"So you want slums."

From the driver's seat Mr. Vaghela's voice: "I can take you to my home, Miss Jennifer. Now this is slum conditions."

When the two young people ignored him, he raised his voice: "Look closely at Mr. Ram B. Vaghela here and you will also find the poor, the downtrodden and the dispossessed." He shrugged. "You know, it is a wonder to me how I have survived this many years."

"We, too, wonder almost daily," Sanjay said.

The old woman pushed herself fully upright, catching sight of herself in the rear-view mirror. Her hair had flattened on one side of her head, and her collar had left a deep red indent in her pale skin.

Jennifer glanced behind her. "You all right, Gran?" Her jeans had ridden a little down her hip, revealing a small tattoo.

"Fine, dear." Had Jennifer told her she'd got a tattoo? She smoothed her hair, unable to remember. "I'm terribly sorry. I must have nodded off."

"Nothing to apologize for," said Mr. Vaghela. "We mature citizens should be allowed to rest when we need to."

"Are you saying you want me to drive, Ram?" Sanjay asked.

"No, no, Mr. Sanjay, sir. I would be reluctant to interrupt your scintillating discourse."

The old man's eyes met hers in the rear-view mirror. Still fogged and vulnerable from sleep, the old woman forced herself to smile in response to what she assumed was a deliberate wink.

They had, she calculated, been on the road for nearly three hours. Their trip to Gujarat, her and Jennifer's last-minute incursion into the otherwise hermetically scheduled touring holiday, had started as an adventure ("My friend from college—Sanjay—his parents have offered to put us up for a couple of nights, Gran! They've got the most amazing place, like a palace. It's only a few hours away") and ended in near disaster when the failure of their plane to meet its scheduled slot left them only a day in which to return to Bombay to catch their connecting flight home.

Already exhausted by the trip, she had despaired privately. She had found India a trial, an overwhelming bombardment of her senses even with the filters of air-conditioned buses and four-star hotels, and the thought of being stranded in Gujarat, even in the palatial confines of the Singhs' home, filled her with horror. But then Mrs. Singh had volunteered the use of their car and driver to ensure "the ladies" made their flight home. Even though it was due to take off from an airport some four hundred miles away. "You don't want to be hanging around at railway stations," she said, with a delicate gesture toward Jennifer's bright blonde hair. "Not unaccompanied."

"I can drive them," Sanjay had protested. But his mother had murmured something about an insurance claim and a driving ban, and her son had agreed instead to accompany Mr. Vaghela, to make sure they were not bothered when they stopped. That kind of thing. Once it had irritated her, the assumption that women traveling together could not be trusted to take care of themselves. Now she was grateful for such old-fashioned courtesy. She did not feel capable of negotiating her way alone through these alien landscapes, found herself anxious with her risk-taking granddaughter, for whom nothing seemed to hold any fear. She had wanted to caution her several times, but stopped herself, conscious that she sounded feeble and tremulous. The young are right to be fearless, she reminded herself. Remember yourself at that age.

"Are you okay back there, madam?"

"I'm fine thank you, Sanjay."

"Still a fair way to go, I'm afraid. It's not an easy trip."

"It must be very arduous for those just sitting," muttered Mr. Vaghela.

"It's very kind of you to take us."

"Jay! Look at that!"

She saw they had come off the fast road now and were traveling through a shanty town, studded with warehouses full of steel girders and timber. The road, flanked by a long wall created from sheets of metal haphazardly patchworked together, had become increasingly pockmarked and rutted so that scooters traced Sanskrit trails in the dust and even a vehicle built for breakneck speed could travel at no more than fifteen miles an hour. The black Lexus now crept onward, its engine emitting a faint growl of impatience as it swerved periodically to avoid the potholes or the odd cow, ambling with apparent direction, as if answering some siren call.

The prompt for Jennifer's exclamation had not been the cow (they had seen plenty of those) but a mountain of white ceramic sinks, their wastepipes emerging from them like severed umbilical cords. A short distance away sat a pile of mattresses and another of what looked like surgical tables.

"From the ships," said Mr. Vaghela, apropos apparently nothing.

"Do you think we could stop soon?" she asked. "Where are we?"

The driver placed a gnarled finger on the map beside him. "Alang."

"Not here." Sanjay frowned. "I don't think this is a good place to stop."

"Let me see the map." Jennifer thrust herself forward between the two men. "There might be somewhere off the beaten track. Somewhere a bit more . . . exciting."

"Surely we are off the beaten track," said her grandmother, viewing the dusty street, the men squatting by the roadside. But no one seemed to hear her.

"No . . ." Sanjay was gazing around him. "I don't think this is the kind of place . . ."

The old woman shifted in her seat. She was now desperate for a drink, and the chance to stretch her legs. She would also have appreciated a visit to the lavatory, but the short time they had spent in India had taught her that outside the bigger hotels this was often as much of an ordeal as a relief.

"I tell you what," said Sanjay, "we'll get a couple of bottles of cola and stop out of town somewhere to stretch our legs."

"Is this, like, a junkyard town?" Jennifer squinted at a heap of refrigerators.

Sanjay waved at the driver to stop. "Stop there, Ram, at that shop. The one next to the temple. I'll get some cold drinks."

"*We'll* get some cold drinks," said Jennifer. The car pulled up. "You all right in the car, Gran?" She didn't wait for an answer. The two of them sprang out of the doors, a blast of hot air invading the artificial chill of the car, and went, laughing, into the sunbaked shop.

A short way along the road another group of men squatted on their haunches, drinking from tin mugs, occasionally clearing their throats with nonchalant relish. They eyed the car incuriously. She sat in the car, feeling suddenly conspicuous, listening to the tick of the engine as it idled. Outside, the heat shimmered off the earth.

Mr. Vaghela turned in his seat. "Madam, may I inquire—what do you pay your driver?" It was the third such question he'd asked her, every time Sanjay was absent from the car.

"I don't have one."

"What? No help?"

"Well, I have a girl who does," she faltered. "Annette."

"Does she have her own quarters?"

She thought of Annette's neat railwayman's cottage, the geraniums on the windowsill. "Yes, in a manner of speaking."

"Paid holiday?"

"I'm afraid I'm not sure." She was about to attempt to elaborate on her and Annette's working relationship, but Mr. Vaghela interrupted.

"Forty years I work for this family and only one week's paid holiday a year. I am thinking of starting a trade union, *yaar.* My cousin has the Internet at his house. We have been looking at how it works. Denmark. Now, there's a good country for workers' rights." He turned back to the front and nodded. "Pensions, hospitals . . . education . . . we should all be working in Denmark."

She was silent for a few moments. "I've never been," she said eventually.

She watched the two young people, the blonde head and the black, as they moved within the roadside store. Jennifer had said they were just friends, yet two nights previously she had heard her granddaughter sneak along the tiled corridor into what she assumed was Sanjay's room. The following day they had been as easy with each other as children. "In love with him?" Jennifer had looked appalled at her tentative question. "God, no, Gran. Me and Jay . . . oh, no . . . I don't want a relationship. He knows that."

Again, she remembered herself at that age, her stammering horror at being left alone in male company, her determination to stay single, for quite different reasons. And then she looked at Sanjay, who, she suspected, might not be as understanding of the situation as her granddaughter believed.

"You know this place?" Mr. Vaghela had started to chew another piece of betel. His teeth were stained red.

She shook her head. With the air-conditioning turned off, she could already feel the elevating temperatures. Her mouth was dry, and she swallowed awkwardly. She had told Jennifer several times that she didn't like cola.

"Alang. Biggest shipbreaker's yard in the world."

"Oh." She tried to look interested, but felt increasingly weary and keen to move on. The Bombay hotel, some unknown distance ahead, seemed like an oasis. She looked at her watch: how could anyone spend nearly twenty minutes purchasing two bottles of drink?

"Four hundred shipyards here. And men who can strip a tanker down to nuts and bolts in a matter of months."

"Oh."

"No workers' rights here, you know. One dollar a day, they are paid, to risk life and limb."

"Really?"

"Some of the biggest ships in the world have ended up here. You would not believe the things that the owners leave on cruise ships—dinner services, Irish linen, whole orchestras of musical instruments." He sighed. "Sometimes it makes you feel quite sad, *yaar*. Such beautiful ships, to become so much scrap metal."

The old woman tore her gaze from the shop doorway, trying to maintain a semblance of interest. The young could be so inconsiderate. She closed her eyes, conscious that exhaustion and thirst were poisoning her normally equable mood.

"They say on the road to Bhavnagar one can buy anything—chairs, telephones, musical instruments. Anything that can come out of the ship they sell. My brother-in-law works for one of the big shipbreakers in Bhavnagar, *yaar*. He has furnished his entire house with ship's goods. It looks like a palace, you know?" He picked at his teeth. "Anything they can remove. Hmph. It would not surprise me if they sold the crew too."

"Mr. Vaghela."

"Yes, madam?"

"Is that a tea-house?"

Mr. Vaghela, diverted from his monologue, followed her pointing finger to a quiet shopfront, where several chairs and tables stood haphazardly on the dusty roadside. "It is."

"Then would you be so kind as to take me and order me a cup of tea? I really do not think I can spend another moment waiting for my granddaughter."

"I would be delighted, madam." He climbed out of the car, and held open the door for her. "These young people, *yaar*, no sense of respect." He offered his arm, and she leaned on it as she emerged, blinking, into the midday sun. "I have heard it is very different in Denmark."

The young people came out as she was drinking her cup of what Mr. Vaghela called "service tea." The cup was scratched, as if from years of use, but it looked clean, and the man who had looked after them had made a prodigious show of serving it. She had answered the obligatory questions about her travels, through Mr. Vaghela, confirmed that she was not acquainted with the owner's cousin in Milton Keynes, and then, having paid for Mr. Vaghela's glass of *chai* (and a sticky pistachio sweetmeat, to keep his strength up, you understand), she had sat under the canopy and gazed out at what she now knew, from her slightly elevated vantage-point, to lie behind the steel wall: the endless, shimmering blue sea.

A short distance away, a small Hindu temple was shaded by a neem tree. It was flanked by a series of shacks that had apparently evolved to meet the workers' needs: a barber's stall, a cigarette vendor, a man selling fruit and eggs, and another with bicycle parts.

It was some minutes before she grasped that she was the only woman in sight.

"We wondered where you'd gone."

"Not for long, I assume. Mr. Vaghela and I were only a few yards away." Her tone was sharper than she'd intended.

"I said I didn't think we should stop here," said Sanjay, eyeing first the group of men nearby, then the car with barely hidden irritation.

"I had to get out," she said firmly. "Mr. Vaghela was kind enough to accommodate me." She sipped her tea, which was surprisingly good. "I needed a break."

"Of course. I just meant—I would have liked to find somewhere more picturesque for you, it being the last day of your holiday."

"This will do me fine." She felt a little better now: the heat was tempered by the faintest of sea breezes. The sight of the azure water was soothing after the blurred and endless miles of road. In the distance, she could hear the muffled clang of metal against metal, the whine of a cutting instrument.

"Wow! Look at all those ships!"

Jennifer was gesticulating at the beach, where her grandmother could just make out the hulls of huge vessels, beached like whales upon the sand. She half closed her eyes, wishing she had brought her glasses out of the car. "Is that the shipbreaking yard you mentioned?" she said to Mr. Vaghela.

"Four hundred of them, madam. All the way along ten kilometers of beach."

"Looks like an elephant's graveyard," said Jennifer, and added portentously, "where ships come to die. Shall I fetch your glasses, Gran?" She was helpful, conciliatory, as if to make amends for her prolonged stay in the shop.

"That would be very kind."

In other circumstances, she thought afterward, the endless sandy beach might have graced a travel brochure, its blue skies meeting the horizon in a silvered arc, behind her a row of distant blue mountains. But with the benefit of her glasses, she could see that the sand was gray with years of rust and oil, and the acres of beachfront punctuated by the vast ships that sat at quarter-mile intervals and huge unidentifiable pieces of metal, the dismantled innards of the defunct vessels.

At the water's edge, a few hundred yards away, a group of men squatted in a row on their haunches, dressed in faded robes of blue, gray and white, watching as a ship's deckhouse swung out from a still-white hull anchored several hundred feet from the shore and crashed heavily into the sea.

"Not your usual tourist attraction," said Sanjay.

Jennifer was staring at something, her hand lifted to shield her eyes against the sun. Her grandmother gazed at her bare shoulders and wondered if she should suggest the girl cover up.

'This is the kind of thing I was talking about. Come on, Jay, let's go and have a look."

"No, no, miss. I don't think this is a good idea." Mr. Vaghela finished his *chai*. "The shipyard is no place for a lady. And you would be required to seek permission from the port office."

"I only want a look, Ram. I'm not going to start wielding a welder's torch."

"I think you should listen to Mr. Vaghela, dear." She lowered her cup, conscious that even their presence at the tea-house was attracting attention. "It's a working area."

"And it's the weekend. There's hardly anything going on. Come on, Jay. No one's going to mind if we go in for five minutes."

"There's a guard on the gate," said Sanjay.

She could tell that Sanjay's natural disinclination to venture further was tempered by his need to be seen as a fellow-adventurer, a protector, even. "Jennifer dear—" she said, wanting to spare his embarrassment.

"Five minutes." Jennifer jumped up, almost bouncing with impatience. Then she was half-way across the road.

"I'd better go with her," said Sanjay, a hint of resignation in his voice. "I'll get her to stay where you can see her."

"Young people," said Mr. Vaghela, chewing meditatively. "There is no telling them."

A huge truck trundled past, the back filled with twisted pieces of metal to which six or seven men clung precariously.

After it had passed, she could just make out Jennifer in conversation with the man on the gate. The girl smiled, ran her hand through her blonde hair. Then she reached into her bag and handed him a bottle of cola. As Sanjay caught up with her, the gate opened. And then they were gone, reappearing several seconds later as tiny figures on the beach.

———

It was almost twenty minutes before either she or Mr. Vaghela could bear to say what they both thought: that the young people were now not just out of sight but way over time. And that they would have to go and look for them.

Revived by her tea, she struggled to suppress her irritation that her granddaughter had again behaved in such a selfish, reckless manner. Yet she knew that her response was due partly to fear that something would happen to the girl while she was in her charge. That she, helpless and old, in this strange, otherworldly place, would be responsible in circumstances she could not hope to control.

"She won't wear a watch, you know."

"I think we should go and bring them back," said Mr. Vaghela. "They have obviously forgotten the time."

She let him pull back her chair and took his arm gratefully. His shirt had the soft papery feel of linen washed many, many times.

He pulled out the black umbrella that he had used on several occasions and opened it, holding it so that she could walk in the shade. She stayed close to him, conscious of the stares of the thin men behind, of those who passed by on whining buses.

They halted at the gate, and Mr. Vaghela said something to the security guard, pointing through at the shipyard beyond. His tone was aggressive, belligerent, as if the man had committed some crime in allowing the young people to go through.

The guard said something apparently conciliatory in reply, then shepherded them in.

The ships were not intact, as she had first believed, but prehistoric, rusting hulks. Tiny men swarmed over them like ants, apparently oblivious to the shriek of rent metal, the high-pitched squeal of steel cutters. They held welding torches, hammers, spanners, the beating chimes of their destruction echoing disconsolately in the open space.

Those hulls still in deeper water were strung with ropes from which dangled impossibly frail platforms on which metal moved to the shore. Closer to the water, she lifted her hand to her face, conscious of the pervasive stench of raw sewage, and something chemical she could not identify. Several yards away a series of bonfires sent toxic plumes of thick smoke into the clear air.

"Please be careful where you walk," said Mr. Vaghela, gesturing toward the discolored sand. "I do not think this is a good place." He glanced back, apparently wondering whether the old woman should remain at the tea-house.

But she did not want to sit and face those young men alone. "I shall hold on to you, Mr. Vaghela, if you don't mind."

"I think this would be recommended," he said, squinting into the distance.

Around them, on the sand, stood chaotic piles of rusting girders, what looked like oversized turbines, and crumpled steel sheets. Huge barnacle-encrusted chains snaked around everything or were piled in seaweedy coils, like giant sleeping serpents, dwarfing the workers around them.

Jennifer was nowhere to be seen.

A small group of people had gathered on the sand, some clutching binoculars, others resting against bicycles, all looking out to sea. She took a firmer hold of Mr. Vaghela's arm and paused for a second, adjusting to the heat. Then they moved forward slowly down to the shore, to where men with walkie-talkies and dusty robes moved backward and forward, talking excitedly to each other, and children played unconcernedly at their parents' feet.

"Another ship is coming in," said Mr. Vaghela, pointing.

They watched what might have been an old tanker, towed by several tugs, becoming gradually distinct as it drew toward the shore. A Japanese four-wheel drive roared past, screeching to a halt a few hundred yards ahead. And it was then that they became aware of voices raised in anger and, as they turned past a huge pile of gas cylinders, of a small crowd further along, standing in the shadow of a huge metallic hull. In their midst, there was some kind of commotion.

"Madam, we should probably head this way," said Mr. Vaghela.

She nodded. She had begun to feel anxious.

———

The man, whose generous pot-belly would have marked him out from the others even without the aid of his smart car, was gesturing at the ship, his indignant speech accompanied by sprays of spittle. Sanjay stood before him in the circle of men, his hands palms down in a conciliatory gesture, trying to interrupt. The object of the man's ire, Jennifer, was standing in a pose her grandmother remembered from her adolescence, hips jutted, arms folded defensively across her chest, head cocked in an insolent manner.

"You can tell him," she interjected periodically, "that I wasn't trying to do anything to his bloody ship. And that there's no law against looking."

Sanjay turned to her. 'That's the problem, Jen. There *is* a law against looking. When you're trespassing on someone else's property."

"It's a beach," she yelled at the man. "It's ten kilometers long. With thousands of bloody people. How is me looking at a few rusting ships going to make the slightest difference to anything?"

"Jen, please . . ."

Around Sanjay, the men stood watching with unconcealed interest, nudging each other at Jennifer's jeans and vest-top, some bowed under the weight of the oxygen cylinders they carried on their shoulders. As the old woman approached, several moved back, and she caught the smell of stale sweat, overlaid with incense and something sulfurous. She fought the urge to put a hand over her mouth.

"He thinks Jennifer is from some environmental group, that she's here to gather evidence against him," Sanjay told her.

"It's obvious I'm only looking," said Jennifer. "I haven't even got a camera on me," she enunciated at the man, who scowled at her.

"You're really not helping," Sanjay remonstrated.

The old woman tried to assess how much of a threat the man might be. His gestures had become increasingly abrupt and dramatic, his expression florid with rage. She looked at Mr. Vaghela, almost as if he were the only adult present.

Perhaps mindful of this, he detached himself from her and moved through the men, his carriage suddenly erect. He went to the ship-breaker and thrust out his hand, so that the man was forced to take it. "Sir. I am Mr. Ram B. Vaghela," he announced.

The two men began to talk rapidly, in Urdu, Mr. Vaghela's voice wheedling and conciliatory one minute, determined and assertive the next.

The conversation was evidently going to take some time. Without Mr. Vaghela's arm, the old woman found she felt wobbly. She glanced to each side of her, searching for somewhere to sit down, then backed a little way from the group, trying not to feel self-conscious—or fearful—of the blatant curiosity of some of the men. She spied a steel drum and walked slowly toward it.

She sat on it for several minutes, watching as Mr. Vaghela and Sanjay tried to placate the shipowner, to convince him of the naïveté and commercial innocence of his visitors. Occasionally they waved toward her and she fanned herself under the umbrella, conscious that her presence, an apparently frail old lady, would probably aid their cause. Despite her benign appearance, she was furious. Jennifer had willfully ignored everyone else's wishes and, in the process, set back their journey at least an hour. Shipyards were dangerous places, Mr. Vaghela had muttered as they crossed the sand, not just for the workers, but for those who were thought to be "interfering." Property had been known to be confiscated, he had said, looking back nervously at the car.

Now she mulled over the fact that she was going to have to walk the same distance back across the hot sand, and that it was entirely possible they would have to pay these people before they could leave, which would eat further into her already depleted budget. "Foolish, inconsiderate girl," she muttered.

In an attempt at nonchalance, she stood up and began to walk toward the bow of the ship, keen to be away from her irresponsible granddaughter and the blank-eyed men. She raised the umbrella and held it low over her head, kicking up dustclouds of sand as she went toward a shaded area. The ship was half dismantled and ended abruptly, as if some giant hand had cut it in two and removed the back half. She lifted the umbrella high to get a better view. It was hard to see much from so far underneath, but she could just make out a couple of gun turrets that had yet to be removed. She studied them, frowning at their familiarity, at the peeling pale gray paintwork, a soft color you saw nowhere but on British naval ships. After a minute, she lowered the umbrella, stepped back, and stared up at the broken hull looming above her, stiff neck temporarily forgotten.

She lifted her hand to shield her eyes from the fierce sun until she could see what remained of the name on the side.

And then, as the last of the letters became distinct, the arguing voices receded, and even in the oppressive heat of an Indian afternoon, the old woman beneath the ship felt herself possessed of a sudden and icy cold.

––––––

The shipbreaker, Mr. Bhattacharya, was unconvinced, yet even in the face of his mounting hostility, the growing restlessness of the crowd and even that they were now a good hour behind schedule, the young people were still bickering. Mr. Vaghela wiped his forehead with a handkerchief. Miss Jennifer was kicking sand angrily behind her, her expression one of sulky acquiescence. Mr. Sanjay wore the uncomfortably flushed countenance of someone who feels himself to be defending an unwinnable argument. Periodically he would look at Miss Jennifer, then away, as if he, too, were annoyed with her.

"I don't need you to have my arguments for me, okay?"

Mr. Vaghela tapped her arm. "If you will forgive me for saying so, Miss Jennifer, I do not believe your grasp of Urdu leaves you up to the task."

"He understands English. I heard him."

"What is the girl saying now?" Mr. Bhattacharya, he could tell, was offended by her barely decent mode of dress. Mr. Vaghela suspected that while he secretly knew the young people were innocent of his charges, he had worked himself into such a rage that he was determined to continue the argument. Mr. Vaghela had met many such men in his life.

"I don't like the way he's talking to me."

Mr. Sanjay moved toward the girl. "You don't even know what he's saying! You're making things worse, Jen. Go back to the car and take your gran with you. We'll sort this out."

"Don't tell me what to do, Jay."

"Where is he going? Where are they going?" Mr. Bhattacharya was watching Mr. Sanjay with increasing fury.

"I think it would be better if the girl left your yard, sir. My friend is just persuading her of that."

"I don't need you to—" Miss Jennifer stopped abruptly.

There was a sudden silence, and Mr. Vaghela, who was uncomfortably warm, followed the eyes of the crowd to the shaded area under the hull of the next ship.

"What is wrong with the old lady?" said Mr. Bhattacharya.

She was sitting slumped forward, her head supported in her hands. Her gray hair looked silver white.

"Gran?" The girl sprinted over to her.

As the old woman raised her head, Mr. Vaghela exhaled. He was forced to admit he had been alarmed by her stance.

"Are you all right?"

"Yes. Yes, dear." The words seemed to come out automatically, Mr. Vaghela thought. It was as if will hadn't had anything to do with them.

Forgetting Mr. Bhattacharya, he and Mr. Sanjay walked over and squatted in front of her.

"You look rather pale, Mammaji, if I may say so." She had one hand on the ship, he noticed, a curious gesture, which she had to bend awkwardly to make.

The shipbreaker was beside them, cleaning his expensive crocodile shoes on the back of his trousers. He muttered to Mr. Vaghela. "He wants to know if you'd like a drink," he told her. "He says he has some iced water in his office."

"I don't want her to have a heart-attack in my yard," Mr. Bhattacharya was saying. "Get her some water and then please take her away."

"Would you like some iced water?"

She looked as if she was going to sit upright, but instead lifted a hand feebly. "That's very kind, but I'll just sit for a minute."

"Gran? What's the matter?" Jennifer had knelt down, hands pressed on her grandmother's knee. Her eyes were wide with anxiety. The posturing arrogance had evaporated in the heat. Behind them, the younger men were murmuring and jostling, conscious that some unknown drama was being played out before them.

"Please ask them to go away, Jen," the old woman whispered. "Really. I'll be fine if everyone just leaves me alone."

"Is it me? I'm really sorry, Gran. I know I've been a pain. I just didn't like the way he was talking to me. It's because I'm a girl, you know? It gets up my nose."

"It's not you—"

"I'm sorry. I should have been more thoughtful. Look, we'll get you back to the car."

Mr. Vaghela was gratified to hear the apology. It was good to know that young people could acknowledge their irresponsible behavior. She should not have caused the old lady to walk such a distance in this heat, not in a place like this. It indicated a lack of respect.

"It's not you, Jennifer." The old woman's voice was strained. "It's the ship," she whispered.

Uncomprehending, they followed her gaze, taking in the vast pale gray expanse of metal, the huge, rusting rivets that dotted their way up the side.

The young people stared at each other, then down at the old lady, who seemed, suddenly, impossibly frail.

"It's just a ship, Gran," said Jennifer.

"No," she said, and Mr. Vaghela noted that her face was as bleached as the metal behind it. "That's where you're quite wrong."

———

It was not often, Mr. Ram B. Vaghela observed to his wife on his return, that one saw an old lady weeping. Evidently they were much more free with their emotions than he had imagined, these British, not at all the reserved stiff-upper-lips he had anticipated. His wife, rather irritatingly, raised an eyebrow, as if she could no longer be bothered to make an adequate response to his observations. He remembered the old woman's grief, the way she had had to be helped back to the car, the way she had sat in silence all the way to Mumbai. She was like someone who had witnessed a death.

Yes, he had been rather surprised by the English madam. Not the kind of woman he'd had her down as at all.

He was pretty sure they were not like that in Denmark.

Part One

1

Money in rabbits! At recent sales in Sydney best furred full-grown bucks
made 19s 11d per pound, the highest price I ever heard of in Australia. The
percentage of top pelts would be small, but at about five to the pound just on
4s each is a remarkable return.

"THE MAN ON THE LAND," BULLETIN, AUSTRALIA, 10 JULY 1946

AUSTRALIA, 1946
FOUR WEEKS TO EMBARKATION

Letty McHugh halted the pick-up truck, wiped non-existent soot
from under her eyes, and noted that on a woman with "handsome
features," as the saleswoman had tactfully defined hers, Cherry Blossom lipstick was never going to alter much. She rubbed briskly at her
lips, feeling stupid for having bought it at all. Then, less than a minute later, she reached into her bag and carefully reapplied it, grimac-
ing at her reflection in the rear-view mirror.

She straightened her blouse, picked up the letters she had collected on her weekly visit to the post office and peered out at the
blurred landscape through the windscreen. The rain probably
wouldn't let up no matter how long she waited. She pulled a piece of
tarpaulin over her head and shoulders and, with a gasp, leapt out of
the truck and ran for the house.

"Margaret? Maggie?"

The screen door slammed behind her, muffling the insistent timpani of the deluge outside, but only her own voice and the sound of
her good shoes on the floorboards echoed back at her. Letty checked
her handbag, then wiped her feet and walked into the kitchen, calling a couple more times, even though she suspected that no one was
in. "Maggie? You there?"

The kitchen, as was usual since Noreen had gone, was empty. Letty put her handbag and the letters on the scrubbed wooden table and went to the stove, where a stew was simmering. She lifted the lid and sniffed. Then, guiltily, she reached into the cupboard and added a pinch of salt, some cumin and cornflour, stirred, then replaced the lid.

She went to the little liver-spotted mirror by the medicine cupboard and tried to smooth her hair, which had already begun to frizz in the moisture-filled air. She could barely see all of her face at once; the Donleavy family could never be accused of vanity, that was for sure.

She rubbed again at her lips, then turned back to the kitchen, her solitude allowing her to see it with a dispassionate eye. She surveyed the linoleum, cracked and ingrained with years of agricultural dirt that wouldn't lift, no matter how many times it was mopped and swept. Her sister had planned to replace it, had even shown Letty the design she fancied, in a book sent all the way from Perth. She took in the faded paintwork, the calendar that marked only this or that agricultural show, the arrival of vets, buyers or grain salesmen, the dogs' baskets with their filthy old blankets lined up round the range, and the packet of Bluo for the men's shirts, spilling its grains on to the bleached work surface. The only sign of any female influence was a copy of *Glamor* magazine, its straplines advertising a new story by Daphne du Maurier, and an article entitled "Would You Marry A Foreigner?" The pages, she noted, had been heavily thumbed.

"Margaret?"

She glanced at the clock: the men would be in shortly for lunch. She walked to the coathooks by the back door and pulled off an old stockman's jacket, wincing at the smell of tar and wet dog that, she knew, would linger on her clothes.

The rain was now so heavy that in places around the yard it ran in rivers; the drains gurgled a protest, and the chickens huddled in ruffled groups under the shrubs. Letty cursed herself for not having brought her gumboots but ran from the back door of the house to the yard and round to the back of the barn. There, as she had half expected, she made out what looked like a brown oil-proofed lump on a horse, circling the paddock, no face visible under the wide-brimmed hat that fell down to the collar, almost mirrored with slick channels of rainwater.

"Margaret!" Letty stood under the eaves of the barn and shouted to be heard over the rain, waving half-heartedly.

The horse was plainly fed up: its tail clamped to its soaking hind-quarters, it was tiptoeing sideways round the fence, occasionally cowkicking in frustration while its rider patiently turned it to begin each painstaking maneuver again.

"Maggie!"

At one point it bucked. Letty's heart lurched and her hand flew to her mouth. But the rider was neither unseated nor concerned, and merely booted the animal forward, muttering something that might or might not have been an admonishment.

"For God's sake, Maggie, will you get over here!"

The brim of the hat lifted and a hand was raised in greeting. The horse was steered round and walked toward the gate, its head low. "Been there long, Letty?" she called.

"Are you insane, girl? What on earth do you think you're doing?" She could see her niece's broad grin under the brim of the hat.

"Just a bit of schooling. Dad's too big to ride her and the boys are useless with her, so there's only me. Moody old girl, isn't she?"

Letty shook her head, exasperated, and motioned for Margaret to dismount. "For goodness' sake, child. Do you want a hand getting off?"

"Hah! No, I'm fine. Is it lunchtime yet? I put some stew on earlier, but I don't know what time they'll be in. They're moving the calves down to Yarrawa Creek, and they can be all day down there."

"They'll not be all day in this weather," Letty responded, as Margaret clambered down inelegantly from the horse and landed heavily on her feet. "Unless they're as insane as you are."

"Ah, don't fuss. She looks worse than she is."

"You're soaked. Look at you! I can't believe you'd even consider riding out in this weather. Good gracious, Maggie, I don't know what you think you're doing . . . What your dear mother would say, God only knows."

There was a brief pause.

"I know . . ." Margaret wrinkled her nose as she reached up to undo the girth.

Letty wondered if she had said too much. She hesitated, then bit back the awkward apology that had sprung to her lips. "I didn't mean—"

"Forget it. You're right, Letty," said the girl, as she swung the saddle easily under her arm. "She wouldn't have had this mare doing circles to balance her up. She'd have put her in a pair of side reins and be done with it."

———

The men returned shortly before one o'clock, arriving in a thunderous cluster of wet overshoes and dripping hats, shedding their coats at the door. Margaret had set the table and was dishing up steaming bowls of beef stew.

"Colm, you've still got mud all the way up the back of your heels," said Letty, and the young man obligingly kicked off his boots on the mat rather than waste time trying to clean them.

"Got any bread with that?"

"Give us a chance, boys. I'm going as fast as I can."

"Maggie, your dog's asleep in Dad's old hat," said Daniel, grinning. "Dad says if he gets fleas off it he'll shoot her."

"I said no such thing, eejit child. How are you, Letty? Did you get up to town yesterday?" Murray Donleavy, a towering, angular man whose freckles and pale eyes signaled his Celtic origins, sat down at the head of the table and, without comment, began to work his way through a hunk of bread that his sister-in-law had sliced for him.

"I did, Murray."

"Any post for us?"

"I'll bring it out after you've eaten." Otherwise, the way these men sat at a table, the letters would be splashed with gravy and fingered with greasemarks. Noreen had never seemed to mind.

Margaret had had her lunch already, and was sitting on the easy chair by the larder, her socked feet on a footstool. Letty watched the men settle, with private satisfaction, as they lowered their heads to eat. Not many families, these days, could boast five men round a table with three of them having been in the services. As Murray muttered to Daniel, his youngest, to pass more bread, Letty could still detect a hint of the Irish accent with which he had arrived in the country. Her sister had occasionally mocked it good-humoredly. "That one!" she'd say, her accent curled round a poor approximation of his own. "He's got more fight in him than a Dundalk wedding."

No, this table lacked someone else entirely. She sighed, pushing Noreen from her thoughts, as she did countless times every day. Then she said brightly, "Alf Pettit's wife has bought one of those new Defender refrigerators. It's got four drawers and an icemaker, and doesn't make a sound."

"Unlike Alf Pettit's wife," said Murray. He had pulled over the latest copy of the *Bulletin*, and was deep in "The Man on the Land," its farming column. "Hmph. Says here that dairy yards are getting dirtier because all the women are quitting."

"They've obviously never seen the state of Maggie's room."

"You make this?" Murray lifted his head from his newspaper and jerked a thumb at his bowl, which was nearly empty.

"Maggie did," said Letty.

"Nice. Better than the last one."

"I don't know why," said Margaret, her hand held out in front of her the better to examine a splinter. "I didn't do anything any different."

"There's a new picture starting at the Odeon," Letty said, changing the subject. That got their attention. She knew the men pretended not to be interested in the snippets of gossip she brought to the farm twice a week, gossip being the stuff of women, but every now and then the mask of indifference slipped. She rested against the sink, arms crossed over her chest.

"Well?"

"It's a war film. Greer Garson and Tyrone Power. I forget the name. Something with *Forever* in it?"

"I hope it's got lots of fighter planes. American ones." Daniel glanced at his brothers, apparently searching for agreement, but their heads were down as they shoveled food into their mouths.

"How are you going to get to Woodside, short-arse? Your bike's broke, if you remember." Liam shoved him.

"He's not cycling all that way by himself, whatever," said Murray.

"One of youse can take me in the truck. Ah, go on. I'll pay for your ices."

"How many rabbits you sell this week?"

Daniel had been raising extra cash by skinning rabbits and selling the pelts. The price of good ones had risen inexplicably from a penny each to several shillings, which had left his brothers mildly envious of his sudden wealth.

"Only four."

"Well, that's my best price."

"Oh, Murray, Betty says to tell you their good mare is in foal finally, if you're still interested."

"The one they put to the Magician?"

"I think so."

Murray exchanged a glance with his eldest son. "Might swing by there later in the week, Colm. Be good to have a decent horse around the place."

"Which reminds me." Letty took a deep breath. "I found Margaret riding that mean young filly of yours. I don't think she should be riding. It's not . . . safe."

Murray didn't look up from his stew. "She's a grown woman, Letty. We'll have little or no say over her life soon enough."

"You've no need to fuss, Letty. I know what I'm doing."

"She's a mean-looking horse." Letty began to wash up, feeling vaguely undermined. "I'm just saying I don't think Noreen would have liked it. Not with things . . . the way they are . . ."

The mention of her sister's name brought with it a brief, melancholy silence.

Murray pushed his empty bowl to the center of the table. "It's good of you to concern yourself about us, Letty. Don't think we're not grateful."

If the boys noted the look that passed between the two "olds," as they were known, or that their aunt Letty's was followed by the faintest pinking of her cheeks, they said nothing. Just as they had said nothing when, several months previously, she had started to wear her good skirt to visit them. Or that, in her mid-forties, she was suddenly setting her hair.

Margaret, meanwhile, had risen from her chair and was flicking through the letters that lay on the sideboard beside Letty's bag. "Bloody hell!" she exclaimed.

"Margaret!"

"Sorry, Letty. Look! Look, Dad, it's for me! From the Navy!"

Her father motioned for her to bring it over. He turned the envelope in his broad hands, noting the official stamp, the return address. "Want me to open it?"

"He's not dead, is he?" Daniel yelped as Colm's hand caught him a sharp blow to the back of the head.

"Don't be even more of a mongrel than you already are."

"You don't think he's dead, do you?" Margaret reached out to steady herself, her normally high color draining away.

"Course he's not dead," her father said. "They send you a wire for that."

"They might have wanted to save on postage but—" Daniel shot backward on his chair to avoid an energetic kick from his elder brother.

"I was going to wait until you'd all finished eating," Letty said, and was ignored.

"Go on, then, Mags. What are you waiting for?"

"I don't know," said the girl, apparently now in an agony of indecision.

"Go on, we're all here." Her father reached out a comforting hand and laid it on her back.

She looked at him, then down at the letter, which she now held. Her brothers were on their feet, standing tightly around her. Letty, watching from the sink, felt superfluous, as if she were an outsider. To hide her own discomfort she busied herself scrubbing a pan, her broad fingers reddening in the scalding water.

Margaret ripped open the letter, and began to read it, murmuring the words under her breath, a habit she had held since childhood. Then she gave a little moan, and Letty whirled round to see her sit down heavily on a chair that one of her brothers had pushed out for her. She looked at her father, apparently grief-stricken.

"You all right, girl?" His face was creased with anxiety.

"I'm going, Dad," she croaked.

"What? To Ireland?" said Daniel, snatching the letter.

"No. To England. They've got me aboard a ship. Oh, my God, Dad."

"Margaret!" Letty admonished her, but no one heard.

"Mags is going to England!" Her older brother read the letter. "She's really going! They've actually managed to squeeze her on!"

"Less of your cheek," said Margaret, but her heart wasn't in it.

"'Due to the change in status of another war bride, we can offer you a passage on the—' What does that spell? 'Will leave from Sydney' blah-blah-blah."

"Change in status? What do you suppose happened to that poor soul, then?" Niall scoffed.

"It's possible the husband might have been married already. It happens, you know."

"Letty!" Murray protested.

"Well, it's true, Murray. All sorts has happened. You only have to read the papers. I've heard of girls who've gone all the way to America to be told they're not wanted. Some with . . ." She tailed off.

"Joe's not like that," said Murray. "We all know he's not like that."

"Besides," said Colm cheerfully, "when he married Mags I told him if he ever let her down I'd hunt him down and kill him."

"You did that too?" said Niall, surprised.

"God," said Margaret, ignoring her aunt but crossing herself in mute apology. "With you lot looking after me it's a wonder he stuck around at all."

A hush descended as the import of the letter settled on the occupants of the room. Margaret took her father's hand and held it tightly, while the others affected not to notice.

"Does anyone want tea?" said Letty. A lump had risen in her throat:

she had been picturing the kitchen without Margaret in it. There were several subdued murmurs of assent.

"There's no guarantee you're getting a cabin, mind," said Niall, still reading.

"They could store her with the luggage," said Liam. "She's tough as old hide."

"Is that it?" said Daniel, who, Letty saw, looked profoundly shocked. "I mean, do you go to England and that's it?"

"That's it," said Margaret, quietly.

"But what about us?" said Daniel, his voice breaking, as if he had not yet taken seriously his sister's marriage or its possible ramifications. "We can't lose Mum *and* Mags. I mean, what are we supposed to do?"

Letty made to speak and found she had no words.

Across the table, Murray had been sitting in silence, his hand entwined with his daughter's. "We, son, are to be glad."

"What?"

Murray smiled reassuringly at his daughter—a smile that Letty could not believe he truly felt. "We are going to be glad, because Margaret is going to be with a good man. A man who's fought for his country and ours. A man who deserves to be with our Margaret just as much as she deserves him."

"Oh, Dad." Margaret dabbed at her eyes.

"And more importantly," here his voice rose, as if to stave off interruption, "we should be glad as anything because Joe's grandfather was an Irishman. And that means . . ." he laid a roughened hand gently on his daughter's expanded belly ". . . this little fellow here is going to set foot, God willing, in God's own country."

"Oh, Murray," whispered Letty, her hand pressed to her mouth.

"Brace yourself, lads," muttered Colm to his brothers, and began to pull on his boots, "we're in for an evening of 'Oh Danny Boy.' "

———

They had run out of places to put wet washing. The indoor dryer was loaded to the point where it threatened to pull down the ceiling; damp linen hung from every indoor hook and cable, pegged to hangers hooked over the tops of doors or laid flat on towels on work surfaces. Margaret hauled another wet undershirt from the bucket and handed it to her aunt, who fed the hem into the mangle and began to turn the handle.

"It's because nothing dried yesterday," Margaret said. "I didn't get the stuff off the line in time so it was soaked again, and I still had lots more to do."

"Why don't you sit down, Maggie?" Letty said, eyeing her legs. "Take the weight off your feet for a minute or two."

Margaret sank gratefully into the chair in the laundry room, and reached down to stroke the terrier that sat by her side. "I could put some in the bathroom, but Dad hates that."

"You know you should rest. Most women have their feet up by now."

"Ah, there's ages yet," Margaret said.

"Less than twelve weeks, by my reckoning."

"African women just drop them behind a bush and carry on working."

"You're not African. And I doubt anyone 'drops' a baby like they're . . ." Letty was conscious of her inability to talk of childbirth with any authority. She continued wringing in silence, the rain drumming noisily on the tin roof of the outhouse, the sweet smell of newly drenched earth rising up through the open windows. The mangle squeaked, a geriatric creature forced unwillingly into effort.

"Daniel's taken it worse than I thought," Margaret said eventually.

Letty continued to work the handle, grunting as she hauled it toward her. "He's still young. He's had a lot to deal with this past couple of years."

"But he's really angry. I didn't expect him to be angry."

Letty paused. "He feels let down, I suppose. What with losing his mum and you . . ."

"It's not like I did it on purpose." Margaret thought of her brother's outburst, of the words "selfish" and "hateful" hurled at her in temper until the flat of her father's hand brought the diatribe to an abrupt halt.

"I know," said Letty, stopping and straightening. "They know it too. Even Daniel."

"But when Joe and I got married, you know, I didn't think about leaving Dad and the boys. I didn't think anyone would mind too much."

"Of course they mind. They love you."

"I didn't mind when Niall went."

"That was war. You knew he had to go."

"But who's going to look after them all? Dad can just about press a shirt or wash the dishes, if he has to, but there's not one of them can put together a meal. And they'd leave the sheets on their beds until they walked themselves to the linen basket."

As she spoke, Margaret began almost to believe in this picture of herself as a domestic lynchpin, which position she had held with quiet resentment for the past two years. She had never anticipated having to cook and clean for anyone. Even Joe had understood when she told him she was hopeless at it and, more importantly, had no intention of remedying the situation. Now, forced to spend hours of every day tending the brothers she had once treated as equals, grief, guilt and mute fury fought within her. "It's a huge worry, Letty. I really think they won't be able to cope without . . . well, a woman around the place."

There was a lengthy silence. The dog whined in her sleep, her legs paddling in some unseen chase.

"I suppose they could get someone in, like a housekeeper," said Letty eventually, her voice deceptively light.

"Dad wouldn't want to pay for that. You know how he goes on about saving money. And, besides, I don't think any of them would like a stranger in the kitchen. You know what they're like." She sneaked a glance at her aunt. "Niall hasn't liked anyone new being around since he came back from the camps. Oh, I don't know . . ."

Outside, the rain was easing off. The drumming on the roof had lightened, and small patches of blue could be seen amid the gray clouds toward the east. The two women were silent for a few minutes, each apparently absorbed in the view from the screened window.

When no answer was forthcoming, Margaret spoke again: "Actually, I'm wondering whether I should leave at all. I mean, there's no point in going if I'm going to spend my whole time worrying about the family, is there?"

She waited for her aunt to speak. When nothing came, she continued, "Because I—"

"I suppose," Letty ventured, "that I could help out."

"What?"

"Don't say 'what,' dear. If you're that worried about them all," Letty's voice was measured, "I might be able to come most days. Just to help out a bit."

"Oh, Letty, would you?" Margaret had ensured that her voice held just the right amount of surprise, just the right level of gratitude.

"I wouldn't want to be treading on anyone's toes."

"No . . . no . . . of course not."

"I wouldn't want you or the boys thinking . . . that I was trying to take your mother's place."

"Oh, I don't think anyone would think that."

Both women digested what had finally been said aloud.

"There might be people who will . . . interpret things the wrong way. People in town and suchlike." Letty smoothed her hair unconsciously.

"Yes, there might," said Margaret, still looking deadly serious.

"But, then, it's not like I've got a job or anything. Not now they've shut the munitions factory. And family should come first."

"It certainly should."

"I mean, those boys need a feminine influence. Daniel especially. He's at that age . . . And it's not like I'm doing anything wrong. Anything . . . you know . . ."

If Margaret noticed the faint blush of pleasure creeping across her aunt's face she said nothing. If there was something else in her aunt's face, in the new lipstick, that made Margaret feel a little more complicated about the arrangement, she made a game attempt to push it away. If the price of her own guiltless freedom was for her mother's place to be usurped, she would be careful only to see the benefits.

Letty's angular face was lit now by a smile. "In that case, dear, if it will help you, I'll take good care of them all," she said. "And Maudie there. I'll take good care of her. You won't need to worry."

"Oh, I'm not worried about her." Margaret raised herself with an effort. "I'm going to—"

"Yes, I'll make sure they're all all right," Letty continued. Anticipation had apparently made her garrulous. "If it will really make you feel a little easier in yourself, Maggie dear, I'll do what I can. Yes, you won't need to worry about a thing." Suddenly galvanized, she wrung out the last shirt by hand and dumped it in the washing basket, ready for the next drying session.

She wiped her large, bony hands on her apron. "Right. Now. Why don't I go and make us both a cup of tea? You write your letter to the Navy, telling them you'll accept, and then we'll know you're all set. You don't want to miss your place, do you? Not like that other poor soul."

Margaret made her smile seem readier than it felt. The *Glamour* article had said she might never see any of them again. You had to be ready for that.

"Tell you what, Maggie, I'll go through your drawers upstairs. See if there's anything I can darn for you. I know you're not the best with a needle, and we'll want you to look as nice as pie when you see Joe again."

You were not to resent them, the magazine had said. You had to make sure you never blamed your husband for separating you from your family. Her aunt was now hauling the basket across the room with the same proprietorial familiarity as her mother once had.

Margaret shut her eyes and breathed deeply as Letty's voice echoed across the laundry room: "I might fix up a few of your father's shirts, while I'm at it. I couldn't help noticing, dear, that they're looking a bit tired, and I wouldn't want anyone saying I don't . . ." She shot a sideways look at Margaret. "I'll make sure everything's shipshape here. Oh, yes. You won't need to worry about a thing."

Margaret didn't want to think of them on their own. Better this way than with someone she didn't know.

"Maggie?"

"Mm?"

"Do you think . . . do you think your father will mind about it? I mean, about me?" Letty's face was suddenly anxious, her forty-five-year-old features as open as those of a young bride.

Afterward, on the many nights when she thought back, Margaret wasn't sure what had made her say it. She wasn't a mean person. She didn't want either Letty or her father to be lonely, after all.

"I think he'll be delighted," she said, reaching down to her little dog. "He's very fond of you, Letty, as are the boys." She looked down and coughed, examining the splinter on her hand. "He's often said he looks on you like . . . a kind of sister. Someone who can talk to him about Mum, who remembers what she was like . . . And, of course, if you're washing their shirts for them you'll have their undying gratitude." For some reason it was impossible to look up but she was aware of the acute stillness of Letty's skirts, of her thin, strong legs, as she stood a few feet away. Her hands, habitually active, hung motionless against her apron.

"Yes," Letty said at last. "Of course." There was a slight choke in her voice. "Well. As I said. I'll—I'll go and make us that tea."

2

The two male kangaroos—both only 12 months out of the pouch—which will fly to London shortly . . . will eat 12 lb of hay en route. Qantas Empire Airways said yesterday the kangaroos would spend only 63 hours in the air.

SYDNEY MORNING HERALD, 4 JULY 1946

THREE WEEKS TO EMBARKATION

Ian darling,
You'll never guess what—I'm on! I know you won't believe it, as I hardly can myself, but it's true. Daddy had a word with one of his old friends at the Red Cross, who has some friends high up in the RN, and the next thing I had orders saying I've got a place on the next boat out, even though, strictly speaking, I should be low priority.

I had to tell the other brides back at home that I was going to Perth to see my grandmother, to prevent a riot, but now I'm here, holed up at the Wentworth Hotel in Sydney, waiting to nip on board before them.

Darling, I can't wait to see you. I've missed you so terribly. Mummy says that when we've got our new home sorted she and Daddy will be over ASAP. They are planning to travel on the new Qantas "Kangaroo" service—did you know you can get to London in only 63 hours flying on a Lancastrian? She has asked me to ask you for your mother's address so she can send on the rest of my things once I'm in England. I'm sure they'll be better about everything once they've met your parents. They seem to have visions of me ending up in some mud hut in the middle of an English field somewhere.

So, anyway, darling, here I am practicing my signature, and remembering to answer to "Mrs.," and still getting used to the sight of a wedding band on my finger. It was so disappointing us not having a proper honeymoon, but I really don't mind where it happens, as long as I'll be with you. I'll end now, as I'm spending the afternoon at the American Wives' Club at Woolloomooloo, finding out what I'll need for the trip. The American Wives get all sorts, unlike us poor British wives. (Isn't it a gas, my saying that?) Mind you, if I have to listen to one more rendition of "When The Boy From Alabama Meets A Girl From Gundagi" I think I shall sprout wings and fly to you myself. Take care my love, and write as soon as you have a moment.

    Your Avice

In the four years since its inception the American Wives' Club had met every two weeks at the elegant white stucco house on the edge of the Royal Botanic Gardens, initially to help girls who had traveled from Perth or Canberra to while away the endless weeks before they were allowed a passage to meet their American husbands. It taught them how to make American patchwork quilts, sing "The Star Spangled Banner," and offered a little matronly support to those who were pregnant or nursing, and those who could not decide whether they were paralyzed with fear at the thought of the journey or at the idea that they would never make it.

Latterly the club had ceased to be American in character: the previous year's U.S. War Brides Act had hastened the departure of its twelve thousand newly claimed Australian wives, so the quilts had been replaced by bridge afternoons and advice on how to cope with British food and rationing.

Many of the young brides who now attended were lodged with families in Leichhardt, Darlinghurst or the suburbs. They were in a strange hinterland, their lives in Australia not yet over and those elsewhere not begun, their focus on the minutiae of a future they knew little about and could not control. It was perhaps unsurprising that on the biweekly occasions that they met, there was only one topic of conversation.

"A girl I know from Melbourne got to travel over on the *Queen Mary* in a first-class cabin," a bespectacled girl was saying. The liner had been held up as the holy grail of transport. Letters were still arriving in Australia with tales of her glory. "She said she spent almost all her time toasting herself by the pool. She said there were dinner-dances, party games, everything. And they got the most heavenly dresses made in Ceylon. The only thing was she had to share with some woman and her children. Ugh. Sticky fingers all over her clothes, and up at five thirty in the morning when the baby started to wail."

"Children are a blessing," said Mrs. Proffit, benignly, as she checked the stitching of a green hat on a brown woolen monkey. Today they were Gift-making for the Bombed-out Children of London. One of the girls had been sent a book called *Useful Hints from Odds and Ends* by her English mother-in-law, and Mrs. Proffit had written out instructions on how to make a necklace from the metal rings for chickens' legs, and a bed-jacket from old cami-knickers for next week's meeting. "Yes," she said, glancing fondly at them all. "You'll understand one day. Children are a blessing."

"No children is more of one," muttered the dark-eyed girl next to Avice, accompanying the remark with a rather vulgar nudge.

In other times, Avice would not have spent five minutes with this peculiar mixture of girls—some of whom seemed to have landed straight off some outback station with red dust on their shoes—or, indeed, have wasted so many hours enduring interminable lectures from middle-aged spinsters who had seized upon the war as a way to enliven what had probably been dismal lives. But she had been in Sydney for almost ten days now, with her father's friend, Mr. Burton, the only person she knew there, and the Wives' Club had become her only point of social contact. (She still wasn't sure how to explain Mr. Burton's behavior to her father. She had had to tell the man no less than four times that she was a married woman, and she wasn't

entirely sure that as far as he was concerned that made any difference.)

There were twelve other young women at today's gathering; few
had spent more than a week at a time with their husbands, and more
than half had not seen them for the best part of a year. The shipment
home of troops was a priority; the "wallflower wives," as they had become known, were not. Some had filed their papers over a year previously and heard little since. At least one, tiring of her dreary
lodgings, had given up and gone home. The rest stayed on, fueled by
blind hope, desperation, love or, in most cases, a varying mix of all
three.

Avice was the newest member. Listening to their tales of the families with whom they were billeted, she had silently thanked her parents for the opulence of her hotel accommodation. It would all have
been so much less exciting if she had been forced to stay with some
grumpy old couple. As it was, it became rather less exciting by
the day.

"If that Mrs. Tidworth says to me one more time, 'Oh dear, hasn't
he sent for you yet?' I swear I'll swing for her."

"She loves it, the old bitch. She did the same to Mary Knight when
she stayed there. I reckon she actually wants you to get the telegram
saying, 'Don't come.'"

"It's the you'll-be-sorrys I can't stand."

"Not much longer, eh?"

"When's the next one due in?"

"Around three weeks, according to my orders," said the dark-eyed
girl. Avice thought she might have said her name was Jean, but she
was hopeless with names and had forgotten them all immediately
she'd been introduced. "She'd better be as nice as the *Queen Mary*.
She even had a hair salon with heated dryers. I'm desperate to get
my hair done properly before I see Stan again."

"She was a wonderful woman, Queen Mary," said Mrs. Proffit,
from the end of the table. "Such a lady."

"You've got your orders?" A freckled girl on the other side of the
table was frowning at Jean.

"Last week."

"But you're low priority. You said you didn't even put in your papers until a month ago."

There was a brief silence. Around the table, several girls exchanged glances, then fixed their eyes on their embroidery. Mrs. Proffit looked up; she had apparently picked up on the subtle cooling in the atmosphere. "Anyone need more thread?" she asked, peering over her spectacles.

"Yes, well, sometimes you just get lucky," said Jean, and excused herself from the table.

"How come she gets on?" said the freckled girl, turning to the women on each side of her. "I've been waiting nearly fifteen months, and she's getting on the next boat out. How can that be right?" Her voice had sharpened with the injustice of it. Avice made a mental note not to mention her own orders.

"She's carrying, isn't she?" muttered another girl.

"What?"

"Jean. She's in the family way. You know what? The Americans won't let you over once you're past four months."

"Who's doing the penguin?" said Mrs. Proffit. "You'll need to keep that black thread for whoever's doing the penguin."

"Hang on," said a redhead threading a needle. "Her Stan left in November. She said he was on the same ship as my Ernie."

"So she can't be in the family way."

"Or she is . . . and . . ."

Eyes widened and met, accompanied by the odd smirk.

"Are you up for a little roo, Sarah dear?" Mrs. Proffit beamed at the girls and pulled some pieces of fawn felt out of her cloth bag. "I do think the little roos are rather sweet, don't you?"

Several minutes later Jean returned to her chair, and folded her arms rather combatively. She seemed to realize that she was no longer the topic of conversation and visibly relaxed—although she might have wondered at the sudden industriousness of the toy-making around her.

"I met Ian, my husband, at a tea-dance," said Avice, in an attempt to break the silence. "I was part of a young ladies' reception committee, and he was the second man I offered a cup of tea to."

"Was that all you offered him?"

That was Jean. She might have known. "From what I've heard I don't suppose everyone's idea of hospitality is quite the same as yours," she retorted. She remembered how she had blushed as she poured; he had been staring conspicuously at her ankles—of which she was rather proud.

Petty Officer Ian Stewart Radley. At twenty-six, a whole five years older than her, which Avice considered just right, tall and straight-backed with eyes the color of the sea, a gentlemanly British accent and broad, soft hands that had made her tremble the first time they ever brushed hers—even holding a shortbread finger. He had asked her to dance—even though no one else was on the floor—and with him being a serviceman, she had thought it mean-spirited to refuse. What was a quickstep or a Gay Gordons when he was looking death in the face?

Less than four months later they were married, a tasteful ceremony in the Collins Street register office. Her father had been suspicious, had made her mother quiz her—in a discreet woman-to-woman way, of course—as to whether there was any reason for such a hasty marriage other than Ian's imminent departure. Ian had told her father, rather honorably, she thought, that he was happy to wait, if that was what Avice's parents wanted, that he would do nothing to upset them, but she had been determined to become Mrs. Radley. The war had hastened everything, foreshortened the natural timescale of such things. And she had known, from that first cup of tea, there was no one else in the world she could envisage marrying; no one else upon whom she could consider bestowing her many gifts.

"But we know nothing about him, dear," her mother had said, wringing her hands.

"He's perfect."

"You know that's not what I mean."

"What do you need to know? He's been out there holding the Brisbane line, hasn't he? Doesn't protecting our country, putting his own life at risk twelve thousand miles from his home to save us from the Japs, make him worthy of my hand?"

"No need to be melodramatic, sweetheart," her father had said.

They had given in, of course. They always did. Her sister Deanna had been furious.

"My Johnnie was billeted with my aunt Vi," said another girl. "I thought he was gorgeous. I sneaked into his room the second night he was there and that was that."

"Best to get in early," said another, to raucous laughter. "Stake your claim."

"Especially if Jean's around."

Even Jean found that funny.

"Now, who wants to practice making one of these lovely necklaces?" Mrs. Proffit held up an uneven-looking chain of aluminum coils. "I'm sure it's what the best-dressed ladies are wearing in Europe."

"Next week it'll be how to make couture evening cloaks from horse blankets."

"I heard that, Edwina." Mrs. Proffit placed the necklace carefully on the table.

"Sorry, Mrs. P, but if my Johnnie saw me wearing one of those he wouldn't know whether to kiss me or check my rear to see if I'd laid an egg."

There was an explosion of laughter, an outburst of barely suppressed hysteria.

Mrs. Proffit sighed and laid down her craftwork. Really! It was only to be expected, as embarkation drew closer—but really! These girls could be so wearying.

———

"So, when are you out?"

Jean's host family were two streets away from the Wentworth, and the girls had ended up walking back together, dawdling. Despite the air of mutual dislike between them, they were reluctant to sit alone in their rooms for yet another evening.

"Avice? When are your orders for?"

Avice wondered whether to answer truthfully. She was pretty sure that Jean—immature and coarse as she was—was not the kind of girl she would normally want to associate with, especially if what had been said about her condition was true. But neither was Avice a girl used to self-restraint, and the effort involved in keeping quiet for an entire afternoon about her own plans had been a strain. "Same as you. Three weeks. What's she called? The *Victoria*?"

"It's a bugger, isn't it?" Jean lit a cigarette, cupping her hands against the sea breeze. As an afterthought, she offered one to Avice.

Avice wrinkled her nose and declined. "What did you say?"

"It's a bugger. They get the bloody *Queen Mary* and we get the old tin can."

A car drove past slowly, and two servicemen hung out of the windows, shouting something crude. Jean grinned at them, waving her cigarette, as the car disappeared round the corner.

Avice stood in front of her. "I'm sorry, I don't understand what you mean."

"Didn't you hear Mrs. Proffit? The one who's married to the commander?"

Avice shook her head.

Jean laughed humorlessly. "I don't think it's quite hair salons and first-class cabins for you and me, girl. Our *Victoria* is a bloody aircraft-carrier."

Avice stared at the girl for a minute, then smiled. It was the kind of smile she reserved at home for the staff when they did something particularly stupid. "I think you must be mistaken, Jean. Ladies don't travel on aircraft-carriers." She pursed her lips, as smoke trickled her way. "Besides, there'd be nowhere to put us all."

"You really don't know anything, do you?"

Avice fought back irritation at being addressed in this manner by someone who had to be at least five years younger than herself.

"They've run out of decent transport. They're going to stick us on anything to get us over there. I reckon they figure whoever really wants to go will put up with whatever they throw our way."

"Are you sure?"

"Even old Mrs. P seemed a bit concerned. Think she's worried about her young ladies arriving in England wearing overalls and covered with fuel. Not quite the impression she wants for Australia's finest."

"An aircraft-carrier?" Avice felt a little wobbly. She reached for a nearby wall and sat down.

Jean seated herself comfortably beside her. "That's what she is. I never bothered to check the name of it. I just assumed . . . Oh, well, they'll have modified it a bit, I should think."

"But where will we sleep?"

"Dunno. On the deck with the planes?"

Avice's eyes widened.

"Strewth, Avice, you're even more gullible than I thought." Jean cackled, stubbed out her cigarette, stood up and began to walk on.

It might have been her imagination but Avice thought she sounded increasingly coarse.

"They'll find some way to fit us on. Got to be better than sticking around here, anyway. We'll get a bed and our food, and the Red Cross will look after us."

"Oh, I don't think so." Avice's face had clouded. She walked briskly. If she rang now she might catch her father before he left for his club.

"What do you mean?"

"I can't possibly travel on something like that. My parents wouldn't have it, for a start. They thought I'd be traveling on a liner. You know, one of the ones that had been requisitioned for transport. That's almost the only reason they let me go."

"You take what you're given in times like these, girl. You know that."

Not me, said Avice silently. She was now running toward the hotel. Not a girl whose family owned the biggest radio manufacturer in Melbourne.

"They'll be providing us with engineers' uniforms too, just in case they need us to do a little scrubbing down."

"I don't think that's very funny, actually."

"You've got to laugh."

Go away, you horrid girl, Avice thought. I wouldn't set foot on the same ship as you for a trip round Sydney Harbor, even if it were the *Queen Mary*.

"Don't worry, Avice. I'm sure they'll be able to fix you up with a first-class berth in the boiler room!" She could still hear Jean's unpleasant cackle half-way down the street.

———

"Mummy?"

"Avice darling, is that you? Wilfred! It's Avice!" She could hear her mother yelling down the hallway, could picture her on her telephone seat, the Persian rug on the parquet floor, the ever-present vase of flowers on the table beside her. "How are you, sweetheart?"

"Fine, Mummy. But I need to speak to Daddy."

"You don't sound all right. Are you really fine?"

"Yes."

"Has Ian sent any word yet?"

"Mummy, I need to speak to Daddy." Avice struggled to keep her impatience out of her voice.

"You would tell me?"

"Is that my littlest princess?"

"Oh, Daddy, thank goodness. There's a problem."

Her father said nothing.

"With the transport."

"I spoke to Commander Guild myself. He promised me you'd be on the next—"

"No, that's not it. He's got me on a boat."

"So what's the problem?"

She could hear her mother behind her father: "It's the young man. Ten to one it's the young man."

And Deanna: "Has he told her not to come?"

"Tell them it's nothing to do with Ian. It's the ship."

"I don't understand, Princess."

"It's an aircraft-carrier."

"What?"

"Maureen," he hissed. "Be quiet. I can't hear a word she's saying."

Avice let out a short sigh.

"Exactly. It's an aircraft-carrier. They're expecting us to sail to England on an *aircraft-carrier*."

There was a brief silence. "They want her to travel on an aircraft-carrier," her father told her mother.

"What? An airplane?"

"No, you stupid woman. One of the ships they put the planes on."

"A warship?"

Avice could almost hear her reeling theatrically in horror. Deanna had started laughing. She would: she hadn't forgiven Avice for marrying first.

"You're going to have to get me on to something else," Avice said urgently. "Talk to whoever it was who got me on. Tell him I need to travel on something else. Get me on another ship."

"You never said anything about an aircraft-carrier!" her mother was saying now. "She can't travel on one of those. Not with all those planes going off the deck all the time. It'll be dangerous!"

"Daddy?"

"They sank the *Vyner Brooke*, didn't they?" her mother clamored. "The Japs might try to sink the aircraft-carrier, like they sank the *Vyner Brooke*."

"Shut *up*, woman."

"What's the matter? Are you the only girl on board, Princess?"

"Me? Oh, no, there's six hundred or so wives traveling." Avice frowned. "It's just that it will be awful. They'll have us sleeping on bedrolls and there won't be any facilities. And, Daddy, you should see the kind of girls they've got me going over with—the language! I can hardly say—"

Her mother broke through on to the line. "I knew it, Avice. They're just not your sort. I really don't think this is a good idea."

"Daddy? Can you sort it out?"

Her father sighed heavily. "Well, it's not as easy as that, Princess. I had to pull quite a few strings to get you on board. And most of the brides have gone now, anyway. I'm not sure how many more transports there are going to be."

"Well, fly me over. I'll go with Qantas."

"It's not as easy as that, Avice."

"I can't go on that awful ship!"

"Listen, Avice, I paid a lot of money to get you on to it, you hear me? And I'm shelling out a damn sight more to keep you in that ruddy hotel because you didn't fancy naval lodgings. I can't pay out even more for a flight to Blighty just because you don't like the facilities on board the ship."

"But, Daddy—"

"Sweetheart, I'd love to help, really, but you've no idea how hard it was to get you on board."

"But, Daddy!" She stamped her foot and the receptionist glanced at her. She lowered her voice to a whisper: "I know what you're doing—don't think I don't know why you're refusing to help me."

Her mother broke in, her voice firm. "Avice, you're right. I think the ship thing is a very bad idea."

"You do?" Avice felt a flicker of hope. Her mother understood the importance of traveling comfortably. She knew that things should be done properly. What would Ian think if she turned up looking like a navvy?

"Yes. I think you should come home today. Get on a train first thing tomorrow morning."

"Home?"

"The whole thing has just too many ifs and buts. This ship business sounds absolutely awful, you haven't heard from Ian in goodness knows how long—"

"He's at sea, Mummy."

"—and I just think all the signs are against you. Cut your losses, darling, and come home."

"What?"

"You know nothing about this man's family. Nothing. You have no idea if there's even going to be anyone to meet you at the other end.

That's if this warship even gets there. Come home, darling, and we'll sort it all out from here. Plenty of girls change their minds. You read about them all the time."

"Plenty of girls get dumped too," called Deanna.

"I'm married, Mummy."

"And I'm sure we can do something about that. I mean, hardly anyone over here even knows."

"What?"

"Well, it was only a little do, wasn't it? We could have it annulled or something."

Avice was incredulous. "Annulled? Ugh! You're both such hypocrites! I *know* what you're doing. You got me on the rottenest old ship you could find just so I wouldn't want to travel."

"Avice—"

"Well, too bad. You're not going to make me change my mind about Ian."

The receptionist had given up any pretense of not listening and was agog, leaning over her counter. Avice placed her hand over the receiver and raised her eyebrows at the girl. Embarrassed, she busied herself with some paperwork.

Her father broke back in: "You there? Avice?" He sighed heavily. "Look, I'll wire you some money. Leave it a while, if you want. Sit tight at the Wentworth. We'll talk about this."

Avice could hear her mother still wittering in the background. Her sister was demanding to know why she was staying at Sydney's best hotel. "No, Daddy," she said. "Tell Mummy and Deanna I'll be on the damned ship to meet my husband. I'll get there my own way, even if it does mean swimming in diesel fuel and stinking troops, because I love him. *I love him.* I won't ring again, but you can tell her—tell Mummy I'll wire her at the other end. When Ian—my husband—has met me."

3

*To be eligible for an appointment in the Australian Army Nursing Service,
the applicant had to be a trained registered nurse, a British subject, single,
without dependents . . . medically fit and of good character and personal
attributes essential to the making of an efficient army nurse.*

JOAN CROUCH, "A SPECIAL KIND OF SERVICE,"
THE STORY OF THE 2/9 AUSTRALIAN
GENERAL HOSPITAL 1940—46

MOROTAI, HALMAHERAS ISLANDS, SOUTH PACIFIC, 1946
ONE WEEK TO EMBARKATION

There was a full moon over Morotai. With a melancholy lucidity, it illuminated the still night, the heat so stifling that even the gentle sea breezes that could normally be relied on to filter through the sisal screens were deadened. The leaves of the palm trees hung limp. The only sound was a periodic muffled thud as a coconut hit the ground. There was no one left to take down the ripe ones, and they fell unchecked, a hazard to the unwary.

For the most part now the island was dark, only a few lights winking in the buildings that lined the road, which stretched the length of the peninsula. For the past five years that end of the island had been clamorous with the traffic of the Allied Forces, the air filled with the roar of aircraft engines and the belch of exhaust fumes, but now there was silence, broken only by bursts of distant laughter, the crackle of a gramophone and, just audible in the still night, the clink of glasses.

In the tented confines of the nurses' mess, a few hundred yards from what had been the American base Matron, Audrey Marshall of the Australian General Hospital finished her day's entry in the Unit War Diary.

- *Hospital ship movements for POW evacuation from Morotai in hand.*
- *Movement orders to hand for unit—12 POWs and 1 nursing sister move to Australia per Ariadne tomorrow.*
- *Bedstate: occupied 12, vacant 24.*

She gazed at the last two figures, wondering at the years of entries in which those figures had been reversed, at the hundreds of days in which she'd had another column to enter: "those deceased." The ward was one of the few still open: forty-five of the fifty-two were now closed, their patients restored to families in England, Australia, or even India, nurses discharged, supplies waiting to be sold to the occupying Dutch authorities. The *Ariadne* would be the last hospital ship, carrying with it this raggle-taggle of men, some of the last POWs to leave the island. From now on it would be just the odd car accident and civilian illnesses until she, too, received her orders to return home.

"Nurse Frederick says I should tell you Sergeant Wilkes is foxtrotting Nurse Cooper around the operating theater . . . She's fallen over twice already." Staff Nurse Gore had stuck her head round the sheeted doorway. Her complexion, which always bloomed in the heat, was flushed with excitement and the last of the whisky. With the hospital so close to abandonment, the girls were skittish and silly, singing songs and re-enacting scenes from old movies to entertain the men, their former reserve and authority evaporating in the moisture-filled air. Although, strictly speaking, they were still on duty, she didn't have the heart to reprimand them—not after what they'd seen these last weeks. She couldn't forget their shocked, drained faces when the first POWs arrived from Borneo.

"Go and tell the silly girl to bring him back in. I couldn't care less if she injures herself, but he's only been on his feet forty-eight hours. We don't want him breaking a leg to add to his troubles."

"Will do, Matron." The girl was gone, the curtain falling back limply into place. Her face reappeared briefly. "Are you coming? The boys are asking where you are."

"I'll be along shortly, Nurse," she said, shutting her book, and raising herself from the folding stool. "You go along now."

"Yes, Matron." With a giggle she departed.

Audrey Marshall checked her hair in the little mirror she kept above the wash-basin, then blotted her face with a towel. She slapped at a mosquito that had launched itself into the back of her arm, straightened her gray cotton slacks and walked out through the nurses' mess, past the operating theaters (now, thankfully, silent) toward Ward G, thinking what a rare pleasure it was to be following the sound of laughter and music rather than the howling of men in pain.

———

The majority of beds in the long tent known as Ward G had been moved back so that half of the room now formed an unofficial, sand-based dance floor and those men still confined to their beds could see it. On the desk in the corner the gramophone huskily issued the songs that had not been scratched to nothing through years of sand and overuse. An impromptu bar had been set up at what had been the dressings station, the drips converted for use with whisky and beer bottles.

Many were out of uniform tonight, the women in pale blouses and floral skirts, the men in shirts with trousers that had to be winched round their waists with narrow belts. Several sisters were dancing, some with each other, a couple with the remaining Red Cross staff and physiotherapists, stumbling over the more elaborate moves. A couple stopped when Audrey Marshall entered, but she nodded at them in a way that suggested they should carry on. "I suppose I should do my final rounds," she said, her voice mock-stern, which prompted a weak cheer from the tent's occupants.

"We'll miss you, Matron," said an emotional Sergeant Levy in the corner. She could just make out his face behind his raised legs, which were still in plaster.

"You'll miss the bed-baths, more like," said his mate. More laughter.

She moved along the row of beds, checking the temperatures of those with suspected dengue fever, peering under dressings that covered tropical ulcers, which refused obstinately to heal.

This lot weren't looking so bad. When the Indian prisoners-of-war had arrived at the beginning of the year even she had had nightmares for weeks. She remembered the shattered bones, the maggoty bayonet wounds, the starving, distended stomachs. Reduced to an almost inhuman state, many of the Sikhs had fought the nurses as they tried to treat them—over the years they had become used to brutality and, in their weakened state, were unable to anticipate anything else. The nurses had cried in their mess tents afterward, especially for the men whom the Japanese had deliberately overfed as they left the camps, and who had died painful deaths from their first taste of freedom.

Some of the Sikhs had hardly been men: they were light enough to be carried by a single nurse, mute or incoherent. For weeks they had fed them like newborn babies: two-hourly doses of powdered milk, followed by teaspoons of mashed potato, minced rabbit, boiled rice, trying to coax their collapsed digestive systems back into life. They had cradled skeletal heads, mopped spilled food from chapped lips, slowly convinced the men with whispers and smiles that this was not the precursor to some further terrible act of violence. Gradually, their hollow eyes bleak with whatever they had seen, the men had begun to understand where they had come.

The nurses had been so moved by their plight, their wordless gratitude and the fact that many had not heard from home in years, that some weeks later they had got one of the interpreters to help them prepare a curried dish for those able to stomach it. Nothing too ambitious, just a little mutton and spices, some Indian flatbread to go with the boiled rice. They had presented it on trays decorated with flowers. It had seemed important to convince the men that there was still a little beauty in the world. But as they entered the ward, and proudly laid out the trays before them, many of the POWs had finally broken down, less able to cope with kindness than with hard words and blows.

"Share a nip with us, Matron?"

The captain lifted the bottle, an invitation. The record finished and at the far end of the room someone cursed as the next disc slid out of slick hands on to the floor. She eyed him for a moment. He shouldn't be drinking with the medication he was taking. "Don't mind if I do, Captain Baillie," she said. "One for the boys who aren't going home."

The girls' faces relaxed. "To absent friends," they murmured, glasses upheld.

"Wish the Americans were still here," said Staff Nurse Fisher, mopping her brow. "I don't half miss those buckets of crushed ice." Only a few British patients now remained.

There was a swell of agreement.

"I just want to get to sea," said Private Lerwick, from the corner. "I keep dreaming of the breezes."

"Cups of tea without chlorinated water."

"Cold English beer."

"No such thing, mate."

Normally heat like this would have left them all listless, the patients dozing on their beds, the nurses moving slowly between them, wiping damp faces with cool cloths, checking for ulcers, infection, dysentery. But the imminent departure of the POWs, the fact that they were mending, that they were here at all, had injected something into the atmosphere. Perhaps it was the sudden realization that long-standing units, tightly knit groups that had supported each other through the horror of the last years, were about to be disbanded, separated by miles, in some cases continents, and might not meet again.

Audrey Marshall, watching the people before her, felt her throat constrict—a sensation so rare that she was briefly perplexed by it. Suddenly she understood the girls' need to party, the men's determination to drink, dance and plow their way with forced merriment through these last hours together. "Tell you what," she said, gesturing toward the drip in the corner, where one of the physiotherapists was drinking beer from a false limb, "make mine a large one."

The singing started not long afterward: "Shenandoah." The reedy, drink-lubricated voices drifted through the canvas into the night sky.

It was half-way through the chorus that the girl entered. Audrey didn't see her at first—the whisky had perhaps dulled the sharp senses that usually ensured she missed nothing. But as she raised her own voice in song, enjoying the sight of the recovering men singing in their beds, the nurses clutching each other, their eyes occasionally welling with sentimental tears, she became aware of a sudden *froideur*, the sideways glances that told her something had changed.

She was standing in the doorway, her pale, freckled face porcelain still, her thin shoulders erect in her uniform as she took in the scene before her. She was holding a small suitcase and a kitbag. Not much to show for six years in the Australian General Hospital. She stared into the crowded tent as if it had altered her resolve to come in, as if she were about to change her mind. Then she caught Audrey Marshall looking at her, and walked over slowly, staying as close as she could to the side of the tent.

"Packed already, Sister?"

She hesitated before she spoke. "I'll be boarding the hospital ship tonight, Matron, if it's all right by you. They could do with a bit of help with the very sick men."

"They didn't ask me," said Audrey, trying not to sound aggrieved.

The girl looked at the floor. "I—I offered. I hope you don't mind. I thought I could be of more use . . . that you probably didn't need me anymore." With the music it was difficult to hear her.

"You don't want to stay and have a last few drinks with us?" Even as she said it Audrey wasn't sure why she'd asked. In the four years they had worked together Sister Mackenzie had never been one for parties. Now she probably understood why.

"You're very kind, but no, thank you." She was already looking at the doorway, as if calculating how soon she could leave.

Audrey was about to press the point, unwilling to let her drift off, to let this be the way her years of service should end. But as she tried to find the right words, she became aware that for the most part the girls had stopped dancing. Several of them stood in huddles, their eyes cold, assessing. "I'd like to say—" she began, but one of the men interrupted.

"Is that Sister Mackenzie? You hiding her there, Matron? Come on, Sister, you can't go without saying a proper goodbye."

Private Lerwick was trying to get out of bed. He had put his feet on the ground and was steadying himself with one hand on the iron bedhead. "Don't you go anywhere, Sister. You made me a promise, remember?"

Audrey caught the knowing smirk between Nurse Fisher and the two girls beside her. She glanced at Sister Mackenzie, and realized that she had seen it too. Sister Mackenzie's hands had tightened on her two bags. She stiffened, then said quietly, "I can't stay, Private. I've got to board the hospital ship."

"Ah, will you not take a drink with us, Sister? A last drink?"

"Sister Mackenzie has work to do, Sergeant O'Brien," the matron said firmly.

"Ah, come on. At least shake my hand."

The girl took a step forward, then went to shake the hands of those men who proffered them. The music had started up again, deflecting attention from her, but even as she moved, Audrey Marshall noted the narrowed eyes of the other nurses, the deliberate turning away of several men. She walked behind her, making sure she wasn't kept at each bed for too long.

"You've meant the world to me, Sister." Sergeant O'Brien held her pale hand in both of his, voice tearful with drink.

"Nothing that any of us wouldn't have done," she said, a little curtly.

"Sister! Sister, come here." Private Lerwick was beckoning. Audrey saw the girl register him, and then the number of people she would have to pass to get to him. "Come on, Sister Mackenzie. You made me a promise, remember?"

"I really don't think—"

"You wouldn't break a promise to a wounded man, would you, Sister?" Private Lerwick's expression was comically hangdog.

The men on each side of him joined in chorus: "Come on, Sister, you promised."

Then the room went very quiet. Audrey Marshall saw the girls step back as they waited to see what Sister Mackenzie would do.

Finally, unable to bear the girl's dilemma any longer, she intervened: "Private, I'll thank you to get back into your bed." She walked briskly across to where he sat. "Promise or no promise, you're not ready to be out of it."

"Aw, Matron. Give a guy a break."

She was lifting his leg back on to the mattress when a voice said, "It's all right, Matron." She turned to see the girl standing behind her, face bright. Only the fluttering of her pale hands betrayed her discomfort. "I did promise."

Audrey felt, rather than saw, the gaze of the other women and, despite the heat, felt her skin prickle. "If you're sure, Sister."

She was a tall girl so she had to stoop as she helped the young man to a sitting position, and then, arm under his shoulders in a long-practiced maneuver, hauled him to his feet.

For a moment, no one spoke. Then Sergeant Levy yelled for music, and someone jigged the gramophone back into life.

"Go on, Scottie," said the man behind her. "Just don't step on her toes."

"I couldn't dance before," he joked, as they moved slowly on to the sandy area that had passed as the dance floor. "Two pounds of shrapnel in my knees isn't going to help none."

They began to dance. "Ah, Sister," Audrey heard him say, "you don't know how long I've been wishing for this."

Those men still nearby broke out a spontaneous round of applause. Audrey Marshall found she was clapping too, moved by the sight of the frail man standing tall and proud, beaming to have achieved his modest ambition: to stand on a dance floor again with a woman in his arms. She watched the girl, braving her own discomfort for him, rangy arms tensed to support him if he lost his balance. A kind girl. A good nurse.

That was the saddest part of it.

The music stopped. Private Lerwick sank gratefully into his bed, still grinning despite his obvious exhaustion. Audrey felt her heart sink, knowing that the simple act of kindness would count against the young nurse. Knowing that, as the girl searched with her eyes for her bags, she was aware of it too. "I'll see you out, Sister," she said, wanting to save her further exposure.

Private Lerwick was still hanging on to her hand. "We know what you've all done, coming here in your time off . . . You've all been like—like our sisters." He broke down and, after a brief hesitation, Sister Mackenzie bent over him, murmuring to him not to upset himself. "That's what I'll think of when I think of you, Sister. Nothing else. I just wish poor Chalkie . . ."

Audrey placed herself swiftly between them. "I'm sure we're all very grateful to Sister Mackenzie, aren't we? And I'm sure we'd like to wish her all the best for the future."

A few nurses clapped politely. A couple of the men exchanged a smirk.

"Thank you," the girl said quietly. "Thank you. I'm glad to have known you . . . all . . ." She bit her lip and glanced toward the door of the tent, apparently desperate to be away.

"I'll see you out, Sister."

"You take care now, Sister Mackenzie."

"Give the boys at home our best."

"Tell my missus to warm up my side of the bed." This was accompanied by ribald laughter.

Audrey, lifted briefly from her strange, low-level anxiety, observed this with satisfaction. Several weeks ago, some of the men could not have told her their wife's name.

———

The two women walked slowly toward the ship, only the sound of their starched uniforms and the soft thud of their shoes on the sand breaking the silence as the sounds of the party faded. They walked the length of the perimeter fence, past the now-deserted rows of hospital tents, the corrugated-iron staff quarters, cookhouse and latrines. They nodded at the security guard on the gate, who saluted, and then, free of the camp, they walked the length of the deserted road to the end of the peninsula, footsteps echoing on the Tarmac, to where the hospital ship sat in the glinting water, illuminated by the moon.

They reached the checkpoint and stopped. Sister Mackenzie stared at the ship, and Audrey Marshall wondered what was going through the girl's head, suspecting she knew the answer. "Not long to Sydney, is it?" she said, when the silence became awkward.

"No. Not long at all."

There were too many inappropriate questions, too many trite answers. Audrey fought the urge to place an arm round the girl, wishing she could better express some of what she felt. "You're doing the right thing, Frances," she said, eventually. "I'd do the same if I were you."

The girl looked at her, back straight, eyes level. She had always been guarded, Audrey thought, but in the past weeks her expression had closed over as completely as if it had been cast in marble. "Don't pay any attention to the others," she said suddenly. "They're probably just jealous."

They both knew that wasn't it.

"Fresh start, eh?" she said, holding out her hand.

"Fresh start." Sister Mackenzie shook it firmly. Her hand was cool, despite the heat. Her expression was unreadable. "Thank you."

"You take care now." Audrey was not a woman given to sentiment or high emotion. As the girl turned toward the ship, she nodded, brushing off her slacks, and went back toward the camp.

Part Two

4

Sydney's most stirring show last week was the departure for England of HMS Victorious *with 700 Australian wives of British servicemen aboard. Hours before the ship sailed the road outside the wharf was dense with relatives and friends . . . Mostly the brides were amazingly young."*

THE BULLETIN, 10 JULY 1946

EMBARKATION

Afterward, she realized she wasn't sure what she had expected; perhaps some orderly queue of women, suitcases in hand, making their way past the captain. With a shake of his hand and some discreet, perhaps tearful goodbyes, they would walk up the gangplank on to their big white ship. She would wave until her family were out of sight, call a few last-minute instructions about the feeding of the mare, the whereabouts of Mum's good boots for Letty, then finally her love and goodbyes, her voice echoing across the harbor as the ship slowly pulled out to sea. She would be brave, keep her eyes trained on what she was going to, not what she was leaving behind.

What she had not imagined was this: the traffic jams all the way to Sydney Harbor, cars snaking in bad-tempered queues, bumper to bumper under the gray city skies, the crowds of people thronging the entrance to the docks, yelling and waving greetings to people too far away or just too deafened by the noise to answer. The brass band, ice-cream sellers, lost children. The jostling of a million elbows and stumbling feet, all trying to force their way to the quayside. The hysteria of innumerable young women, clutching parents, bawling grief-stricken or giddy with excitement as they attempted to haul baggage and food parcels through the thick crowd toward the huge gray vessel. The air of nervous anticipation, hanging like sea mist over the docks.

"Bloody hell! We'll never make it at this rate." Murray Donleavy sat behind the wheel of the pickup truck, smoking yet another cigarette, his freckled face set.

"Be fine, Dad." Margaret laid a hand on his arm.

"Man's driving like an idiot. Look, he's so busy chinwagging he hasn't even noticed they're moving. Get *up* there." He slammed his hand on the horn, causing the car in front to judder and stall.

"Dad, he's not one of your cows, for God's sake. Look, it's fine. We'll be fine. If it gets any worse I can always get out and walk."

"She can bat them out the way with her bloody stomach." Daniel, behind her, had been increasingly rude about her "lump," as he called it.

"I'll bat you out of the way, if you don't mind your language. With the back of my hand." Margaret leaned forward to stroke the terrier that sat in the footwell between her feet. Every so often, Maude Gonne's nose would twitch at the unfamiliar scents that came in through the window: sea salt, traffic fumes, popcorn and diesel. She was an old dog, half-blind, her nose speckled with salt-and-pepper flecks of gray, and had been Margaret's tenth birthday gift from her mother because, unlike her brothers, she wasn't going to get a gun.

She leaned down and pulled her hand basket on to her knee, then checked for the fourteenth time that her papers were in order.

Her father glanced over. "Looks like you've got bugger all in that basket. I thought Letty put a few sandwiches in for you."

"I must have taken them out when I was fussing with it at home. Sorry—too much on my mind this morning."

"Let's hope they feed you on board."

"Course they'll feed us, Dad. Especially me."

"They'll need another ship just to carry the food she needs."

"Daniel!"

"Dad, it's okay." Her brother's fierce features were half hidden behind his overgrown fringe. He seemed to find it increasingly difficult to look at her. She thought about reaching out a hand to say she understood, that she wouldn't hold this uncharacteristic meanness against him, but she suspected he would repel that too—and now that they were near to saying goodbye, she wasn't sure that she was robust enough to take it.

Letty hadn't wanted him to come, had seen the boy's sullenness as a bad omen for the voyage. "You don't want a face like that to be the last thing you see of your family," she said, as Daniel slammed the door for the umpteenth time.

"He's all right," Margaret had replied.

Letty had shaken her head and redoubled her efforts on the food parcel. Twenty-five pounds they were allowed; and Letty, afraid that Joe's mother might not think her new Australian family hospitable enough, had weighed and reweighed until she had utilized every last bit of the allowance.

Margaret's dowry thus contained, among other things, Letty's best tinned fruitcake, a bottle of sherry, tinned salmon, beef and asparagus, and a box of jellied fancies that she'd put by with the coupons on a visit to Hordern Brothers. She had wanted to pack a dozen eggs, but Margaret had pointed out that even if they survived the car journey to Sydney, after six weeks on board ship they would be less a gift than a health hazard. "It's not like the Poms are the only ones who've got rationing," Colm had complained. He was rather partial to Letty's fruitcake.

"The nicer we treat them, the better they're likely to treat Maggie," Letty had said crossly. Then after staring into the middle distance, she had fled the kitchen, dabbing her eyes with a tea-towel.

She no longer bothered to set her hair.

"Got your papers?" They had reached the gates of Woolloomooloo wharf. In his new uniform the officer was stiff with the importance of the day. He leaned through the window of the truck, and Margaret pulled her well-thumbed documents out of her basket and handed them to him.

His finger traced the line of names until, apparently satisfied, he waved them on. "All brides, *Victoria*. Number six berth. You'll probably have to drop her by the post. There's no space to stop."

"Can't do that, mate. Look at her."

The officer ducked down to her father's window then glanced away, scanning the crowds. "You might be lucky and find a space over on the left. Follow the signs to the quayside, then head left by the blue pillar."

"Cheers, mate."

The man banged twice on the roof of the truck. "Try not to run anyone over. It's madness in there."

"Do me best." Murray shoved his hat further down on his head, and negotiated his way toward the quayside. "Can't promise anything, mind."

The truck growled and whined as Murray steered through the crowd, braking now and then as some stray person fell off the curb into the road, or swerving round a weeping mother and daughter, clutching each other, oblivious to their surroundings. "Too right they're not like cows," he muttered to himself. "Cows have more sense."

He didn't like crowds at the best of times. Despite Woodside's relative proximity to the city, Margaret thought he had probably been to Sydney no more than a handful of times since she was born. Noisy, stinking place, full of sharks. He couldn't walk a straight line, he would complain. All the people had him dodging about just to get from A to B. She didn't much like them herself, but today she felt curiously detached, as if she were an observer, unable to take in the magnitude of what she was about to do.

"How we doing for time?" he said, as they sat, engine idling, waiting for another crocodile of people to pass, dragging bulging suitcases or recalcitrant children.

"Dad, we're fine, I've told you. I could get out and walk from here if you like."

"As if I'd leave you alone with that lot!"

Suddenly she realized he felt a huge responsibility for getting her there; that, much as he hated to lose her, he was afraid he would not do right by her this last time. "It's only a couple of hundred yards and I'm hardly an invalid."

"I promised I'd see you on to your ship, Maggie. You just sit tight." His jaw had tightened and she wondered absently to whom he had made the promise.

"There! Look, Dad!" Daniel was rapping on the back window, gesticulating wildly to where an official-looking car was just leaving a parking space.

"Right." Her father's chin jutted, and he revved the engine, causing the people in front of him to skip out of the way. "Get up there," he roared through his window and, within seconds, had wedged the truck into the little space, thwarting several other cars which had edged toward it. "There!" He turned off the ignition, and as the engine ticked its way to sleep, he turned to his daughter. "There," he said again, not quite as firmly.

She reached across and took his hand. "I knew you'd get me here," she said.

———

The ship was huge; big enough to take up the entire length of the dockside, blocking out the sea and the sky so that only its flat gray surfaces met the crowds who now swarmed up to the barriers, trying frantically to communicate with those already on the water. Big enough to knock Maggie's breath clean into the back of her throat.

On its side, gun turrets bulged like balconies, some with cannons still poised or bearing spindly gantries, bent like the necks of elegant birds. On the flight deck, just visible from this far back, aircraft were poised in three formations, their wings folded above them, Corsairs, Fireflies and, possibly, a Walrus. Margaret, imbued by osmosis with her brother's passion for aircraft, could name them all. Hundreds of girls were aboard already, lining the flight deck or sitting astride gun barrels, waving from walkways, their gestures tiny and metronomic against the aircraft-carrier, coats and headscarves tied tight against the brisk sea breeze. A few peered from portholes, mouthing silent messages to those below. It was impossible to hear anything in the overall din, so many signaled in a kind of manic semaphore.

To one side a brass band was playing: she could just identify "The Maori's Farewell" and "Bell-bottomed Trousers" as snatches carried over the noise of the crowd. As they stood, a girl was being helped down the gangplank, crying, brightly colored paper streamers stuck to her coat. "Changed her mind," she heard one of the officers say. "Someone take her to the cargo sheds with the others."

Margaret allowed herself to feel the slightest trepidation, and knew how easy it would be to let hysteria engulf her.

"Nervous?" said her father. He had seen the girl too.

"Nope," she said. "I just want to see Joe again."

Her answer seemed to satisfy him. "Your mum would be proud."

"Mum would say I should be wearing something smarter."

"That too." He nudged her and she nudged him back, then reached up to adjust her hat.

"Any more brides?" A Red Cross woman with a clipboard elbowed her way past. "Brides, you need to board now. Have your papers ready." As each girl made her way up the gangplank, she was showered with streamers, and cries of "You'll be sorry," from the dockers in a tone that might or might not have been jovial.

Her father had taken her trunk to Customs. Now she peered round him to where her youngest brother was standing, eyes averted from her and the ship. "Look after that mare for me, Daniel," she said, now having to shout a little. "Don't let any of those deadweights anywhere near her." He stared at the ground, refusing to look at her. "And keep her in a snaffle as long as you can. She's not pulling at the moment, and she'll go better in the long run if you can keep her mouth soft."

"Daniel. Answer your sister." Her father elbowed him.

"All right."

She stared at his thin shoulders, at the face resolutely turned from hers, overwhelmed by the urge to hug him, to tell him how much she loved him. But he had found her pregnant form increasingly repellent, had recoiled from contact with her since she had confirmed she was leaving. It was as if he blamed her bump, not Joe, for taking her away.

"Shake my hand?"

There was a long pause, weighted by the prospect of their father's opprobrium, then Daniel's hand snaked out and took hers in a brief, firm clasp. Then he dropped it. Still he would not look at her.

"I'll write you," she said. "You'd better bloody reply."

He said nothing.

Her father stepped forward and hugged her tightly. "Tell that man of yours he's to look after you," he said, his voice strangled as he spoke into her hair.

"Not you too, Dad." She breathed in the mothball smell of his good jacket, and the bovine scent that mingled with hay. "You'll be all right, you lot. Letty will look after you better than I ever did."

"Well, that wouldn't be hard."

She could hear the effort in his joke, and held him tighter.

"I wish—I wish . . ."

"Dad . . ." Her voice held a warning.

"Right." He pulled away from her, took several swift glances around him, as if his mind was already elsewhere. He swallowed. "Well, we'd better let you get on board. Want me to carry your bags?"

"I'll be fine." She slung the big bag over her shoulder, jamming her hand basket and food parcel under her free arm as she balanced herself. Then she took a deep breath, and made toward the ship.

Her father's hand shot out. "Hang on, girl! You've got to go through Customs first."

"What?"

"Customs. Look—they're sending everyone that way before they get on board."

She peered through the jostling crowds to where he was pointing: a huge corrugated-iron shed across the quayside.

"That's what the Red Cross woman was saying. Everyone through there first."

Two girls were talking to the officers at the doorway. One was gesturing at her bag and laughing.

Her father peered at her. "You all right, girl? You've gone awful pale."

"I can't, Dad," she whispered.

"I can't hear you, girl. What's the matter?"

"Dad, I don't feel good," she said.

Her father stepped forward and took her arm. "What is it? Do you need to sit down?"

"No . . . It's the crowds. I'm feeling a bit faint. Tell them they've got to get me aboard." She closed her eyes. She heard her father bark at Daniel, and him sprinting off.

Several minutes later, two naval officers were standing beside her. "Are you all right, madam?"

"I just need to get aboard."

"Right. Have you been—"

"Look, you can see I'm expecting. I feel faint. The baby's pressing on my bladder and I'm afraid of embarrassing myself. I can't stay in this crowd a minute longer." Desperation had made her tearful, and it embarrassed them, she could tell.

"This isn't like her," her father was saying, his voice concerned. "She's a strong lass. Never seen her come over faint before."

"We've had a few already," said one of the officers. "It's all this commotion. We'll get her aboard. Give us your bags, madam."

She let go of her bag and the food parcel, the brown paper now softened with the sweat of her hands.

"She going to be okay? You got a doctor aboard?" Her father hovered by them, his face drawn.

"Yes, sir. Please don't worry." She felt him pause beside her. "Sorry, sir. You can't come any further."

One of the officers had reached for her basket. "Want me to take this for you?"

"No," she snapped, pulling it to her. "No, thank you," she added, and tried to smile. "It's got all my papers and things in it. Be terrible if I lost it."

He grinned at her. "You're probably right, madam. Today's not the day to lose anything."

They had each supported her under an elbow and were now propelling her toward the ship. Unlike the *Victoria* itself, she noted absently, the gangplank looked tired, its wooden struts half rotten from years of feet and seawater. " 'Bye then, Maggie," her father called.

"Dad." Suddenly it seemed too hurried. She wasn't sure if she was ready after all. She tried to blow a kiss with her free hand in an attempt to convey something of what she felt.

"Dan? Daniel? Where is he?" Her father had spun round to locate the boy. He waved his hand for her to wait, to hang on, but the crowd was pushing against the barrier and he was already being swallowed into it.

"I haven't said goodbye properly."

"Bloody boy." Her father was almost in tears. "Dan! I know he wants to say goodbye. Look, don't take any notice of all that—"

"We should really get you aboard, madam," said the officer beside her.

She looked at him, then at the Customs shed. Her feet were on the gangplank now. She could feel the pressure of her suitcase on her leg as the officer stood behind her, impatient to move on.

"I can't see him, love," Murray called. "I don't know where he is."

"Tell him it's okay, Dad. I understand." She could see that her father was blinking hard.

"You'll be sorry!" A young navvy, cap pulled low over his head, grinned at her slyly.

"You take care," her father yelled. "You hear me? You take care of yourself." Then his voice, his face and the top of his battered hat were lost in the mêlée.

———

The executive officer, or XO as he was known to the men, had tried three times to get his attention. Bloody man kept standing there, bobbing up and down, like a child begging permission to visit the little boys' room.

Dobson. Always a little more informal than the occasion deserved. Captain Highfield, already in a foul mood, was determined to ignore him. He turned away, rang down to the Engine Control Room.

The damp was making his leg ache. He rested it briefly by placing his full weight on the other in a lopsided stance unusual to him. He was a stocky man, whose ramrod-straight posture had become ingrained over years of service—and led to countless irreverent imitations below decks.

"Hawkins, let me know about the port outer engine. Is it still locked?"

"I've got two men down there at the moment, sir. We're hoping to free it up in the next twenty minutes or so."

Captain Highfield exhaled. "Do your best, man. Otherwise we're going to need another two tugs to get us clear, and that's not going to look too clever today, is it?"

"Not quite the image we want to give the old colonials when we're running off with their daughters."

"Bridge, wheelhouse, Coxswain at the wheel."

"Very good, Coxswain. Stand by to steer one-two-zero." Captain Highfield stood up from the voice-pipe.

"What?"

Dobson hesitated. "I . . . was just agreeing with you, sir. Not the kind of image we want to project."

"Yes, well, not something you need to worry about, Dobson. What was it you wanted?"

From the bridge, the whole harbor was visible: the huge, teeming crowds that stretched as far as the dry docks, the bunting strung below, and, one by one, the women who made their way slowly up the gangplank, waving as they came. Highfield had groaned inwardly at every one.

"I came to talk to you about the mess report, sir. We're still missing a few."

Captain Highfield glanced at his watch. "At this hour? How many?"

Dobson consulted his list. "At this moment, sir, almost half a dozen."

"Bloody hell." Captain Highfield slammed his hand down on the dial. The slipping off was turning into a farce. "What on earth were the men doing last night?"

"Sounds like there was something of a shindig at one of the drinking clubs, sir. We've had a few back been caught scrapping, a few who were frankly incapable. One man missed the gangplank and fell into the soup. Lucky we had Jones and Morris on watch, sir, or we might have lost him altogether. And then there are the six still absent."

Highfield stared out of the bridge. "Bloody shambles," he said. Those around him knew that the ferocity in his voice did not relate entirely to the missing men. "Six hundred flapping girls can make their way aboard on time, but not England's finest. Bloody embarrassment, the lot of them."

"There's something else. Four of the brides are in with the Red Cross already."

"What? They've only been on board five minutes."

"Didn't listen when we said they'd need to duck through the hatches. Too excited, I suppose." He smacked his forehead, mirroring the most common injury on board ship. "One's a stitches job."

"Can't the surgeon see to it?"

"Ah. He's—erm—one of those missing."

There was a lengthy silence. The men around him were silent and expectant.

"Twenty minutes," Highfield said eventually. "Just till we get the port outer engine working again. After that you can tell the mess men to start offloading their belongings. I won't have this ship held up. Not today of all days."

Avice leaned on the rail, one hand keeping her new hat in place. Astride a gun turret, Jean was making a spectacle of herself. The dark-haired girl had become hysterical, and after yelling until she was hoarse at anyone who would listen, now had her arms slung over two ratings, as if she were drunk and leaning on them for support. Perhaps she *was* drunk: with that kind of girl little would have surprised Avice. It was why she had been rather careful to disassociate herself the moment they had come aboard half an hour earlier.

She looked down at the pleats on her new suit, satisfied by how superior her outfit was compared with those of the girls around her. Her parents, who had been unable to see her off, had sent a telegram and some money, and her mother had arranged for the suit to be delivered that morning to the hotel. Avice had been worried about what to wear, unsure of the etiquette for such an occasion. Now, with a clear view of at least a hundred other girls, hardly any of whom seemed to have dressed for the occasion, she wondered why she had fretted.

The ship was shabby. Avice had had her picture taken, been interviewed by the *Bulletin* for its society pages, and someone whom she had been pretty sure was the captain had shaken her hand, but it didn't alter the fact that the *Victoria* was rusting in places, and bore no more resemblance to the *Queen Mary* than Jean did to her namesake Jean Harlow. As Avice had made her way up the rickety gangplank, her nostrils had curled at the faint but definite aroma of boiled cabbage, which reinforced the second-class nature of her transport.

Still, no one could accuse Avice of lack of fiber. Oh, no. She straightened her shoulders and forced herself to think about what she was heading to. In six weeks, she would discover what her new life held. She would get to know his parents, take tea at the Rectory, meet the ladies of the quaint English village where they lived, perhaps the odd duke or duchess. She would be introduced to his friends, those outside the RAF, who had known him as a child. She would begin to make their home.

She would finally be Mrs. Ian Radley, rather than just Avice—or, as her mother put it, "Oh, Avice . . ."—who might be married but, as far as her family was concerned, seemed no more deserving of respect or adult consideration than she had been as a child.

"Watch her!"

Avice glanced down to the deck below: Jean had just slipped off the side of the gun turret. She was hanging, giggling, from the trouser pocket of one of the ratings, her slip and a good deal of leg exposed to anyone who cared to look. She was about to say something, when she realized that the deck was vibrating gently under her feet: the engines must have started, not that they could be heard in the din. She looked over the edge and saw, with a start, that the gangplank had been hauled up. There was a swell of noise, and a short distance away a winch was hoisting up several sailors who had apparently missed their opportunity to get aboard by normal means. They were laughing and cheering, covered with lipstick kisses. Possibly even drunk.

Disgraceful, thought Avice, smiling despite herself as they were dumped unceremoniously on the flight deck above. Around them, small tugs bossed and bullied the vast ship, negotiating its slow release from the harbor. The women were chattering excitedly, waving with greater urgency, their voices lifting as each tried to make sure their message was heard over the hubbub.

"Mum!" a voice below Avice yelled, increasingly hysterically. "Mum! Mum!"

Someone beside her was praying, then broke off to exclaim to herself: "I can't believe it! I can't believe it!"

The crowd, a sea of Australian flags and the odd Union Jack, frothed and bubbled as people pushed toward the edge of the quay, bobbing above their neighbors to be seen by those aboard. Several placards were held aloft: "God Speed, Audrey," "Good Luck from the Dockyard Workers of Garden Island." She found herself gazing around the port, then at the hills beyond. Is this it? she thought suddenly, her breath catching in her throat. My last view of Australia? Then, with a lurch, the streamers snapped, their cobwebby strands releasing the ship from the rails of the dockside and, with an audible groan, she lurched away from the quay, sinking a few degrees as she slipped anchor.

There was a collective gasp. The engines began to power. A girl shrieked and over the din the band, now clearly visible on the quayside, struck up with "Waltzing Matilda."

A few items were hurled from the ship's berth and fell short, sending up small splashes of futility. The thin ribbon of blue water widened beneath them, then became an expanse. The ship, as if oblivious to the madness around it, glided, surprisingly quickly, away from the harbor.

"You'll be sorry!" came a solitary cry, over the music. It sounded like a joke. "You'll all be sorry!"

It was at this point that the ship's passengers descended briefly into silence. Then, breaking it, the first of the girls began to cry.

———

Murray Donleavy placed his arm round his sobbing son, and sat silently as the crowds melted away, the sound of grieving women becoming more distinct. Finally, only a few huddles of people remained, staring out as the ship gradually merged with the horizon. It was getting chilly and the boy was shivering. He took off his jacket and threw it about Daniel's shoulders, then hauled the boy against him for warmth.

Every now and then Daniel raised his head as if he wanted to speak, but was unable to find words and sank back into silent weeping, his face thrust into his hands as if the tears were a cause of shame.

"Nothing to be sorry for, boy," he murmured. "It's been a tough day."

Theirs was one of the few vehicles remaining, sitting in a sea of muddied streamers and discarded sweet wrappers. Murray walked round to the driver's side of the pickup, then halted when he noticed that his son was standing still and staring at him. "You all right now?"

"Do you think she'll hate me, Dad?"

Murray moved round and hugged his boy again. "Don't be so bloody soft." He ruffled his hair. "She'll be banging on about you visiting her before you know it."

"In England?"

"Don't see why not. You keep saving up that rabbit money and you'll be able to fly there before you know it. Things are changing fast."

The boy gazed ahead at nothing, transported to a world of richly rewarded pelts and huge airplanes. "I could fly there," he repeated.

"Like I said, boy, you save your money. The rate you're going, you'll be able to pay for all of us."

Daniel smiled then, and his father's heart ached to see him meet another loss so bravely. This must be how it had felt for the women during the war, he observed, as he climbed into the truck. Except that they hadn't known if we were coming back. Take care of her, he told the ship silently. Look after my girl.

They sat in the cab for a few moments, watching people trail out through the dockyard gates, seeing exposed the vast expanses of ground that had been invisible, hidden under human traffic. The wind was picking up now, sending bits of paper scuttling around the quayside, to be dived on by seagulls. He sighed, suddenly conscious of the length of the drive home.

"Dad, she's left her sandwiches." Beside him, Daniel held aloft the greaseproofed package that Letty had put together that morning. "It was here, on the floor. She's left her lunch behind."

Murray frowned, trying to remember what his daughter had said about leaving them at home. Oh, well, he thought. She must have been mistaken. That's women when they're carrying. All over the place. Noreen had been the same.

"Can I have them, Dad? I'm starving."

Murray stuck his key into the ignition. "Don't see why not. They're no use to her now. Tell you what, save one for me."

It had finally begun to rain: the gray skies that had threatened to discharge their load all day were spitting against the windscreen. Murray started the truck, and reversed out slowly on to the dockside. Suddenly he hit the brake, sending Daniel shooting forward, his mouthful of sandwich spraying over the dashboard.

"Hang on," he said, his face electrified with the memory of an empty basket and his daughter's inexplicable hurry to get on board. "Where's the bloody dog?"

5

An Australian bride missed sailing for England in HMS Victorious *because at the last moment a charge, subsequently dismissed, was laid against her. Immediately she was released, she was rushed in a police car to No. 3 Wharf Woolloomooloo, but the brideship aircraft-carrier had sailed.*

SYDNEY MORNING HERALD, 4 JULY 1946

ONE DAY IN

HMS *Victoria* was seven hundred and fifty feet long, and weighed twenty-three thousand tons, comprising nine floors below the flight deck and four decks above it up to the vertiginous heights of the bridge and island. Even without the brides' specially created berths it would have housed in its gigantic belly some two hundred different rooms, stores and compartments, equaling the size, perhaps, of several department stores or upmarket apartment blocks. Or even, depending on where the brides had come from, several large barns. The hangars alone, where most of the brides were housed, fed and entertained, were nearly five hundred feet long and situated on the same floors as the canteens, bathrooms, the captain's sleeping area and at least fourteen sizable storerooms. They were linked by narrow passageways, which, if one confused the decks, were as likely to lead to an aircraft repair shop or engineers' mess as a brides' bathroom—a situation that had already caused several red faces. Someone had pinned a plan of the ship in the brides' canteen, and Avice had found herself studying it several times, mulling bad-temperedly over Vegetable Stores, Parachute Packing Rooms and Pom-Pom Magazines that should, by rights, have been grand ballrooms and first-class cabins. It was a floating world of unintelligible rules and regulations, of ordered and as yet unrevealed routines, a labyrinthine rabbit warren of low-ceilinged rooms, corridors and lockers, the vast majority of which led to places where the women were not meant to be. It was vast yet cramped, noisy—especially for those billeted near the engine rooms—battered, and filled to bursting point with chattering girls and men trying, in some cases half-heartedly, to do their work. With the sheer numbers of people moving around and a general unfamiliarity with the placing of the different flights of stairs and gangways it frequently took the best part of half an hour simply to traverse one deck, alternately pushing past people or pressing against the pipe-laden walls to give way to others.

And still Avice could not lose Jean.

From the moment she discovered they had been allocated the same cabin (more than six hundred brides and they had lumped her with Jean!) the girl had decided to take on a new role: that of Avice's Best Friend. Having conveniently forgotten the mutual antipathy that had characterized their meetings at the American Wives' Club, she had spent the greater part of the last twenty-four hours trailing after her, interrupting whenever Avice struck up conversation with anyone else to stake her claim with a suggestion of a shared history in Sydney.

So it was that they were both on the early sitting for breakfast ("Avice! Do you remember that girl who used to sew everything blanket stitch? Even her undies?"), walking the decks to try to get their bearings ("Avice! Do you remember when we had to wear those necklaces made out of chicken rings? Have you still got yours?") or sharing a packed queue for the bathroom ("Avice! Did you wear those cami-knickers on your wedding night? They look a bit posh for every day . . . or are you trying to impress someone? Eh? Eh?"). She knew she should be nicer to Jean, especially since she had discovered she was only sixteen—but really! The girl was awfully trying.

And Avice wasn't convinced that she was entirely truthful either. There had been an exchange when Jean had chattered on at breakfast about her plans to get a job in a department store where her husband's aunt held a managerial post. "How can you work? I thought you were expecting," Avice had said coldly.

"Lost it," said Jean blithely. Avice gave her a hard, skeptical look. "It was very sad," Jean said. Then, after a pause: "Do you think they'll let me have a second helping of bacon?"

Jean, Avice noted as she walked briskly up the last flight of stairs, hardly ever mentioned her husband, Stanley. She herself would have mentioned Ian more often, but on the few occasions when she had Jean had tried to elicit from her some smutty confidence ("Did you let him do it to you before your wedding night?" And, even worse: "Did it give you a fright the first time you saw it . . . you know . . . sticking up?"). Finally Avice gave up trying to shake her off by movement. They were all due upstairs on the flight deck at eleven for the captain's address. It should be simple enough to lose her among more than six hundred other women, shouldn't it?

"Do you fancy going to one of these lectures?" Jean shouted, chewing gum as they made their way past the projection room. "There's one on the strains of marrying a foreigner next week." Her voice, as it had all morning, carried over the noisy vibrations of the engines and the repeated piped calls, summoning Petty Officer Gardner or special sea dutymen to the commander's office.

Avice pretended not to hear her.

"I quite fancy the one on common difficulties in the first year," Jean went on. "Except our first year has been dead easy so far. He wasn't even there."

———

"The ship's company of HMS *Victoria* will do their best to make your passage to the United Kingdom an enjoyable one . . . At the same time you must remember you are not in a liner, but are privileged to be a passenger in one of His Majesty's ships. Life on board must be governed by service rules and customs."

Margaret stood on the flight deck, three deep in the rows of brides, some of whom were giggling with nerves as they listened to the captain. He moved, she thought, as if someone had sewn his sleeves to the body of his jacket.

The sea, sparkling blue, was benign and calm, and the deck—the size of a two-acre field—hardly moved. Margaret cast surreptitious glances along its shining length, sniffing the salted air, feeling the breeze-blown sea mist on her skin, enjoying her first sense of space and freedom since they had slipped anchor the previous day. She had thought she might be a little frightened once they could no longer see land but instead she relished the sheer size of the ocean and wondered—with curiosity, not terror—what lay beneath the surface.

At each end of the deck, reflected in shallow, prismed puddles of seawater and aircraft fuel, the airplanes stood tethered, their gleaming noses pointing upward as if hankering for flight. Between them, at the base of the tower known as the "island," groups of men in overalls stood watching.

"Every person aboard one of His Majesty's ships is subject to the Naval Discipline Act, which means no spirits, wine or beer, and that gambling in any form is forbidden. There is to be no smoking near the aircraft at any time. Most importantly, do not get in the way of or distract men who are on duty. You are allowed nearly everywhere on the ship except the men's living spaces, but work must not be interrupted."

At this some of the girls glanced around and one of the ratings winked. A giggle rippled through the female ranks. Margaret shifted her weight to her other foot and sighed.

Jean, one of the girls allocated to share her cabin, had nipped into the space in front of her two minutes after the captain had started talking, and stood, one leg bent under her, biting her nails. She had been buoyant that morning, chattering away from daybreak about her excitement, about the ship, her new shoes. Anything that came to mind had spewed out, unfiltered, to the ears of her new companions. Now, faced with the captain's stern manner and his litany of possible misdemeanors, she was looking temporarily wobbly, her excitement giving way to trepidation.

"You may have heard from other brides that they had the chance to disembark at various ports on their journey. It must be remembered that in a troopship you will probably get no leave. There may be a chance to land at Colombo and possibly at Bombay, if the international situation allows, but this cannot be looked upon as certain. I would add that persons failing to return to the ship by the stated time are liable to be left behind."

The captain's gaze traveled along them. There was nothing speculative in it.

"If there is a general complaint about some matter, the duty women's service officer should be informed, and she will bring the matter to the notice of one of the lieutenant commanders. Meanwhile, the following spaces are out of bounds to women: ratings' living spaces and messes, officers' cabins and messes, below the level of the hangar deck, one deck above the flight deck, gun positions and galleries, and inside boats.

"A more comprehensive guide, in booklet form, will be distributed to each of you later this afternoon. I'd like you all to read it and ensure you follow its regulations to the letter. I cannot emphasize strongly enough how grave the consequences will be for those who choose to disobey them."

A silence descended on the deck, as he allowed the weight of his words to resonate. Margaret felt her cheeks flush as she thought of her cabin on the hangar deck below. A little way along, a woman was crying.

"Eight women's service officers are on board to advise, help and assist you on the journey." Here, he indicated the women standing by the Corsairs, each looking almost as grim and self-important as the captain himself. "Each WSO has a group of cabins under her special care and will always be available to help you." He fixed the women in front of him with a stern gaze. "The WSOs will also go rounds during the night."

"That's my evening's entertainment buggered," whispered the girl beside Margaret, and was met by a muffled snort of laughter.

"Just as women are not allowed in naval personnel's quarters, the ship's company is not allowed in the women's quarters and living spaces, except as required for duty. I would remind you of my previous statement, that the duty women's service officers will go rounds during the night."

"And naughty girls will have to walk the plank." There was

another surreptitious but clear outbreak of giggling, a pressure valve loosening.

"Lord knows what he takes us for," said the girl beside Margaret, fiddling with a brooch.

The captain appeared to be at the end of his interminable speech. He looked down at a note attached to his booklets, apparently determining whether or not to continue. After a moment or two, he raised his head. "I have also been asked to tell you that . . . a small hair-dressing salon . . ." here the captain's jaw tightened ". . . has been created in the after end of the lounge adjacent to B Cabin. It will be staffed by volunteers from among the passengers, if anyone would . . . like to offer their services."

He stared at his papers, then fixed them all with a look that might have been cold or simply weary resignation.

"Friendly soul," said Margaret, under her breath, as the group dispersed.

"I feel like I'm back at school," murmured Jean, in front of her, "but with fewer places to smoke."

———

Highfield looked at the women in front of him, nudging, whispering, fidgeting, not even capable of standing still for long enough to hear him list the rules and regulations that would govern their lives for the next six weeks. Even in this last twenty-four hours, he had watched every new outrage, every new example of why this had been a catastrophic idea, and wanted to telegraph McManus to say, "See? Didn't I tell you this would happen?" Half of them were hysterical, and didn't seem to know whether to laugh or cry. The other half were already clogging up the place, getting lost below decks, forgetting to duck and injuring their heads, getting in the way of his men, or even stopping him to demand, as one had this morning, where she might find the canteen with the ice-cream. To top it all, he had walked along the upper gallery earlier this morning and found himself in a fine mist, not of aircraft fuel but of perfume. Perfume! They might as well tie their undergarments in place of the ship's pennant and be done with it.

Admittedly there was no dramatic difference in the men's behavior, but he knew it was only a matter of time: at this very minute the women would be the main topic of conversation in the seamen's and stokers' mess, in the officers' mess and even the marines'. He could feel a subtle sense of disquiet in the air, as when dogs scent an approaching storm.

Or perhaps it was simply that nothing had felt settled since Hart's death. The company had lost the cheerful sense of purpose that had characterized its last nine months in the Pacific. The men—those who remained—had been withdrawn, more prone to argument and insubordination. Several times since they had slipped anchor, he had caught them muttering among themselves and wondered to what extent they blamed him. He concluded his speech, and forced the thoughts, as he often did, from his mind. The women looked wrong. The colors were too bright; the hair was too long; scarves dangled all over the place. His ship had been an ordered thing of grays and whites, of monochrome. The mere introduction of color was unbalancing, as if someone had unleashed a flock of exotic birds around him and left them, flapping and unpredictable, to create havoc. Some women were wearing high-heeled shoes, for goodness' sake.

It's not that I don't like women, he thought, as he did several times an hour. It's just that everything has its place. *People* have their place. He was a reasonable man. He didn't think this was an unreasonable point of view.

He folded the booklet under his arm and caught sight of some ratings loitering by the lashings—the chains that secured the aircraft to the deck. "Haven't you got anything bloody better to do?" he barked, then turned on his heel and strode into the lobby.

———

Dear Joe,

Well, here I am on the Victoria with the other brides, and I can tell you this: I'm definitely a land girl. It's awful cramped, even in a ship this size, and wherever you go you're bumping into people, like being in the city but worse. I suppose you're used to it, but I'm already dreaming of fields and empty spaces. Last night I even dreamt of Dad's cows . . .

Our four-berth cabin is one of many in what was apparently a giant liftwell, and I am sharing with three girls, who seem to be all right. One girl, Jean, is only sixteen—and guess what? She's not the youngest. There are evidently two girls of fifteen on board— both married to Brits and traveling alone. I can't say what Dad would have done if I'd come home at fifteen and announced I was getting married—even to you, dear. I'm also sharing with a girl who has been working for the Australian General Hospital out in the Pacific, and says almost nothing, and another who I think is a bit of a society type. I can't say any of us has much in common, other than that we are all wanting the same thing.

One bride apparently missed the boat at Sydney and they're flying her to Fremantle, where we will pick her up. So I guess you can't say the Navy aren't doing all they can to get us to you.

The men are all pretty friendly, although we're not meant to talk to them much. Some girls go silly whenever they walk past one. Honestly, you'd think they'd never seen a man before, let alone married one. The captain has read us the Riot Act already, and everyone keeps going on about water and how we're not meant to use any. I only had a flannel wash this morning—I can't see how I'm going to run the ship dry on that. I think of you often, and it is a comfort to me to think that we are probably, even at this minute, sailing on the same ocean.

Joe Junior, I'm sure, sends his love (kicks like a mule when I'm trying to sleep!).

Your Maggie

These were the other things that she hadn't told Joe: that she had lain awake for most of the first night, listening to the clanking of chains, doors slamming above and below, the hysterical giggling and shrieking of other women behind thinly constructed walls, and feeling the vibrations of the great ship moving under her, like some groaning prehistoric beast. That among the incomprehensible pipes that sounded every fifteen minutes or so ("Hands to action stations," "Stand by to receive gash barge alongside," "Special Sea Dutymen, close up") their wake-up call had been a rendition over the Tannoy of "Wakey, wakey, show a leg" (and that at five thirty, she had overheard the less savory men's version: "Wakey, wakey, rise and shine, hands off cocks, pull on socks"). That the ship was a bewildering mass of ranks and roles, from marines to stokers to airmen. That the canteen was big enough to seat three hundred girls at once, that together they made a noise like a huge flock of starlings descending, and that she had eaten better food at last night's supper than she had for the last two years. That almost the first naval custom they had been taught—with great emphasis on its importance—was the "submariner's dhobi": a shower of several seconds to soak oneself, a soaping with the water turned off, then a brief rinse under running water. It was vital, the Red Cross officer had impressed upon them, that they conserve water so that the pumps could desalinate at a rate fast enough to replace it, and they could make the crossing hygienically. From what she had heard in the shower rooms, she was pretty well the only bride to have followed those instructions.

Behind her, hidden by her size and a carefully folded blanket, Maude Gonne lay sleeping. After the captain's address, Margaret had raced back to their cabin (Daniel would have said "lumbered") and subdued the little dog's yelps with stolen biscuits, then smuggled her along to the bathroom to make sure she didn't disgrace herself. She had only just got back to the bunk when Frances came in, and she had thrust herself on to her bed, a warning hand on the dog's hidden head, willing her to stay quiet.

It was a problem. She had thought she would be allocated a single cabin—most of the pregnant brides had been. It hadn't occurred to her that she might have to share.

She wondered whether Frances, on the bunk opposite, could be trusted. She seemed all right, but she had said little that suggested anything at all. And she was a nurse—some of whom got awfully tied up in rules and regulations.

Margaret shifted on her bunk, trying to get comfortable, feeling the engines rumbling beneath her. There was so much she wanted to tell Joe, so much she wanted to convey about the strangeness of it all—of being thrust from her home into a world where girls became hysterical not just about their future but over brands of shampoo or stockings ("Where did you get those? I've been looking everywhere for them!") and exchanged the kind of intimate confidences that suggested they'd known each other for years, not twenty-four hours.

Mum would have been able to explain it, thought Margaret. She would have been able to speak their language, translate it, and afterward would have defused its power with a few pithy remarks. If I'd known she was going, she thought, I would have listened harder. I would have treated it all with a little more respect, rather than spending my life trying to live up to the boys. They never told you it wasn't just a gaping hole of grief but that it went on and on, myriad questions that wouldn't be answered.

She glanced at her watch. They would be out now, perhaps on the tractor, clearing the saplings at the bottom of the steers' field, as they had been meaning to do all summer. Colm had joked that spending all these weeks surrounded by women would drive her mad. Dad had said it might teach her a few things. Margaret gazed surreptitiously at the feminine trappings around her, of silk, nylon and floral patterns, of face creams and manicure sets. She hadn't anticipated that it might leave her feeling alien.

"You want my pillow?" Frances had emerged from her novel. She was gesturing toward Margaret's stomach.

"No. Thanks."

"Go on—you can't be comfortable."

It had been the longest sentence she had uttered since introducing herself. Margaret hesitated, then accepted the pillow with thanks and wedged it under her thigh. It was true: the bunks offered all the width and comfort of an ironing-board.

"When's it due?"

"Not for a couple of months or so." Margaret sniffed, pushed tentatively at her mattress. "It could have been worse, I suppose. They might have given us hammocks."

The other girl's smile faltered, as if, having opened the conversation, she was now unsure what else to say. She returned to her book.

Maude Gonne shifted and whined in sleep, her paws scrabbling against Margaret's back. The noise was disguised by the thrum of the engines and the chatter of girls passing outside the half-open door. But she would have to do something. Maude Gonne couldn't stay in here for the whole six weeks. Even if she only left to go to the bathroom there were bound to be occasions when the other girls were here. How would she keep her quiet then?

Bugger it, she thought, shifting her belly again. What with the baby moving constantly, and all these women around, night, day and every single minute in between, it was impossible to think straight.

———

The cabin door was open and Avice stepped in, remembering to duck—she had no intention of meeting Ian with a bruised forehead—and raised a smile for the two girls lying on the bottom bunks. Made of a naval-issue bedroll lying in a raised platform of webbing, they were less than five feet apart, and the women's small cases, containing the minimum of their belongings, were stacked securely against the temporary sheet-metal wall that divided them from the next cabin.

The entire space was rather smaller than her bathroom at home. There was no concession to the femininity of the passengers: the fabrics were utilitarian at best, the floor uncarpeted, the color a uniform battleship gray. The only mirrors were in the steamy confines of the shower rooms. Their larger cases, with the main part of their clothes and belongings, were stored in the quarterdeck lockers, which smelled of aircraft fuel and to which they had to beg access from a spectacularly sour WSO, who had already reminded Avice twice—with what Avice felt was obvious envy—that life on board was not a fashion parade.

Avice was desperately disappointed in her traveling companions. Almost everywhere she had been this morning she had seen girls in smarter clothes, with the right sort of look, the kind that spoke to Avice of a social standing not dissimilar to her own. She might have found consolation in their company for the awfulness of the ship. But instead she had been landed with a pregnant farm girl and a surly nurse. (She did so hope she wasn't going to be one of those superior types, as if the terrible things she had supposedly witnessed made the rest of them shallow for trying to enjoy themselves.) And, of course, there was Jean.

"Hey there, shipmates." Jean scrambled on to the bunk above Margaret, her thin bare limbs like a monkey's, and lit a cigarette. "Avice and me have been checking out the action on board. There's a cinema up near the bow, on the lower gallery. Anyone fancy coming to the pictures later?"

"No. Thanks anyway," said Frances.

"Actually, I think I'll stay here and write some letters." Avice had made her way on to her top bunk, holding her skirt down over her thighs with one hand. It took some effort. "I'm feeling a little weary."

"How 'bout you, Maggie?" Jean leaned over the side of her bunk.

Her head heaving suddenly into view made Margaret jump and contort into a peculiar shape. Avice wondered if this traveling companion was going to prove even odder than she had suspected. Margaret seemed to sense that her reaction had been a little strange: she reached behind her, picked up a magazine and flicked it open with studied nonchalance. "No," she said. "Thank you. I—I should probably rest."

"Yeah. You do that," said Jean, hauling herself back into her bunk and taking a long drag on her cigarette. "The last thing we want is you dropping it in here."

Avice was searching for her hairbrush. She had been through her vanity case several times, and climbed down from her bunk to gaze at the others. Now that the excitement of the slipping off had dissipated, and the circumstances in which she was going to have to spend the next six weeks had come into focus, her mood had darkened. She was finding it difficult to keep smiling through. "I'm sorry to bother you all, but has anyone seen my brush?" She thought it rather noble of her not to direct this at Jean.

"What's it look like?"

"Silver. It has my initials on the back. My married ones—AR."

"Not up here," said Jean. "A few things spilled out of our cases when the engines did that juddery thing earlier. Have you looked on the floor?"

Avice knelt down, cursing the inadequate light from the one un-shaded overhead bulb. If they'd had a window, she would have been able to see better. In fact, everything would have been more pleasant with a sea view. She was sure some of the girls had got windows. She couldn't understand why her father hadn't made it a requirement. She was just stretching her arm under Frances's bunk when she felt a cold wet touch high on the inside of her thigh. She shrieked and jumped up, smacking the back of her head on Frances's bunk.

"What, in heaven's name—"

Pain shot through the top of her head, making her stumble. She pulled her skirt tight round her legs, twisting round in an effort to see behind her. "Who did that? Was it someone's idea of a joke?"

"What's the matter?" asked Jean, wide-eyed.

"Someone goosed me. Someone stuck their cold wet . . ." Here, words failed Avice, and she gazed round suspiciously, as if perhaps some madman had stowed away when no one was looking. "Someone goosed me," she repeated.

No one spoke.

Frances was watching her silently, her face impassive.

"I'm not imagining it," Avice told her crossly.

It was then that all eyes fell on Margaret, who was leaning over the edge of her bunk, muttering to herself. Avice, cheeks flushed, heart racing, legs crossed defensively, stared at her.

Margaret looked up at her with a guilty expression. She stood up, went to the door, closed it and sighed. "Oh, hell. I need to tell you all something. I'd thought I'd get a cabin to myself because of be-ing . . . like this."

Avice took a step backward—which was a difficult maneuver in so little space. "Like what? Oh, Lord! You're not one of those . . . deviant types? Oh, my goodness."

"Deviant?" said Margaret.

"I knew I shouldn't have come."

"Pregnant, you eejit! I thought I'd get a cabin to myself because I'm pregnant."

"Are you making a nest under your bunk?" said Jean. "My cat did that when she had kittens. Made a terrible mess."

"No," said Margaret. "I was not making a ruddy nest. Look, I'm trying to tell you all something." Her cheeks were flushed.

Avice crossed her hands protectively over her chest. "Is this your way of apologizing?"

Margaret shook her head. "It's not what you think." She lowered herself on to her hands and knees and uttered a soft crooning sound. Seconds later, her broad hand emerged from under her bunk. In it she held a small dog. "Girls," she said, "meet Maude Gonne."

Four sets of eyes stared at the dog, who stared back with rheumy disinterest.

"I knew it! I knew you were up to something!" crowed Jean, triumphantly. "I said to myself, when we were on the flight deck, 'That Margaret, she's as furtive as a fox in long grass eating guts.'"

"Oh, for goodness' sake." Avice grimaced. "You mean that was what . . . ?"

"Those cami-knickers really do the job, eh, Avice?" scoffed Jean.

Frances studied the dog. "But you're not allowed pets on board," she said.

"I know that."

"I'm sorry, but you can't hope to keep it quiet," Avice said. "And it'll make the dorm smell."

There was a lengthy silence as unspoken thoughts hung in the air.

In the end, anxiety overrode Avice's natural delicacy. "We're on this thing for almost six weeks. Where's it going to do its business?"

Margaret sat down, ducking to avoid banging her head on the top bunk. The dog settled on her lap. "She's very clean—and I've worked it all out. You didn't notice anything last night, did you? I ran her up and down the end gangway after you'd gone to sleep."

"Ran her up and down the gangway?"

"And cleaned up afterward. Look, she doesn't bark. She doesn't smell. I'll make sure I keep her 'business' well out of your way. But please, please, don't dob me in. She's . . . old . . . My mum gave her to me. And . . ." she blinked furiously ". . . look, she's all I've got left of my mum. I couldn't leave her, okay?"

There was silence as the women exchanged looks. Margaret stared at the floor, flushed with emotion. It was too soon for this level of confidence, she knew it, and so did they. "It's just for a few weeks, and it's real important to me."

There was another lengthy silence. The nurse looked at her shoes. "If you want to try to keep her in here, I don't mind."

"Nor me," said Jean. "Long as she doesn't chew up my shoes. She's quite sweet. For a rat."

Avice knew she couldn't be the only one to complain: it would make her seem heartless. "What about the Royal Marines?" she asked.

"What?"

"The ones they're posting outside our doors from tomorrow night. Didn't you hear that WSO? You won't be able to get her out."

"A marine? For what?"

"He's coming at nine thirty. I suppose it's to stop the men below coming up and ravishing us," said Jean. "Think about it—a thousand desperate men lying just a few feet below us. They could storm the doors if they wanted to and—"

"Oh, for goodness' sake!" Avice's hand flew to her throat.

"Then again," said Jean, grinning lasciviously, "it might be to keep us lot in."

"Well, I'll have to get her out before the marine comes."

"Gangway's too busy," said Jean.

"Perhaps we should just tell someone," said Avice. "I'm sure they'd understand. And perhaps they'll have . . . facilities for this kind of thing. A room they can put her in. She'd probably be much happier with a bit of space to run around, wouldn't she?" It wasn't just the dogginess that bothered her, she realized, it was the sense that someone was getting away with something. They had all had their luggage weighed to the last ounce, their food parcels restricted, and had been made to leave behind their favorite belongings. And this girl had had the gall to bypass it all.

"No," said Margaret, her face darkening. "You heard the captain this morning. We're still way too close to home. They'd put her off in a boat and send her back to Sydney and that would be the last I ever saw of her. I can't take the risk. Not yet, anyway."

"We'll keep it quiet," said Jean, stroking the little dog's head. Avice thought that Jean would have been up for anything that smacked of subverting authority. "Won't we, girls? It'll be a gas. I'm going to sneak her a bit of dinner later."

"Avice?" said Margaret. It was as if, Avice thought afterward, she had already been earmarked as a killjoy.

"I won't say a word," she said, her voice strained. "Just keep her well away from me. And if you do get discovered, make sure you tell them it was nothing to do with us."

6

Among the ship's complement were about thirty-five to forty Royal Marines, their smartness in appearance and manner was usually in direct contrast to us "matelots," and was the subject of some amused wonderment on our part . . . The brass buttons and spit and polished boots shone, they were so fastidious in their appearance.

L. TROMAN, SEAMAN, HMS VICTORIOUS,
IN WINE, WOMEN AND WAR

TWO DAYS IN

In an effort to keep occupied those brides whose initial excitement might have given way to homesickness, HMS *Victoria* offered, on the second full day of the voyage, the following activities—neatly documented in the inaugural issue of the *Daily Ship News*:

1000 hrs	Protestant Devotions (E Deck)
1300 hrs	Recorded Music
1430 hrs	Deck Games (Flight Deck)
1600 hrs	Knitting Corner (4oz of pink or white wool and two pairs of needles per girl to be provided by the Red Cross)
1700 hrs	Lecture: "Marriage and Family Life," to be given by the Ship's Chaplain
1830 hrs	Bingo Party (Recreation Area, Main Deck)
1930 hrs	Roman Catholic Mass

Of these, the Deck Games and the Bingo Party looked to be the most popular, and the lecture the least. The chaplain had an unfortunately forbidding manner, and at least one of the brides had remarked that they didn't need a lecture on marriage from a man who looked like he wanted to wash himself whenever a woman happened to brush past him.

Meanwhile, the imaginatively titled newspaper, edited by one of the women's officers with the help of two brides, also noted the birthdays of Mrs. Josephine Darnforth, 19, and Mrs. Alice Sutton, 22, and appealed to its readers to come forward with little snippets of gossip and good wishes that "might make the journey pass in a pleasant and congenial manner."

"Gossip, eh?" mused Jean, to whom this piece had been read aloud. "Betcha by the end of the trip they'll have enough to fill twenty bloody newspapers."

Avice had left the dormitory early for Protestant Devotions. She suspected she might meet more her sort of people at church. She had felt a little perturbed when Margaret announced that she would be attending the Roman Catholic Mass. She had never met a papist before, as her mother called them, but she was careful not to let her pity show.

Jean, who had already announced her aversion to any kind of religion (an unfortunate experience with a Christian Brother) was making up, ready for Recorded Music. She suspected there might be dancing and pronounced herself as "itchy as a bare-arsed wallaby on a termite hill" to escape the cabin and take to the floor.

Margaret was lying on her bed, a hand on the dog, reading one of Avice's magazines. Occasionally she would snort derisively. "Says here you shouldn't sleep on one side of your face too often in case it gives you wrinkles. How the hell else are you meant to sleep?" Then she had recalled the sight of Avice the night before, lying flat on her back above Frances, despite the obvious discomfort of a headful of rollers, and made a mental note not to comment publicly again.

This left Frances free to disappear without comment and, dressed in pale khaki slacks and a short-sleeved shirt—the closest she could come to her old uniform—she had slipped out, nodding a brief greeting to the girls she passed, and made her way down the gangway.

———

She had had to knock twice before she got a response, and even then she drew back, checking and rechecking the name on the door.

"Come in."

She stepped into the infirmary, whose walls were lined from floor to ceiling with bottles and jars, secured on narrow shelves behind glass doors. The man behind the desk had short red hair, slicked close to his head like a protective shell, and was dressed in civilian clothes. His face was freckled, his eyes creased from years of what might have been squinting but, judging from his actions now, was probably smiling.

"Come right in. You're making the place look untidy."

Frances flushed briefly, realized he had been joking, then took a few steps toward him.

"What seems to be the problem, then?" He was sliding his hand back and forth along the desk as if to some unheard rhythm.

"I don't have one." She straightened, stiff in her starched shirt. "Are you the surgeon? Mr. Farraday?"

"No." He gazed at her, apparently weighing up whether to enlighten her. "Vincent Duxbury. Civilian passenger. I'm probably not the man you had in mind. He—er—he failed to make the trip. Captain Highfield asked me to step in. And, frankly, given the standard of entertainment on board, I'm happy to oblige. How can I help you?"

"I'm not sure that you can," she said, perplexed. "At least, not in that way. I was—I mean, I'm a nurse." She held out a hand. "Frances Mackenzie. Sister Frances Mackenzie. I heard that some of the brides were to be allowed to help out with secretarial duties and such, and I thought I might offer my services here."

Vincent Duxbury shook her hand, and motioned to her to sit down. "A nurse, eh? I thought we might have a few on board. Seen much duty?"

"Five years in the Pacific," she said. "Last posting was the Australian General Hospital 2/7 Morotai." She fought the urge to add "sir."

"My cousin was out in Japan, back in 'forty-three. Your husband?"

"My? Oh." She looked briefly wrongfooted. "Alfred Mackenzie. Royal Welsh Fusiliers."

"Royal Welsh Fusiliers . . ." He said it slowly, as if it had significance.

She folded her hands in front of her.

Dr. Duxbury leaned back in his chair, fiddling with the top of a brown-glass bottle. It looked as if he had been in the room for some time, although he was still in his jacket. Suddenly it dawned on her that the smell of alcohol was not necessarily medicinal.

"So . . ."

She waited, trying not to look too hard at the label on the bottle.

"You want to carry on serving. These six weeks."

"If I can be useful, yes." She took a deep breath. "I've had special experience in burns, treatment of dysentery, and revival of impaired digestive systems. That was the POWs," she added. "We had significant experience of those."

"Uh-huh."

"I don't have much specialist feminine or obstetric knowledge, but I thought at least I could help with the men. I asked someone aboard the hospital ship *Ariadne*, where I last served, and they said that aircraft-carriers sustain a disproportionate number of injuries, especially during flight training."

"Well researched, Mrs. Mackenzie."

"So . . . it's not even that I'd like to occupy my time usefully, Doctor. I would appreciate the chance to gain a little more experience . . . I'm a good learner," she added, when he didn't speak.

There was a brief silence. She looked at him, but was discomfited by the intensity of his gaze.

"Do you sing?" he said eventually.

"I'm sorry?"

"Sing, Mrs. Mackenzie. You know, show tunes, hymns, opera." He began to hum something she didn't know.

"I'm afraid not," she said.

"Pity." He wrinkled his nose, then slapped his hand on the desk. "I thought we might get some of the girls together and put on a show. What a perfect opportunity, eh?"

The brown bottle, she saw, was empty. She still could not make out what was written on the label, but now the scent of what it had contained burst softly on to the air with his every utterance.

She took a deep breath. "I'm sure that would be a . . . a useful idea, Doctor. But I really wondered whether we could just discuss—"

"'Long ago and far away' . . . Do you know 'Showboat'?"

"No," she said. "I'm afraid I don't."

"Pity. 'Old Man River' . . ." He closed his eyes and continued to sing.

She sat, her hands clasped in her lap, unsure whether or not to interrupt. "Doctor?"

His singing segued into a low melodic humming. His head was thrown back.

"Doctor? Do you have any idea of when you might like me to start?"

"'He just keeps rollin' . . .'" He opened an eye. Continued to the end of the line. "Mrs. Mackenzie?"

"I can start today, if you'd like. If you'd find it . . . useful. I have my uniform in my dormitory. I kept it deliberately in my small bag."

He had stopped singing. He smiled broadly. She wondered if he would be like this every day. She'd have to start secretly counting bottles, as she had with Dr. Arbuthnot.

"You know what I'm going to say to you, Frances? May I call you Frances?" He was pointing at her now with his bottle. He looked as if he was enjoying his moment of possible munificence. "I'm going to tell you to go away."

"I'm sorry?"

He laughed. "That got you, didn't it? No, Frances Mackenzie. You've been serving your country and mine for five years. You deserve a little break. I'm going to prescribe a six-week holiday."

"But I want to work," she said.

"No buts, Mrs. Mackenzie. The war's over. In a few short weeks you're going to be engaged in the hardest job of your career. You'll be raising children before you know it and, believe me, those sick soldiers will look like a holiday then. That's the real work. Take it from someone who knows. Three boys and a girl. Each one a little dynamo." He counted them off on his fingers, then shook his head, as if lost in distant appreciation of his offspring.

"That's the only work I want you interested in from now on. *Real* women's work. So, much as I enjoy the company of an attractive young woman, right now I'm going to insist you enjoy your last days of freedom. Get your hair done. Watch some movies. Make yourself look pretty for that old man of yours."

She was staring at him.

"So go. Go on—now."

It took her several seconds to grasp that she had been dismissed. He waved away her offered hand.

"And enjoy yourself! Come and sing a few tunes! 'Make way for tomorrow . . .'"

She could hear him singing the entire length of the gangway.

———

That evening the marine arrived at a minute before nine thirty. A slim man with dark, slicked hair, who moved with the economy of someone used to making himself invisible, he positioned himself at the entrance to their dormitory, placed his feet a little more than eighteen inches apart and stood with his back to the door, eyes focused on nothing. He was responsible for watching over the two cabins on each side of theirs, and the five above. Other marines were posted at similar intervals by the others.

"Trust us to have one actually outside our door," muttered Margaret.

The brides had been lying on their bunks reading or writing, and Avice had been painting her nails with a polish she had bought at the PX shop in the wardroom lounge. It was not a particularly pretty shade, but she had felt she needed a treat to help her through what was already proving a testing journey.

Hearing his footfall, able to see a sliver of his body through the half-open door, they glanced at each other. Almost unconsciously, Margaret looked down at her sleeping dog. They waited in case he uttered some greeting or perhaps an instruction, but he just stood there.

At a quarter to ten Jean stepped outside with her cigarettes, and offered him one. When he refused, she lit one for herself and began to ask him questions: where was the cinema? Did the men get the same food as the brides? Did he like mashed potato? He answered monosyllabically, smiling only once when she asked him what he did when he needed to visit the dunny. ("Oh, Jean," muttered Avice, behind the door.) "I'm trained not to," he said drily.

"So, where do you sleep?" she asked coquettishly, leaning against one of the pipes that ran up the wall.

"My mess, ma'am."

"And where's that?"

"Official secret," he said.

"Oh, come on," said Jean.

The marine looked straight ahead.

"I'm only curious . . ." She stepped closer to him, peering into his face. "Oh, come on, I've had toy soldiers that talked more than you."

"Ma'am."

She apparently assessed her remaining firepower. Conventional weapons were going to be ineffective. "Actually," she said, stubbing out her cigarette, "I wanted to ask you something . . . but it's a bit embarrassing."

The marine looked wary. As well he might, thought Avice.

Jean traced a pattern on the floor with her toe of her shoe. "Please don't tell anyone, but I keep getting lost," she said. "I'd like to walk around but I've got lost twice already, and it's made me a bit of a joke with the other girls. So I don't really like to ask them. I even missed dinner because I couldn't find the canteen."

The marine had relaxed a little. He was intent, listening.

"It's because I'm sixteen, you see. I didn't do too good at school. Reading and stuff. And I can't . . ." she let her voice drop to a whisper ". . . I can't understand the map. The one of the ship. You couldn't explain it to me, could you?"

The marine hesitated, then nodded. "There's one pinned up on that noticeboard. Want me to talk you through it?" His voice was low, resonant, as if he was about to break into song.

"Oh, would you?" said Jean, a heartbreaking smile on her face.

"Golly, Moses, she's brilliant," said Margaret, who was listening from behind the door. When Margaret and Avice looked out the pair were standing in front of the map, fifteen or so feet along the gangway. Margaret, carrying an oversized washbag, gave them a merry wave as she hurried along in her dressing-gown. The marine saluted her, then turned back to Jean to explain how she might use the map to get from the hangar deck to, for example, the laundry. Jean was apparently concentrating intently on whatever he had to say.

"It's not ideal," said Margaret afterward, sitting down heavily on her bunk as the dog plodded round the dormitory, sniffing at the floor. "It's not like a proper walk for her. I mean, she's used to fields."

Avice stifled the urge to remark that she should have thought of that beforehand. She was now smoothing cold cream into her face in front of her little traveling mirror. The sea air was meant to do terrible things to one's skin, and she was darned if she was going to meet Ian looking like a strip of Bombay duck.

The door opened.

"Great," said Margaret, as Jean came in, grinning, and closed it behind her. "You were great, Jean."

Jean simpered. "Well, girls, you've either got it—" She stopped. "Blimey, Avice, you look like a haddock with your mouth like that."

Avice closed it.

"I'm ever so grateful, Jean," Margaret told her. "I didn't think he was going to move. I mean, that bit about not being able to read was a masterstroke."

"What?"

"I'd never have come up with it. You must really be able to think on your feet."

Jean gave her an odd look. "No thinking about it, mate." She directed her next words at the floor. "Can't read a word. 'Cept my name. Never have."

There was an awkward silence. Avice tried to gauge if this was another of Jean's jokes, but she wasn't laughing.

Jean broke the silence. "What the bloody hell is that?" She stood up, flapping her hands.

There was a second's grace, then a putrid smell explained her outburst.

Margaret winced. "Sorry, ladies. I said she was clean. I never said she wasn't windy."

Jean burst out laughing, and even Frances managed a rueful smile.

Avice raised her eyes to heaven and thought, trying to keep bitterness from her heart, of the *Queen Mary*.

————

It was on the second night that homesickness struck. Margaret lay awake in the darkened cabin, listening to the odd creak and sniff as her traveling companions shifted on their bunks, her exhaustion swept away paradoxically by the opportunity to sleep. She had thought she was fine: the strangeness of it all and the excitement of leaving the harbor had conspired to stop her thinking too hard about her new environment. Now, picturing the ship in the middle of the ocean, heading out into the inky blackness, she was gripped by an irrational terror, a childlike desire to turn round and run for the familiar safety of the only house in which she had ever spent a night. Her brothers would be going to bed now: she could picture them round the kitchen table—they had barely used the parlor since her mother had died—their long legs stretched out as they listened to the wireless, played cards or, in Daniel's case, read a comic, perhaps with Colm leaning over his shoulder. Dad would be in his chair, hands tucked behind his head, the frayed patches showing at his elbows, eyes closed as if in preparation for sleep, occasionally nodding. Letty would be sewing, or polishing something, perhaps sitting in the chair her mother had once occupied.

Letty, whom she had treated so shabbily.

She was overwhelmed by the thought of never seeing any of them again, and bit down on her fingers, hoping that physical pain might force away the image.

She took a deep breath, reached out and felt Maude Gonne under the blanket, tucked into the restricted area where her thigh met her belly. She shouldn't have brought the little dog: it had been selfish. She hadn't thought of how miserable she would be, stuck inside this noisy, stuffy cabin for twenty-four hours a day. Even Margaret was finding it difficult, and she could go to the other decks at will. I'm sorry, she told the dog silently. I promise I'll make it up to you when we get to England. A tear trickled down her cheek.

Outside, the marine shifted position on the metallic floor and murmured a quiet greeting to someone passing. She heard his shirt brush against the door. In the distance, several sets of heavy footfalls tramped down the metal stairs. Above her, Jean murmured to herself, perhaps in sleep, and Avice pulled the blanket further over her rollered hair.

Margaret had never shared a room in her life; it had been one of the few advantages of growing up female in the Donleavy household. Now the little dormitory, without the door open, without light or a breath of air, felt stifling. She swung her legs over the side of the bunk and sat there for a minute. I can't do this, she told herself, dragging her oversized nightdress over her knees. I've got to pull it together. She thought of Joe, his expression warm and faintly mocking. "Get a grip, old girl," he said, and she closed her eyes, trying to remind herself of why she was making this journey.

"Margaret?" Jean's voice cut into the darkness. "You going somewhere?"

"No," said Margaret, sliding her feet back under the covers. "No, just . . ." She couldn't explain. "Just having trouble getting to sleep."

"Me too."

Her voice had sounded uncharacteristically small. Margaret felt a swell of pity for her. She was barely more than a child. "Want to come down here for a bit?" she whispered.

She could just make out Jean's slender limbs climbing rapidly down the ladder, and then the girl slid in at the other end of her bunk. "No room at the top end." She giggled and, despite herself,

Margaret giggled back. "Don't let that baby kick me. And don't let that dog slip its nose up my drawers."

They lay quietly for a few minutes, Margaret unable to work out whether she found Jean's skin against hers comforting or unsettling. Jean fidgeted for a while, legs twitching impatiently, and Margaret felt Maude Gonne lift her head in inquiry.

"What's your husband's name?" Jean asked eventually.

"Joe."

"Mine's Stan."

"You said."

"Stan Castleforth. He's nineteen on Tuesday. His mum wasn't too happy when he told her he'd got wed, but he says she's calmed down a bit now."

Margaret lay back, staring at the blackness above her, thinking of the warm letters she had received from Joe's mother and wondering whether courage or foolhardiness had sent a half-child alone to the other side of the world. "I'm sure she'll be fine once you get to know each other," she said, when continued silence might have suggested the opposite.

"From Nottingham," said Jean. "D'you know it?"

"No."

"Nor me. But he said it's where Robin Hood came from. So I reckon it's probably in a forest."

Jean shifted again, and Margaret could hear her rummaging at the end of the bunk. "Mind if I have a smoke?" she hissed.

"Go ahead."

There was a brief flare, and she glimpsed Jean's illuminated face, rapt in concentration as she lit her cigarette. Then the match was shaken out, and the cabin returned to darkness.

"I think about Stan loads, you know," she said. "He's dead handsome. All my mates thought so. I met him outside the cinema and he and his mate offered to pay for me and mine to go in. *Ziegfeld Follies*. In technicolor." She exhaled. "He told me he hadn't kissed a girl since Portsmouth and I couldn't really say no in the circumstances. He had a hand up my skirt before 'This Heart Of Mine.'"

Margaret heard her humming the tune.

"I got married in parachute silk. My aunt Mavis got it for me from a GI she knew who did bent radios. My mum's not really up all that stuff." She paused. "In fact, I get on better with my aunt Mavis. Always have done. My mum reckons I'm a waste of skin."

Margaret shifted on to her side, thinking of her own mother. Of her constancy, her bossy, exasperated maternal presence, her freckled hands, lifting to pin her hair out of the way several hundred times a day. She found her mouth had dried.

"Was it different, when you got . . . you know?"

"What?"

"Did you have to do it differently . . . to have a baby, I mean."

"Jean!"

"What?" Jean's voice rose in indignation. "Someone's got to tell me."

Margaret sat up, careful not to bang her head on the bunk above. "You must know."

"I wouldn't be asking, would I?"

"You mean no one's ever told you . . . about the birds and the bees?"

Jean snorted. "I know where he's got to put it, if that's what you're talking about. I quite like that bit. But I don't know how doing that leads to babies."

Margaret was shocked into silence, but a voice came from above: "If you're going to be so coarse as to discuss these matters in company," it said, "you could at least do it quietly. Some of us are trying to sleep."

"I bet Avice knows," giggled Jean.

"I thought you said you'd lost a baby," said Avice, pointedly.

"Oh, Jean. I'm so sorry." Margaret's hand went involuntarily to her mouth.

There was a prolonged silence.

"Actually," Jean said, "I wasn't exactly carrying as such."

Margaret could hear Avice shifting under her covers.

"I was . . . well, a bit late with my you-know-what. And my friend Polly said that meant you were carrying. So I said I was because I knew it would help me get on board. Even though when I worked out the dates I couldn't really have been, if you know what I mean. And then they had to postpone my medical check twice. When they did it I said I'd lost it and I started crying because by then I'd almost convinced myself that I was and the nurse felt sorry for me and said no one needed to know one way or the other, and that the most important thing was getting me over to my Stan. It's probably why they've stuck me in with you, Maggie." She took a deep drag of her cigarette. "So, there you are. I didn't mean to lie exactly." She rolled over, picked up a shoe and stubbed out her cigarette on the sole. Her voice took on a hard, defensive edge: "But if any of you dob me in, I'll just say I lost it on board anyway. So there's no point in telling."

Margaret laid her hands on her stomach. "Nobody's going to tell on you, Jean," she said.

There was a deafening silence from Avice's bunk.

Outside, an unknown distance away, they could hear a foghorn. It sounded a single low, melancholy note.

"Frances?" said Jean.

"She's asleep," whispered Margaret.

"No, she's not. I saw her eyes when I lit my ciggie. You won't tell on me, Frances, will you?"

"No," said Frances, from the bunk opposite. "I won't."

Jean got out of bed. She patted Margaret's leg, then climbed nimbly back up to her bunk, where she could be heard rustling herself into comfort. "So, come on, then," she said eventually. "Who likes doing it, and what is it that makes you actually get a baby?"

On the flight deck, a thousand-pound bomb from a Stuka aircraft looks curiously like a beer barrel. It rolls casually from the underbelly of the sinister little plane, with the same gay insouciance as if it were about to be rolled down the steps of a beer cellar. Surrounded by its brothers, flanked by a bunched formation of fighter planes, it seems to pause momentarily in the sky, then float down toward the ship, guided, as if by an invisible force, toward the deck.

This is one of the things Captain Highfield thinks as he stares up at his impending death. This, and the fact that, when the wall of flame rises up from the armored deck, engulfing the island, the ship's command center, its blue-white heat clawing upward, and he is possessed of the immobilizing terror, as he had always known he would be, he has forgotten something. Something he had to do. And in his blind paralysis even he is dimly aware of how ridiculous it is to be casting around for some unremembered task while he faces immolation.

Then, in the raging heart of the fire, as the bombs rain around him, bouncing off the decks, as his nostrils sting with the smell of burning fuel and his ears refuse to close to the screams of his men, he looks up to see a plane, where there is no plane. It, too, is engulfed, yellow flames licking at the cockpit, the tilted wings blackened, but not enough to obscure, within, Hart's face, which is untouched, his eyes questioning as he faces the captain.

I'm sorry, Highfield weeps, unsure if, through the roar of the fire, the younger man can hear him. I'm sorry.

When he wakes, his pillow damp and the skies still dark above the quiet ocean, he is still speaking these words into the silence.

7

I, like many others, had developed a love-hate relationship with the Vic. We hated the life, but we were proud of her as a fighting unit. We cursed her between ourselves, but would not hear anyone outside of the ship say anything derogatory about her . . . she was a lucky ship. Sailors are so superstitious.

L. TROMAN, SEAMAN, HMS VICTORIOUS, IN WINE, WOMEN AND WAR

TWO WEEKS PREVIOUSLY

According to her log, HMS *Victoria* had seen action in the north Atlantic, the Pacific and, most recently, at Morotai where, carrying Corsairs, she helped force back the Japanese and bore the scars to show it. She, and many like her, had stopped repeatedly over the past few years at the dockyards at Woolloomooloo to have her mine-damaged hull repaired, bullet and torpedo holes plugged, the brutal scars of her time at sea put straight before she was sent out again, bearing men who had themselves been patched up and readied for battle.

Captain George Highfield was much given to fanciful thinking, but as he walked along the dry dock, staring up through the sea mist at the hulls of *Victoria* and her neighbors, he often allowed himself to think about the vessels as his fellows. Hard not to see them as suffering some kind of hurt, as having some kind of personality when they had allied themselves to you, given you their all, braved high seas and fierce fire. In forty years' service, he'd had his favorites: those that had felt undeniably his, the occasional alchemic conjunction of ship and crew in which each man knew he would lay down his life willingly for its protection. He had bitten back private tears of grief when he left them, less privately when they had been sunk. He often supposed this was how previous generations of fighting men must have felt about their horses.

"Poor old girl," he muttered, glancing at the hole ripped in the aircraft-carrier's side. She looked so much like *Indomitable*, his old ship.

The surgeon had said he should use a stick. Highfield suspected that the man had told others he shouldn't be allowed back to sea at all. "These things take longer to heal at your age," he had observed, of the livid scar tissue where the metal had sliced through to the bone, the ridged skin of the burns around it. "I'm not convinced you should be up and about on that just yet, Captain."

Highfield had discharged himself from the hospital that morning. "I have a ship to take home," he had said, closing the conversation. As if he would allow himself to be invalided out at this stage.

Like everyone else, the surgeon had said nothing. Sometimes it seemed to Highfield that no one knew what to say to him now. He hardly blamed them: in their shoes he would probably have felt the same.

"Ah, Highfield. They told me you were out here."

"Sir." He stopped and saluted. The admiral approached through the light rain, waving away the umbrella-bearing officer beside him. Above them, the gulls wheeled and dived, their cries muffled by the mist.

"Leg all better?"

"Absolutely fine, sir. Good as new."

He watched the admiral glance down at it. When you spotted an admiral out in the open air, his men used to say, you'd not know whether to polish your buttons for a ceremony or brace yourself for a roasting. But McManus was a good sort, who always knew somehow what was going on. So many of them spent their time behind their desks, breaking off only to go aboard ship the day before she was due back in, thus claiming some of her glory. But this admiral was a rare bird: always wanting to know what was going on at the docks, mediating in disputes, testing the political waters, questioning everything, missing nothing.

Highfield fought the urge to shift the weight off his leg again. He was conscious suddenly that McManus probably knew all about that too. "Thought I'd go and take a look at *Victoria*," he said. "Haven't seen her in a few years. Not since I went aboard during the Adriatic convoys."

"You may find her a little changed," said McManus. "She's taken a bit of a bashing."

"I suppose you could say the same for most of us." It was the closest Highfield would come to a joke, and McManus acknowledged it in his quiet smile.

The two men walked slowly along the dock, unconsciously stepping in time with each other.

"So you're A1 and ready to go again, eh, Highfield?"

"Sir."

"Terrible business, what happened. We all felt for you, you know."

Highfield kept his face to the front.

"Yes," McManus continued. "Hart would have gone all the way to the top. Not your usual crabfat . . . Bloody shame when you were all so close to getting home."

"I contacted his mother, sir, while I was in hospital."

"Yes. Good man. Best coming from you."

It was embarrassing to be praised for so small an achievement. Then Highfield found, as often happened when the young man was mentioned, that he could no longer speak.

When the silence had lasted several minutes, the admiral stopped and faced him. "You mustn't blame yourself."

"Sir."

"I hear you've been a little . . . down about it. Well, we've all suffered such losses, and we've all lain awake at nights wondering if we could have prevented them." His assessing gaze passed over Highfield's face. "You had no choice. Everyone is aware of that."

Highfield tensed. He found it impossible to meet the admiral's eye.

"I mean it. And if your remaining company's careers last as long as yours they'll see worse. Don't dwell on it, Highfield. These things happen." McManus tailed off, as if he were deep in thought, and

Highfield stayed silent, listening to the sound of his feet on the now slick dockside, the distant grind and thump of cranes.

They had almost reached the gangplank. Even from here he could see the engineers on board, replacing the metal that had been buckled by impact, hear the banging and drilling that told him welders were busy inside the hangar space. They had been working hard, but a huge charred cleft in the starboard side was still partly visible in the smooth gray metal. She would win no beauty contests but, as his eyes rested upon her, Highfield felt the misery of the past weeks melt away.

They paused at the foot of the gangplank, squinting up into the light rain. Highfield's leg twinged again and he wondered whether he could hold on to the sides inconspicuously.

"So, what next when you get back, Highfield?"

Highfield hesitated. "Well, I'll be retired, sir."

"I know that, man. I meant what are you going to do with yourself? Got any hobbies? No Mrs. Highfield that you've been hiding all these years?"

"No, sir."

"Oh."

Highfield thought he detected pity in the word. He wanted to say he had never felt the lack of a female presence in his life. Get too close to a woman, and you were never happy anywhere. He'd seen men hankering for their wives while they were afloat, then irritated by the confines of femininity and domesticity when they were on land. He didn't bother saying this anymore: on the occasions when he had, the men had looked at him rather curiously.

The admiral turned back toward *Victoria*. "Well, there's nothing like a 'lifer,' is there? I suppose we wouldn't have had the best of you if you'd always had your mind on some woman somewhere."

"Indeed, sir."

"Golf's my thing. I plan to be on the links morning till evening. Think my wife'll like it that way too." He laughed. "She's got used to doing her own thing, over the years, you know."

"Yes," said Captain Highfield, although he didn't.

"Doesn't relish the prospect of me under her feet all the time."

"Still."

"Not something you'll have to worry about, eh? You can play all the golf you like."

"I'm not really a golfing man, sir."

"What?"

"Think I'm happier on the water." He nearly said what he thought: that he wasn't sure what he was going to do. And that he felt discomfited at not knowing. He had spent the last four decades with his life planned out in minutes, knowing days, weeks ahead what he would be doing, even where, according to his typewritten short or long cast, in what part of the world he would be.

Some thought him lucky to be finishing his career as the war ended: a blaze of glory, they joked, then realized what they'd said. I'll bring my men home, he said. It'll be a good way to end. He could sound very convincing. Several times he had fought the urge to beg the admiral to let him stay on.

"Going up then?"

"Thought I might inspect the work. Sounds like they've been busy." Now that he was on board again, Highfield felt a little of his authority return, the sense of surety and order that had ebbed away from him during his time in hospital. The admiral said nothing, but went briskly up the gangplank, his hands linked behind his back.

The pegging-in board had been turned toward the wall. The captain paused at the doorway, turned it round and slid his name tag across to confirm his presence aboard; a reassuring gesture. Then they stepped over the sill of the doorway, ducking simultaneously as they entered the cavernous hangar.

Not all of the lights were illuminated, and it took Highfield a couple of minutes to adjust to the gloom. Around him, ratings were strapping huge boxes of equipment to narrow shelves, raising and lowering black buckets of tools for those working above them. At one end, three young dabbers were repainting the pipework. They glanced behind them, apparently unsure whether they should salute. He recognized one, a young lad who had nearly lost a finger a few weeks previously when it got caught in the lashings. The boy saluted, revealing a leather pocket strapped to his hand. Highfield nodded in acknowledgment, pleased that he was already back to work. Then he looked in front of him at the huge liftwell that transported the planes to the deck. Several men were at work, one on a scaffold platform, apparently securing metal struts at regular intervals all the way up to the flight deck. He stared at the scene, trying to work out a possible explanation. He failed.

"Hey! You!" The young welder on the platform lifted his safety helmet. The captain moved to the edge of the liftwell. "What on earth do you think you're doing?"

The man didn't answer, his expression uncertain.

"What are you doing to the liftwells? Have you gone mad? Do you know what liftwells do? They allow the bloody planes to go up and down. Who on earth told you to do—"

The admiral placed his hand on Highfield's arm. It was several seconds before the captain, all his senses still trained on the improbable sight before him, registered the gesture. "This is what I came to talk to you about."

"The damn fool's putting metal supports in the liftwells. Bunk supports, for goodness' sake. Don't you know what you're doing, man?"

"He's doing it under my orders, Highfield."

"I'm sorry, sir?"

"The *Victoria*. There have been a few developments while you were in the sick bay. New orders from London. This trip isn't going to be quite as straightforward as you thought."

Highfield's face fell. "More POWs?"

"No."

"Not enemy POWs? You remember the trouble we had on—"

"Worse, I'm afraid, Highfield." He let out a long breath, his eyes steady on the captain's face. "They're for women."

There was a long silence.

"You'll still be taking your men home. But you've got extra cargo. Six hundred-odd Australian war brides bound for their men in Blighty. The liftwells will be used for the extra berths."

The welder resumed his work, his torch sending sparks skittering off the metal frame.

Captain Highfield turned to the admiral. "But they can't go on my ship."

"It's the war, Highfield. People are having to make do."

"But they travel on troop ships, sir. Liners, where they can cater for them. You can't have girls and babies and suchlike on an aircraft-carrier. It's madness. You must tell them."

"I can't say I was entirely happy about it either. But needs must, old chap. All the liners have already been commandeered." He patted Highfield's shoulder. "It's only six weeks. Be gone before you know it. And after all that business with Hart and the mine, it might perk the men up. Take their minds off things."

But it's my last voyage. My last time with my men. With my own ship. Highfield felt a great wail build inside him, a fury at the humiliation of it. "Sir—"

"Look, George, the telephone lines to London have been burning up on this one. There's a bit of a political row brewing up over these wives. The British girls are holding demonstrations outside Parliament because they feel they've been forgotten about. Both the top brass and the Australian government are keen not to have that kind of thing repeated over here. It's caused a lot of bad feeling with the Aussie men, having so many of their women marry out. I think all sides feel the best thing is to get the women away as soon as possible and let the whole thing settle down."

His tone became conciliatory: "I know this is difficult for you, but try to look at it from the girls' point of view. Some of them haven't seen their men for two years or more. The war's over, and they're desperate to be reunited." He noted the rigid set of the other man's jaw. "Put yourself in their shoes, George. They just want to get home to their loved ones as fast and with as little fuss as possible. You must understand how that feels."

"It's a recipe for disaster, women on board." The strength of Highfield's feelings hardened his voice and several men nearby stopped work to watch. "I won't have it! I won't have this ship disrupted by women. They must understand. They must see."

The admiral's voice was soothing, but it had taken on the impersonal bite of someone losing their patience. "There's no babies or children traveling. They've picked this lot very carefully. Just fit young women—well, possibly a few in the family way."

"But what about the men?"

"No men. Oh, there might be the odd extra, but we won't know about that until a few days before boarding. Haven't had the final short cast on this one yet." The admiral paused. "Oh, you mean yours. Well, they'll be on different decks. The liftwells—with the cabins—will be closed off. There's a few—the, er, ones in the family way—in single cabins. Your men's work will continue as normal. And we're putting in all sorts of safeguards to stop any improper mixing—you know the sort of thing."

Captain Highfield turned to his superior. The urgency of his position had stripped his face of its habitual impassiveness: his whole self was desperate to convey how wrong this was and how impossible. "Look, sir, some of my men have been without—without female company for months. This is like sticking a match in a box of fireworks. Did you not hear about the incidents on *Audacious*? We all know what happened, for God's sake."

"I think we've all learned lessons from *Audacious*."

"It's impossible, sir. It's dangerous and ridiculous and it stands to destabilize the whole atmosphere on the ship. You know how fragile these things are."

"It's really not negotiable, Highfield."

"We've worked for months to get the balance right. You know what my men have been through. You can't just drop a load of girls in there and think—"

"They'll be under strict orders. The Navy is to issue guidelines—"

"What do women know of orders? Where there's men and women in close quarters, there's going to be trouble."

"These are married women, Highfield." The admiral's voice was sharp now. "They're going home to be with their husbands. That's the whole point."

"Well, with respect, sir, that shows just how much you understand about human nature."

His words hung in the air, shocking both men. Captain Highfield took a quivering breath. "Permission to be dismissed. Sir." He hardly waited for the nod. For the first time in his naval career, Captain Highfield turned on his heel and walked in anger from his superior.

The admiral stood and watched him travel the length of the hangar and disappear into the bowels of his ship, like a rabbit finding safety in its warren. In some cases such disrespect could prompt the end of a man's career. But, grumpy old stick that Highfield was, McManus had a lot of respect for him. He didn't want him to end his working life in ignominy. Besides, the admiral mused, as he nodded to the young ratings to carry on, much as he loved his wife and daughters, if he was truthful, and if it were his ship, he would probably have felt the same.

8

The brides had lectures and demonstrations during the voyage to help them with the shopping and cooking problems of rationing. Their diet on the later stages of the trip was slightly pruned so that the effect of the change to rationed food would not be too severe.

DAILY MIRROR, 7 AUGUST 1946

FIVE DAYS

With a change of mood as abrupt and capricious as those of the brides on board, the sea conditions altered dramatically outside the stretch of water known as Sydney Heads. The Great Australian Bight, the men said, with a mixture of glee and foreboding, would sort out the sailors among them.

It was as if, having lulled them into a false sense of security, the fates had now decided to demonstrate their vulnerability, the unpredictability of their future. The cheerful blue sea darkened, muddied and swelled into threatening peaks. The winds, born as whispered breezes, grew to stiff gusts, then amplified to gale force, spitting rain on the men who, smothered with oilcloth, attempted repeatedly to secure the planes more firmly to the decks. Beneath them, the ship bucked and rolled her way through the waves, groaning with the effort.

It was at this point that the passengers, who had spent the previous days meandering round the decks like a restless swarm, retired, at first one by one, then in greater numbers, to their bunks. Those remaining on their feet made their way unsteadily along the passageways, legs braced, leaning whey-faced against the walls. Lectures were canceled, as was the planned lifeboat drill when the ship's company realized that too few women could stand to make it worthwhile. The women's service officers still able to walk did their best to distribute anti-nausea pills.

The pounding of the seas, the periodic sounding of the ship's horn and the incessant clanging of the chains and airplanes above them made sleep impossible. Avice and Jean (it would be Jean, wouldn't it?) were lying on their bunks locked into their private worlds of nauseous misery. At least, Avice's world had been private: she thought she knew Jean's every symptom—how her stomach felt like it had curdled, how even a piece of dry bread had led her to disgrace herself outside the flight-deck canteen, how that horrible stoker who kept following them along by the laundry had eaten a cheese and Vegemite sandwich right in front of her, just to make her go even more green. It had all been hanging out of his mouth and—

"Yes, yes, Jean. I get the picture," Avice had said, and blocked her ears.

"You not coming for some tea, then?" said Margaret, standing in the doorway. "It's potted steak." The dog was asleep on her bed, apparently unaffected by the rough weather.

Jean was turned to the wall. Her reply, perhaps fortuitously, was unintelligible.

"Come on, then, Frances," said Margaret. "I guess it's just you and me."

———

Margaret Donleavy had met Joseph O'Brien eighteen months previously when her brother Colm had brought him home from the pub, along with six or seven other mates who became regular fixtures in the Donleavy household in the months leading up to the end of the war. It was her brothers' way of keeping the house busy after their mother had gone, she said. They couldn't cope with the emptiness at first, the deafening silence caused by the absence of one quiet person. Neither her father nor her brothers had wanted to leave her and Daniel alone while they drowned their sorrows in the pub (they were mindful sorts, even if they didn't always come across that way) so for several months they had brought the pub to the farm, sometimes fourteen or fifteen men hanging off the back of the pickup truck, frequently Americans bearing spirits and beer, or Irishmen singing songs that made Murray's eyes brim with tears, and the house was filled nightly with the sound of men singing, drinking, and occasionally Daniel weeping as he tried to make sense of it all.

"Joe was the only one who didn't ask me out or make a nuisance of himself," she told Frances, tucking into mashed potato as they sat in the near-empty canteen. "The others either treated me like some kind of barmaid, or tried to give me a squeeze when my brothers weren't looking. I had to whack one with a shovel when he came on a bit fresh in the dairy." She grabbed her metal tray as it slid across the table. "He didn't come back." A week later Colm had caught another peeping through the door when she was in the bathroom, and he, Niall and Liam had thrashed him to within an inch of his life. After that they had stopped bringing men home.

Except Joe, who had come every day, had teased Daniel into good humor, had offered her father advice gleaned from his father's own smallholding in Devon, and had cast surreptitious glances at her with offerings of too-small nylons and cigarettes.

"I had to ask him in the end," she said, "why he hadn't made a move on me. He said he thought if he hung on long enough I'd decide he was part of the furniture."

They had walked out for the first time three months to the day before the U.S. Air Force dropped the atom bomb on Hiroshima, and had wed several weeks afterward, Margaret in her mother's wedding dress, on the last occasion Joe could get leave. She had known they'd be all right together. Joe, she said, was like her brothers. He didn't take himself or her too seriously.

"Was he pleased about the baby?"

"When I told him I was expecting, he asked me whether it was due at lambing season." She snorted.

"Not the romantic kind." Frances smiled.

"Joe wouldn't know romance if it smacked him in the face," Margaret said. "I don't mind, though. I'm not really one for all that sappy stuff. Live with four farming men long enough, it's hard to associate romance with the same sex that have spent years flicking nose-pickings at you under the kitchen table." She grinned, took another mouthful. "I wasn't even going to get married. To me marriage was just more cooking and wet socks." She glanced down at herself, and the grin disappeared. "I still ask myself every now and then how I've managed to end up like this."

"I'm sorry about your mum," said Frances. She had had a second helping, Margaret noted—the baby's position meant she couldn't manage very much without indigestion—yet she was as thin as a rake. Pudding had been a "bathing beauty," blancmange, so named, the chef had said, smirking, because it shivered and had lovely curves.

"How did she die? Sorry," said Frances, hurriedly, as Margaret's pale skin colored. "I don't mean to be . . . indelicate. It's the nursing."

"No . . . no . . ." said Margaret.

They clutched the table, which was clamped to the floor, arms shooting out to stop salt, pepper or beakers sliding off.

"It came out of nowhere," she said eventually, as the wave subsided. "One minute she was there, the next minute she was . . . gone."

The canteen was almost silent, apart from the low muttering of those women brave or hardy enough to contemplate food, and the occasional crash as a piece of crockery or a tray fell victim to another swell. The queues of the early days had evaporated, and the few girls with an appetite dawdled in front of the serving dishes, taking their time to choose.

"I'd say that was rather a good way to go," said Frances. Her eyes, when she looked at Margaret, were clear and steady, a vivid blue. "She wouldn't have known a thing." She paused, then added, "Really. There are far worse things that could have happened to her."

Margaret might have dwelt on this peculiar statement longer had it not been for the giggling in the corner. Distantly audible as background noise for some minutes, it had now built up into a peak, rising and falling in volume as if in conjunction with the waves outside.

The two women turned in their chairs to see that some women in the corner were no longer alone: they had been joined by several men in engineers' overalls. Margaret recognized one—she had exchanged a greeting with him as he had scrubbed the decks the previous day. The men had closed in around the women, who appeared to be enjoying a little male attention.

"Jean should be here," said Margaret, absently, and turned back to her food.

"Do you think we should take them something? Some mashed potato?"

"Be cold by the time we get it there," said Margaret. "Besides, I don't fancy Jean bringing it up over my bunk. It smells bad enough in there as it is."

Frances stared out of the window at the water heaving and churning around them, occasionally meeting the salt-stained windows with an emphatic slap.

She was reserved, thought Margaret, the kind who always seemed to have a second conversation taking place in her head even as she spoke. "I hope Maude Gonne's all right," she said aloud.

Frances turned, as if brought back reluctantly from distant thoughts.

"I'm torn between wanting to make sure she's okay, and feeling like I can't stand one more minute in that bloody cabin. It's driving me nuts. Especially with those two moaning."

Frances nodded almost imperceptibly. It was the furthest she would come, Margaret suspected, to outright agreement. But she leaned forward, so that her voice could just be heard over the noise in the canteen. "We could take a walk round the decks later, if you want. Give her a bit of air. Maybe you could put her in that wicker basket and we could hide her with a cardigan."

"Hello, ladies."

It was the engineer. Margaret jumped, then glanced behind him at the skittish girls he had just left, some of whom were peering over their shoulders at him. "G'day," she said neutrally.

"I've just been speaking to my friends over there, and I thought I'd let you ladies know that there's a little 'welcome aboard' party in the stokers' mess tonight." He had an accent, and an ease born of long-rewarded confidence.

"Nice thought," said Margaret, sipping her tea. "But we've got a bloke posted outside our door."

"Not tonight you haven't, ladies," he said. "Big shortage of morality monitors because of the weather. We'll have a night or two of freedom." He winked at Frances. He had probably been born winking. "It'll just be a bit of a laugh. We've got some grog, we'll play cards and maybe introduce you to a few English customs."

Margaret raised her eyes to the ceiling. "Not for us, thanks."

"Cards, missus, cards." His expression was of shock and offense. "I don't know what you had in mind. Blimey, you a married woman and all . . ."

Despite herself Margaret laughed. "I don't mind a game of cards," she said. "What do you play?"

"Gin rummy. Newmarket. Perhaps the odd game of poker."

"Only card game there is," she said, "but I only play for stakes."

"My kind of girl," he said.

"I'll probably thrash you," she said. "I've learned from the best."

"I'll take my chances," he said. "I'm not fussy who I take money off."

"Ah. But will there be room for me?" she said, pushing herself back in her chair, so that the full expanse of her belly was revealed. She was waiting to see his reaction.

His hesitation lasted a fraction of a second. "We'll make room for you," he said. "Any decent poker player's welcome in the stokers' mess."

It was as if they had recognized something in each other.

"Dennis Tims." He thrust out a hand.

She took it. "Margaret—Maggie—O'Brien."

He nodded at Frances, who had failed to proffer her own hand. "We're four decks below, almost directly under you. Make your way down the stairs by the officers' bathrooms, then follow the sound of a good time." He saluted, made as if to walk away, then added, in a stage whisper, "If you get wedged in the stairs, Mags, give us a shout and I'll get a few of the lads to come and give you a shove."

The prospect of a few hours in male company made Margaret feel distinctly chipper. It was not the flirtation she craved—unlike many of the other women—just the uncomplicated maleness of home. She let out a huge sigh: Dennis's arrival had shown her what a strain she had found her new all-female existence. "He seemed all right," she said cheerfully, heaving herself out from behind the table.

"Yes," said Frances. Already she was taking her tray toward the washing-up trolley.

"You coming with me? Frances?"

Margaret had to jog to keep up as the tall, slim girl strode down the passageway, barely shifting her weight despite the violent rocking of the floor. Frances had kept her face turned away from Dennis for almost the entire time he was talking, she thought. It was several minutes more before she realized that during the entire two hours they had spent together Frances had told her not a thing about herself.

———

Dear George,

I hope this letter finds you well, and that your leg is much recovered. I was not sure that you received my last letter as I have not had a reply for so long. I have taken the liberty of numbering this one so that you might tell which order mine were sent in. We are all well here in Tiverton. The garden is looking simply lovely, and my new borders are filling out nicely. Patrick is working hard, as always, and has taken on a new chap to help him with some of the bigger accounts. That will bring his total staffing to five, which is quite a tally for these thin years.

I am rather anxious to hear from you, George, as I have asked you several times now whether you want to take up the rental of the cottage on the edge of the Hamworth estate. I have spoken to Lord Hamworth personally (we have met occasionally at his wife's social gatherings) and he has said he is happy to consider you, with your glowing service record, but he does need to know soon, dear, as other people have indicated an interest. There is a retired teacher next door, Mrs. Barnes, a nice sort, from Cheltenham. And we have already lined up a lady to do for you, so you need not worry about your hot dinners!

And as I have mentioned before, Patrick is quite happy to introduce you to the better side of Tiverton society—he is a not inconsiderable force in the local Rotary Club and could make sure you have an "in" with the right sort around here. Now that you will have some more time at your disposal, perhaps you might like to join the local car club? Or even do a bit of yachting? I'm sure you will want to carry on "messing about in boats," even in your twilight years.

Another retired serviceman and his wife have just moved in locally, although I think he might be RAF, so you would have someone to exchange your "war stories" with. He is a quiet sort—said hardly a word to me in the lane!—and seems to have something wrong with his eye. I assume it is a war injury, but Marjorie Latham swears he is winking at her.

I must go now, George. But I thought I should let you know that our sister is a little better. She says to tell you she is grateful for all you did, and hopes to be able to write herself soon. She has borne her loss so bravely.

I pray, as always, that your voyage is a safe one.

　　Your loving sister
　　Iris

Captain Highfield sat in his rooms, one steadying hand on his lead-crystal wine-glass as he read the letter he had put off opening since Sydney, a fork raised absently to his mouth. It had remained there, in mid-air, for several paragraphs now, and when he reached the end of the letter he put it down, then pushed away the congealing gammon steak and boiled potatoes.

He had been rather glad of the change in the weather: the women were easier to manage in the confines of their berths and cabins and, apart from a couple of cases of severe vomiting and the girl who had bruised herself rolling out of an upper bunk, the sick bay had not been unduly troubled. That said, the doctor was much on his mind at the moment.

At first he had wanted to ascribe it to the damp, the rheumatic twinge caused by the sudden drop in pressure. But the ache in his leg had become steadily more insistent, had mutated in form so that occasionally it sharpened, became a signal of malevolent intent. He knew he should go and get it seen to: the doctor in Sydney had impressed upon him the necessity of it. But he knew that if they found what he suspected they would have a reason to deprive him of this last voyage. They'd have him flown home. And even a ship full of women was preferable to no ship at all.

There was a knock on his door. Reflexively, Captain Highfield pushed his leg further under the table. "Enter."

It was Dobson, bearing a thick sheaf of papers. "Sorry to disturb you, sir, but I've brought you the revised sick list. I thought you'd want to know that we're down five of the eight WSOs."

"All sick?"

"Four sick, sir. One confined to bed. She fell down the stairs by the transmitter room and sprained her ankle."

Dobson was staring at the untouched food. No doubt that would be reported to his mess later, and the possible reasons for it discussed, Highfield thought. "What on earth was she doing outside the transmitter room?"

"Lost, sir." Dobson shifted his balance expertly as the floor rose beneath him and spray obliterated the view from the window. "One of the engineers found two girls in the number-two flour store this morning. Somehow managed to lock themselves in. Seems an awful lot of them can't read a map."

The wine had soured in his mouth. Highfield exhaled silently. "So what will we do about going rounds tonight?"

"I thought we could get a few of the marines to do it, sir. Clive and Nicol are pretty responsible fellows. To be honest, I can't see there'll be too much trouble with the ladies while we're coming through the Bight. I'd say at least half are too busy moaning on their bunks to get up to any mischief. The canteens are almost empty."

Dobson was right. Highfield hoped absently that the foul weather would last the entire six weeks. "Fine. Get the men to do it. How's the water level?"

"Not too bad, sir. We're just about keeping on top of things, although I have to say the systems on this old girl are pretty tired. Some of the machinery looks like it's held together with baling twine and good luck. Still, it's helped that so many of the women are in bed." He grinned. "Less hair-washing, that sort of thing."

"Yes, well, I've been thinking about that. Make sure we introduce another lecture on the dhobi. Make it compulsory. And for those who fail to implement it, the threat that they will be allowed no water for three days before they meet their husbands should do the trick."

Dobson left, something a little irritating in his swagger. He fancied himself for captain, Rennick, Highfield's steward, had told him, more than once. He had been glad to see other men who had served beneath him promoted, but there was something about Dobson's manner that simply stuck in his craw. Something in the man's eyes told him that, whether it was due to Hart or his own imminent retirement, he was written off; despite his history, his position, he was no longer a man to be reckoned with.

"Man's an ass," Rennick said, arriving to take the captain's plate. He had been with Highfield almost ten years and his opinions were expressed with the confidence of their long acquaintance.

"He's an ass, but he's the only executive officer I've got."

"The men have no respect for him. He'll do you no good on this voyage."

"You know what, Rennick? Right now, ass or not, Dobson is the least of my worries."

The steward shrugged, his lined Scottish face fixing the captain with an expression that suggested they both knew more than they chose to say. As he left the room, Highfield's eyes fell to the letter in front of him. Then he took his wine-glass in his other hand and swept the piece of paper off the mahogany table into the bin below.

———

Dennis had been wrong about the marine. When Margaret and Frances arrived back at their cabin, he was standing outside, his hand raised as if to knock. "Hey!" yelped Margaret, trying, against her own lumbering weight, and the swaying floor, to run down the passageway. "Hey!"

He lowered his hand long enough for Margaret to slide between him and the door.

"Can I help?" she said, panting, one hand under her belly.

"I've brought you some crackers. Captain's orders, ma'am. We're doing it for everyone who's sick."

"They're asleep," said Margaret. "Best not to disturb them, wouldn't you say, Frances?"

Frances glanced at the man, and then away. "Yes."

"Frances here's a nurse," said Margaret. "She knows what's best for sickness."

There was a short silence.

"Crackers tend to help." The marine was holding the box stiffly in both hands. "Shall I leave them with you, then?"

"Yeah. Thanks." Margaret took the box, wincing: the baby hadn't enjoyed being rattled.

The man was staring at Frances. When he realized Margaret was watching him, he looked away quickly. "I won't be here tonight," he said. "There's a few gone sick because of the weather so I'll be helping with the rounds. I've got permission to look in on you later if you'd prefer." He had a clipped way of talking, as if uncomfortable with casual conversation.

"No," said Margaret. "We'll be fine." She smiled broadly. "Thanks for offering, though. And you don't have to call us 'ma'am.' Seems a little . . . formal."

"Orders, ma'am."

"Oh. Orders."

"Right." He lifted a hand in a half-salute.

" 'Bye, then. And thanks for the crackers." Margaret fluttered her fingers. She was praying that Maude Gonne, alerted by her voice, wouldn't bark.

When they opened the door Jean woke, raising a pale face from under her blanket. She refused the crackers and sat up slowly, revealing the upper half of a flannelette nightgown garlanded with little pink rosebuds. She looked, Margaret thought, shockingly young.

"Do you think we should take anything?" Maude Gonne had leapt on to her lap and was trying to lick her face.

"Take anything where?"

"The stokers' mess. A drink or something."

"I'm not going," Frances said.

"You must! I can't go by myself."

Jean squinted. Her eyes were shadowed. "Go where?" she murmured.

"Bit of a do downstairs," said Margaret. "I'm promised a game of poker. I'm going to head down there once I've given Maudie a quick run. Come on, Frances, you can't sit here all night. You'll be miserable."

"It's really not my thing," said Frances. But she sounded half-hearted.

"Then I'll teach you."

"You're not leaving me here," said Jean, and swung her legs over the edge of the bunk.

"Are you sure?" said Margaret. "It's pretty rough outside."

"Better than puking my guts up in the company of Miss Prim," she said, jerking a thumb at the sleeping figure of Avice in the bunk opposite. A long silk robe in shell pink hung from it. "I'll come with you. I'm not missing out if there's a party. It'll be the closest thing I've had to a laugh since we set off."

———

If Margaret had thought the brides' cabins cramped, little had prepared her for the sheer numbers of men who could be crowded into a single mess area, not much bigger than a working-man's parlor. The first indicator was the odor: the musk that had characterized her brothers' rooms at home had been condensed, amplified, until it met them in an unsavory blast even outside the door. It was the smell of male bodies in permanent too-close contact, washed and unwashed, of sweat and alcohol and cigarettes and unlaundered linen and things that neither Frances nor Margaret wanted to think about. It was little surprise: four floors down, bang on the waterline, it was unlikely the mess had ever enjoyed more than the faintest whisper of fresh air. Directly above the starboard engine room, it was also in a state of almost constant vibration, the noise juddering away below their feet with an awesome, leviathan constancy.

"I think we should go back," said Frances. She had dragged her feet all the way there, had anticipated trouble at the end of every passageway. Margaret had ended up clutching her sleeve, determined that the girl was going to have a good time, just once, if it killed her.

"Past the officers' bathrooms, right? Do you think those are the bathrooms?"

"I'm not looking to see," said Jean. In the minutes between sneaking out of their dormitory and coming down the stairs she had recovered her color. Behind her, Frances stumbled, and tried to catch her balance as the ship pitched again.

"Here it is," said Margaret. "Hello?" she called, and knocked tentatively, unsure if she would be heard above the din. "Is Dennis there?"

There was the briefest silence, then an outburst of catcalling and whistling. A cry of "Chaffer up, lads, we've got visitors." Then, after several minutes, in which Margaret and Frances wondered whether to leave, and Jean attempted unsuccessfully to peep through the inch-wide illuminated gap, the door swung open. A sweet-smelling Dennis, wearing a pressed shirt and clutching a bottle of amber liquid, waved his arm in the manner of someone proposing a grand entry.

"Ladies," he said, stooping to address them, "welcome to the real engine of the *Victoria*."

Thirty-two men were billeted in the stokers' mess, and even with only half of that number present, the women found themselves in a proximity to the opposite sex that in normal circumstances would have left them awaiting imminent betrothal. Frances spent the first half an hour pressed up against the only spare six inches of wall, apparently too terrified, faced with the presence of several semi-dressed males, to sit down. Jean was giggling and blushing, saying, "Saucy!"

in a scolding voice whenever she couldn't think of anything sensible to say, which was often. Margaret was perhaps the least perturbed: her condition and her ease in the company of large numbers of men enabled them to treat her like an honorary sister. Within an hour, she had not only won several hands of cards, but had answered several queries about the best things to write in letters to sweethearts, how to handle interfering mothers-in-law and, on one occasion, which tie to wear for a civilian event. The air was thick with cigarette smoke, alcohol fumes and the occasional curse—followed by an apology, as a concession to the presence of ladies. In the far corner, a rake-thin man with slicked red hair played a trumpet quietly. He was ignored, which made Margaret think this was probably a nightly occurrence.

"You ladies want a drink?" said Dennis, leaning over them with a couple of tumblers. They had quickly established that he did not operate by the normal rules of the ship. Alcohol, smokes, a sub till payday—all of these flowed either to or from him like water. Frances, who had been persuaded to sit down beside Margaret, shook her head. She was apparently immune to the men's admiring looks, and had spent so much time staring at her shoes that Margaret felt guilty for having insisted she come. Jean, meanwhile, had drunk two tumblers already and was getting sillier by the second.

"Steady now, Jean," Margaret whispered. "Remember how sick you were earlier."

"Davy here says it will settle my stomach," said Jean, prodding the man beside her.

"Sittle yer stummick?" One of the ratings, Jackson, had found their accents fascinating, and had made a point of parroting whatever they said.

"You don't want to believe anything this lot tell you," said Margaret, raising her eyebrows. "Settle your stomach, indeed."

"That what your Joe told you, was it?" said Dennis, pointing at hers, to the sound of ribald laughter.

There were bars on the walls to support the hammocks, and rows of lockers, their owners identified by postcards or hand-drawn lettering. On what little wall space remained, pictures of scantily clad starlets jostled for elbow room with grainy, less glamorous shots of wives and girlfriends, beaming children, a nicotine-stained reminder of other, wider worlds far from here. Around them, those men not playing cards at the wooden tables lay in their hammocks, writing letters, sleeping, smoking, reading or just watching—simply enjoying the presence of women. Most had covered themselves, out of deference, and many had proffered boiled sweets, cigarettes, or even photographs of their sweethearts for admiration. Despite the close confines, there was no undercurrent of threat as there had been in the days when Dad brought all those blokes back from the pub. The men were hospitable, friendly and only mildly flirtatious. Margaret thought she understood; having spent months away from those they loved, just having someone there as a reminder of world away from war and men and fighting was enough. She had felt it herself when she had seen men in the same uniform that Joe wore.

"Frances? You sure you won't play a hand?" Margaret had won again. Dennis had whistled and thrown down his cards, threatening dire revenge on the next occasion they met. There seemed no doubt in his mind that there would be another.

"No. Thank you."

"You'd be great at it." She would. Her face was almost entirely impassive; her neat, slightly sharpened features revealed none of the discomfort that Margaret knew she felt. Several times now she had mentioned that Frances was a nurse, and several times Frances had rebuffed any attempt to get her to talk about her time in service. There was just enough grace in her manner to prevent the suggestion of rudeness. But only just.

"Your mate all right?" Dennis murmured to her.

"I think she's a little shy." Margaret had no other explanation. She had kept her head down, embarrassed to be claiming familiarity with a woman she had only recently met.

"A liddle shoi," murmured the rating behind her.

"Shut up, Jackson. So, who's your man with, then?"

"Navy," said Margaret. "Joseph O'Brien. He's an engineer on the *Alexandra*."

"An engineer, eh? Hey, lads, Mags here's one of us. An engineer's wife. I knew you had taste, Mags, as soon as I laid eyes on you."

"And I bet you lay eyes on plenty of women." Margaret raised her eyebrows.

"Very few with taste," said his mate.

They played four or five more hands, the game and the surroundings swiftly displacing the women's sense of being strangers. Margaret knew she was a safe prospect to someone like Dennis: he was the kind of man who enjoyed female company if the possibility of sexual conquest was removed. She had feared her pregnancy might make things difficult on the voyage; now she saw it might make things easier.

Even better, paradoxically, was that these men didn't define her by her belly. Almost every woman she had met so far on this ship had asked her how far gone she was, whether it was a "good" baby (what, she thought, was a bad one?), whether she hoped for a boy or a girl. It was as if she had ceased to be Margaret at all but had become a walking incubator. Some wanted to touch it, and whispered unwanted confidences about how they longed for their own. Others, like Avice, eyed it with vague distaste, or failed to mention it at all, as if they were afraid it might be contagious in some way. Margaret rarely broached the subject: haunted by images of her father's cows giving birth, she had still not reconciled herself to her biological fate.

They played two, three, several more hands. The room grew smokier. The man in the corner played two songs she didn't recognize, then "The Green Green Grass of Home," unusually fast, on his trumpet. The men had stopped the game to sing. Jean broke in with an unrepeatable ditty, and forgot the last few lines. She collapsed into squawks of laughter.

It grew late, or at least it felt late: without natural light or a clock it was impossible to tell whether time had stalled or sped on into the early hours. It became a matter of good or bad hands, of Jean's giggling, the trumpet in the corner, and sounds that, with a little imagination, bore the faintest resemblance to home.

Margaret put down her hand, gave Dennis a second to register. "I think you owe me, Mr. Tims."

"I'm all out," he said, in good-natured exasperation. "Settle for cigarette cards? Something to give the old man?"

"Keep them," she said. "I'm feeling too sorry for you to take anything else off you."

"We'd better get back to the dorm. It's getting late." Frances, the only one of them who was still stiff and formal, looked pointedly at her watch, and then at Jean, who, helpless with giggles, was lying on a hammock, looking at a young rating's comic book.

It was a quarter to twelve. Margaret stood up heavily, sad to have to leave. "It's been great, guys," she said, "but I suppose we should go while the going's good."

"Don't want to get sent home in a lifeboat."

Frances's face revealed that, for several seconds, she had taken this remark seriously.

"Thanks ever so much for the hospitality."

"Hospidaliddy," murmured Jackson.

"Our pleasure," said Dennis. "Want one of us to check the passageway's clear for you?" Then his voice hardened. "Oi, Plummer, have a little respect."

The music stopped. All eyes turned toward Dennis's line of sight. The owner of Jean's comic book had rested a hand casually on the back of her thigh, which was now removed. It was unclear whether Jean was too drunk to have noticed it. Either way, there was a subtle shift in the atmosphere. For a second or two, nobody spoke.

Then Frances stepped forward. "Yes, come on, Jean." It was as if she had been galvanized into life. "Get up. We must get back."

"Spoilsports." Jean half slid, half fell off the hammock, blew a kiss to the rating, and allowed her arm to be linked by Frances's rigid one. " 'Bye, lads. Thanks for a lovely time." Her hair had fallen across her face, half concealing a beatific smile. "Got to shake a leg in the morning." She wiggled one of hers clumsily, and Frances reached forward to pull her skirt down to a demure level.

Margaret nodded to the men round the table, then made her way to the door, suddenly awkward, as if only just aware of the potential pitfalls of their position.

Dennis seemed to grasp this. "Sorry about that," he said. "It's just the drink. No harm meant."

"None taken," said Margaret, raising a neutral smile.

He held out a hand. "Come again." He stooped forward and murmured, "I get sick of the sight of this lot."

She knew what he was trying to say, and was grateful.

"I'd appreciate another game," he added.

"I'm sure we'll be back," she said, as Frances dragged Jean out of the door.

———

Avice was awake when they sneaked into their cabin as silently as they could with Jean giggling and snorting between them.

They had seen only two others: wary girls, who had shared with them the briefest complicit grin before vanishing into a shadowy doorway. Margaret, however, had seen spectral monitors everywhere: her ears had burned with anticipated cries of "Hey! You! What do you think you're doing?" She knew from Frances's serious face that she felt the same. Meanwhile, Jean had been sick twice, thankfully in the officers' bathroom, which had been empty at the time, but was now giggling as she tried to relate to them the story she had been reading. "It was awful funny. Every time this girl does anything. Anything." Her face opened in exaggerated amazement. "All her clothes fall off."

"Hilarious," muttered Margaret. She was a strong girl ("a bit of a heifer," her brothers used to say), but the baby, combined with Jean's almost dead weight and the incessant lurching of the ship, had caused her to grunt and sweat along the passageway. Frances had taken most of Jean's weight and hauled her along silently, one hand gripping at pipes and rails, her face set with the effort.

"Most times it's down to her undies and whatnot. But there were at least two pictures where she had nothing on at all. Nothing. She had to do this with her hands." Jean wrestled herself out of their grasp—she was surprisingly strong for such a small girl—and made as if to cover her bosom and groin, her face an exaggerated *ooh!* of surprise.

"Oh, come on, Jean."

Margaret had peeped round the corner to where their dormitory was, and saw thankfully that the marines were not on duty. "Quick! We might only have a minute."

It was then that the woman had stepped out of the darkness.

"Oh!" Frances gasped.

Margaret felt herself flush.

"What's going on, ladies?"

The officer came toward them at a trot, her bosom arriving shortly before she did. She was one of the WSOs, a short, auburn-haired woman who had directed them earlier to the laundry. There was something almost indecent in her haste, as if she had been waiting for some misdemeanor to take place. "What's going on? You know brides are not allowed out of their dormitories at this time of night."

Margaret felt her tongue swell to fill her mouth.

"Our friend is ill," said Frances, coolly. "She needed to go to the bathroom, and we weren't sure she would manage by herself."

As if in corroboration, the deck lifted under them, sending all four staggering against the wall. As she slipped to her knees Jean swore, then belched.

"Seasickness, is it?"

"Terrible," said Margaret, heaving Jean up.

"Well, I'm not sure—"

"I'm a nurse," interrupted Frances. That thin little voice could hold a surprising amount of authority, Margaret thought. "I decided it would be more hygienic if she was ill away from the bunks. We've got another inside," she said, pointing toward their door.

The woman stared at Jean, whose head was hanging down. "Are you sure it's just seasickness?"

"Oh, yes," said Frances. "I've examined her and she's fine otherwise."

The woman's expression was guarded.

"I've seen it before," said Frances, "when I was serving on the hospital ship *Ariadne.*" She had emphasized "serving." She held out a hand. "Sister Frances Mackenzie."

The woman had been outmaneuvered. She was bothered by it, Margaret could tell, not least because she was not sure how it had happened.

"Yes. Well . . ." she said. She did not take Frances's hand, but left it in mid-air. The apparent ease with which Frances eventually lowered hers made Margaret wonder briefly how many times the gesture had been refused.

"Well, I'll ask you to return to your bunks, ladies, and not to come out again unless it's an emergency. You know we don't have our marine guard tonight, and there's meant to be a strict curfew in place."

"I'm sure we'll be fine now," said Frances.

"Orders, you know," said the officer.

"Yes, we know," replied Frances.

Margaret made as if to move, but Frances was waiting for the woman to go.

Of course, Margaret thought. The dog.

The woman broke. She walked on, casting one brief, uneasy backward look at them as she headed unsteadily toward the canteen.

9

Rounds of all weather decks, galleries and gun positions were carried out frequently, and at irregular periods after dark. All women had to be in their bunks by 11p.m. and the duty woman officer went round to see that no women were missing . . . These measures were the best that could be devised and although by no means perfect, at any rate, acted as a deterrent to bad behavior and broke up many petting parties before their logical conclusion.

CAPTAIN JOHN CAMPBELL ANNESLEY,
QUOTED IN HMS VICTORIOUS, NEIL MCCART

SEVEN DAYS

The sound of the bugle echoed tinnily through the Tannoy, and bounced down the walls of B Deck. Beneath it several men grimaced, and at least one put his hands over his ears—delayed, tentative movements, which were testament to eight unofficial "parties" alleged to have taken place during the previous nights. Of the fifteen men lined up outside the Captain's office, eleven awaited summary trial for some related misdemeanor and the remainder were up for offenses dating back to the last shore leave. Normally such disciplinary matters would take place when the ship was not a day or two out of dock, but the extraordinary nature of its cargo, and the unusual level of offenses meant that, to some extent at least, normal service on board HMS *Victoria* had not yet been resumed.

The master-at-arms stood squarely in front of one of the younger boys who was being supported under each arm by two pustulent mates. He shot out a broad, pudgy finger, and chucked the offender under the chin, frowning as he caught a whiff of his breath. "I don't know what your mother would say to you, my old flower, if she could see you in this state, but I've got a good idea." He turned to the boys. "He your mate?"

"Sir."

"How'd he get like this?"

The boys, for they were not much more, looked at their feet. "Dunno, sir."

"Scotch mist, is it? As opposed to just Scotch?"

"Dunno, sir."

"Dunno, sir," the man repeated, fixing them with a well-practiced glare. "I bet you don't."

Henry Nicol, Marine, stepped back against the wall. The young dabber beside him was wringing his cap in bruised, bloodied hands. He breathed out, bracing himself against the movement of the ship. They were out of the worst of the Bight, now, but it could still catch the unwary.

"Soames, eh?"

The younger man nodded unhappily at the master-at-arms. "Sir."

"What's he in for, Nicol?"

"Quarrels and disturbances, sir. And drunkenness."

"Not like you, Soames."

"No, sir."

The older man shook his head. "You speaking for him, are you, Nicol?"

"Yes, sir."

"Make sure you get some sleep afterward. You're on watch again tonight. You look bloody awful." He nodded at the younger man. "Soames, it's a bad business. Use your loaf next time, not your fists."

The master-at-arms moved slowly on to the next man—conduct to the prejudice of good order, drugs/alcohol—and Soames slumped against the wall.

"You're all for it," the master-at-arms said. "It's the captain today, not the executive officer, and I can tell you he's not in the best of moods."

"I'm going to get it, aren't I?" Soames groaned.

In normal circumstances Nicol might have disputed this, might have been reassuring, upbeat. But with one hand still resting against the letter in his trouser pocket, he had neither the energy nor the desire to make someone else feel better. He had put off opening it for days, guessing, dreading the nature of its contents. Now, seven days after they had left Sydney, he knew.

As if knowing could ever make anything any better.

"You'll be all right," he said.

> *Dear Henry,*
>
> *I'm disappointed but not surprised I haven't heard back from you. I want to say again how sorry I am. I never set out to hurt you. But we have had hardly a word from you in so long, and I am really very fond of Anton. And he is a good man, a kind man, who pays me a lot of heed . . .*
>
> *This is not meant to be a criticism of you. I know we were awfully young when we married, and perhaps if the war had not come when it did . . . Still, as we both know, our world today is full of such if-onlys . . .*

He had read the first paragraph and thought that, ironically, life was easier when his letters were still censored.

It was almost twenty minutes before they were up. They paused outside the captain's office, then Nicol followed the younger man in and they saluted. Captain Highfield was seated behind the desk, flanked by the marine captain and a lieutenant Nicol didn't recognize, who was writing something in a ledger. For some seconds he gave no sign that he was aware of the new occupants of the room.

Nicol nudged the younger man. "Cap," he hissed, his own black beret held in front of him. Soames removed his.

The officer beside the captain read out the charge: the boy had been scrapping with another dabber in the seamen's mess. He had also been drinking—spirits, far in excess of the daily "sippers" ration to ratings.

"How do we plead?" said Captain Highfield, still writing. He had tall, elegant script, somehow at odds with his short, stubby fingers.

"Guilty, sir," said Soames.

Yes, I am guilty. And weak. But, to be truthful, for the last four years I might as well have been a widow for the word I have had from you. I spent three of those years lying awake week after week praying for your safety; that you might come back to us, talking to the children of you daily, even when I suspected you did not remember us. When you did come back you were like a stranger.

Finally, the captain looked up. He eyed the young man, then addressed the marine. "Nicol, isn't it?"

"Sir."

"What can you tell me about this young man's character?"

Nicol cleared his throat, gathered his thoughts. "He's been with us a little over a year, sir. A dabber. He's been very steady during that time, hard-working, quiet." He paused. "A good sort."

"So, Soames, given this glowing character reference, what turned you into a brawling idiot?"

The boy's head dipped. "Look up, man, when you're talking to me."

"Sir." He blushed. "It's my girl, sir. She . . . she was to see me off in Sydney. We've been stepping out some time. But she's been . . . well, it's one of the others in C Deck, sir."

When Anton came, and started paying me some attention, Henry, it's not even that he stepped into your shoes. There were no shoes for him to step into.

". . . and he started taunting me . . . and then the others, well, they said as how I couldn't keep hold of a woman, and you know what it's like in the mess, sir, well, I'd had a bellyful of it and—well—I suppose I saw red."

"You suppose you saw red."

The children are very fond of him. You will always be their father, and they know that, but they will love America and have all sorts of chances there that they would never have had in a sleepy old village in Norfolk.

"Yes, sir." He coughed into his hand. "I'm very sorry, sir."

"You're very sorry," said the captain. "So, Nicol, you say he's been a good sort up to this point?"

"Yes, sir."

The captain put down his pen and clasped his hands. His voice was icy. "You know I don't like fighting on my ship. I especially don't like fighting when there's alcohol involved. Even more, I dislike discovering that there may be social events taking place on my ship without my knowledge that involve alcohol."

"Sir."

"Do you understand? I don't like surprises, Soames."

But here, dear, I have to tell you something hard. If there is an urgency to my letter it is because I am carrying Anton's child, and all we are waiting for is your permission to divorce, so that we can marry and bring this baby up together.

"You're a disgrace."

"Yes, sir."

"You're the fifth person I've seen in here this morning on a drink-related charge. Did you know that?"

The boy said nothing.

"Rather surprising for a ship that supposedly contains no alcohol except your weekly allocation."

"Sir."

Nicol cleared his throat.

The captain stared at the boy from under his brows. "I'm conscious of your previous good character, Soames, and you should consider yourself lucky you have someone of better character to speak for you."

"Sir."

"I'm going to let you off with a fine. But I want you to be clear on one thing—and you can tell your friends this, and all those waiting outside too. Little escapes me on this ship. Very little. And if you think I am not aware of the little get-togethers that are springing up at an hour when our crew and our female cargo should be separated not just by walls but by whole bloody passageways, then you are very much mistaken."

"I didn't mean any harm, sir."

I did not intend things to turn out this way. Please do not make this child grow up a bastard, Henry, I implore you. I know I have hurt you terribly, but please do not inflict whatever you feel for me on the little one.

"You meant no harm," Highfield muttered, and began to write. "You meant no harm. None of you ever does."

There was a brief silence in the room.

"Two pounds. And don't let me see you in here again."

"Sir."

"Left turn, quick march," called the lieutenant.

The two men saluted, and left the office.

"Two bloody pounds," said Soames, as they shuffled past the queue of offenders, ramming his cap back on to his head. "Two bloody pounds," he muttered to one of his mates. "He's a miserable bloody bastard, that Highfield."

"Bad luck."

Soames's pace increased with his sense of injustice. "I don't know why he had to pick on me, going on and on like that. I haven't even spoken to one of those bloody Aussie brides. Not so much as a bloody one of them. Not like bloody Tims. He has girls in that mess most nights. Jackson told me."

"Best stay away from the lot of them," said Nicol.

"What?" The younger man turned, perhaps sensing the barely suppressed tension in the marine's voice. "You all right?"

"I'm fine," he said, removing his hand from his pocket.

Please write me or wire me when you can. I am happy to leave you the house and everything. I have kept it all in good order, the best I could. I do not want to cause you more trouble. I just want your permission to go.

Yours,

Fay

"Yes," said Nicol, striding down the passageway. "I'm fine."

———

The summary trials ended a few minutes after eleven. Captain Highfield laid down his pen and motioned to Dobson, who had entered some minutes previously, and the marine captain that they should sit down. A steward was sent for tea.

"It's not good, is it?" he said, leaning back in his chair. "We're hardly a week in and look at it."

The marine captain said nothing. The marines were a disciplined lot and never drank on board; they tended to appear only as character witnesses, or occasionally when the natural friction between marines and seamen boiled over into blows.

"It's bringing tension into the ship. And alcohol. When did we last have so many drunkenness offenses at sea?"

The two men shook their heads. "We'll organize a locker search, captain. See if we can flush it out," said Dobson. Out of the window, behind them, the skies had cleared to a bright, vivid blue, the sea becalmed. It was the kind of sight that couldn't help but fill the heart with optimism. But Highfield took no joy from it: his leg had throbbed dully all morning, a permanent, intermittent reminder of his failure.

He had avoided looking at it when he dressed this morning: its color disturbed him. A faint purplish tinge told not of the steady creation of new, healthy tissue but of some terrible struggle taking place beneath. If Bertram, the ship's regular surgeon, had been aboard, he could have asked him to take a look at it. He would have understood. But Bertram had failed to show at Sydney, was now the subject of a court-martial, and that damn fool Duxbury was in his place.

Dobson leaned forward, his elbows resting on his knees. "The women's officers tell me they're pretty sure there's movement at night. The one on B Deck had to break up a situation only last night."

"Fighting?"

The two seated men glanced at each other, then at the captain.

"No, sir. Er . . . physical contact between a bride and a rating."

"Physical contact?"

"Yes, sir. He had hold of her round the—round the back of the bilge pump."

Highfield had suspected this might happen, had warned his superiors of it. Yet the reality struck him like a punch. The thought that, even as he sat there, such things were going on aboard his own ship . . .

"I knew this would happen," he said, and saw that the other two men seemed markedly less disturbed by it than he felt. In fact, Dobson looked as if he was trying to contain mirth. "We'll have to post more marines outside the hangar area, the stokers' and seamen's messes."

"With respect, sir," the marine captain interjected, "my boys are on rotating seven-day shifts as it is, as well as all their other tasks. I can't ask them to do more. You saw how exhausted Nicol was, and he's not the only one."

"Do we really need them outside the men's messes?" said Dobson. "If we've got marines keeping the brides in, plus the monitors doing the chastity rounds, surely that should be adequate?"

"Well, it's obviously not, is it? Not if we're already breaking up petting parties and goodness knows what else. Look, we're only a week out of port. If we let it slip now, heaven knows where we'll end up." He was besieged by images of fornicating couples in the flour store, of irate husbands and puce-faced admiralty.

"Oh, come on, sir. I'd say it's important to keep it in perspective."

"What?"

"There are bound to be a few hiccups to begin with, especially with so many crew new together, but it's nothing we can't manage. In fact, after the business with *Indomitable*, it's probably a good thing. It shows that the men are perking up a bit."

Until that point, perhaps through diplomacy or even a desire not to wound their captain further, no one had talked of the sunken ship—at least, not in relation to the men's morale. At the mention of its name Highfield's jaw tightened. It might have been reflexive. More likely it was because of who had spoken.

As he gathered his thoughts, Dobson added silkily, "If you'd rather, Captain, you could leave disciplinary matters to us. It would be sad, sir, if, because of a few youthful high jinks, you couldn't enjoy this last voyage a little."

In Dobson's barbed words, in his relaxed, confident manner, lay everything the men thought about Highfield now but would not say aloud. Once, Dobson would never have dared speak to him in this way. Highfield was so stunned by this barely veiled insubordination that he couldn't speak. When the steward arrived with his tea, he had to wait for several seconds before the captain noticed his presence.

The marine captain, a more diplomatic sort, leaned forward. "I think, sir, that much of the problem this past week may have been to do with the conditions over the Bight," he said. "I believe that both the seamen and the women may have taken advantage of the fact that so many of the monitors were absent to increase the levels of— erm—interaction. Give it a few days more and the women will be less excitable and the men will have got used to having them around the place. I suspect things will settle down."

Highfield, now suspicious, studied the marine captain. There was a transparency in his expression visibly lacking in that of the man beside him. "You think we should let things be?"

"Yes, I do, sir."

"I agree, sir," said Dobson. "Best not to rattle things up too much at this stage."

Highfield ignored him. As he closed the ledger, he turned to the marine captain. "Very well," he said. "We'll go softly for now. But I want to know everything, every footstep, that takes place below deck after ten p.m. Shake the monitors up—get them to use their eyes and ears. And if there is the slightest hint of misbehavior—the slightest hint, mind—I want us to be down on it like a ton of bricks. I will not have anyone charge this voyage with lowering naval standards. Not under my command."

Dear Deanna,

I hope you, Mother and Father are all well. I'm not sure when I will be able to post this, but I thought I would write and let you know a little of our voyage. It is all terribly exciting. I often think how much you would enjoy being here, and how surprising are the conditions we travel in, given my reservations.

I have made three delightful new friends: Margaret, whose father owns a large estate not far from Sydney; Frances, who is terribly elegant and has been doing admirable things in nursing; and Jean. They are all so much more interesting than our old crowd. One girl here has brought fifteen pairs of shoes with her! I am very relieved that I was able to go shopping before I came on board. It is so nice to have new things, isn't it?

My accommodation is situated in the largest part of the boat, a short distance from the part known as the bridge and the captain's "sea cabin." We are told there may well be some cocktail parties once we get to Gibraltar as it is entirely possible that several governors are coming aboard, so that is something to look forward to.

The staff really cannot do enough for us. Every day they lay on new entertainments to keep us girls busy; needlework, dancing, all the latest films. I am off to watch National Velvet *this afternoon. I don't believe it has reached Melbourne yet but, believe me, you must go when it does. The girls who have already seen it say Elizabeth Taylor is perfectly wonderful. The sailors are charming, and helpful, and are always bringing one little things to eat. And, Deanna, you would die for the food. It's as if no one had ever heard of rationing. Not quite the powdered egg we had all feared! So you can tell Mother and Father they do not need to worry in the slightest.*

There is a fully fitted hair salon at the far end of the ship. After I finish writing I think I might take a look. Perhaps I might even offer some help! Remember how Mrs. Johnson always said no one could set hair like me? I shall have to find a decent salon as soon as I reach London. I shall, of course, let you know all about London. I am hoping to hear from Ian before we meet, as to the plans for our little holiday there.

As I said, I hope my letter finds you all well, and please do pass on my happy news to the old crowd. Oh, yes, your little recital will have taken place by the time you get this. I trust it went well. I'll write again when I'm not so busy!

   Your loving sister
   Avice

Avice was sitting in the small canteen on the flight deck, staring out of the salt-spattered window at the seagulls swooping alongside the ship and the bright skies beyond. For the half-hour it had taken her to write her letter, she had almost begun to believe in the version of the voyage she had created. So much so, in fact, that she had felt rather deflated when she signed off to find herself back in this rusting waterborne hangar, surrounded not by cocktail parties and adorable new friends but by the scarred noses of the airplanes on the deck, the shuffling, incoherent boys in their grubby overalls, the brine and salt, the smells of fried food, oil and rust.

"Cup of tea, Avice?" Margaret was leaning over her, that huge belly almost resting on the wood-topped table. "I'm going to get some. You never know, it might settle your stomach."

"No. Thank you." Avice swallowed, then allowed herself to imagine the taste. An immediate wave of nausea confirmed her refusal. She was still having trouble coping with the pervasive droplets of jet fuel that seemed to follow her everywhere, clung to her clothes and in her nostrils. It didn't matter how much perfume she applied, she still felt she must smell like a mechanic.

"You've got to have something."

"I'll have a glass of water. Perhaps a dry cracker, if they've got some."

"Poor old you, eh? Not many get it so bad."

There were three puddles in the middle of the floor. They reflected the light from the windows.

"I'm sure I'll get over it soon enough." Avice made sure to smile brightly. Very few troubles in life couldn't be lessened by a nice smile—that was what her mother always said.

"I was like that in my early months with this." Margaret patted her bump. "Couldn't even keep down dry toast. I was really miserable. I'm surprised I didn't get as seasick as you and Jean."

"Would you mind if we talked about something else?"

Margaret laughed. "Sure thing. Sorry, Ave. I'll go and get the tea."

Ave. If Avice had been feeling less awful, she would have corrected her: there was nothing worse than an abbreviated name. But Margaret had already waddled off toward the counter, leaving her with Frances, an even more uncomfortable proposition.

Over the past few days, Avice had decided there was something profoundly discomfiting about Frances. There was something watchful about her, as if even as she sat there in silence she was judging you. Even when she was being nice, bringing pills to make Avice feel less sick, checking that she wasn't too dehydrated, there was something reserved in her demeanor, as if there were elements of Avice that meant she did not want to engage too closely with her. As if *she* were something special!

Margaret had told her that Frances had been turned down when she offered to work in the infirmary. The less generous-spirited part of Avice wondered what the Navy had felt was not fitting about the girl; the other thought how much easier life would have been without her hanging around all day, with her awkward conversation and serious face. She glanced at the tables of other girls, most of whom were chatting away as if they had known each other for years. They had settled into little cliques now, tight bands already impenetrable to outsiders. Avice, gazing at one particularly happy group, fought the urge to appeal to them, to demonstrate that she was not with this strange, severe girl by choice. But that, of course, would have been rude.

"Have you anything planned for this afternoon?"

Frances had been studying a copy of *Daily Ship News*. She looked up sharply with the guarded expression that made Avice want to yell, "It isn't a trick question, you know." Her pale red hair was pulled into a tight chignon. If she had been anyone else, Avice would have offered to do her something more flattering. She'd be pretty if she brightened herself up a little.

"No," said Frances. Then, when the ensuing silence threatened to overwhelm them both, "I thought I might just sit here for a while."

"Oh. Well, I suppose the weather's improved, hasn't it?"

"Yes."

"I thought the lecture sounded rather dull today," said Avice. She abhorred a conversational vacuum.

"Oh?"

"Rationing and somesuch." She sniffed. "Frankly, once we get to England I plan to do as little cooking as possible."

Behind them a group of girls pushed back their chairs noisily and rose from their table, barely breaking their conversation.

The two women watched them go.

"Have you finished your letter?" Frances asked.

Avice's hand closed over her writing-pad, as if its contents might somehow become visible. "Yes." It had come out sharper than she'd intended. She made a conscious effort to relax. "It's to my sister."

"Oh."

"I've written two others this morning. One to Ian, and another to an old schoolfriend. She's the daughter of the McKillens?"

Frances shook her head.

Avice sighed. "They're very big in property. I hadn't written to Angela since I left Melbourne . . . I don't know when we'll be able to post them, though. I'd love to know when I'll get one from Ian." She examined her fingernails. "I'm hoping it will be Ceylon. I've been told they might bring aboard post there."

She had dreamt of a fat little cushion of Ian's letters, waiting in some sweltering tropical post office. She would tie them with red ribbon and read them in private, luxuriously, one at a time, like someone enjoying a box of chocolates. "It's rather strange," she said, almost to herself, "going all this way and not speaking for so long." Her finger traced Ian's name on the envelope. "Sometimes it all feels a bit unreal. Like I can't believe I married this man, and now I'm on this boat in the middle of nowhere. When you can't speak to them, it's hard to keep hold of the fact that it's all real."

Five weeks and four days since his last letter. The first she had received as a married woman.

"I try to imagine what he's thinking now, because the worst thing about waiting so long for letters is that you know all the feelings are out of date. Things he might have been upset about then will have passed. Sunsets he described are long gone. I don't even know where he is. The one thing we all count on, I suppose, is that their feelings for us haven't changed, even if we're not speaking. I suppose that's our test of faith."

Her voice had dropped, become contemplative. She realized that for several minutes she had forgotten to feel sick. She sat up a bit. "Don't you think?"

Something odd happened to Frances's expression: it closed over, became neutral, mask-like. "I suppose so," she said.

And Avice knew she might as well have said that the sky had gone green. She felt unbalanced and irritated, as if her gesture toward intimacy had been deliberately rebuffed. She was almost tempted to say something to that effect but at that moment Margaret waddled back to the table bearing a tea tray. Propped in her mug was a large vanilla ice-cream, the third she had eaten since they had sat there.

"Listen to this, girls. Old Jean will love it. There's going to be a crossing-the-line ceremony. It's a sailors' tradition, apparently, about crossing the equator, and there's going to be all sorts of fun on the flight deck. The guy at the tea urn just told me."

Frances's rudeness was forgotten. "Will we have to get dressed up?" Avice's hand had risen to her hair.

"Dunno. I know nothing about it—they're going to post something on the main noticeboard later. But it'll be a laugh, right? Something to do?"

"Ugh. I'm not joining in. Not with my stomach."

"Frances?" Margaret had bitten the top off her cone. A small blob of ice-cream was stuck to the tip of her nose.

"I don't know."

"Ah, come on," said Margaret. The chair creaked in protest as she sat down. "Let your hair down, woman. Cut loose a little."

Frances gave her a tentative smile, showing small white teeth. She might even, Avice saw, with a start, be beautiful. "Perhaps," she said.

———

Frances had thought she would resent the man outside. On the first night he had stood there, on the other side of their door, she had been unable to sleep, conscious of the stranger's proximity. Of her own state of undress, her vulnerability. Of the fact that, in theory at least, he was in authority over her. She had been acutely conscious of his every movement, every shift of his feet, every sniff or cough, the sound of his voice as it murmured a greeting or instruction to a passer-by. Occasionally, lying in the dark, she would ponder on his significance: his presence highlighted the fact that they were cargo, a consignment to be ferried safely from one side of the world to the other, in many cases from fathers to husbands, one set of men to another.

Those heavy feet, that rigid stance, the rifle told her they were to be constrained, imprisoned, yet guarded, protected from the unknown forces below. Sometimes, when the nearness of so many people, so many strange men, teamed with their isolation made her feel anxious, she was glad that he was stationed outside the door. But more usually she resented him for making her feel like a possession, someone's property to be safeguarded.

The others seemed to indulge in little such philosophical consideration. In fact, they didn't notice him; for them, like so much on board, he was part of the nightly furniture, someone to call good evening to, to smuggle the dog past, or even themselves, if they were tiptoeing downstairs to another party. As they were tonight. Margaret and Jean were off to meet Dennis for another poker session, chatting in surreptitious whispers as they brushed their hair, fiddled with stockings and shoes and, in Jean's case, borrowed everyone else's cosmetics. It was nearly nine, not late enough to confine them to their cabin, according to the curfew, but after both supper shifts: late enough to warrant a legitimate query about where they were going, should their movement be noticed.

"You sure you won't come with us, Frances?" They had been to several parties now. Jean had stayed sober during at least one.

Frances shook her head.

"You don't need to behave like a nun." Margaret finished doing up her shoe. "I'm sure your old man won't mind you enjoying a bit of company, for goodness' sake."

"We won't tell," said Jean, shaping her mouth into a *moue* as she reapplied her lipstick.

Margaret lifted her dog on to what remained of her lap. "You'll go nuts if you spend every evening in here, you know."

"They'll have to walk you off in a straitjacket when we get to Plymouth." Jean cackled, tapping the side of her head with a forefinger. "They'll think you've got kangaroos loose in the top paddock."

"I'll take my chances." Frances smiled.

"Avice?"

"No, thank you. I'll rest this evening." Avice's nausea had worsened again, and she lay, pale and limp, on her bunk, periodically lifting and lowering her book. "If you could keep the dog well away from me I'd be grateful. Its smell is making me feel even worse."

They had not expected the marine to be standing outside. He had not been there the previous evening, and none of them had heard the footsteps that usually signaled his arrival. Jean, then Margaret, stopped dead in the doorway. "Oh . . . we're just going for some fresh air," said Margaret, speedily closing the door behind her.

"We'll be back by eleven," said Jean.

"Or thereabouts."

Frances, who had stood up to retrieve her dressing-gown from a hanger, paused on the other side of the door, hearing the male voice, the surprise and slight strain in the women's.

"I'd avoid the Black Squad, if that's how you like your fresh air," he said now, so quietly that no one could be sure of what they'd heard.

Frances leaned closer to the door, her dressing-gown raised in the air.

"The stokers' mess. Bit of a crackdown tonight," he explained.

"Oh. Right," said Margaret. "Well. Thanks."

She heard their shoes clattering down the passageway, then the marine coughing quietly. They would say nothing until they reached the corner by the fire hose. Then, out of sight, they would explode with shock and laughter, clutching each other briefly before, with a furtive glance behind them, they made for the stokers' mess.

Avice wasn't asleep. It would have been easier, Frances thought, if she had been. Stuck together in the little cabin, they moved silently around each other. Then Avice lay down, facing the wall, and Frances flicked self-consciously through a magazine, hoping her concentration appeared more genuine than it was.

They had rarely spent any time alone together. Margaret was easy, straightforward, her uncomplicated nature written in her ready smiles. Jean was less predictable, but there was no side to her: she expressed everything she felt, every minor irritation and enthusiasm directly, unpalatable as it might be.

But Avice, Frances guessed, found her difficult. Not only did they have nothing in common, but her personality, her way of being, rubbed Avice up the wrong way. She suspected that in other circumstances Avice might have been openly hostile: experience had shown her that that kind of girl often was. They needed to look down on someone to reassure themselves of their own position.

But there was no room for such honest emotion in a cabin not quite ten feet by eight. Which left the two of them locked in their own excruciating worlds of genteel diplomacy. Frances would inquire occasionally whether Avice needed anything, whether her sickness had lifted a little; Avice would ask if Frances minded her leaving the light on a little longer; both would spend the rest of the evening pretending politely that they believed the other to be asleep.

Frances lay back on her bunk. She tried to read, found she had scanned the same paragraph several times without taking anything in. She forced herself to concentrate and discovered she had read the magazine before. Finally she stared up at the sagging webbing above her, watching it shift.

The dog whimpered quietly in sleep, just visible under Margaret's cardigan. She glanced down to check that its water bowl was full.

Way above them, she heard a bump, followed by a muffled burst of laughter.

Outside, the marine muttered to someone as they passed. Time stretched out, became elastic.

Frances sighed. Quietly, so that Avice would not hear. Margaret was right. If she spent another evening in here, she'd go insane.

———

He turned when she opened the door. "Stretching my legs," she said.

"Strictly speaking, ma'am, you shouldn't be leaving your cabin at this time."

She didn't protest, or plead, just stood, waiting, and he nodded her on. "Stokers' mess?"

"No," she said, smiling at her feet. "No. Not my cup of tea."

She walked briskly along the passageway, conscious of his eyes on her back, fearful that he might call out to her that he had changed his mind, that it was already too close to the curfew, and instruct her to stay where she was. But he said nothing.

Out of his range, she went up the stairs near the cinema projection room, nodded a polite greeting to two girls who, arm in arm, stood back to let her pass. She hurried along, head down, past cabins, past rows of tin trunks secured to the wall with webbing straps, the redundant stores for lifejackets, weaponry, ammunition, the painted instructions—"Keep Dry," "Do Not Use After 11:47," "Do Not Smoke." She strode up the temporary steps toward the captain's sea cabins two at a time, ducking to avoid hitting her head on the metal struts.

She reached the hatch, glanced back to check no one was watching, then opened it and stepped out on to the flight deck. Then she stopped abruptly, almost reeling from the sudden expanse of inky black sea and sky.

Frances stood there for some time, breathing in the cool, fresh air, feeling the breeze tighten the skin of her face, enjoying the gentle movement of the ship. Down below the throbbing of the engines often made her feel as if she was in the bowels of some prehistoric animal: it vibrated through her, chugging and groaning bad temperedly with effort. Up here, the movement was a low purr, the creature benign and obedient, carrying her safely forward, like some mythical beast, across the vast ocean.

Frances peered across the deserted deck, out of bounds after dark. Some moonlit, some in shadow, the silhouettes of the aircraft stood around her, like children congregated in a playground. There was something oddly appealing about their profiles, noses up, as if they were scenting the air. She walked slowly among them, allowing herself to stroke the shining metal, relishing its cool, damp feel under her hand. Finally, she sat down under a narrow streamlined belly. In her vantage-point on the concrete floor, between two webbing lashes, she folded her hands round her knees and stared out at the million stars, the never-ending trails of white foam that charted their course through the water, the unknowable point where the inky sea met the infinite black sky. And for possibly the first time since they had embarked, Frances Mackenzie closed her eyes and, with a shudder that passed through her entire body, allowed herself to breathe out.

———

She had been sitting there for almost twenty minutes when she saw the captain. He had stepped out of the same door she'd closed behind her, his rank clearly visible in his white cap and his curiously accentuated upright posture. She recoiled at first, and maneuvered herself so that she was protected by the shadows, already anticipating the choleric shout "Hey! You!" that would bring about her disgrace. She watched him close the door carefully so that it did not slam. Then, with the same furtive air as, presumably, she had displayed, he stepped forward and began, increasingly obviously, to limp toward the starboard side of the ship and a point just out of sight of the bridge. He stopped by one of the larger airplanes, his uniform spotlit by the moonlight, and reached out as if to support himself on a wing strut. Then, as she held her breath, he bent and rubbed his leg.

He stood there for some minutes, his weight on one leg, shoulders slumped, staring out to sea. Then he straightened his shoulders and walked back to the hatch. By the time he reached it, his limp was no longer perceptible.

Afterward, she could not articulate what it was about this brief scene that she had found comforting—whether it was the sea itself, her ability to carve out twenty minutes' freedom unnoticed, or the small suggestion of humanity contained in the captain's limp, a reminder of men's fallibility, their capacity to conceal their hurt, to suffer—but as she came back down the stairs she had found herself somehow less conscious of the glances of those who passed, with a little of her confidence restored to her.

She would not normally have asked a man for a cigarette. She would not have allowed herself to be drawn into conversation. She would certainly not have begun one. But she felt so much better. The sky had been so beautiful. And there was something so melancholy about his face.

He was leaning against the wall beside their door, cigarette cupped between thumb and forefinger, eyes fixed on a point on the floor in front of him. His hair had flopped forward and his shoulders were hunched, as if he was lost in some less-than-happy thought. As he caught sight of her he pinched out the cigarette and dropped it into his pocket. She thought he might have flushed. Afterward, she remembered feeling mildly shocked: up to that point, he had seemed a kind of automaton. Like so many marines. She had hardly considered there might be room for something as human as embarrassment, or even guilt, behind the mask. "Please don't bother," she said. "Not on my account."

He shrugged. "Not meant to, really, on duty."

"Still."

He had thanked her gruffly, not quite meeting her eye.

And for some reason, instead of disappearing into the cabin, she had stood there, her cardigan round her shoulders and, unexpectedly even to herself, asked whether she might have one too. "I don't feel like going in yet," she explained. Then, self-conscious, she had stood beside him, already regretting her decision.

He pulled a cigarette from the pack, and handed it to her wordlessly. Then he lit it, his hand briefly touching hers as it cupped the flame. Frances tried not to flinch, then wondered how quickly she could smoke it without making herself dizzy and disappear. He had plainly not wanted company. She, of all people, should have seen it. "Thanks," she said. "I'll just have a few puffs."

"Take your time."

Twice she found herself in the unusual position of smiling, an instinctive, conciliatory gesture. His, in answer, was fleeting. They stood, one on each side of the door frame, looking at their feet, the safety notice, the fire extinguisher until the silence became uncomfortable.

She looked sideways at his sleeve. "What rank are you?"

"Corporal."

"Your stripes are upside-down."

"Three-badge marine."

She took a deep drag of her cigarette. She was already nearly a third of the way down it. "I thought three stripes meant sergeant."

"Not if they're upside-down."

"I don't understand."

"They're for long service. Good conduct." His eyes flickered over them, as if he had rarely considered them. "Stopping fights, that kind of thing. I suppose it's a way of rewarding someone who doesn't want promotion."

Two ratings walked along the passageway. As they passed Frances, their gaze flicked from her to the marine and back again. She waited until they'd gone, their footsteps echoing. A moment later the brief rise and fall in the sound of chatter told of the opening and closing of a cabin door.

"Why didn't you want promotion?"

"Don't know." Possibly he realized this had sounded a little abrupt, because he went on, "Perhaps I never saw myself as sergeant material."

His face seemed frozen into disappointment, she thought, and his eyes, while not unfriendly, told of his discomfort with casual conversation. She knew that look: she wore it habitually too.

His gaze briefly met hers and slid away. "Perhaps I never wanted the responsibility."

It was then that she spotted the photograph. He must have been looking at it before she came. A black and white picture, a little smaller than a man's wallet, tucked into his right hand between finger and thumb. "Yours?" she said, nodding toward his hand.

He lifted it, and looked at it as if for the first time. "Yes."

"Boy and girl?"

"Two boys."

She apologized, and they smiled awkwardly. "My youngest needed a haircut." He handed it to her. She took it, held it under the light and studied the beaming faces, unsure what she was meant to say. "They look nice."

"Picture's eighteen months old. They'll have grown some."

She nodded, as if he had shared with her some piece of parental wisdom.

"You?"

"Oh. No . . ." She handed back the picture. "No."

They stood in silence again.

"You miss them?"

"Every day." Then his voice hardened. "They probably don't even remember what I look like."

She did not know what to say: whatever she was intruding on would not be eased by a cigarette and a few minutes of small-talk. She felt suddenly that engaging him in conversation had been rash and misjudged. His job was to stand outside their door. He had no choice if she chose to talk to him. He would not want to be bothered by women at all hours.

"I'll leave you," she said, quietly, then added, "Thank you for the cigarette." She trod it out, then bent down to pick up the butt. She was afraid to take it into the cabin—what would she do with it in the dark? But if she put it into her pocket it might burn through the fabric. He had failed to notice her predicament, but as she hesitated by the door he turned. "Here," he said, holding out a hand. The palm was weathered, leathery with years of salt and hard work.

She shook her head, but he held his hand closer, insistent. She placed the little butt on it, and blushed. "Sorry," she whispered.

"No problem."

"Goodnight, then."

She opened the door, was sliding silently round it into the darkness when she heard his voice. It was quiet enough to reassure her that her judgment of him had been right, but light enough to show he had not taken offense. Light enough to suggest some kind of offering.

"So, whose is the dog?" it asked.

10

The voyage was a nightmare. Due to breakdowns, it took eight weeks. We had one murder, one suicide, one Air Force Officer who went crazy etc. All of this against the background of a crew neglecting their work in order to have time to pursue "brides" and later to engage in virtually public, gymnastic sexual activity with them. They appeared to use every available location on the ship, including one couple who specialized in the "Crows Nests."
FROM THE PAPERS OF THE LATE RICHARD LOWERY,
NAVAL ARCHITECT

SIXTEEN DAYS

The first Not Wanted Don't Come arrived on the morning of the sixteenth day the brides had been on board. The telegram arrived just after eight a.m. in the radio room, shortly after the long-range weather reports. Its content was noted by the radio operator. He carried it swiftly to the captain, who was eating toast and porridge in his rooms. He read it, then summoned the chaplain, who summoned the relevant WSO, and all three spent some time pontificating on what was known of the character of the bride concerned, and how well—or otherwise—she was likely to take the news.

The subject of the telegram, a Mrs. Millicent Newcombe (née Sumpter) was called in to the captain's office at ten thirty a.m.—it had been thought only fair to let the girl enjoy a good breakfast first; many had not yet entirely recovered from seasickness. She arrived white-faced, convinced that her husband, a pilot, flying Seafires, had been shot down and was missing, presumed dead. So great had been her distress that none of the three was quick enough to tell her the truth, and merely stood uncomfortably as she sobbed into her handkerchief. Eventually Captain Highfield put matters straight, telling her in a sonorous voice that he was terribly sorry but it wasn't that. It really wasn't that at all. Then he had handed her the telegram.

Afterward, he told his steward, she had gone quite pale—paler even than when she had suspected her husband's death. She had asked, several times, whether they thought it was a joke, and when she heard that all such telegrams were investigated and verified as a matter of course, she had sat down, squinting at the words in front of her as if they didn't make sense. "It's his mother," she said. "I knew she'd do for me. I knew it."

Then, as they stood in silence around her, "I bought two pairs of new shoes. They cost me all my savings. For going ashore. I thought he'd want to see me in nice shoes."

"I'm sure they're very nice shoes," the chaplain murmured help-lessly.

Then, with a heartbreaking look round the room, she said, "I don't know what I do now."

Captain Highfield, along with the women's officer, had wired the girl's parents, then contacted London, who had advised that they should put her off at Ceylon where a representative of the Australian government would take charge of the arrangements to bring her home. The radio operator would make sure that her parents or other family members had any relevant information. They would not let her go until they were sure that arrangements were in place to meet her at the other end. These procedures were laid out in the paper-work recently sent from London and had been put in place for the earlier return of GI brides.

"I'm very sorry," she said, once the arrangements had been made, thin shoulders straightening as she pulled herself together. "To put you all to so much trouble, I mean. I'm very sorry."

"It's really no trouble, Mrs. . . . erm . . . Millicent."

The women's officer had placed an arm round the girl's shoulders to steer her out; it was hard to tell whether the gesture was protective or merely indicative of her determination to get her away from the captain's office.

For several moments after she had left the room was silent, as if, in the face of such emotional devastation, no one knew what to say. Highfield, sitting down, the girl's forlorn voice still echoing round his walls, found he was developing a headache.

"I'll get on to the Red Cross in Ceylon, sir," said the chaplain, eventually. "Make sure there's someone who can stay with her a little. Give her a bit of support."

"That would be a good idea," said Highfield. He scribbled something meaningless on the notepad in front of him. "I suppose we should contact the pilot's supervising officer as well, just to make sure there are no extenuating circumstances. You take charge of that, Dobson, will you?"

"Yes, sir," said Dobson. He had entered just as Millicent was leaving, and was whistling a jaunty tune that Highfield found intensely annoying.

He wondered whether he should have spent more time with the girl, whether he should get the WSO to bring her to dinner. A meal at the captain's table might be consoling after her humiliation. But he had always found it difficult to judge these things.

"She'll be all right," Dobson said.

"What?" said Highfield.

"She'll probably have found another young dope by the time she leaves Ceylon. Pretty girl like that." He grinned. "I don't think these Aussie girls are too fussy, as long as they find someone to get them off the old sheep farm."

Highfield was speechless.

"Besides, it's one less bride on board, eh, Captain?" Dobson laughed, apparently pleased with his own humor. "Bit of luck we could have jettisoned the lot by the time we reach Plymouth."

Rennick, who had been standing in the corner, briefly met his captain's eye, then quietly left the room.

———

Until that point the world as the brides had known it had steadily receded by nautical miles, and the *Victoria* had become a world of its own, existing discretely from the continuing life on land. The routines of the ship had become the routines of the women, and those faces who daily moved around them, scrubbing, painting or welding, their population. This new world stretched from the captain's office at one end to the PX store (purveyors of lipstick, washing-powder, writing paper and other essentials—without a ration book) at the other, and from the flight deck, surrounded by its endless blue horizon, to the bowels of the bilge pumps, the port and starboard engines.

The days were marked off for some women by letter-writing and devotions, for others by lectures and movies, punctuated by walks round the free sections of the blustery deck or by the odd game of bingo. With food provided, and their lives dictated by the rules, there were few decisions to make. Marooned on their floating island, they became passive, surrendered themselves to these new rhythms, surrounded by nothing except the slowly changing climate, the increasingly dramatic sunsets, the endless ocean. Gradually, inevitably, in the same way as a pregnant woman cannot imagine the birth, it became harder to look forward to their destination, too much of a struggle to imagine the unknown.

Still harder to think back.

In this stilled atmosphere, news of the Not Wanted Don't Come filtered through the ship as rapidly and pervasively as a virus. The collective mood, which had taken on a hint of holiday as the girls felt less nauseous, was suddenly, distantly, fraught. A new low note of anxiety underlay the conversation in the canteen; a spate of headaches and palpitations presented themselves to the sick bay. There was a rapid rise in the number of queries about when the next batch of letters was to arrive. At least one bride confided in the chaplain that she thought she might have changed her mind, as if by saying the words, and hearing his reassurance, she could ward off the possibility of her husband doing the same.

That one piece of paper, and its four bald words, had brought home to them rudely the reality of their situation. It told them that their future was not necessarily their own, that other unseen forces were even now dictating the months and years to follow. It reminded them that many had married in haste, and that no matter what they felt, what sacrifices they had made, they were now waiting, like sitting ducks, for their husbands to repent at leisure.

Despite this, or perhaps because of it, the arrival that afternoon of King Neptune and his cohorts prompted an atmosphere on board that could at best be described as fevered and at worst as manic.

After lunch Margaret had dragged the others up on to the flight deck. Avice had declared she would rather rest on her bunk, that she was feeling too delicate to enjoy herself. Frances had said, in her cool little voice, that she didn't think it was her kind of thing. Margaret, who had not failed to notice the chill in the air between the two, and a little unbalanced herself by the discovery in the bathroom that morning of a weeping girl convinced—in the face of no evidence— that she was about to get a telegram, had determined it would do them all good to go.

Her motives were not entirely selfless: she didn't want to act as a buffer for the others' jangling moods, couldn't face yet another afternoon ricocheting aimlessly between the canteen and the confines of the dormitory.

Jean, at least, had needed no persuading.

When they had emerged outside, the flight deck—normally deserted apart from rows of attentive seagulls, lost brides, or lonely pairs of seamen scrubbing their way backward in steady formation—was a seething mass of people, the sun bouncing off the deck around them, their chatter lifting above the sound of the engines as they seated themselves around a newly constructed canvas tank. It was several seconds before Margaret noticed the chair suspended above it from the mobile crane.

"Good God! They're not going to stick us in that, are they?" she said.

"Need a dockyard crane for you," said Jean, as she pushed, elbows out like elephants' ears, through the crowd, oblivious to sharp looks and muttering. "Come on, girls. Plenty of room over here. Mind your backs! Pregnant lady coming through."

Now that most were seated, Margaret could see that the crowd was mixed. It was the first time since they had slipped anchor that so many men and women had been gathered together without formal separation. The officers, though, stood apart in their whites. The heat on the deck evoked an expectant, festival atmosphere, and as she lumbered through the crowd, she was conscious of the women's bare arms and legs, the bolder attention of the men.

A short distance away another heavily pregnant woman was looking for somewhere to sit, a sunhat on her head, her pale skin mottled in some uncomfortable reaction to the heat. She caught sight of Margaret and her face twisted into acknowledgment, part smile, part sympathy. Behind her, a man in overalls offered a laughing girl a paper cup, and she thought wistfully of Joe, buying her lemonade at a local fair on one of the first times they had walked out together.

She lowered herself into the space Jean had cleared for her, trying to prop herself on the hard surface in a way that wouldn't make her limbs ache. Minutes later she found herself ducking inelegantly as a large crate was passed over the women's heads by one of the ratings to a mustachioed engineer, whom she recognized from Dennis's mess. "There you go, missus," he said, placing it beside her. "Sit yourself on that."

"Very civil of you," she said, embarrassed, a small part of her resentful that her condition meant she required it.

"Not at all," he said. "We're drawing lots over there, and none of us wanted the job of hauling you to your feet."

Considering Margaret's facility with bad language, it was perhaps fortunate that at that moment "Neptune" arrived, in a wig made of unbraided rope, his face painted a violent green. He was surrounded by a number of equally outlandishly dressed companions, who were introduced as (a rather hairy) Queen Amphitrite, the Royal Doctor, Dentist and Barber, and the oversized Royal Baby, modesty protected by a toweling napkin and slathered in a layer of the grease more commonly associated with a well-tuned engine. Behind them, accompanied by the red-haired trumpet-player, came a band of bare-chested men, cheered loudly by the assembled troops and women, who were apparently to act as enforcers. They were introduced without explanation as "Bears."

"I'd dare to 'bear.' Hey! I'd 'bear all' for you, mate!" Jean's face was glowing with excitement. "Look at him! He's as fit as a Mallee bull!"

"Oh, Jean," sighed Avice.

Despite her air of exasperation, it was clear to everyone that Avice was feeling better. It was apparent in the way she had spent a full twenty minutes doing her hair, even without the aid of a proper mirror or hairspray. It was apparent in the way that she sprayed herself so liberally with scent that Maude Gonne had sneezed for almost half an hour. But it was mostly apparent in the sudden lifting of her spirits at being in mixed company. "Look. There's all sorts of ranks here," she said happily, neck craned to make out who was in the crowd. "Look at all the stripes! I thought it was just going to be a load of horrid old engineers."

Margaret and Frances exchanged a look.

"And horrid old engineers' wives?" said Margaret, drily, but Avice didn't appear to hear.

"Oh, I wish I'd got out my dress with the blue flowers," she said, to no one in particular, as she eyed her cotton skirt. "It's so much nicer."

"You all right?" said Frances, nodding at Margaret's belly. Despite her large, floppy sunhat, she seemed ill at ease.

"Fine," said Margaret.

"Need a drink or anything? It's quite warm."

"No," said Margaret, a little impatiently.

"I don't mind going to the canteen." It was as if Frances was desperate to go.

"Oh, stop fussing," said Avice, straightening her hem. "If she wants something, she'll ask for it."

"I'll speak for myself, thanks. I'm fine," said Margaret, turning to Frances. "I'm not ill, for goodness' sake."

"I just thought—"

"Well, don't. I'm perfectly capable of looking after myself." She lowered her head, fighting her ill-temper. Beside her, Frances had gone very still, reminding Margaret uncomfortably of Letty.

"Hear ye, hear ye," said Neptune, lifting his trident so that it glinted in the sun. Slowly the noise subsided to a barely suppressed communal giggle, the odd whisper rippling through the crowd like a breeze across a cornfield. Satisfied that he had the women's full attention, he lifted a scroll of paper.

"You ladies now by Britain claim'd
Will find our company is shamed.
And offenses grave and numerous here
Old Neptune's court has come to hear.
Rating, captain, all the same,
Before our sea king's judgment famed
And all will find their sins are met
With punishment both foul and wet,
Whether failing to share with friends his grog
Or being termed a pollywog,
You'll hear the charge, and then we'll see
How Neptune choose to punish thee."

"It's hardly Wordsworth, is it?" sniffed Avice.

"Who?" said Jean.

"Now our ratings, our tadpoles, pollywogs
Will have to fight like cats and dogs
To save themselves from Neptune's pack
And earn the right to be 'Shellback.'
Captain, chaplain, or humble docker,
They've sent too many to Davy Jones' locker.
So we will decide, O ladies fair,
Just who gets a spell in our dunking chair."

Eventually, after much catcalling and something that might have qualified as a scuffle, the first "tadpole" was called up: a young rating whose squint was explained by the spectacles borne aloft like a prize behind him. His guilt, apparently, was predicated on it being only his second time of crossing the line—the first had been in wartime, and had not been commemorated. As the women howled their approval, he was first charged with "failing to acknowledge the territory of Neptune," then, as the enforcers held him down, the Royal Dentist filled his mouth with what looked like soapsuds, leaving him gagging and choking. He was then lifted into the chair and, at the lowering of Neptune's trident, summarily ducked, as the women clapped and cheered.

"It's not very dignified, is it?" said Avice, leaning forward for a better view.

At this point, the Bears moved into the crowd, eyeing the women with theatrical intent. The brides, in turn, shrieked obligingly and clutched each other, vowing loudly and without any intent whatsover, to protect each other. They were melodramatic enough for Margaret to roll her eyes. Beside her, Frances didn't flinch. But, then, she seemed so little moved by the presence of men that Margaret wondered how she had ever come to be married at all.

One of the Bears stopped in front of them. His chest still wet from some previous assault, green-faced with a string of shells around his neck, he bent low and peered at the women. "What sinners and miscreants do we have here, then?" he said. "Which of you is deserving of punishment?" He was met by a collective shriek as the brides parted like biblical waves around him.

Except Frances. As he paused in front of her, she sat very still and stared back at him, until, realizing he would get no sport from her, he turned to Margaret. "Aha!" he cried, advancing toward her. Margaret was about to protest smilingly that there was no way they were putting her in that bloody chair when he swiveled round, like a pantomime villain, to face the delighted audience around him. "I see I shall have to find another victim," he said, thrusting a hand toward her, "for it is Neptune's law that one must not offend a whale!"

The brides around them fell about. Margaret, who had been about to make some smart retort, found herself tongue-tied. They were all laughing at her. As if her pregnancy made her some kind of joke. "Oh, rack off," she said crossly. But that only made everyone laugh louder.

She sat there as he prowled off after other game, her eyes filled inexplicably with tears. Frances's hat was pulled low on her head, her hands folded tightly in her lap.

"Bloody eejit," Margaret muttered, then louder: "Bloody eejit." As if saying it might make her feel better.

The sun grew fiercer and she could feel her nose and cheeks burning. Several other ratings were brought forward, and similarly charged; some were writhing and swearing, or carried bodily, allegedly having attempted to hide in different parts of the ship. Most laughed.

Margaret envied Frances her hat. She shifted on her crate, one hand raised to her hairline as she watched the entertainment, the staged misfortunes of others gradually forcing aside her own bad mood. "You've been on ships before. Is it always like this?" she said to Frances, who was now wearing sunglasses. She couldn't bear an atmosphere.

Frances forced a smile, and Margaret felt ashamed for having been so sharp with her. "I couldn't tell you," she murmured. "I've always been working." Then she was distracted by something off to her right.

"Who are you nodding at?"

"That's our marine," Frances said.

"It is?" Margaret squinted at the dark-haired man standing a short distance away from them. She hadn't ever really looked at his face, had been too busy hurrying past him, hunched over her concealed dog. "He looks bloody awful. Shouldn't he be asleep if he's on watch all night?"

Frances didn't answer. The marine had spotted them and her eyes were now on her feet.

"He's nodding at you," said Margaret, waving cheerfully. "There! You not going to wave back?"

But Frances didn't appear to have heard.

"Look!" interrupted Jean, grabbing Margaret's elbow. "Bloody hell! They've got one of the officers!"

"And he's no ordinary officer," said Avice. "He's the executive officer. He's terribly high up, you know. Oh, my goodness!" Her mouth twitched under her hand, as if she thought that, for the sake of propriety, she shouldn't be seen to enjoy this quite so much.

Swearing and spluttering, the XO had been carried from beside the captain to the ducking stool and strapped in. There, set upon by Bears, his shirt was removed and, as the brides shrieked their approval, he was smothered in grease and his face plastered with what might have been oatmeal.

Several times he twisted in the seat, as if to appeal to someone behind him, but syrup was rubbed into his hair and feathers scattered on top. With every humiliation the noise level grew higher, until even the gulls circling the scene were shrieking. It was as if, having been made brutally aware of their own lack of control over their lives, the women took a cathartic pleasure in determining what happened to someone else's.

"Off! Off! Off!" yelled the crowd, men's voices mingling with women's.

Margaret's own humiliation was forgotten. She was grinning and shouting, reminded of her brothers' rough-housing, of the way, as children, they had pinned each other to the dirt and forced cow dung into each other's mouths.

She was distracted by a tap on her shoulder. Frances was mouthing something at her. It was impossible to hear what she was saying, but she seemed to be gesturing that she was leaving. She looked pale, Margaret thought, then turned back to the XO's misery.

"Look at him," yelled Avice, marveling. "He looks absolutely furious."

"Mad as a cut snake," said Jean. "I didn't think they'd do it to someone that high up."

"Are you okay—" Margaret began, then saw that Frances had already gone.

At the urging of the now delirious crowd, the Royal Barber applied foam to the officer's hair, then took a pair of oversized scissors and hacked at it. Then his mouth was cranked open by gleeful men and he was fed what Neptune announced as "seafarer's medicine." As he retched and spluttered, his face now all but unrecognizable, one of the Bears walked round the assembled women, proudly detailing its ingredients—castor oil, vinegar, soapsuds, and powdered egg. Two rotting fish were stuck into the XO's ears, a woman's scarf tied around his neck. There was a brief countdown, and then he was ducked, emerging twice to express his outrage.

"You'll all bloody well pay for this," he was shouting, through the suds. "I'll get your names and take this up with your superiors."

"Hold your tongue, Dobbo," ordered Queen Amphitrite, "or you may find something even fishier on it."

The women laughed louder.

"I really can't *believe* they're meant to do that," said Avice, fizzing with excitement. "I'm sure someone so high up isn't meant to be included." Then she took on the stillness of a gun-dog scenting sport. "Oh, my goodness! That's Irene Carter!"

Neptune's court—and her companions—forgotten, she stood up and pushed her way through the jeering crowd, one hand raised to her hair as she went. "Irene! Irene! It's Avice!"

"Do you think the captain will report them for it?" Jean said, wide-eyed, as the noise subsided and the spluttering victim was unstrapped from the ducking chair. "You'd think someone like that was off-limits, wouldn't you?"

"I've no idea," said Margaret.

She scanned the deck for Frances and spotted the captain. He was standing beside the island, his face partially obscured by the men around him. A shorter man with a heavily lined face stretched up to mutter something into his ear. It was hard to tell from that distance, what with the captain wearing his cap, and with so many people moving around, but she could have sworn he was laughing.

———

It was almost two hours before she found Frances. *National Velvet* was playing and she was seated alone in the cinema, several rows from the front, her sunglasses pushed back on her head, apparently absorbed in the sight of Mickey Rooney drunk in a saloon bar.

Margaret paused at the side of the little aisle, squinting in the dark to confirm to herself that it was Frances, then went over to her. "You all right?" she said, easing in beside her.

"Fine," Frances murmured.

Margaret thought she had never met someone so determinedly emotionless in her life. "The ceremony was a good laugh," she said, raising her feet on to the seat in front. "The chef was charged with cooking inedible food. They stuck a dead squid on his head and made him eat yesterday's slops, all mixed up. I thought it was a bit unfair. I mean, I couldn't do any better."

In the light from the screen she saw Frances smile in a way that suggested a complete lack of interest.

Margaret continued doggedly: "Jean's gone to take tea with the able seamen. Oh, and Avice has left us. Found some old friend and they fell on each other like long-lost sweethearts. They even looked like each other—perfect hair, lots of makeup, that kind of thing. My guess is she'll drop us like a hot brick now. I got the feeling we were a bit of a disappointment to her. Or I was," she said hurriedly. "You know, the fat old milkmaid with the stinky little dog. Probably not her idea of a social scene." The baby was kicking. Margaret shifted, scolding it silently.

"I . . . was wondering why you left," she said. "I thought . . . well, I just wanted to check you were all right."

At this point Frances evidently realized she was not going to be allowed to watch the film. Her posture softened a little and her head dipped toward Margaret. "I'm not very good with crowds," she said.

"That it?" said Margaret.

"Yes."

Elizabeth Taylor mounted her horse with the kind of easy leap that suggested weightlessness, a joy in the simple act of movement. Margaret watched her, reminded of her mother's bad-tempered mare, remembering how, months earlier, she had been able to vault lithely on to its back, and then, showing off to her brothers, spin round athletically to face its rear. She had been able to do hand-stands on the older, quieter horse.

"I'm sorry," she muttered. "About being a bit sharp earlier."

Frances kept her eyes on the screen.

"I just find—I find being pregnant a bit difficult. It's not really me. And sometimes . . . I say things without thinking." Margaret rested her hands on her belly, watching as they lifted with the baby's squirms. "It's because of my brothers. I'm used to being direct. And I don't always think about how it comes across."

Frances was looking down now and the screen was illuminated briefly by cinematic sunlight. It was the only sign by which she could tell that the other woman was listening. "Actually," she continued, the darkness and their solitude allowing her to say the things she had kept to herself for so long, "I hate it. I shouldn't say that but I do. I hate being so big. I hate not being able to walk up two bloody stairs without puffing like an old codger. I hate the look of it, the idea that I can't do a bloody thing—eat, drink, walk around in the sun—without having to think of the baby."

She fiddled with her hem. She was heartily sick of this skirt and of wearing the same things day after day. She had hardly worn a skirt in her life until she had become pregnant. She smoothed it distractedly.

Eventually she spoke again. "You know, almost as soon as Joe and I got married he was gone and I was living with Dad and my brothers. Married in theory, I guess you could call it. It certainly didn't feel like being married. But I didn't complain because we were all in the same boat, right? None of us had our men with us. And then the war ended. And then I discovered . . . you know . . ." She looked down. "And instead of finally getting my passage overseas and meeting Joe again and just being able to enjoy me and him being together, finally being together, which was all I really wanted, we've already got this thing to take into account. No honeymoon. No time to ourselves. By the time it's born we'll have been alone together for about four weeks of our married life."

She rubbed her face, grateful that Frances couldn't see it. "You probably think I'm awful for saying all this. You've probably seen all sorts of death and sickness and babies and are sitting there thinking I should be grateful. But I can't be. I just can't. I hate the thought that I'm meant to feel all these feminine, maternal things that I can't make myself feel." Her voice caught. "Most of all, I hate the thought that once it's born I'm never going to be free again . . ."

Her eyes had filled with tears. Awkwardly she tried to wipe her eyes with her left hand so that Frances would not know. This was what it was turning her into: a stupid, weeping girl. She blew her nose on a damp handkerchief. Tried to get comfortable again and flinched as the baby delivered another sharp kick to her ribs, as if in retribution. It was then that she felt a cool hand on her arm.

"I suppose it's to be expected," Frances said, "that we'll get a bit tense with each other. I mean, living so close and all."

Margaret sniffed again. "I didn't mean to cause offense."

It was then that Frances turned to her. Margaret could just discern her huge eyes. She swallowed, as if what she had to say required effort. "None taken." And, after the briefest of squeezes, she took her hand back into her lap and returned to the film.

———

Margaret and Frances walked back along the hangar deck, having joined the second shift, rather than their allotted one, for dinner, due to the late finish of the film. This request had prompted as much cheek-sucking and ill-tempered acquiescence among the women's officers, Margaret said, as if they had asked to eat in the nude. "Lukewarm corned-beef pie as opposed to warm corned-beef pie. It hardly requires an international treaty, does it?"

Frances had smiled for the second time that evening; Margaret had noted it because each time her face had been transformed. That porcelain stillness, the melancholy air of withholding, had evaporated briefly and this sweetly beautiful stranger had broken through. She had been tempted to comment on it, but what little she knew of Frances had told her that any remark would bring down the shutters again. And Margaret was not a stickybeak.

Frances was talking about life on board a hospital ship. As her quiet, precise voice detailed the rounds, the injuries of a young marine she had treated outside the Solomon Islands, Margaret thought of that smile, then of Letty. Of the brief, blushing youthfulness of her, that strange almost-prettiness that beset her features when she had dared briefly to believe in a future with Murray Donleavy. She pushed away the memory, feeling darkly ashamed.

The temperature had not cooled as much as it had on previous evenings, and a balminess in the air reminded her of summer at home, of sitting out on the front porch, bare feet warm against the rough boards, the sound of the occasional slap as one of her brothers abruptly ended the night flight of some carnivorous insect. She tried to imagine what they would be doing that night. Perhaps Daniel would be sitting on the porch skinning rabbits with his penknife . . .

Suddenly she became aware of what Frances was telling her. She stopped. Got Frances to repeat herself. "Are you sure? He knows?" she said.

Frances's hands were thrust deep into her pockets. "That's what he said. He asked whose she was."

"Did you tell him?"

"No."

"So what did you say?"

"I didn't say anything."

"What do you mean, you didn't say anything?"

"I didn't say anything. I shut the door."

They fell back against the pipe-lined wall as two officers walked past. One tipped his hat, and Margaret smiled politely. She waited until they were far down the gangway before she spoke again. "He told you he knew about the dog and you didn't ask him whether he was going to tell on us? Or how long he had known? Nothing?"

"Well, he hasn't told on us yet, has he?"

"But we don't know what he's going to do." Frances's jaw, Margaret realized, was peculiarly set.

"I just . . . I didn't want to get into a discussion about it."

"Why not?" Margaret asked incredulously.

"I didn't want him to get any ideas . . ."

"Ideas? About what?"

Frances managed to look furious and defensive at once. "I didn't want him to think he could use the dog as a bargaining ploy."

There was a lengthy silence, Margaret frowning in incomprehension.

"It's a big deal. I thought he might want something . . . in return."
She seemed faintly embarrassed now, as if she had understood how
this logic might sound.

Margaret shook her head. "Jeez, Frances. You've got a strange view
of how people go about things."

They had arrived at their cabin. Margaret was trying to think
whether there had been some hidden meaning in the way the marine had waved to them and was about to suggest that she should be
the one to talk to him when he arrived, but she was distracted by the
sight of a girl running up the passageway. She had shoulder-length
dark hair secured off her face with bobby pins, one of which had become detached and was hanging loose. She skidded to a halt when
she reached them, and scanned their door. "You live here? 3G?" she
panted.

"Yeah." Margaret shrugged. "So?"

"You know a girl called Jean?" she asked, still breathless. And when
they nodded: "You might want to get downstairs. Keep an eye on
your little mate, before someone official finds her. She's got herself
into a bit of trouble."

"Where?" said Margaret.

"Seamen's mess. E Deck. Go left by the second flight of stairs. It's
the blue door near the fire extinguisher. I've got to go. The marines
are going to be here in a minute. You'll have to hurry."

"I'll go," said Frances to Margaret. "I'll be faster. You catch me up."
She slipped off her shoes, dumped her cardigan and bag at their
door, then sprinted down the passageway, her long thin legs flying up
behind her as she went.

———

There were all manner of hardships one could endure, Avice thought,
if one happened to be in the right company. Since she had found
Irene Carter that afternoon, and had been invited to join her and her
friends for tea, then a lecture (Irene had sewn some simply marvelous peg-bags) and finally supper, they had talked for so long and so
animatedly that she had forgotten not only the time but how much
she detested the old ship.

Irene Carter's father owned Melbourne's most prominent tennis club. She was married to a sub-lieutenant just returned from the Adriatic; the son of (here Avice paused for breath) someone high up in the Foreign Office. And she had brought no less than eleven hats with her, in case one couldn't get them in England. Irene Carter was most definitely the right sort. And, with a rigor Avice suspected was rather lacking in her own character, she had determined to surround herself only with other girls of the right sort, in one case going so far as to organize a bunk swap so that the dark-skinned girl with glasses had been reallocated to a cabin where she would "find girls like herself." She hadn't needed to spell out what criteria this might include. Avice, looking at Irene and the perfectly lovely girls around her, could see that they were all alike, not just in dress and manner but in their attitudes.

"Of course, you know what happened to Lolicia Tarrant, don't you?" Irene was saying, her arm lightly linked through Avice's as they tripped down the steps into the main hangar. The others were walking a couple of steps behind.

"No." Irene's shoes were the same as the ones Avice's mother had seen in a Paris magazine. She must have had them flown over.

"Well, you know she was engaged to that pilot? The one with the . . . unfortunate mustache? No? Well . . . he wasn't five weeks in Malaya when she took up with an American soldier." She lowered her voice. "Awful man. So coarse. You know what he used to say about Melbourne? 'Half as big as New York City's largest cemetery— and twice as dead.' Ugh. Used to repeat it endlessly, as if he were being terribly original every time."

"So what happened?" Avice was wide-eyed, picturing Lolicia with the American.

"Well, that was it. Her fiancé came back and was not best pleased to find Lolly promenading around with this GI, as you can imagine. Let's just say it was more than the Brisbane line he'd been holding, you get my drift?"

"Goodness," said Avice.

"And nor was Lolly's father best pleased when he found out.

They'd been wary of the Americans since the murders, of course." All of the girls remembered the scandal there had been when four Melbourne women were murdered by Private Edward J. Leonski and Australia's relationship with the GIs had soured.

"He wasn't a murderer."

"Oh, Avice, you are funny! No. But he did let all his GI friends know what he'd been up to with Lolly. In the most graphic detail. And his commanding officer apparently got the wrong end of the stick and sent Lolly's father a letter, suggesting he keep better watch on his daughter."

"Oh, my goodness!"

"Her reputation was shredded. Her fiancé wants nothing to do with her, even though half of what this officer said was untrue, of course."

"Is she all right?"

"I don't know," said Irene.

"I thought you and she were friends," said Avice.

"Now?" Irene pulled a face and she shook her head, as if she were trying to dislodge an annoying insect. There was a long silence. "So," she continued, "are you going to enter for Queen of the *Victoria*? They're having a Miss Lovely Legs contest next week, you know."

They were half-way along the hangar deck when they came across Margaret. She was leaning against a noticeboard, one hand above her head, palm down, as if to support herself, while the other was clutching the point where her giant belly took a right-angled leap from her body.

"Are you all right?" said Avice, paralyzed with the fear that the farm girl was about to give birth. She would have to get involved. Goodness only knew what Irene would think.

"Stitch," said Margaret, through gritted teeth.

Avice felt almost faint with relief.

"Would you like some help getting back to your cabin?" asked Irene, courteously.

"No." Margaret looked at Avice, then at her friend. Her nose, Avice noticed, had reddened with the sun. "I've got to go downstairs. Jean's got herself involved in a little . . . episode."

"She shares our cabin," Avice explained.

"You want some help?" said Irene. She had bent her knees to look into Margaret's flushed face.

"I need to catch my breath."

"Well, you can't possibly go and get your friend like that. Not down all those stairs. We'll come with you."

Avice began to remonstrate: "No . . . I don't think we should . . . I mean, Jean is . . ."

But Irene had already slid her arm from Avice's and was reaching for Margaret. "Better? Come on, take my arm. We'll have a little adventure."

Come on, girls, she had said. Haven't had the remotest bit of excitement since setting foot on board. Let's go and rescue a damsel in distress. And Avice heard Jean's bawdy laugh in her ears, heard her saying that Margaret was "as itchy as an itchybug in Itchyville" or some such and watched Irene—her only lifeline to a proper social life during this voyage—prepare to float away from her on a mist of disapproval. She closed her eyes, rehearsing her excuses and ways to distance herself from Jean's vulgarity.

But Jean, when they found her, was not laughing. She wasn't even standing.

They saw her legs before they saw her, emerging awkwardly from behind a stack of canisters by the overheated starboard engine room, her shoes, half on her feet, pointing toward each other. As they came closer their voices, which had been hushed down the long, narrow gangway, stilled as they took in the tableau before them. They could see enough of her top half to gather that she was drunk—drunk enough to murmur incoherently at nobody in particular. Drunk enough to half sit, half lie, legs splayed, on the hard, oily floor. Drunk enough not to care that her blouse was unbuttoned and a small pale breast had spilled out of a dislodged brassière.

Frances stood over her, her usually pale, grave face flushed and animated, her hair somehow uncoiling from its usually severe pinning, her being radiating electricity. A man, possibly a seaman, equally drunk, was reeling away from her, clutching his shoulder. His flies were undone, and there was a flash of something purple and obscene in the fleshy gap they exposed. As the new arrivals stared in mute, shocked horror, another man peeled out of the shadows behind Jean and, with a guilty glance at them, straightened his dress and rushed away. Jean stirred, muttered something, her hair in dark, sweaty fronds over her face. Amid the shocked silence, Margaret knelt down and tried to pull Jean's skirt over those pale thighs.

"You bastard," Frances was screaming at the man. They could see she was holding a large spanner in her bony hand. He moved and her arm came down, the spanner connecting with his shoulder in an audible crack. As he ducked away, tried to shelter, the blows rained down on him with the relentless, manic force of a jackhammer. As one hit the side of his head, a fine arc of blood spattered into the air from above his ear.

Before they had a chance to digest this scene, to let its meaning, the ramifications, sink in, Dennis Tims was running toward them, his taut bulk bringing renewed threat. "What the hell's going on?" he said, cigarette still in hand. "Mikey said—What the hell . . . ? Oh, Jesus," he said, taking in Frances, the man's trousers, Jean on the floor, now supported by Margaret. "Oh, Jesus. Jesus . . . Thompson, you bloody—" He dropped his cigarette and grabbed at Frances, who tried to shake him off, her face contorted. "You bastard!" she yelled. "You dirty bastard!"

"All right, girl," he said. "All right now. All right." As his mate pulled the man away from her, he closed his broad forearms around Frances's collarbone and pulled her back, until the spanner was waving futilely in the air.

Tims's mate released the man who, too shocked or perhaps too inebriated to react, fell like a stone. The noise of the engines was deafening, a never-ending timpani of thumping and grinding, yet even over this the sound his head made was a sick, echoing thud, like that of a watermelon when it is dropped to the floor.

Irene shrieked.

Tims let go of Frances and shoved the man on to his side, at first, one might have suspected, to inflict further damage. But he was roughly checking the head wound, muttering something unintelligible under his breath.

Two of the girls who, until then, had been whispering together ran off, hands pressed to their faces.

Avice was shaking. Tims was on his knees, shouting at the man to get up, get up, damn him.

Margaret, behind the men, had begun to haul Jean away.

Frances was standing, legs hip-width apart, the spanner loose in her fingers, shaking convulsively. She was possibly unaware that she was weeping.

"We should call someone," said Avice to Irene. There was a terrible energy in the air. Her breath emerged in short bursts, as if, even as an observer, she had been overfilled with adrenaline.

"I don't . . . I . . ."

It was then that they caught sight of the women's officer running toward them, her feet echoing on the metal floor. "What is going on here?" Scraped-back dark hair, large bosom. She was still twenty feet from them.

Tims stopped, a fist raised. One of his mates said something to him, put a hand to his elbow, then the man melted into the darkness. Tims straightened, ran a hand through his short, straw-colored hair. He looked at Margaret, as if he had only just noticed she was there, his eyes wide and strained, his hand still moving involuntarily. He shook his head, as if to say something, to apologize perhaps. And then she was there, in front of them all, her eyes darting between them, a regulatory air emanating from her like a bad perfume.

"What is going on here?"

———

At first she didn't seem to see Jean on the floor, Margaret still trying to make her decent. Her stockings, Avice saw, were looped round her knees.

"Bit of an accident," said Tims, wiping bloodied hands on his trousers. He did not look at the woman. "We've just been sorting it out." He mouthed the words as much as spoke them.

The officer looked from his hands to Avice, to Margaret, was briefly distracted by Margaret's belly. "What are you girls doing down here?"

She waited for an answer. No one spoke. Beside her, Avice realized, Irene's hand was pressed to her chest, clutching a handkerchief, in the manner of a consumptive heroine. Her social assurance and confidence had deserted her and her mouth hung a little open.

When she turned back Tims had disappeared. The injured man now sat lopsidedly on the floor, his knees drawn up to his chest.

"You do know there are grave penalties for being in the men's area?"

There was a heavy silence. The officer bent down, took in the state of the man, the fact that the other had vanished. Then she saw Jean. "Oh, my goodness. Please don't tell me this is what I think it is."

"It's not," said Margaret.

The woman's eyes moved to her. "Oh, my goodness," she said again. "The captain will have to be informed."

"Why? It wasn't us." Avice had yelled to be heard over the engines. "We only came to get Jean."

"Avice!" Frances was scrambling to her feet. She stood between the woman and Jean's prostrate form. "Leave it to us. We'll get her back to her room."

"I can't do that. I've been told to report any parties, any drinking, any . . . misdemeanors. I'll need all your names."

"But it wasn't us!" said Avice, with a glance at Irene. "It's only Jean who's disgraced herself!"

"Jean?"

"Jean Castleforth," said Avice, desperately. "We really are nothing to do with it. We just came down because we heard she was in trouble."

"Jean Castleforth," said the woman. "And yours?"

"But I haven't so much as looked at another man! I don't even like alcohol!"

"I said we'll take her home," said Frances. "I'm a nurse. I'll look after her."

"You're not suggesting I ignore this? Look at her!"

"She's just—"

"She's no better than a brass, is what she is!"

"How dare you?" Frances was surprisingly tall when she stood straight. Her features had sharpened. Her fists, Avice noted, were balled. "How dare you?"

"Are you telling me they forced her to come down here?" The woman wrinkled her nostrils against the smell of alcohol on Jean's breath.

"Why don't we all just—"

Quivering with rage, Frances turned on Avice. "Get out of here! Just get away from me. And listen, you—you women's officer, or whatever you are—you can't report her for this, you hear? It wasn't her fault."

"My orders are to report any misdemeanors."

"She's sixteen years old. They've obviously got her drunk and . . . abused her. She's sixteen!"

"Old enough to know what she's doing. She shouldn't be down here. None of you should be."

"They got her drunk! Look at her! She's virtually unconscious! You think she should lose her reputation, possibly her husband, because of this?"

"I don't—"

"You can't ruin the girl's whole life because of one drunken moment!" Frances was standing over the woman now, some sense of barely concealed—what was it?

Avice, shocked by this unrecognizable Frances, found herself instinctively stepping backward.

The officer could see it too: she had squared up a little, in a manner that suggested some defensive strategy. "As I said, my orders are to—"

"Oh, shut up about your bloody orders, you officious—"

It was impossible to say why Frances, flushed and electric, had lifted her arm but Margaret was already pulling her backward. "Frances," she was murmuring, "calm down, okay? It's okay."

It was a few moments before Frances appeared to hear her. She was rigid, filled with tension. "No, it's not okay. You've got to tell her," she said, her eyes glittering.

"But you're not helping her," said Margaret. "You hear me? You've got to back off."

Something in Margaret's eyes stayed Frances. She blinked several times, then let out a deep, shuddering breath.

Irene's hand—she was still clutching the handkerchief—was shaking. As Avice looked away from it, the officer had turned and, as if grateful for the means of escape, was walking briskly, with purpose, down the passageway.

"She's just a kid!" Frances yelled. But the woman was gone.

11

Congratulations to Mrs. H. Skinner and Mrs. H. Dill who both have wedding anniversaries this week. Mrs. Skinner has been married two years and Mrs. Dill a year and although this happy occasion may find them separated from their husbands we sincerely hope that this will be the last anniversary they will spend apart and wish them every happiness in their future life.

"CELEBRATION TIME," DAILY SHIP NEWS,
FROM THE PAPERS OF AVICE R. WILSON, WAR BRIDE,
IMPERIAL WAR MUSEUM

EIGHTEEN DAYS

At sea, it was impossible to say at what time dawn broke, not because it varied from day to day, or continent to continent, but because across the flattened arc of a marine horizon the glowing crack that sheared into the darkness could be seen hundreds, perhaps thousands of miles away, long before it might be visible on land, long before it meant a new day. And, more importantly, because below decks, in a narrow passageway without windows or doors, without anything but artificial light, it was impossible to tell whether it had happened at all.

This was one, but not the only, reason Henry Nicol did not like the hour between five and six in the morning. Once he had enjoyed the early watch, when the seas had been new and magical to him, when, unused to living in such close quarters with other men, he had relished the quietest time aboard ship: those last dark minutes before the ship segued into the mechanics of its day and woke, by degrees, around him. The one time he could imagine himself the only person in the world.

Later, when he had been home on leave and the children were babies, one or both would inevitably wake at this time, and he would hear his wife slide heavily out of bed, half seeing, if he chose to open an eye, her hand reaching unconsciously to her pin curls, the other reaching for her dressing-gown as she whispered, "Hold on, Mother's coming." He would turn over, pinned to his pillow by the familiar mix of guilt and impatience, aware even in half-sleep of his own failure to feel what he should for the woman padding across the linoleum: gratitude, desire, even love.

For some time now 0500 had become not the herald of a new dawn but a bald figure of timing for conversion: in America, it would be five o'clock the previous evening. And in America, his 1900 hours would be waking-up time for his boys. But this time the distance in geography would be only half of it: their whole lives would be running on different time lines. He had often wondered how they would remember him, if they could not imagine him existing half a day, even a whole day ahead. Now there would be no more thinking of them in the present tense, imagining, as he sometimes did, They'll be having breakfast now. They'll be brushing their teeth. They might be outside, playing with a ball, a car, the wagon I made for them from bits of wood. Now he would think of them historically.

Some other man's hands throwing the ball.

On the other side of the steel door a woman murmured in sleep, her voice rising as if in a question. Then silence.

Nicol stared at his watch, adjusted the previous day as they entered another time zone. My hours are speeding toward nothing, he thought. No home, no sons, no heroic return. I have given up my best years and watched my friends freeze, drown and burn. I have given up my innocence, my friends their lives, so that I might grieve for what I was never sure I even wanted. At least, until it was too late.

Nicol leaned back, hardened his mind against the familiar thoughts, trying to dislodge the huge weight that had settled upon him, that pulled on his heart and lungs. Willing the last hour to pass faster. Willing the dawn to come.

———

"Off caps!"

The paymaster failed to look up as the seaman stepped forward, swiveled his cap from his head and laid it on the table before him. The two men at his side were flicking through drawers of banknotes, passing each other handwritten slips.

"Andrews, sir. Air mechanic, first class. Seven two two one nine seven two. Sir."

As the younger man stood expectantly before him, the paymaster flipped pages, then ran his finger swiftly down his accounts book. "Three pounds twelve shillings."

"Three pounds twelve shillings," repeated the paymaster's assistant, beside him.

The mechanic cleared his throat. "Sir—with respect, sir—that's less than we were getting before Australia, sir."

The paymaster wore the expression of one who had heard every complaint, every financial try-on not once but several thousand times. "We were serving in the Pacific, Andrews. You were getting extra pay for operating in a war zone. Would you like us to organize a couple of kamikaze guests to warrant your extra two shillings?"

"No, sir."

"No . . . Don't spend it all ashore. And steer clear of those women. Don't want a queue outside the sick bay in two days' time, do we, lads?"

The money was counted, pushed across the table. The cap was replaced on the mechanic's head and he walked off, a little pink, counting the notes between keen fingers.

"Off caps!"

"Nicol."

Lost in the gentle rhythm of the line that snaked along what remained of the hangar deck, he heard his name spoken twice before he registered it. He was bleary from another night of lost sleep and deep in unwelcome thoughts.

Tims, a broad, taut figure, stood beside him, smoking, for several seconds before he spoke again. Nicol knew him as a bluff man, one of those larger-than-life sorts who liked to be thought of as a "mess character." There were rumors that he was involved in money-lending, and those who fell foul of him often became terribly accident prone.

Nicol had tended instinctively to steer clear of him, recognizing that with someone like Tims it was often better not to get too close or, indeed, know too much. One neither wanted to make an enemy of him nor find oneself indebted to him. These men, with their strange charisma, their intricately built power bases, were to be found on every ship. It was, he supposed, inevitable in a self-contained world that relied on silence and hierarchy.

Now, however, Tims was subdued; when he spoke, his words were careful and considered. There might be a bit of bad blood between the seamen and the stokers, he said. There had been an incident with a woman a couple of nights ago. He had shaken his head as he said this, as if even he could not believe the foolishness of the Aussie girls. Things, he said, had got a little out of hand.

Such a bald admission was out of character. And at first Nicol wondered if he was asking him obliquely to make an arrest. But before he had a chance to ask why this should be of any more than passing interest to him, Tims spoke again: "It's your lot who were involved."

Your lot. What a strange, almost familial intimacy the phrase suggested. Nicol had felt a flush of incomprehension that the reserved bride who had chatted with him that evening might have been the cause of some kind of drunken fracas. That was women for you, he thought bitterly. Unable to stay faithful—sober, even—for a six-week voyage.

Then Tims, a bloodsoaked bandage visible round his knuckles, explained further. It had not been the tall girl, Frances, but the young silly one Nicol had spoken to on his first watch. The one who was always giggling. Jean.

He was somehow less shocked and, although disturbed by what he heard, felt something that might have been relief. Frances hadn't seemed the type. Too awkward in company. Too self-conscious. He supposed he wanted to believe that there were still good women out there. Women who knew how to behave.

Women who understood the notion of loyalty.

"I need you to do us a favor, Marine. I can't go along there, obviously." Here Tims jerked a thumb toward the cabins. "Just make sure Maggie's all right, will you? The one who's expecting. She's a nice girl, and she was a bit shocked. What with her condition and all . . . Well, I don't like to think of her being troubled."

"She'll go to the sick bay if she's shook up, surely."

Tims grimaced. "To see that idiot? He's been drunk as a skunk every day he's been on board so far. I wouldn't trust him with a splinter." Tims stubbed out his cigarette. "No. I think it would be a good idea if you kept an eye on her. And if anyone says anything, the girls were in their bunks all night. Right?"

It was not the norm for a marine to be addressed in such a way by a stoker. And something in Tims's tone might normally have caused Nicol to bristle. But he suspected this unusual confidence was prompted by chivalry, perhaps even genuine concern, and he let it go. "No problem," he said.

Now he thought back, there had been some subtle change in atmosphere that evening. From the other side of the door he had heard none of the usual intermittent conversation, but instead urgent whispering. At one point, there had been the sound of crying, a brief argument. The tall girl had been out three times "for water" and barely muttered a hello. He had assumed it was one of those bouts of feminine hysteria. They had been warned that such things could happen once they were on board, especially with the women unused to living at close quarters.

"I tell you," Tims was saying, "Thompson's lucky I didn't get to that spanner first."

"Spanner?" He glanced behind him.

"One of the girls had it. The tall one. By all accounts it was her who got the bastard off. Gave him a good crack on the shoulder, then tried to stove his head in for good measure." Tims laughed humorlessly. "You've got to hand it to these Aussie girls, they're not short of balls. You couldn't imagine an English girl doing the same, could you?" He took a long drag of his cigarette. "Then again, I suppose you wouldn't get an English girl heading below decks with a load of foreign johnnies."

"Don't be too sure," muttered Nicol, and regretted it.

"Anyway, I'm going to lie low for a bit. The mess is closed to visitors for a while. But tell Mags I'm sorry. If I'd got to her little mate first . . . well, it wouldn't have happened."

"Where's Thompson?" said Nicol. "In case they ask. Is he in custody?"

Tims shook his head.

"Shouldn't we be taking him in?"

"Think about it, Nicol. If we haul him in for what he's done, the girl gets done too, right? The WSO who came down didn't have a clue, only got Jean's name. But little Jean's not going to tell the truth about what went on. Not if she wants to get to Blighty and her old man without a fuss, which I'm pretty sure she does." He stubbed out his cigarette. " 'Sides, I'm sure you don't want a fuss made about your girls getting into trouble. Can't look good on you, can it? Them all being down in the engine rooms that close to the start of your watch . . ." He kept his voice soft, at odds with the implied threat in his words. "I'm just letting you know, out of courtesy, like, that me and the boys will deal with Thompson and his shabby little mate our way. Even if we have to wait till we're ashore."

"It'll get out," said Nicol. "You know it will."

Tims glanced behind him at the long queue. When he turned back, his eyes held something that made Nicol feel vague pity for the unknown offender. "Not if everyone keeps their gobs shut it won't."

Margaret leaned over the rail as far as her belly would allow, and hauled up the wicker basket, murmuring to herself as it bumped off the sides of the ship. Below her, in the glinting waters, lithe brown boys dived over the sides of their small craft for coins that the sailors threw from the deck. Alongside them slim canoes, hollowed from single tree-trunks, wobbled under the movements of thin, tanned men holding armfuls of trinkets. The port of Colombo, Ceylon, shimmered in the heat, punctuated by the occasional tall building and set behind with dense, dark forest.

There had been several reported cases of smallpox and it had been announced earlier that it was not considered wise for the women to go ashore. Here, anchored in the clear blue waters several hundred feet from shore, was as close as they were going to get to Ceylon.

Margaret, who had been desperate to leave the ship, who had spent days anticipating the feel of solid earth under her feet, had been furious. "Your man at the PX says they're still going to allow the men ashore so it's okay for us to catch the bloody smallpox off our own." She had almost wept with the unfairness of it.

"I suppose it's because the men are inoculated," said Frances. Margaret chose not to hear her.

Perhaps in consolation, one of the storemen had lent them a cable to which he had attached a basket. They were to lower it and pull it up when it was full, so they could examine the goods at their leisure. He had pointed out two other warships anchored in the harbor, where she could see clusters of little boats involved in the same activity. "French and American. You'll find most of the traders end up round the Americans." He rubbed his thumb and forefinger together, grinning and raising an eyebrow. "If you can swing your basket that far you might get yourself some new stockings."

"This batch looks good, girls. Get your purses ready."

Margaret, puffing with exertion, brought the basket carefully over the rail, then placed it on the floor of the gun turret where they were seated. She rummaged through, holding up beads, strings of shell and coral that rippled through her fingers. "Mother-of-pearl necklace, anyone? Better than that thing with all the chicken rings, eh, Jean?" Jean raised a thin smile. She had been silent all morning. Before the "wakey-wakey" call, Margaret had heard her exchanging whispered words with Frances. Then they had disappeared to the bathroom for some time. Frances had taken her medical kit. No one had talked of what might have taken place, and Margaret hadn't liked to ask, wasn't sure even of the question. But now, pale and subdued, looking frighteningly young, Jean sat mutely between them. When she walked, she did so gingerly.

"Look, Jean. This would go well with your blue dress. See how the mother-of-pearl catches the light."

"Nice," said Jean. She lit another cigarette, her shoulders hunched around her ears as if she were cold, despite the heat.

"We should get something for poor old Avice. Might make her feel better."

She heard her voice, determinedly cheerful, and in the answering silence the suggestion that Frances might not want Avice to feel better.

There had been a terrible argument between the two after they had returned to the cabin the previous night. Frances, her normal reserve dissolved, had screamed at Avice that she was selfish, a traitor, merely concerned with saving her own skin. Avice, flushed with guilt, had retorted that she couldn't see why she should jeopardize her future because Jean had the morals of an alleycat. They would have found out her name in the end. Her own temper had been sharpened because her friend Irene had vanished. It had been all Margaret could do to stop the pair coming to blows. The following morning, when Avice had left the cabin, the others had assumed they would probably not see her again that day.

The voices of the traders floated up to them: "Mrs. Melbourne! Mrs. Sydney!" They gestured prices with their fingers. In the midst of their boats, a small boy's head broke through the shining surface of the water. He was grinning as he held aloft something metallic. Then he looked closely at it and his face darkened. He hurled it at the ship. It pinged off the side like a bullet.

"What's that all about?" said Margaret, peering down.

"The sailors throw them old nuts and dowels. They let them dive thinking they're coins," said Frances. "Their idea of fun." She stopped. They had new views on sailors' ideas of fun.

But Jean didn't appear to have heard. She had been examining a little pearl necklace, and now stuffed it into her pocket.

"Want me to get that for you?" said Margaret. "I don't mind if you forgot your purse."

Jean's eyes were still pink-rimmed. "Nah," she said. "I'm not paying. More fool them for sending it up."

There was a brief silence. Then, wordlessly, Margaret got up, removed a few coins from her purse and lowered them, with the remaining trinkets, to the boat below. Then, perhaps to comfort herself as much as the younger girl, she said to Jean, "Did I ever tell you how Joe proposed to me?"

She sat down, nudged her. "This'll make you laugh. He'd already decided he wanted to ask me. He'd got Dad's permission. And he'd bought a ring. Oh, I'm not wearing it now," she explained. "Fingers are too swollen. Anyway, he decides Wednesday's the day—it's his last but one day before the end of his shore leave, and he turns up, nervous, his boots shining like mirrors and his hair slicked. He's got it all planned in his head. He's going to go down on one knee and make the one romantic gesture of his life."

"Wasted on you," said Frances.

"Well, he knows that now," Margaret grinned, "so, anyway, he gets to ours, and he knocks on the door, and just as he's stepping in, I'm screaming at Daniel about him not leaving all his clothes on the floor because I'm darned if I'm going to run around after him like Mum did. Poor old Joe's standing in the hallway and me and Dan are going at each other hammer and tongs. Then Dad runs in, yelling that the cows have got out. Joe's standing there, still in shock at the sight of me swearing like a navvy, and Dad grabs him and says, 'Come on, lad. Look alive,' and hauls him out to the back."

Margaret leaned back. "Well," she said, "it was chaos. There's around forty of them out and they've brought down one of the fences, and there's two tearing up what's left of Mum's garden, so Dad's beating them with a stick, tears falling down his face, trying to prop up Mum's flowers. There's Colm racing down the track in the truck, horn blaring, trying to head off the ones stampeding toward the road. Liam's on one of the horses, acting like John Wayne. And then there's me and Joe trying to corner the rest of them in the shed."

She looked around the faces opposite her. "Ever seen a frightened cow, girls?" She lowered her voice. "They shit like you've never seen. And where they're wheeling around, it's going everywhere. Poor old Joe is covered with it, top to toe, his beautiful shoes, everything."

"How disgusting," said Jean, raising a small smile.

"And then, to add insult to injury, our biggest girl decides to make a break for it, and she goes straight over him. Don't get me wrong, he's no pushover—but the way she went into him it was as if he wasn't even there. Bam." She mimed falling backward.

Even Margaret, supposedly immune to the farmyard smell, had held her nose when she helped him get up, tried to wipe him down. She had thought he was swearing, but eventually realized he was saying, "The ring, the ring." The two of them had spent almost half an hour on their hands and knees in the cowshed, trying to find Joe's token of everlasting devotion in the slurry.

"And you—you still wear it?"

"Cow dung included. To me that's part of the romance." Then, as Jean's hand went to her mouth, "Oh, Jean! Of course I washed it before I put it on. I had to do the same for Joe. My first evening as his fiancée was spent washing and ironing his uniform so that he wouldn't get into trouble back at base."

"Stan asked me while we were at a dance," said Jean. "I reckon I was the youngest there—I was still fifteen. But it was lovely. I was wearing a blue shantung silk two-piece, it belonged to my friend Polly, and he said I was the most beautiful girl in the room. He'd had a few, but when they struck up with 'You Made Me Love You' he turned to his mate and said, 'This is the girl I'm going to marry. You hear that?' And then he said it louder. And I made out I was dead embarrassed but, to be honest, I really liked it."

"I'm sure you did," said Frances, smiling.

"He was the first person to tell me he loved me." Her eyes glittered with tears. "No one ever told me that. Not my mum. Never even met my dad." She pushed her hair off her face. "Nope. I got nothing back there, nothing. He's the best man I ever met."

———

They had sat, in near silence, for almost half an hour more, Margaret calling to the traders to come closer, to take these back, bring those over. She had bought, at ridiculous cost, two necklaces for Letty, telling herself they would be a lovely gift, knowing it was a feeble attempt to atone. As the heat grew fiercer, and the sun moved across, taking their vantage-point out of the shade, she thought about moving. But no entertainments had been planned for the day, owing to the former expectation that they would be ashore, and the thought of them bickering with each other in the little dormitory was unbearable.

She was squinting listlessly at a small propeller craft humming toward them, the naval cap of its skipper, the clumsy gray shapes on board, watching them become increasingly distinct at it drew closer. She heard exclamations along the length of the ship as other women realized what it was.

"Girls!" she yelled. "It's the post! We've got post!"

An hour later, they sat in the canteen, the normally cabbage-scented air now thick with anticipation, as a Red Cross officer collected all mail to be sent and distributed small bundles of letters from a trestle table at the end. The announcement of each name was greeted with squeals from the recipient and her friends, as if she was being called up to collect an award, rather than correspondence. Around them the windows were propped open to allow the sea breezes to penetrate the room. The light bounced off them, echoing the glimmering ocean low.

Jean had been among the first called to the table: her impressive seven letters from Stan had restored some of her vitality. She had handed them to Frances, who read them aloud in her low, sonorous voice, while Jean puffed nervously at a cigarette. "Did you hear that?" she kept interrupting. "My name tattooed on his right arm. In two colors! And it hurt like buggery."

Margaret and Frances had exchanged a glance. "And," Frances continued, "he's won four pounds in a boxing match. He says the other fellow's idea of boxing involved trying to block Stan's punches with his nose."

"Hear that?" Jean nudged Margaret. "Trying to block punches with his nose!" If her laughter was a little too high to suggest genuine mirth, no one said anything. It was enough that she was laughing at all.

Later Frances would confide that she had left out several

paragraphs: those that warned Jean to "behave herself," and the story of a sweetheart deserted by one of his friends once he heard she had been "playing fast and loose."

"Margaret O'Brien?"

Margaret was out of her chair with a speed that belied her cumbersome frame. Breathless, she launched herself at the sheaf of letters proffered toward her, and returned, glowing and triumphant, her failure to get ashore forgotten. She wondered, briefly, whether she could go to the cabin and read them in private without causing offense. But just as she was about to ask, she heard a chair scrape back, and looked up from the envelopes to see Avice seat herself carefully in front of them.

There was a brief pause. Margaret, a little taken aback that Avice had chosen to seat herself among them after the previous evening's quarrel, wondered if she might be about to apologize.

"I've got news," Avice said.

"So have I," said Jean. "Look. Seven letters. Seven!"

"No," said Avice. She had a contained smile on her face, as if she harbored some great secret. It was a different Avice from the furious, tight-lipped girl who had left their cabin several hours earlier. "I have real news," she said, her chin jutting out. "I'm expecting."

There was a stunned silence.

"Expecting what?" said Jean.

"A baby, of course. I've been to the doctor."

"Are you sure?" said Frances. "Dr. Duxbury doesn't strike me as . . . the most reliable . . ." She thought of the last time she had seen him, singing blindly into a stores cupboard.

"Oh, so nurses know more than doctors now, do they?"

"No, I'm just—"

"Dr. Duxbury has taken a blood test, but in the meantime he asked me lots of questions and did an examination. He's pretty certain." She smoothed her hair and glanced around, perhaps hoping to impart such momentous news to a wider audience.

"I guess it makes sense," said Margaret, "now I think about it."

The two other women looked at each other.

Avice couldn't retain her composure. Her face lit up, cheeks pink with excitement. "A baby! Can you imagine? I knew I couldn't be seasick. I've been yachting loads of times and that didn't make me ill. Margaret, you must tell me everything I need to buy. Do you think they sell baby clothes in England? I shall have to get Mummy to send over all sorts of things."

Margaret stood up and reached over the table to hug her. "Avice," she said, "it's great news. Congratulations. How wonderful for you both."

"Strewth," said Jean, wide-eyed. "So all that seasickness was really you expecting?" She looked genuinely pleased. Frances hasn't told her of Avice's betrayal, Margaret thought, and felt suddenly sad for her.

"He thinks I'm already nine or ten weeks along. I was rather shocked when he told me. But I'm so excited. Ian's going to be thrilled. He'll be such a good father," Avice trilled, one slim hand resting on her flat stomach, already lost in a vision of future family life.

Margaret marveled at her ability to wipe out the events of the past hours.

"Stan got a tattoo of my name," Jean told her, but Avice didn't hear.

"I think I shall put in a special request to the captain to wire my family and tell them the news. I don't think I can bear to wait until we reach England." Her name, called in clipped tones, echoed through the canteen. "Letters!" she said, standing. "Letters! In all the excitement I hadn't even thought—oh, you two have got yours." She looked at Frances, as if suddenly remembering, and said nothing.

"Congratulations," said Frances. She didn't look at Avice.

———

Frances's name was called an hour later; it was almost the last, and cut across the canteen when the once-packed room was nearly empty. Margaret had thought several times about leaving them all to drink in Joe's words in private, then re-examine them with the benefit of silence, but there was such bad blood between the other girls now, and Jean was still fragile, that she felt obliged to wait.

Avice had received two letters from her family, and two very old ones from Ian, sent only days after he had left Sydney. "Look at the date on them," she had said crossly. She had seemed to count it as a personal insult that Jean and Margaret had received more than she had. "Ian's are nearly six weeks old. Honestly, you'd think the least the Navy could do is make sure we get our letters on time. How on earth am I meant to tell him about the baby if he's going to get my next letter a week after we reach Plymouth?"

She studied the postmark bad-temperedly. "It's really not on. I should have had lots more by now. They're probably piled up in some godforsaken outpost somewhere."

"I think you were just unlucky, Avice," said Margaret, absently. She had reread Joe's first several times now. He had numbered them thoughtfully so that she could read them in the correct order. "Hello, love," he had written. "Hoping by the time you get this you'll be on board the *Victoria*. Couldn't believe it when you told me you'd be on that old girl. Keep a lookout for Archie Littlejohn. He's a radio man. We trained together back in '44. Good chap. He'll look out for you. Then again I reckon there's not a man on board who won't look out for you girls. They're a good bunch on the *Vic*."

Margaret gulped as his words became audible in her imagination, and thought of Joe's trusting faith in the good nature of the men around him. She sneaked a look at Jean, who was gazing intently at Stan's letters. "Want me to teach you?" she asked. "While we're on board? Bet we could have you reading by the time we disembark."

"Really?"

"Nothing to it," said Margaret. "An hour or two a day and you'll be a regular bookworm."

"Stan doesn't know . . . about the reading. I always got my mate Nancy to write letters for me, see?" she said. "But then I remembered when I came aboard that if anyone else writes them it'll be in different handwriting."

"All the more reason to get you started," said Margaret. "You'll be able to write your own. And I bet you Stan won't know any different."

Jean's obvious delight lightened the mood. "You really think I could do it?" she kept saying, and grinning when Margaret responded in the affirmative. Her mother had always told her she was thick, Jean revealed, her eyes darting between them. "Mind you, she's gotta be the thick one. She's stuck back there working in the cracker factory, and I'm on a ship to Blighty. Right?"

"Right," said Margaret, firmly. "Here, give us your envelope. I'll write out your ABCs."

Frances had arrived back at the table. Avice glanced up from her letters at Frances's hand. "Only one?" she said loudly. She failed to keep the smile off her face.

Frances was unperturbed. "It's from one of my old patients," she said, with shy pleasure. "He's home and walking again."

"How lovely," said Margaret, patting her arm.

"Nothing from your husband?"

"Avice . . ." said Margaret, warningly.

"Well, I'm only asking."

There was a brief silence.

Margaret made as if to speak, then couldn't think of anything to say. "Oh, well. Perhaps he was overcome at the thought of seeing you again," she said. Avice raised her eyebrows, stood up and strolled away.

———

Having failed to elicit a reply from you to any of my correspondence, I am writing out of courtesy to let you know that I have applied for a divorce, on grounds of three years' desertion. While you and I know this might not be quite correct, I am hoping you will not contest. Anton is paying for the children's and my passage to America, so that we can join him there. We leave Southampton on the 25th. I would have liked us to do this in a civilized manner, for the children's sake as much as anything, but you are obviously determined to show me the same lack of concern as you have displayed the whole time you have been gone.

Where is your humanity? Perhaps there is nothing left of you underneath your rules and regulations. I know things must have been hard for you. I know you have probably seen and coped with no end of horrors. But we, here, are living. We would have been your lifeline if you had let us.

Now I feel no guilt in choosing life, a better life, for me and my children . . .

"What's the matter, Nicol? You look a bit pale. Got a Not Wanted Don't Come?" Jones-the-Welsh was lying on his hammock, flicking through a dozen or so letters. They would be from a dozen or so women.

Nicol stared, unseeing, at his. Crumpled it into his pocket. "No," he said, then coughed to stop his voice cracking. "No . . . just a bit of news from home."

A few of the men around him exchanged glances. "No one ill?" said Jones.

"No," said Nicol. His tone halted further enquiries.

"Well, you look terrible. In fact, you've looked like buggery for weeks. Working middle watch does that to you, doesn't it, lads? You know what you need, man?" Here he punched Nicol's arm. "You need a bit of R and R. You're off tonight, right? Come ashore with us."

"Ah . . . I think I'll just sleep."

"It's called leave, man. Believe it or not, Nicol, even *you* are meant to go off duty occasionally."

"I'll stay here. Got a bit of make and mend to catch up on."

"Sorry, man, can't have it. You've got a pocket full of dosh and a face like a smacked arse. Dr. Jones here says the only cure is to lighten the pair of them. Get a couple of hours' kip now. Then you're coming out with us. And we're going to get absolutely pissed."

Nicol began to refuse, then felt inexplicably relieved by Jones's good-natured bullying. The thought of standing outside that metal door, alone with his thoughts at another dawn, was too much. "Okay," he said, strung up his hammock and hopped lithely into it. "You're on. Wake me up half an hour before you want to head off."

They had eaten together—less, Margaret suspected, out of any great desire on Avice's part to share her meals with them but because Irene and her friends had made it clear, by their whispers and cold stares, that she was no longer welcome in their set. She had watched Avice preparing to bounce over to their table and announce her news until she realized they were being discussed—not in a good way. She had deflated a little, her eyes darting to them at every peal of laughter. Then she had smoothed her hair and sat down opposite Margaret. "You know," she said lightly, "I've just remembered what I couldn't stand about that Irene Carter. She's terribly rude. I can't imagine what I ever saw in her."

"It's nice for us all to eat together for a change," Margaret said equably, ignoring Frances's silence.

"Nice not to have Avice puking anyway," said Jean.

"Did they make a mistake with your post, Frances," said Avice, "or did you really get just one letter?"

"Do you know what, Avice?" said Margaret, loudly. She pushed away her plate. "We had a lovely chat earlier about how our husbands proposed to us. I bet you'd love to tell us how Ian proposed to you, wouldn't you?"

Margaret caught Frances's look. It might have been of gratitude or something else entirely.

"Have I not told you? Really? Oh, it was the best day of my life. Well, next to our wedding, of course. That's always a girl's best day, isn't it? And in our case we couldn't have the kind of wedding I might normally have expected—with my family's position in society and all . . . No, it had to be a bit more intimate. But, oh, Ian's proposal. Oh, yes . . ." She closed her eyes. "Do you know? It still comes back to me so vividly, almost like a scent . . ."

"A bit like Margaret's, then," said Jean.

"I knew he was the one as soon as I saw him. And he says the same about me. Oh, girls, he's so sweet. And it's been so long since we spoke—I can't bear it. He's the most romantic man alive. I didn't think I'd marry into the services, you see. I wasn't one of those uniform-hunters, always fluttering her eyelashes at anything in whites. But I was helping out at one of the tea dances—perhaps you had something similar where you were?—and I saw him and that was it. I knew I had to be Mrs. Radley."

"So what did he do?" said Jean, lighting a cigarette.

"Well, he was terribly gentlemanly. We knew we loved each other—he told me he was actually obsessed with me at one point— can you imagine?—but he was worried about whether I could cope with being a services wife. I mean, what with all the separations and insecurity . . . He told me he didn't know if it was fair to put me through that. But I told him, 'I may look like a delicate flower'— that's what my father used to call me, his little jasmine blossom—'but I'm actually quite strong. Really. I'm very determined.' And I think even Ian recognized that in the end."

"So, what happened?" said Margaret, sucking her teaspoon.

"Well, we were both in agony. Daddy wanted us to wait. And Ian didn't want to upset him, so he said he would. But I couldn't bear the thought of us leaving each other simply 'engaged.' "

"Worried he'd bugger off with someone else?" said Jean.

"So he got permission from his commander and we just ran off and got married in front of a justice of the peace. Just like that. It was terribly romantic."

"What a lovely story, Avice," said Margaret. "I'm going to get some tea. Anyone want a cup?"

Outside the sky was darkening. The sunsets happened rapidly here, day fading into night with some impatience. The ship was quieter than usual, despite the presence of the women, as if the absence of the men had seeped into each deck, subduing them.

"I'll go and see if they're going to show anything at the cinema," said Jean.

"They might have decided to put something on with us all being here."

"There's nothing," said Avice, "just a sign saying the next one's to-morrow afternoon."

"The men will be ashore now," said Margaret, staring out of the window. "Lucky things."

"What about your bloke, Frances?" Jean rested her chin on her hands, her head tilted to one side. "How did he propose?"

Frances stood up, began gathering plates on to a tray. "Oh, it's not very interesting," she said.

"I'm sure we'd be fascinated," said Avice.

Frances gave her a hard look.

Margaret thought she should probably try to steer the conversation toward some other course, but she had to admit to a sneaking curiosity.

So they waited. And Frances, after a moment's hesitation, sat down, the dirty plates piled high in front of her. She told them in quiet, unemotional tones, her words the polar opposite to Avice's gush of love. She had met him in Malaya while she had been nursing. Private Engineer "Chalkie" Mackenzie, twenty-eight years old. From a town called Cheltenham. He had shrapnel wounds, which had become infected because of the tropical humidity. She had nursed him and, over the weeks, he had grown fond of her.

"Sometimes, when he had a fever, he became delirious and thought we were already married. We weren't meant to form attachments with the men, but his captain, who was in the next bed, indulged him. We all did. We went along with all sorts if it made the men feel better."

"So, when did he ask you?" said Jean. Above her, the neon lights came on abruptly, illuminating the women's faces.

"Well . . . he asked me lots of times, actually. There wasn't really one occasion. I think it was about sixteen before I agreed."

"Sixteen times!" said Avice. It was as if she couldn't believe Frances could provoke such persistence.

"What made you say yes?" said Margaret. "In the end, I mean."

"What made him keep asking?" muttered Avice.

But Frances stood up and glanced at her watch. "Goodness, Maggie! Look at the time. That dog of yours will be desperate for her walk."

"Oh, darn. You're right. Better get back downstairs," said Margaret. With a nod to the others, she and Frances half walked, half ran toward the cabin.

———

The girls were kissing. They did it once, briefly, then turned to look at him, and laughed at his failure to react. The shorter one leaned back on her bar stool, eyeing him lazily, then stretched out a bare leg. The other, in a green dress several sizes too big for her slight frame, muttered something he didn't understand, and leaned forward to ruffle his hair. "Two two." She held up two fingers. "Very nice time. Two two." Initially, he had ordered them both another drink. It had taken him several minutes to understand what she was suggesting. Then he shook his head, even when she reduced the price to almost a third of the original amount. "No more money," he said, his words sounding strange and unfocused to his ears. "All gone."

"No no," the girl in the green dress said. It was as if she had heard refusals too many times, and that they had all been meaningless. "Two two. Very nice time."

At some point in the evening he had lost his watch, and no longer had any idea what time it was. Men catcalled or fought incompetently in the street outside. Girls disappeared upstairs, came down again and chattered or squabbled with their colleagues. Outside, the neon bar sign cast the blue light of a cold gray dawn across the entrance.

On the wall behind the girls he could see a picture of Eisenhower, probably donated by some visiting GI. What time was it in America? Nicol tried to recall how he had calculated the difference earlier that evening.

Across the room, half seated, half lying on a banquette, Jones-the-Welsh was placing cigarettes in a girl's mouth and laughing as she coughed them out again. "Don't inhale so much," he was saying, as she hit him playfully with a slim hand. "You're making yourself ill." He caught Nicol watching him. "Ah . . . no . . . Don't tell me you like Annie here too?" he called. "Greedy bastard. You've got two of your own already."

Nicol tried to formulate some reply, but it turned to powder in his mouth.

"To wives and sweethearts," Jones-the-Welsh announced, his drink aloft. "May they never meet."

Nicol raised his glass to his mate and took a slug. "And no rubbish tip," he muttered. Jones, just about hearing him, burst out laughing.

Their last visit to Ceylon had comprised duty, not leave, and they had been charged with the "drunk patrol," looking for ratings who, weighed down by their paypackets but unencumbered by either sense or inhibition, took advantage of their few hours' freedom to drink as much as possible of whatever local brew they could find with disastrous results. Shortly before dawn, he and Jones, having emptied several of the local brothels, had found several young hands lying comatose at the base of a local rubbish tip. Over the course of their night out, they had evidently been relieved of money, watches, paybooks and even station cards, and were now incapable of either thought or speech. Not knowing without those documents who the men were, he and Jones, after some discussion, had dumped them, soiled, stinking uniforms and all, on the nearest Allied ship. There they would await a double dose of wrath—from the superiors of their adopted ship and from those they belonged to.

"Too right. No rubbish tip for us, mate," said Jones, lifting a glass. "Just remember to say *Viceroy*. Got it? Just you remember the name of your ship. *Viceroy*." And he burst out laughing again.

"You come now."

The girl in the green dress was tugging his sleeve. The other had vanished. She closed her hand round his with the proprietorial confidence of a child and led him up the stairs. He had to let go of her to negotiate them, clutching the banister as the wooden steps rose and fell beneath his feet like a deck in a storm.

The door of the room was paper light in his hand; the fragility of the dividing walls apparent in the noises he could hear from the next room.

"Nice time, uh?" The girl followed his gaze and giggled.

He felt suddenly weary, and seated himself heavily on the side of the bed, watching as she undid her dress. The knobs of her spine were distinct under her pale skin. It made him think of Frances, of her bony fingers as she had held the picture of his boys.

"You help me?" she said, twisting nimbly to look at him, and gesturing toward her zip.

The thin coverlet was immaculately laundered. Beside it, on a rickety table, stood a bottle with several beautifully arranged blossoms. These two domestic details, a suggestion of some desire far removed from the depravity he could hear in the next room, made his eyes fill with tears. "I'm sorry," he said. "I don't think—"

She turned, and he caught something raw in her expression. "Yes, yes," she said, her smile rapidly in place again. "You be happy man. I see you before? You know me. I make you happy man."

"I'm sorry," he said.

She clasped his hand then, in a surprisingly firm grip. Her glance toward the door told him that perhaps she had her own reasons for not wanting him to leave. "You wait little while," she pleaded.

"I just want to—"

"Just little while stay-stay."

He realized then that her eyes made her seem older. Something weary and resigned in them, even when she had smiled mischievously, fluttered her eyelids like a young girl. But now that he looked, her breasts were curiously undefined, as if they had not yet reached maturity. And her nails, when he looked at her hands, were bitten as his sister's once were; down to the bloodied quick, childishly uncaring of their appearance. Nicol closed his eyes, feeling suddenly ashamed to have been complicit in such corruption. This is what war does, he said silently. Even we who survived. It does for us in the end.

He felt her weight upon him then, light hands stroking his face.

"Please you wait little while," whispered the voice in his ear. He could smell her perfume, something heavy and cloying, at odds with her youth, the insubstantial nature of her frame.

She had reached round his neck, was pulling him down. "You wait little while with me." She reached down with nimble fingers, let out a muffled exclamation into his neck when he gently stayed her hand.

"There's nothing left in me," he said. "I'm empty."

Then, as she lay against him, her dark eyes searching his for some sign of his intention, he lay back on the pillow. Through the partially open window he could hear shouting. The smell of something frying drifted up, sharp and gingery. He took her hand. "You tell me something," he said. He could feel her breath on his neck, careful, expectant, and realized he was drifting toward sleep.

"I make you happy now?" she whispered.

He hesitated. Knew these would probably be the last words he said tonight: "What time is it in America?"

12

The ship has been in contact with London by telephone! This was done by a broadcast to Sydney over TBS. The TBS receiver in Sydney was fed into a microphone connected to the London—Sydney telephone line . . . This is a great advance in the communication world and promises great things for the future.

**FROM THE PRIVATE JOURNAL OF MIDSHIPMAN HENRY STAMPER,
13 JANUARY 1946, BY COURTESY OF MARGARET STAMPER**

TWENTY-ONE DAYS

It had never happened before. She had certainly never meant it to happen at all. But Frances was forced to concede that she was falling in love.

Every evening she would tell herself that she should stay away, that it would do her no good, that by her actions she was putting her passage in danger. And in spite of that, every evening, with the minimum explanation to her cabin mates, she found herself disappearing through the metal door. With a furtive glance toward each end of the gangway, she would tread swiftly past the other cabins, lightly up the stairs and along the upper length of the hangar deck until she reached the heavy steel hatch that opened out on to the flight deck.

When she thought about it afterward, she realized that part of it was that they had all got used to each other: the sailors, the women and the routines of the ship, the air thick with longing and waiting, the never knowing. She had got used to not having a purpose in the morning, had perhaps lost a little of the institutional briskness that she had carried with her, like armor, for years. She felt easier around people. She might even venture that she liked a few. It was hard not to care about someone like Margaret.

But it was really the ship she loved: the size of it, like a leviathan, surely too huge to have been created by mere men, propelled by an epic strength through the roughest seas. She loved the scars, the streaks of rust that, despite years of painting and repainting, were visible on her skin, testament to the time she had spent at sea. Frances loved the infinite space visible all around her, the sense of boundless, irrevocable movement west. She loved the sense of possibility that the ship bestowed on her. The nautical miles and unfathomable fathoms that it opened up between her and her past as it glided through the water.

If it wasn't too cold at night, she would sit on the flight deck for hours, reading a book or a magazine, glancing up occasionally to make sure she couldn't be seen by whoever was on watch at the bridge. Their attention trained on the seas, no one noticed her. Now, in the increasing heat, it offered sweet relief; she would locate her favored spot under the aircraft and enjoy in solitude the soft breezes, the ceaseless sound of the waves rushing beneath, the taste of salt on her parted lips. She liked the way you could see the sky's mood changing miles away, a distant storm, its power diminished by distance. And there were the sunsets, the primeval oranges and blues that bled into the edge of the earth until you could no longer see where the sky ended and the sea began.

Occasionally, if she was lucky, she would sight a shoal of porpoises and laugh at the joy of their movement. It felt like they were complicit with the ship, the way they eyed her, moving alongside the vessel in perfect accord. But mostly she lay against one of the aircraft wheels, her wide-brimmed hat tipped back, and just stared at the sky. A sky now free of droning enemy aircraft, of silent, malevolent missiles, of the screams of the wounded. Of the judgments of those who thought they knew her. There was nothing between her and her destination—no mountains, no trees, no buildings. No people.

At night, alone, she could shrug off, temporarily, both past and future. She could just sit and be, comforted by the fact that here she was just Frances—a tiny, meaningless nothing amid the sky, the sea and the stars.

———

"So, how's your ship of brides?"

The warship *Alexandra* was the first British vessel the *Victoria* had passed within radio distance since they had left Sydney. But Highfield had taken Captain Edward Baxter's call with less enthusiasm than he might have done in other circumstances, having something of an inkling as to how the exchange would run.

"And how's sports day? Dobson tells me you're letting the girls out for a bit of a hop, skip and jump. Or am I thinking of something else?"

Highfield closed his eyes, listening to the distant rattle of laughter.

In spite of everyone's best efforts, sports day, it was widely agreed afterward, could not be described as an unequivocal success. Despite the mirror-flat sea, whose surface the *Victoria* glided across so smoothly that you could have balanced a penny upright on her bow half-way back to Trincomalee, the deck hockey had had to be abandoned after the pucks, in three successive matches, sailed overboard. The same went for the baton during the relay race, prompting one bride to burst into tears at the booing and jeering that greeted her mistake. Another suffered burns to her legs when she braked too late and skidded along the deck dangerously until she was hauled back from the edge. Girls, the officers observed, were not used to the specialist skills required to play sports in the confines of a ship, even one as large as *Victoria*.

The women's officers, growing impatient in the heat, tried to extend the games area as far as the aircraft. But it had proven impossible to run the wheelbarrow and sack races safely around the planes, and even when they were moved, hoisted around by the gantry or pushed by whistling deck hands, the women, unused to their shape, would repeatedly bang themselves on wings or knock into propellers. The absence of the liftwells meant that it was impossible to place them anywhere else. Meanwhile, as the ship maintained its course across the Indian Ocean it had found itself in the midst of a heat-wave, the vast flight deck absorbing the heat of the sun, so that feet blistered on the decks, and many found it too hot to run, the drinking fountains sent up warm water and throughout the afternoon the competitors drifted away, pleading exhaustion, sunburn, or head-ache. The sweltering temperatures in the cabins meant they were all fractious with lack of sleep. In the midst of this, two brides (one, rather unfortunately, the founder of the Brides' Bible Club) had helped carry a friend with a sprained ankle to the infirmary. There, Dr. Duxbury was reeking of alcohol and engrossed in reading matter that, had he been in a condition to do so, he might have defended at best as "medically informative." The ankle forgotten, the shaken brides had sprinted to the head of the ship's Red Cross to make a for-mal complaint.

"I thought it was important for me to be fully conversant with all aspects of female anatomy," Dr. Duxbury told Captain Highfield.

"I'm not sure that *Hollywood Starlets* was quite the biological text-book our passengers had in mind," the captain replied. And decided that, unorthodox as it was, it might be best if he hung on to the in-firmary keys for the foreseeable future.

It was then that two brides fell into fisticuffs over the egg and spoon. (Pointless, really, as all the eggs were wooden.) The "Carry the Maiden" race had culminated in an argument when a girl ac-cused a rating of hoisting up her skirt. Sports day had officially ended.

"I think the question all the chaps want to know is how's your water consumption?"

"Fine," said Highfield, thinking back to that morning's report. They had had some trouble with one of the desalination units, but the chief engineer had told him they were now running as normal.

Baxter was talking too loudly, as if conscious that he was listened to by other people at his end. "It's just that we hear on the grapevine you've set up a hair salon, and we were wondering how you looked after a shampoo and set . . ." He guffawed heartily, and Highfield thought he heard an echoing laugh behind him.

He was alone in the meteorological office, high above the

shimmering deck, and his leg had throbbed steadily all day. He had felt a vague sense of betrayal when it started; for days it had given him hardly any trouble, to the point at which he had convinced himself that it was healing without the need for medical intervention.

"I spoke to Dobson before they put me through to you. He says those Aussie girls are giving you all a run for your money."

"What do you mean?"

"Causing the odd upset. Getting the men a bit agitated. Can't say I envy you, old man. Load of women littering up the place with their washing and nail varnish and frillies and what-have-you. Wandering around in their next-to-nothings, distracting the men from their work. My boys here have opened a book on how many little Victors and Victorias will be running around in nine months' time."

There had been a noticeable lightening in the way senior naval personnel talked to each other since the end of the war. Now they were determined to poke fun, make jokes. Highfield, not for the first time, found himself hankering after the old ways. He tried to keep the affront from his voice. "My men are conducting themselves properly."

"It's not the men's behavior I'm thinking of, George. I've heard about these colonial girls. Not quite the same reserve as their British sisters, if what I've heard about the nocturnal activities in Sydney are anything to go by . . ."

"These girls are fine. Everything's under control." He thought uncomfortably of the incident the women's service officer had reported the previous week. Baxter and his like would know soon enough.

"Yes. Well. My advice would be to keep 'em locked up as much as you can. We've had all sorts of trouble with our younger lads and women passengers. And that's just the odd Wren or two. Dread to think what it must be like with more than six hundred. I think some of them have lost their heads now they know they're heading home."

In Highfield's answering silence, he seemed finally to acknowledge that he was not going to get the response he desired. Highfield, meanwhile, had pulled up his trouser leg. It might have been his imagination, but the color of the skin surrounding the wound was angrier than it had been when he last examined it. He dropped the fabric, clenching his jaw, as if he could make the damn thing better by a sheer act of will.

"Yes . . . we've all had a bit of a chuckle at the thought of you and the hair salon. Of all the ships . . . of all the captains, eh? Still . . . I suppose it's nice to know there's some use for the old girl after she retires. You and she could set up the world's first mobile beauty parlor."

Highfield's attention snapped away from his leg. "Retires?"

"You know, when she's decommissioned."

"*Victoria*'s being decommissioned?"

There was a brief silence. "I thought you knew, old man. She's done. When the engineers were all over her in Woollomooloo they decided it wasn't worth patching her up again. She's finished when you get back to Blighty. They've decided they want to concentrate on a whole new class of carrier now that the war's over. Not that it's going to affect you too much, eh?"

Highfield sat down. Around him, the dials and maps of the meteorological office stared back mutely, oblivious of their imminent redundancy. So, he told the ship silently, you and me both. He hardly heard the other captain's continuing conversation.

"But jesting aside, how are you, old boy? Heard you took a knock with *Indomitable*. Quite the talk of the town, for a while. You had a few people worried."

"I'm fine."

"Of course, of course. Can't dwell on these things, can you? Shame, though. Young Hart served with me a couple of years ago. Quite shocked, when I heard. Nice young man. Stood out from the crowd."

"Yes. Yes, he did."

"Met his wife once, when we were out in Singapore. Nice little girl. I seem to recall she had just had twins. Which rather brings me to my reason for calling. London wired me this morning. They tell me you might have a few brides on board who are married to my men. We're going to be alongside for a day or two and London thought it would be a nice gesture if we allowed them radio contact. What do you think? I dare say it would be good for my men's morale to have a quick chat with the little woman."

"I don't know . . ."

"Well, don't decide just yet. As I understand it, there's only a handful of them anyway. I don't suppose you'll have hordes of hysterical girls knocking on your door. But it would mean a lot to my boys. And it all helps keep them out of trouble. We're docking in Aden in a few days, and it's always good to give the men a reminder of their responsibilities before they hit the shore." His laugh was low, guttural, confident that he would be understood.

Below on deck men in tropical rig were tidying away the last of the sports-day ropes and chairs, occasionally wiping sweat from their brows. A short distance away two young women strolled toward the deck canteen, the setting sun bouncing off their set, shining hair. They ducked together under the wing of one of the aircraft, one reaching out a slim hand to touch it as she passed and drawing it rapidly away, as if exclaiming that it was too hot. She was laughing at something the other had said and covered her mouth.

Behind them, the other fighter planes stretched across the deck, their smooth surfaces radiating heat. As redundant as the rest of the ship.

"Highfield?"

"Get your man to speak to my number one," Highfield said, eyes still fixed on the deck below. "We'll send over a passenger list and you can let me know who your boys want to speak to. We'll see if we can organize something."

He put down his headphones. Then he turned to the radio operator. "Get me the commander-in-chief of the British Pacific Fleet. And whoever deals with the Lend-lease Agreement."

———

The cabin had been empty that evening; Avice was at a fabric-flower-making session, which apparently counted toward the Queen of the *Victoria* contest. Having decided Irene Carter was now her sworn enemy, she was intent on beating her to the title.

Jean, having whined about the oppressive heat, and tired of her reading lesson, was watching a film with two brides from the dormitory above.

Frances, having enjoyed an hour's solitude and made a fuss of the old dog, was feeling restless, a little too warm for comfort. In the airless confines of the dormitory, her blouse lay stickily against her skin and the sheets moved tackily against the bedroll. She went to the bathroom and splashed her face several times with cold water.

She was about to leave the dormitory for the flight deck when Margaret burst in, flushed and breathless. "Ohmygoodness," she was saying, one plump hand at her throat. "Ohmygoodness."

"Are you all right?" Frances leapt toward her.

Margaret mopped a faint sheen from her face. A heat rash had spread from her chest to her neck. She sat down heavily on her bunk.

"Margaret?"

"I've been summoned to the radio room. You'll never guess—I'm to speak to Joe!"

"What?"

Margaret's eyes were wide. "Tonight! Can you believe it? The *Alexandra* is just a short distance away, apparently, and we can pick her up on radio. There's me and about five others who they say can speak to our husbands. I'm one of the lucky ones! Can you believe it? Can you?"

She grabbed the dog from her bed and kissed her vigorously. "Oh, Maudie, can you believe it? I'm going to speak to Joe! Tonight!" Then she glanced at her reflection in the mirror Avice had propped beside the door and groaned. "Oh, no! Look at the state of me. My hair always goes mad in the humidity." She lifted the unruly fronds in her fingers.

"I don't think he'll be able to see you over the radio," Frances ventured.

"But I still want to look nice for him." Margaret attacked her hair with Avice's brush, vigorous strokes that left it springing up in electric bursts of benign rebellion. She pursed her lips. "Will you come with me? I feel so wobbly—I don't want to make a fool of myself. Would you mind?" She bit her lip. "It's almost three months since I spoke to him. And I need someone to remind me not to swear in front of the captain."

Frances looked at her feet.

"Oh, golly, Moses, I'm sorry. I'm being tactless. I don't mean to gloat. I'm sure you'd love to be speaking to your husband. I just thought if anyone was to be with me I'd like you."

Frances took her hand. It was damp with either heat or nervous excitement. "I'd be delighted," she said.

———

"Joe?"

Around her the light dimmed. Margaret shifted awkwardly, and asked in a whisper whether she was standing in the right place. The radio operator, earphones clamped to his head, fiddled with the myriad dials in front of him. Then, apparently satisfied by a series of chirrups and whistles, he adjusted the microphone in front of her. "Put your face close to there," he said, placing his hand gently on Margaret's back to encourage her in. "That's it. Now try again."

"Joe?"

In the little room tucked beneath the bridge, the handful of chosen brides, some accompanied by friends, nudged each other. The radio room was too small for so many people, and they stood stiffly, arms pressed close to their sides, a few fanning themselves with magazines, their faces shining in the heavy heat. Outside the sky had blackened, and somewhere, many miles away, the objects of their desire floated in the darkness.

"Mags?" The voice was distant, crackly. But, from Margaret's expression, definitely his.

There was a collective sharp intake of breath, the sound a child might make when confronted by a Christmas tree. Margaret had been first up and it was as if until the brides heard this evidence it had been impossible to believe in the proximity of their men, that they might be able, after months of silence, to exchange a few precious words. Now they beamed at each other, as if their joy was contagious.

Margaret put out a hand to the microphone. Then, after a brief, embarrassed smile, "Joe, it's me. How are you?"

"I'm grand, love. Are you keeping well? Are they looking after you?" The disembodied voice broke into the silence.

Margaret closed her hand round the microphone. "I'm fine. Me and Joe Junior both. It—it's good to hear you," she faltered, evidently conscious that just as she was surrounded by strangers it was likely he was too. None of the women wanted to embarrass their men in front of their mates or superiors.

"Are they feeding you well?" came the voice, and the occupants of the radio room laughed. Margaret's eyes flicked toward the captain, who stood back, arms crossed. He was smiling benignly.

"They're looking after us just fine."

"Good. You . . . watch out in this heat. Make sure you drink lots of water."

"Oh, I am."

"I've got to go, sweetheart, give the next fellow a turn. But you take care now."

"You too." Margaret moved in to the microphone, as if she could somehow get closer to him.

"I'll see you in Plymouth. Not long now."

Margaret's voice broke. "Not long at all," she said. " 'Bye, Joe."

As she turned from the microphone, she sagged and Frances stepped forward to hold her, alarmed by the tears coursing down Margaret's cheeks. It had been a pretty mean exchange, she thought. She should have been allowed a few more minutes at least and perhaps some privacy, so that she could say what she felt. There was so much Margaret had needed to say to Joe, Frances thought, about freedom, being a wife, motherhood.

But when Frances looked at her now, Margaret's smile was bright enough to illuminate the darkness. "Oh, Frances, that was wonderful," she whispered.

Frances heard the raw love in Margaret's voice, the evidence of so much gained from so little. And she held her friend for a minute, her mind both blank and racing, as Margaret tried in whispers to revisit what they had said to each other, exclaiming that her mind had gone blank—that in hearing his voice, she had had no idea what to say. "But it doesn't matter, does it? Oh, Frances, I hope you get the chance to talk to your man soon. I can't tell you how much better I feel. Did you hear Joe? Isn't he the best?"

———

All eyes were on the dark girl in the blue dress who had burst into noisy tears at the sound of her husband's voice and was being comforted by the Red Cross officer. So it was only the captain who caught the expression of the tall girl in the corner, who had been jokingly introduced to him as "unofficial midwife." He didn't like to look too hard at any of the women, didn't want things to be misconstrued. But there was something compelling about her erect stance. And in her eyes, which reflected shock, as if she had discovered some great loss. He felt, unaccountably, as if they mirrored his own.

———

Nicol walked along the lower gallery, past the ordnance spares and gun room, past the hangar where normally one might find several aircraft and attendant trunks of spare parts, instead of rows of doors. Most were propped open in the vain hope of attracting a stray breeze, and from behind them emanated the sounds of murmuring women, cards flipping on to makeshift tables or magazine pages turning. Careful to keep his gaze straight ahead, he moved along them and ran silently up the stairs, conscious that tonight even that small exertion caused his skin to stick to his shorts. Nodding at the chaplain, he moved along the half-lit gangway toward the lobby, trying to make himself inconspicuous as he passed the captain's rooms. Finally, with a quick glance to left and right, he opened the hatch door beside the lieutenant commander's office and emerged on to the unlit deck.

He had been told where to find her. He had knocked on the door rather awkwardly (it felt like an intrusion, even speaking into this feminine lair) to tell them what had been decided. To get them, like the others, to prepare. Perhaps he had told them early because he wanted them to have the best spot. They had laughed, incredulous. Made him say it twice before they would believe it. Then, with Avice and Jean galvanized into action, Margaret, still glowing from her radio contact, had whispered confirmation to him of what he already suspected.

The sky was mostly covered with cloud, revealing only a handful of stars, so it was several minutes before he saw her. At first he had thought it a wasted journey, had prepared to turn and leave. Strictly speaking, he should not have been away from his post. But then a shadow shifted, and as a cloud slid back to bathe the deck in moonlight, he found he could just make out her angular shape under the furthest Corsair, her arms wrapped round her knees.

He stood still for a moment, wondering if she had seen him and whether the mere act of him having located her would make her uncomfortable. Then, as he drew closer and she turned to him, he felt a rush of relief. As if her presence there could reassure him of something. Constancy, he supposed. Perhaps even some strange sense of goodness. He thought suddenly of Thompson, of his bloodied face when he was stretchered back on board several days previously. He must have got into a brawl during his shore leave, his mess man said. Stupid boy, ending up on his own. They had drummed it into them from their earliest days that in new territory they should stick together.

Nicol saw that she had been crying. He watched her draw her hand across her eyes, her shoulders straighten, and his pleasure in seeing her was clouded by awkwardness. "I'm sorry if I disturbed you. Your friend told me I might find you here."

She made as if to stand, but he gestured that she should stay where she was.

"Is everything all right?"

She looked so alarmed that he realized his sudden unannounced presence might have suggested a feared telegram and cursed himself for his insensitivity. "Nothing wrong. Please." He motioned again for her to remain seated. "I just wanted to tell you . . . to warn you . . . that you won't be alone for long."

Something even more strange happened then. She looked almost appalled. "What?" she said. "What do you mean?"

"Captain's orders. It's too hot in the liftwells—your cabins, I mean.

He's ordered that everyone should sleep out here tonight. Well, you brides, anyway."

Her shoulders relaxed a little. "Sleep out here? On deck? Are you sure?"

He found himself smiling. It sounded pretty daft even to him. When the XO had told him he had made it clear from his careful use of words that he thought the captain had finally gone mad. "We can't have you all boiling down there. It's about as hot as it gets. We've had one of our engineers pass out in the starboard engine room this evening, so Captain Highfield has decided all brides are to bring their bedrolls up here. You can sleep in your swimwear. You'll be a lot more comfortable."

She looked away from him then, out at the dark ocean. "I suppose this means I'll have to stay away from here now," she said wistfully.

He could not take his eyes off her profile. Her skin, in the milky blue moonlight, was opalescent. When he spoke, his voice cracked and he coughed to disguise it, to pull himself together. "Not on my account," he said. "You wouldn't be the first to need a few minutes alone with the sea."

Alone with the sea? Where had that come from? He didn't talk like that. She probably thought him a fanciful fool. There was something about her self-containment that had made him stumble like that, like an idiot.

But she didn't seem to have noticed. When she turned to him, he saw that her eyes glistened with tears. "It doesn't matter," she said dully. "It wasn't working tonight anyway."

What wasn't? he wanted to ask. But instead, he said quietly, "Are you all right?"

"I'm fine," she said. And as she stood abruptly, brushing her skirt for non-existent dust, the clouds drew back across the moon and her expression was once more hidden from his gaze.

Highfield couldn't help but laugh privately at Dobson's face when the first girl emerged on to the deck, her bedroll under her arm, dressed in a frilled bright pink two-piece swimsuit, the kind of thing that would previously have had him spluttering into his collar. She stopped at the main hatch, glanced warily at the captain, then as he nodded, stepped out and motioned behind her to her friends. She tiptoed across the deck to where a marine was pointing.

She was followed quickly by two more, giggling and bumping into each other under the spotlights, steered into designated spaces, as the aircraft had been on previous voyages. Soon they were pouring out of the open hatches, the larger ones modest in oversized cotton shirts, some a little embarrassed to be seen so publicly in such intimate apparel. He had said that those who felt uncomfortable were welcome to sleep in their dormitories, but he was certain that, the heat being as oppressive as it was, most would prefer the sweet breezes of a deck moving through air to the stuffiness below. And so it proved: they kept on coming, some chattering, some exclaiming as they tried to pitch their bedroll and found there was already not enough room, in their shapes and sizes and hairstyles and manner an endless example of the infinite variety of womanhood.

The marines would watch over them. Oddly enough, it had been one of the few occasions on which the men had not groaned at news of an unexpected night watch. Highfield looked at the marines' faces as they moved around the flight deck; even they, normally poker-faced, could not help laughing and joking with the women at this improbable turn of events. "What the hell?" Highfield muttered to himself periodically, the rare expression making his own mouth turn up at the corners. What the hell?

One of the WSOs appeared at his shoulder, accompanied by Dobson. "Nearly all up, are they?" Highfield asked.

"I think so, Captain. But we were wondering if we could place a few closer to the aircraft. There's not much space for so many. If the men are meant to have room to move round the edges, and if they all want room to stretch out—"

"No," said Highfield, abruptly. "I want them well apart."

Dobson waited several seconds, as if for an explanation. When none was forthcoming, he bad-temperedly sent off the women's officer to sort out two girls who were arguing over ownership of a sheet.

He would tell his colleagues that it was probably something to do with Hart, Highfield knew, that the *Indomitable* business had left the captain peculiar about risk. Let him think what he wants, Highfield thought dismissively.

It was nearly ten o'clock when the last bride had trickled out, and the cabins had been checked to ensure there would be no more arrivals. Highfield stood before the women and motioned for silence. Gradually the chatter of the dimly lit crowd faded until only the distant rumble of the engines and the low hiss of the waves could be heard below.

"I was going to outline a couple of rules," he said, shifting on his leg. He faced the marines, in a neat, silent row to his left. "To make a few things clear about this evening. But I've decided it's too hot. And if you don't have enough common sense not to fall off the side there's not a lot of hope for you, whatever I say. So I'll ask you, as ever, not to distract the men from their work. And I hope this helps you get a better night's sleep."

His words were met with a cheerful swell of chatter from the women and a round of applause. He could see the gratitude on some faces, and felt an unfamiliar swelling of something in him. His mouth twitched into a smile.

"Just make sure it's only marines who are allowed up here," he said to Dobson. And then, while his good mood stalled the pain in his leg, he made his way stiffly toward his rooms.

———

That night, Frances thought afterward, had been the high point of the voyage. Not just for her but for most of them. Perhaps it was something about them all being together, about the freedom and sweet release of the open sea and the sky after the days of encroaching heat and deepening ill-temper, that lifted their spirits. The openness of the deck made them all, briefly, equal, prevented the cliques that made being among large numbers of women such a trial.

Avice, who for the last week had ignored her, had spent several hours making friends with the girls around them, capitalizing on her new status as pregnant wife. Margaret, after fretting a little while about Maude Gonne and being reassured by Frances, who had sneaked down on a pretext and found her sleeping comfortably, had flaked out not twenty minutes after they settled and was now snoring to her left, her belly, under a paper-thin man's shirt, propped on Frances's pillow.

Frances was pleased to see it: she had felt pangs of sympathy for Margaret, swollen and uncomfortable in the heat, twisting and turning on her bunk in a vain attempt to get comfortable.

Initially Frances had felt a little self-conscious in her bathing suit, but confronted with the exposed limbs and midriffs of several hundred women of all shapes and sizes (some in the minuscule new bikinis), she soon realized that such self-absorption was ridiculous. Once the marines had got over the shock of what they were guarding they had lost interest too; several were now playing cards on crates by the bridge, while others chatted among themselves, apparently oblivious to the near-naked sleeping bodies behind them.

Could they really be so uninterested? Frances wondered. Could any man really feel so sanguine, faced with so much bare female flesh? But, try as she might, she could see nothing in their manner to justify her discomfort. Eventually she had allowed her own sheet to drop around her, had adjusted herself so that her semi-upright body caught the maximum of the breeze that whispered across the deck. And when she did see one of the men glance longingly in their direction, still dressed in his high-necked tropical rig, she was forced to the conclusion that it was probably the women's coolness that they coveted, rather than their bodies.

She must have slept for a few hours after midnight. Most of the girls around her had slept soundly, the lack of several nights' sleep a demolition ball against the novel circumstances that might have kept them awake. But she couldn't help herself: being among so many people made her uncomfortable. Eventually, she had sat up and decided, gracefully, to give in to wakefulness, simply to enjoy the freedom to sit out there without fear of discovery. She wrapped her cotton sheet loosely round her shoulders, and trod carefully to the edge of the group, from where she could just make out the foamed movement of the ship in the ocean. Eventually she found a spot away from everyone, and sat, thinking of nothing, staring into the distance.

"You all right?" It was said quietly, so that only she could hear.

The marine was standing a few feet away from her, his face carefully turned to the front.

"I'm fine," she murmured. She kept hers toward the sea, as if they were in mutual pretense that they were not in conversation.

He stood there for some time. Frances was acutely conscious of the stillness of his legs beside her, braced a little as if in preparation for some unseen swell.

"You like it up here, don't you?" he asked.

"Very much. It might sound a little silly. But I've found the sea makes me feel . . . well, happy."

"You didn't look very happy earlier."

She wondered that she could talk to him like this. "I suppose the emptiness of it all overwhelmed me," she said. "I didn't feel comforted . . . the way I usually do."

"Ah." She felt, rather than saw, his nod. "Well, she rarely does what you expect her to."

They were silent for a while, Frances unbalanced because they were no longer divided by a steel door. Initially she had pulled her sheet up round her neck so that she was almost totally enclosed by it. Now, she decided that was silly, a kind of extreme reaction to his presence. And she let it slide down over her shoulders. While reddening at her own audacity.

"Your whole face changes when you're up here."

She glanced up at him quickly. Perhaps he grasped that he had overstepped some mark because he kept his eyes on the ocean. "I know how it feels," he added. "It's why I like to stay at sea."

What about your children, she wanted to ask, but couldn't frame it so that it didn't sound like an accusation. Instead she stole a peep at his face. She wanted to ask him why he seemed so sad when he had so much to return to. But he turned and their eyes locked. Her hand lifted of its own volition to her face, as if to shield herself from him.

"Do you want me to leave you alone?" he said quietly.

"No," she said. The word was out before she had had time to think about it. And then both silenced, by awkwardness or surprise that she had said anything, he stood beside her, her personal sentry, as they stared out over the dark waters.

———

The first slivers of light, fierce and electric, appeared thousands of miles distant on the horizon shortly before five. He told her of how the sunrises could change, depending on which part of the equator they were traveling through, sometimes slow and languorous, a gentle flooding of the sky with creamy blue light, at others a brief, almost aggressive sparking, short-circuiting the sky into dawn. He told her how, as a young recruit, he had been able to list nearly all the constellations, had taken some pride in it, had watched them disappear slowly at daybreak, to enjoy the magic of their reappearance hours later, but that when the war started he couldn't look for more than a minute at a night sky without hearing the distant hum of an enemy plane. "It's spoiled for me now," he said. "I find it easier not to look."

She told him how the exploding shells in the Pacific mimicked the colors of the dawn, and how, on night duty, she would watch through the window flap of her ward tent, wondering at man's ability to subvert nature. You could see a strange beauty even in those colors, she said. War—or perhaps nursing—had taught her to see it in just about anything. "It'll come back, you know," she said. "You just have to give it time." Her voice was low, consoling. He thought of her uttering similar sentiments to the wounded men she tended, and wished, perversely, that he had been among them.

"Have you served on this ship for long?"

It took him a minute to focus on what she was saying.

"No," he said. "Most of us were on *Indomitable*. But she was sunk at the end of the war. Those of us who got out ended up on the *Victoria*."

Such a few tidy words, well rehearsed now. They did little to convey the chaos and horror of the final hours of that ship, the bombs, the screams and the holds that turned into geysers of fire.

She turned her face full toward him. "Did you lose many?"

"A good few. Captain lost his nephew."

She turned to where the captain had stood below the bridge, hours earlier, immaculate in his tropical rig, consulting a chart. "Everyone has lost someone," she said, almost to herself.

He had asked her about the prisoners-of-war, and had listened to her litany of injuries, of those patients she had cared for and lost. He didn't ask her how she had coped. Those who had lived through it rarely did, she remarked. It was unimportant, once you had experienced the fierce gratitude of simply being alive.

"Quite a thing to choose to do," he said.

"Do you really think any of us had a choice?"

It was at that moment, as he looked at her pale, serious face, heard in her reply the determination not to glean even the smallest advantage from other people's suffering, that he knew his feelings for her could no longer be considered appropriate. "I—I—no . . ." The shock of this knowledge drove his voice from him, and he shook his head mutely. He found his thoughts suddenly, inappropriately, drawn to his last shore leave, and he felt exposed, flooded with shame.

"We all have to find some way," she said, "of atoning."

You? he wanted to say incredulously. You didn't start this war. You were not responsible for the damage, the torn limbs, the suffering. You are one of the good things. You are one of the reasons we all kept going. You, of all people, of all these women lying here, have nothing to atone for.

Perhaps it was the strangeness of the hour, or that her bare shoulders, in the encroaching light, glowed like something ethereal. Perhaps it was the simple fact that he had not exchanged for what seemed like years a single word that was not smothered with uniformed bluff and bravery. He wanted to crack open like the dawn in front of her, to reveal himself, faults and all, and be absolved by her warmth and understanding. He wanted to scream at her husband— no doubt some stupid, wisecracking engineer, who, even as they spoke, might be straightening his trousers as he crept out of some Far-Eastern brothel, exchanging sly winks with his messmates—"Do you know what you've got? Do you understand?"

He thought briefly, insanely, that he might try to put at least some of this into words. And then, at the corner of his eye, Captain Highfield appeared on the bridge. Following his gaze, she turned and watched as the captain consulted two officers. He gestured toward the aircraft, then straightened up as they talked to him rapidly. From their raised voices, something seemed to be up.

He drew back reluctantly from Frances. "I'd better go and find out what's going on," he said. He held the warmth of her answering smile close to him for the twenty-four strides it took to join the others.

Several minutes later he returned. "They're going over the side," he said.

"What?"

"The planes. Captain's decided we all need more room. He's just got permission from London to put them overboard."

"But there's nothing wrong with them!"

His voice bubbled uncharacteristically. The long night had caught him, choked him, and now, releasing him, left him emotional. "The bigwigs who oversee the Lend-lease Agreement are okay with it. But he's . . . he's not the kind of captain to make decisions like that." He shook his head, disbelieving.

"But he's right," she said eventually. "It's over. Let the sea take them."

And as dawn broke, touching the near naked bodies with its cold blue light, a few of the girls woke, pulling their sheets round them, watching mutely with sleep-filled eyes as silently, one by one, the aircraft were wheeled to the edge by pairs of engineers. Accompanied by the minimum of instruction, so as not to wake those sleeping, the planes faced the skies for the last time, wings folded upward, some still scarred and scorched from airborne victories. They waited patiently while their last details were read out and checked off. Then they teetered on the edge, spending the shortest moment in mid-air before they disappeared on their concluding flight, the splash of each impact surprisingly muted as they drifted down, silently shifting against the currents of the Indian Ocean, down, down toward a final, gentle landing on some unknown unseen sea bed.

13

My brother brought back an English bride. Before they landed, she was lauded up to the skies as being beautiful, accomplished, helpful and brilliant . . . ; but instead of that we found an ugly, brown-necked, red-complexioned, lazy hussy who had not a good word to say about anyone or anything in this country . . . Speaking personally it was a sorry day for me when an imported minx landed in our family.

LETTER TO MELBOURNE'S TRUTH NEWSPAPER, 1919

TWENTY-TWO DAYS

Dear Mum,

This is a hard letter to write. I guess I've put off writing it for as long as I could. But you probably know without me having to explain what it is I want to tell you I have done, and how I've carried it round ever since. I'm not proud of myself, Mum. I gave myself all sorts of reasons to convince myself I was doing the right thing. But I'm not sure who I thought I was protecting—you or myself . . .

My dearest love,

It's very strange trying to compose this letter, knowing that in all likelihood by the time you get it we will already be in each other's arms. But this voyage is starting to stretch, and I feel increasingly desperate, stuck out here in the middle of the ocean, to maintain some kind of contact. To at least talk to you, even though you might not be able to listen. I suppose some of these brides are more self-sufficient than I am, able to cope with endless days of absent time. But to me, every minute I spend without you is far too long, and infinitely worthless . . .

Sometimes the unspoken conversations taking place on the *Victoria* became clamorous. Now, half-way through the voyage, the weight of these one-sided exchanges hung heavy in the air as brides reread and composed correspondence, trying to express their longing, confiding their fears to their families or chiding their men for lack of emotion. In Cabin 3G two brides sat side by side on their bunks, each buried in thought as they committed their own pens to the tissue-thin Navy-issue writing-paper.

Occasionally, through the partially open door, the sound of passing footsteps was accompanied by a burst of laughter or a murmured conversation, punctuated by discreet exclamations of surprise. The heat of the previous days had broken a little with the arrival of a short storm in the early hours of that morning, and the inhabitants of the brides' cabins had become active again: many were out enjoying the fresher air. None of which was heard apparently by the remaining occupants of Cabin 3G, both of whom were lost in a one-sided conversation with persons far from the confines of the *Victoria*.

. . . darling, in the circumstances it feels rather silly to be writing these words. So perhaps I shall use them simply to say how much I adore you, and how glad I am that this baby is ours. That we will bring him or her up together, and not separated, as we have been, by endless stretches of water. That I can't think of a more wonderful father than I am sure you will be.

Sometimes you can feel something so bad, be so caught up in your own unhappiness, that it's hard to see what's right. Even harder to do it.

Still, I realized something last night: that even after everything that happened you would never have done what I did. That the whole point was, you would have just wanted people to be as happy as they could possibly be. It's hard even to write that, without feeling ~~ashamed~~ *sorry.*

"Avice," said Margaret, "do you have any blotting paper?"

"Here," said Avice, stretching downward. "You can have that sheet. I've got plenty." She adjusted her skirt as she settled down again, her free hand reaching absently to pat her stomach.

*. . . so that's why I'm going to write to Letty, and tell her the truth. That
Dad, while he'll never love anyone like he loved you, deserves to have a bit
of company. He deserves to be looked after. I've finally realized I don't
have to protect some perfect image I have of the two of you. I don't have to
feel angry with her for being in love with him all these years. I can just feel
sad for her that she wasted them on someone she knew she couldn't have.
Didn't even try to have.*

*I know you'll agree with this, Mum. But I think Letty, after all her
years alone, deserves to be loved.*

"I'm going upstairs to sit on the deck for a bit. Are you all right if I
leave you with Maudie?"

Avice glanced up at Margaret, who was standing by the door, her
completed letter in her hand. She looked, Avice thought, a little red
round the eyes. Mind you, with that awful blue dress, which she
must have worn for the last ten days, and those swollen ankles, her
eyes were probably the least of her worries. "Sure," she said.

"It's not so bad up there now the heat has died down a bit."

Avice nodded and, as the door closed behind Margaret, she resumed writing.

*It's very odd, perhaps you might even find it silly, but do you know what,
Ian? I have felt strangely nervous about telling you. I know you're not desperately keen on surprises, but this is a truly special sort of surprise, isn't
it? Of course it would have been nice for us to have a little time to ourselves, but once the baby is born we can sort out a nurse for it, and you and
I can go on being just how we were in Australia—except with a darling
little baby to love too. I know some men rather miss the attention of their
wives once the little ones come along but, darling, I want to assure you
that I AM NOT ONE OF THOSE. No baby would ever come between you and
I. You are first in my heart, and always will be. The important thing is for
us to be together. That's what you always said to me. I hold those thoughts
close to my heart every minute of every day. The important thing is for us
to be together.*

Your Avice

Avice lay back on her bunk, listening to the distant thrum of the ship's engines, the occasional breaking in of the Tannoy, the shrieking of other girls engaged in some activity above. She placed her sealed letter on her chest, holding it to her with both hands, and thought back.

———

The checkout time would normally have been eleven a.m., but it being wartime, and needs being what they were, she had known that even at a quarter past two in the afternoon they were unlikely to be disturbed by the maid. The Melbourne Flower Garden Hotel, like many local establishments, did a brisk trade these days in what were known as "extended checkouts." So extended, in fact, were checkout times that quite frequently the couples did not bother staying at the hotel overnight. It was entirely possible that many were not married. Why else would they require a hotel room? The explanations of "wives" coming into town especially to meet their husbands' ships sounded unconvincing even to the most naïve ears. But with so many troops in town, and need being what it was, the hotel owner had been canny enough to grasp that flexibility and a blind eye would keep the dollars rolling in.

Avice calculated how much time was left before they should get up and return home. If they left in the next hour they could possibly nip into the zoo so that she wouldn't have to lie about where they'd been. Her mother was bound to ask her something pointed about Sumatran tigers or some such.

Ian had been dozing, one heavy arm pinning her to the bed. Now he opened an eye. "What are you thinking?"

She let her head turn slowly until their faces were only inches apart. "I was thinking we were probably not supposed to do this until after the wedding."

"Don't say that, gorgeous girl. I couldn't have waited that long."

"Would it have been so hard?"

"Sweetheart, you know I've only got a forty-eight-hour pass. Wasn't this more fun than fussing about plans for flowers and brides-maids and what-have-you?"

Avice thought secretly that she would probably have liked fussing over flowers and bridesmaids, but she didn't want to spoil the mood so she smiled enigmatically.

"God, I love you."

She could feel his words on her skin, as if he were giving her tiny particles of himself even in his breath. She closed her eyes, savoring them: "I love you too, darling."

"You're not sorry?" he said.

"To be marrying you?" Her eyes widened.

"To have done . . . you know. I didn't hurt you or anything?"

He had, a little, if she was honest. But not in any way that had made her want to stop. She blushed now, shocked at the things she had found herself doing, at how easily she had surrendered to him. She had always suspected, from what her mother had told her, that it would be something she had to endure. The Sleeping Beast, her mother had called it. "Best leave it sleeping as much as possible," she had advised sagely.

"You don't think any less of me . . . ," she murmured ". . . for having let you . . ." She swallowed. "I mean, I'm not sure I was meant to enjoy it quite as much as I did . . ."

"Oh, my darling girl, no! God, no, it was wonderful that you liked it. In fact, that's one of the things I love about you, Avice," Ian pulled her close to him and spoke into her hair. "You're a sensual creature. A free spirit. Not like English girls."

A free spirit. She had found herself believing this new version of herself, as Ian described it. Some time earlier, when she had found herself naked and self-conscious before him, he had said she was a goddess, the most alluring creature he had ever seen, and something else that made her blush, his eyes unfocused in admiration of her, and she had found herself determinedly becoming alluring and goddess-like when she really wanted to reach for a dressing-gown.

This must mean he's right for me, she told herself. He has it in him to make me better than I am.

Outside, the traffic was picking up. Somewhere below the open window a car door slammed and a man shouted insistently, "Davy, Davy," apparently unheeded.

"So," she said, disentangling their legs and sliding round so that she was leaning over him, some small part of her still shocked at the feel of his naked skin against hers. "You really, really love me, do you?"

He smiled at her, his hair matted against the pillow. She thought she'd never seen a more handsome man in her entire life. "Do you really have to ask?"

"And I never do anything to upset you, or irritate you?"

"Couldn't," he said, reaching over to the bedside table for a cigarette. "Impossible."

"And you want to be with me forever?"

"More than. For infinity."

She took a deep breath. "Then I'm going to tell you something, and you're not to be angry with me."

He pulled a cigarette from his packet with neat white teeth, and paused, using the arm looped round her neck to cup the flame of the match as he lit it. "Mm?" he said. A soft plume of blue smoke rose into the still air beside her head.

"We're getting married."

He looked at her for a moment. His eyes creased upward. "Of course we're getting married, my little duck."

"Tomorrow."

She didn't like to think too hard about that next bit. The way those creases hardened and his eyes became less soft.

The way the not-so-Sleeping Beast had suddenly become more so. "What?"

"I've fixed it up. With a justice of the peace. We're getting married tomorrow. At the Collins Street register office. Mum and Dad and Deanna are going to be there and the Hendersons have agreed to be our witnesses." Then, when he didn't say anything, "Oh, darling, don't be cross with me. I couldn't bear the thought of you going off again and us only being engaged. And I thought seeing as you do love me and I love you and we only want to be together there wasn't any point in waiting months and months and months. And you did say you'd got permission from your commander."

Ian sat up abruptly so that she fell against the pillow. She pushed herself upright against the headboard, the sheet gathered round her chest.

Ian had leaned forward, his back to her. It might have been her imagination, but there appeared to be grim determination in the way he was smoking his cigarette.

"Now, darling," she said, playfully, "you're not to be cross. I won't have it."

He didn't move.

She waited several lifetimes, and slumped a little. The pert expression of disapproval slowly faded. Eventually, when she could bear it no longer, she put out a hand to him. His skin, where it met hers, sang to her of the previous hours. "Are you really cross with me?"

He was silent. He put out his cigarette, then turned back to her, running a hand through his hair. "I don't like you organizing things over my head . . . especially not something as—as important as this."

Now she dropped the sheet, leaned forward and put her arms round his neck. "I'm sorry, darling," she whispered, nuzzling his ear. "I thought you'd be pleased." That wasn't strictly true: even as she had made the appointment, she had known that the flicker of nervousness in the pit of her stomach was not purely anticipation.

"It's a man's place, after all, to arrange these things. You make me feel . . . I don't know, Avice. Who wears the trousers here?" His face was clouded.

"You!" she said, and the last of the sheet dropped away as she slid a slim leg over him.

"This isn't some joke, is it? It's all set up? Guests and everything?"

She lifted her lips from his neck. "Only the Hendersons. Apart from family, I mean. It's not like I organized some huge do without you knowing."

He covered his face with a hand. "I can't believe you did this."

"Oh, Ian, sweetheart, please don't—"

"I can't believe you—"

"You do still want me, don't you, darling?" Her voice, tremulous and a little pleading, suggested more doubt than Avice felt. It had never occurred to her that Ian might change his mind.

"You know I do . . . It's just—"

"You want to make sure you're head of the household. Of course you do! You know I think you're simply masterful. And if we had had more time I would have left it as long as anything. Oh, Ian, don't be cross, darling, please. It's only because I wanted to be Mrs. Radley so badly."

She pressed her nose to his and widened her blue eyes so that he might lose himself in them. "Oh, Ian, darling, I do love you so much."

He had said nothing initially, just submitted to her kisses, her murmured entreaties, the gentle exploration of her hands. Then, slowly, she felt him thaw. "It's only because I love you, darling," she whispered, and as he gave himself up to her, as she slowly became lost, felt their bodies restoring him to her, as the Sleeping Beast awoke, a little part of her reflected with satisfaction that, difficult as these things could sometimes be, through intelligence, charm and a bit of luck, Avice Pritchard usually had her way.

———

He had been a little odd at the wedding. She knew her mother thought so. He had been distracted, selectively deaf, bit his nails even (an unbecoming habit in a grown man). Given that there were only eight of them, and that he was an officer, she had thought his nervousness a little excessive.

"Don't be silly," her father had said. "All grooms are supposed to look like condemned men." Her mother had hit him playfully, and tried to raise a reassuring lipsticked smile.

Deanna had sulked. She had worn a blue suit, almost dark enough to be considered black, and Avice had complained about it to her mother, who had told her not to fuss. "It's very hard for her, you being the first to get married," she had whispered. "Do you understand?"

Avice did. Only too well.

"Still love me?" she had said to him afterward. Their parents had paid for everyone's dinner and a night at the Melbourne Grand. Her mother had wept at the table and told her in a stage whisper, as she and Ian left to go upstairs, that it really wasn't all that bad and it might help if she had a little drink or two first. Avice had smiled—a smile that reassured her mother and irritated the bejaysus out of her sister, to whom it said, I'm going to do It: I shall be a woman before you. She had even been tempted to tell her sister she had already done It the previous evening, but the way Deanna had been lately, she thought she was likely to blab to their mother and that was all she needed.

"Ian? Do you still love me, now that I'm just boring Mrs. Radley?"

They had reached their room. He closed the door behind her, took another swig of his brandy and loosened his collar. "Of course I do," he said. He had seemed more like himself then. He pulled her to him, and slid a warm hand chaotically up her thigh. "I love you to bits, darling girl."

"Forgiven me?"

His attention was already elsewhere. "Of course." He dropped his lips to her neck, and bit her gently. "I told you. I just don't like surprises."

———

"I reckon there's a storm brewing." Jones-the-Welsh checked the barometer at the side of the mess door, and lit another cigarette, then generated a shudder. "I can feel it inside me. Pressure like this—it's got to break some time, right?"

"What do you think that was this morning, Scotch mist?"

"Call that a storm? That was a piss and a fart in a teacup. I'm talking about a proper storm, lads. A real wild woman of a storm. The kind that stands your hair on end, whips you round the chops and shreds your trousers afore you can say, 'Ah, come on now, love. I was just calling you her name for a joke.'"

There was a rumble of laughter from various hammocks. Nicol, lying in his, heard the sound as a dull harbinger of darkening skies. Jones was right. There would be a storm. He felt tense, jittery, as if he had drunk too many cups of Arab coffee. At least, he told himself it was the storm.

In his mind Nicol saw, again, the imprint of that pale face, illu-minated by moonlight. There had been no invitation in her glance, no coquettishness. She was not the kind of woman who considered flirting compensation for the condition of marriage. But there was something in her gaze. Something that told him of an understanding between them. A connection. She *knew* him. That was what he felt.

"Oh, for God's sake," he said aloud, swinging his legs out of the hammock. He had not meant to speak, and as his feet hit the floor he felt self-conscious.

"What's the matter, Nicol, my love?" Jones-the-Welsh put down his letter. "Someone done up your corset too tight? Not arrested enough people lately?"

Nicol closed his eyes. They were sore, gritty. Despite his exhaus-tion, sleep eluded him. It let him chase it through the daytime hours, occasionally suggesting that it would be his. Then as he relaxed, the urge evaporated and left him, with that imprint on the back of his eyelids. And an ache in his soul. How can I think like this? he would ask himself. Me of all people.

"Headache," he said now, rubbing his forehead. "As you said. The pressure."

He had told himself he was incapable of emotion. So shocked by the horrors of war, by the loss of so many around him that, like so many men, he had closed off. Now, forced to examine his behavior honestly, he thought perhaps he had never loved his wife, that he had instead become caught up in expectation, in the idea that he should marry. He had had to—after she had revealed the conse-quence of what they had done. You married, you had your children and you grew old. Your wife grew sour with lack of attention; you grew bitter and introverted for your lost dreams; the children grew up and moved on, promising themselves they would not make the same mistakes. There was no room for wishful thinking, for alternatives. You Got On With It. Perhaps, he thought in his darkest moments, he found it hard to admit that war had freed him from that.

"You know, Nic, the stokers are talking of having a party tonight. Now that the old lady's settled down again." He patted the wall beside him. "I must say, it does seem a waste for all that female talent to miss out on the experience of a bit of good old naval hospitality. I thought I might look in later."

Nicol reached for a boot and began to polish it. "You're a dog," he said.

Jones-the-Welsh let out a joyous woof. "Oh, what's the harm?" he said. "Those who don't want a bit of Welsh rarebit must be proper in love with their old men. So that's lovely. Those who find the sea air has . . ." here he raised an eyebrow ". . . given them a bit of an appetite, probably weren't going to go the distance anyway."

"You can't do it, Jones. They're all married, for God's sake."

"And I'm pretty sure some are already a little less married than they were when they set out. You heard about the episode on B Deck, didn't you? And I was on middle watch outside 6E last night. That girl with the blonde hair's a menace. Won't bloody leave me alone. In and out, in and out . . . 'Ooh, I'm just popping to the bathroom,' dressing-gown hanging open. I'm sure us men are the real victims in these things." He fluttered his eyelashes.

Nicol went back to his boots.

"Ah, come on, Nicol. Don't come over all married and judgmental on us. Just because you're happy living by the rule book doesn't mean the rest of us can't enjoy ourselves a little."

"I think you should leave them alone," he said, closing his ears to the communal "woohoo!" that met his words. There was a creeping lack of respect for the women, even among men he considered honorable, that made him uncomfortable.

"And I think *you* should buck up a bit. Lidders here is coming, aren't you, boy? And Brent and Farthing. Come with us—then you can see we're behaving ourselves."

"I'm on duty."

"Of course you are. Pressed up to that dormitory door listening to those girls pant with longing." He cackled and jumped into his own hammock. "Oh, come on, Nicol. Marines are allowed a bit of fun too. Look . . . think of what we're doing, right, as some kind of service. The entertainment of the Empire's wives. For the benefit of the nation."

With an extravagant salute, Jones leaned back again. By the time Nicol had worked out an appropriately pithy response, Jones had fallen asleep, a lit Senior Service hanging loosely from his hand.

———

The men were boxing on the flight deck. Someone had set up a ring where the Corsairs had sat and in it Dennis Tims was battering several shades of something unrepeatable out of one of the seamen. His naked upper body a taut block of sinewy muscle, he moved without grace or rhythm around the ring. He was an automaton, a machine of destruction, his fists pounding bluntly until the darting, weaving young seaman succumbed and was hauled unconscious through the ropes and away. Four rounds in, there was such a terrible inevitability to his victories that the assembled men and brides were finding it hard to raise the enthusiasm to clap.

Frances, who had found it difficult to watch them, stood with her back to them. Tims, punching, was too close a reminder of the night of Jean's "incident." There was something in the power of his swing, in the brutal set of his jaw as he plowed into the pale flesh presented to him, that made her feel cold, even in this heat. She had wondered, when she and Jean had sat down, whether they should move away, for the younger girl's sake. But Jean's benign interest demonstrated that she had been too drunk to know what Tims had seen—or for that matter, what anyone else had done.

"Hope they don't get too hot and bothered," Jean said now, folding herself neatly into the spot beside Margaret. She seemed to find it difficult to sit still: she had spent the last hour wandering backward and forward between the ringside and their deck-chairs. "Have you heard? The water's run out."

Margaret looked at her. "What?"

"Not drinking water, but the pump isn't working properly and there's no washing—not hair, clothes or anything—until they've mended it. Emergency rations only. Can you imagine? In this weather!" She fanned herself with her hand. "I tell you there's a bloody riot in the bathrooms. That Irene Carter might think she's a right lady, but when her shower stopped you should have heard the language. Would have made old Dennis blush."

Over the past week or so, Jean had recovered her good humor, so much so that her ceaseless and largely inconsequential chatter had taken on a new momentum. "You know Avice is taking Irene on for Queen of the *Victoria*? They've got the Miss Lovely Legs competition this afternoon. Avice has been down to the cases and persuaded the officer to let her get out her best pair of pumps. Four-inch heels in dark green satin to match her bathing suit."

"Oh."

Tims followed an upper cut with a left hook. Then again. And again.

"Are you all right, Maggie?"

Frances handed Margaret the ice-cream she had been proffering, unnoticed, for several seconds, exchanging a brief glance with Jean as she did so.

"It—it's not the baby, is it?"

Margaret turned to them. "No, I'm fine. Honest."

She looked neither of them in the eye.

"Oh, Dennis is in again. I'm going to see if anyone wants to have a wager with me. Mind you, I can't see that anyone's going to offer odds against him. Not at this rate." Jean got up, straightened her skirt, and skipped over to the other onlookers.

Margaret and Frances sat in silence with their ices. In the distance, a tanker moved across the horizon, and they followed its steady progress until it was no longer visible.

"What's that?"

Margaret looked at the letter in her hand, evidently having realized that the name of the addressee was showing.

Frances said nothing, but there was a question in her eyes. "Were you . . . going to throw it into the water?"

Margaret gazed out at the turquoise waves.

"It . . . would be a nice thing to do. I had a patient once whose sweetheart got bombed, back in Germany. He wrote her a goodbye letter and we put it into a bottle and dropped it over the side of the hospital ship."

"I was going to post it," Margaret said.

Frances looked back at the envelope, checked that she'd read the name correctly. Then she turned to Margaret, perplexed. Behind her, voices were raised in shock at some misdemeanor in the ring, but she kept her eyes on the woman beside her.

"I lied," said Margaret. "I let you think she was dead but she's not. She left us. She's been gone nearly two and a half years."

"Your mother?"

"Yup." She waved the letter. "I don't know why I brought it up here."

Then Margaret began to talk, at first quietly, and then as if she no longer cared who heard.

It had been a shock. That much was an understatement. They had come home one day to find dinner bubbling on the stove, the shirts neatly pressed over the range, the floors mopped and polished and a note. She couldn't take it anymore, she had written. She had waited until Margaret's brothers were home from the war, and Daniel had hit fourteen and become a man, and now she considered her job done. She loved them all, but she had to claw back a little bit of life for herself, while she still had some left. She hoped they would understand, but she expected they wouldn't.

She had got Fred Bridgeman to pick her up and drop her at the station, and she had gone, taking with her only a suitcase of clothes, forty-two dollars in savings, and two of the good photographs of the children from the front parlor.

"Mr. Leader at the ticket office said she'd got the train to Sydney. From there she could have gone anywhere. We figured she'd come back when she was ready. But she never did. Daniel took it hardest."

Frances took Margaret's hand.

"Afterward, I suppose, we could all have seen the signs. But you don't look, do you? Mothers are meant to be exhausted, fed up. They're meant to shout a lot and then apologize. They're meant to get headaches. I suppose we all thought she was part of the furniture."

"Did you ever hear from her?"

"She wrote a few times, and Dad wrote begging her to come back, but when she didn't, he stopped. Pretty quickly, come to think of it. He couldn't cope with the idea of her not loving him anymore. Once they accepted she wasn't coming back, the boys wouldn't write at all. So . . . he just . . . they . . . behaved as if she had died. It was easier than admitting the truth." She paused. "She's only written once this year. Maybe I'm a reminder of something she wants to forget, guilt she doesn't want to feel. Sometimes I think the kindest thing I could do would be to let her go." She turned the envelope in her free hand.

"I'm sure she wouldn't want to cause you pain," said Frances, quietly.

"But she is. All the time."

"You can get in touch with her, though. I mean, once she hears where you are, who knows? She might write more often."

"It's not the letters." Margaret threw the envelope on to the deck.

Frances fought the urge to pin it down with something. She didn't want a stray breeze to take it overboard.

"It's everything. It's her—her and me."

"But she said she loved you—"

"You don't get it. I'm her daughter, right?"

"Yes . . . but—"

"So what am I meant to feel, if motherhood is so bad that my mum had always been desperate to run away?" She rubbed swollen fingers across her eyes. "What if, Frances, what if when this thing is born, what if when this baby finally gets here . . . I feel exactly the same?"

———

The weather had broken at almost four thirty, just as the boxing finished—or as Tims grew bored: it was hard to say which. The first large drops of rain landed heavily on the deck, and the women had swiftly disappeared, exclaiming from under sunhats or folded magazines, sweeping their belongings into bags and scurrying, like ants, below decks.

Margaret had retreated to the cabin to check on the dog, and Frances sat with Jean in the deck canteen, watching the rain trickling through the salt on the windows and into the rusting frames. Only a few brides had chosen to stay on deck, even under the relative shelter of the canteen: a storm on the sea was a different prospect from one on land. Faced with 360-degree visibility and nothing between human life and the endless expanse of rolling gray seas, with the thunderous clouds coming relentlessly from the south, it was possible to feel too exposed.

Margaret had seemed a little better once she'd spoken out. She had wept a little, crossly blamed the baby for it, and then, smiling, had apologized, several times. Frances had felt helpless. She had wanted to tell her a little about her own family, but felt that to do so would require further explanation, which she wasn't prepared to give, even to Margaret. The other woman's friendship had become valuable to her, which made her vulnerable. Also, it brought with it a sense of foreboding. She toyed with the metal spoon in her empty cup, hearing the ship groan, the sheets of metal straining against each other like fault lines before an earthquake. Outside the lashings clanked disconsolately, and the rain ran in tidal rivers off the deck.

Where is he now? she thought. Is he sleeping? Dreaming of his children? His wife? Just as Margaret's friendship had introduced new emotions into her life, so thoughts of the marine's family now brought out something in her that filled her with shame.

She was jealous. She had felt it first on the night that Margaret had spoken to Joe on the radio; hearing their exchange, seeing the way Margaret had been illuminated by the mere prospect of a few words, made Frances aware of a huge chasm in her own life. She had felt a sadness that wasn't, for once, assuaged by the sight of the ocean. Now, a sense of loss was sharpened by the thought of the marine and his family. She had thought of him as a friend, a kindred spirit. It was as much as she had ever expected of a man. Now she found it had crossed into something she couldn't identify, some nagging impression of separation.

She thought of her husband, "Chalkie" Mackenzie. What she had felt on first meeting him had been quite different. She put down the spoon and forced herself to look at the other women. I won't do this, she told herself. There is no point in hankering for things you can't have. That you have never been able to have. She made herself think back to the beginning of the voyage, to a time when the mere fact of the journey was enough. She had been satisfied then, hadn't she?

"The cook says it's not going to be a bad one," said Jean, returning to the table with two cups of tea. She sounded almost disappointed. "This is about as rough as it's going to get, apparently. Shame. I didn't mind all that rocking when we came through the Bight. Once I stopped chucking my guts up, anyway. Still, he says we'll probably get more bad weather once we get the other side of the Suez Canal."

Frances was getting used to Jean's perverse enthusiasms. "There can't be too many other passengers praying for rough weather."

"I am. I want a real humdinger of a storm. One I can tell Stan about. Oh, I know we won't feel much on a big old girl like this, but I'd like to sit up here and watch. A bit of excitement, you know? Like the movies, but real. Far as I'm concerned, it's all getting a bit boring."

Frances gazed out of the window. Some unfathomable distance away bolts of lightning illuminated the skies. The rain was heavier now, hammering on the metal roof so that they had to speak up to be heard. On the other side of the canteen several brides were pointing at the distant horizon.

"Oh, come on, Frances. You like a bit of excitement too, don't you? Look at that lightning! You telling me that doesn't get you a bit—you know?" Jean jiggled on her seat. "I mean, look at it."

Just for a moment, Frances allowed herself to see the squall as Jean did, to let its raw energy flood over her, illuminate her, charge her up. But the habits of years were too strong, and when she turned to Jean, her demeanor was calm, measured. "You might want to be careful what you wish for," she said. But she kept her eyes on the distant storm.

They were about to leave, standing beside each other at the canteen doorway, waiting for the rain to ease off a little so that they could bolt toward the hatch that led down to the cabins, when the rating arrived. He pushed through the door, dripping wet after having made the short journey across the deck, bringing with him a gust of the rain-soaked cool air.

"I'm looking for a Jean Castleforth," he said, reading from a piece of paper. "Jean Castleforth." His voice had been portentous.

"That's me." Jean grabbed the man's arm. "Why?"

The rating's expression was unreadable. "You've been called to the captain's office, madam." Then, as Jean stood still, her expression rigid, he said to Frances, as if Jean were no longer there, "She's one of the young ones, right? I've been told it's best if someone comes with her."

Those words halted any further questions. He led them on what Frances thought afterward was the longest short walk of her life. Suddenly heedless of the rain, they strode briskly across the hangar deck, past the torpedo store, and up some stairs until they reached a door. The rating rapped on it sharply. When he heard, "Enter," he opened it, stood back, one arm out, and they walked in. At some point during the walk, Jean had slid her hand into Frances's and was now gripping it tightly.

The room, set on three sides with windows, was much brighter than the narrow passageway and they blinked. Three people were silhouetted against one of the windows, and two faced them. Frances noted absently that the floor was carpeted, unlike anywhere else on the ship.

She saw with alarm that the chaplain was there, then recognized the women's officer who had come across them that night in the engine area. The temperature seemed to drop and she shivered.

Jean's eyes darted round the grim faces in front of her and she was shaking convulsively. "Something has happened to him, hasn't it?" she said. "Oh, God, you're going to tell me something's happened to him. Is he all right? Tell me, is he all right?"

The captain exchanged a brief look with the chaplain, then stepped forward and handed Jean a telegram.

"I'm very sorry, my dear," he said.

Jean looked at the telegram, then up at the captain. "M . . . H . . . Is that an H?" She traced the letters with her finger. "A? You read it for me," she said, and thrust it at Frances. Her hand shook so much that the paper made a rattling sound.

Frances took it in her left hand, keeping hold of Jean's hand in the other. The girl's grip was now so tight that the blood was pooling in her fingertips.

She took in the content of the telegram a second before she read it out. The words dropped from her mouth like stones. "'Have heard about behavior on board. No future for us.'" She swallowed. "'Not Wanted Don't Come.'"

Jean stared at the telegram, then at Frances.

"What?" she said, into the silence. Then: "Read it again."

Frances wished that in the telling of those words there was some way to soften their impact.

"I don't understand," said Jean.

"News travels between ships," said the WSO, quietly. "Someone must have told one of the other carriers when we docked at Ceylon."

"But no one knew. Apart from you . . ."

"When we spoke to your husband's superiors to verify the telegram, they said he was rather disturbed by news of your pregnancy." She paused. "I understand that, according to your given dates, it would be impossible for him to be the father." The woman spoke cruelly, Frances thought, as if she were pleased to have found some other stick with which to beat Jean. As if the Not Wanted Don't Come had not been sufficiently damaging.

Jean had gone white. "But I'm not pregnant—that was—"

"I think in the circumstances, he probably feels that is irrelevant."

"But I haven't had a chance to explain to him. I need to speak to him. He's got it all wrong."

Frances stepped in. "It wasn't her fault. Really. It was a misunderstanding."

The woman's expression said she had heard this many times. The men just looked embarrassed.

"I'm sorry," said the captain. "We have spoken to the Red Cross and arrangements will be put in place for your passage back to Australia. You will disembark at—"

Jean, with the ferocity of a whirlwind, launched herself at the women's officer, fists in tight balls. "You bitch! You fucking old bitch!" Before Frances dived in she had landed several flailing punches on the woman's head. "You vindictive old whore! Just because you couldn't find anyone!" she screamed. She was heedless of the men trying to pull her away, to Frances's entreaties. "I never did nothing!" she shouted, tears streaming down her cheeks, as Frances and the chaplain held her back, faces flushed with effort. "I never did nothing! You've got to tell Stan!"

The air had been sucked from the room. Even the captain looked shocked. He had stepped back.

"Shall I take them back, sir?" The rating had entered the room, Frances saw.

Jean had subsided.

The captain nodded. "It would be best. I'll have someone talk to you about the . . . arrangements . . . a little later. When things have . . . calmed down."

"Sir," said Frances, breathing hard, holding the shaking girl in her arms. "With respect, you have done her a great disservice." Her head whirled with the unfairness of it. "She was a victim in this."

"You're a nurse, not a lawyer," hissed the women's officer, one hand at her bleeding head. "I saw. Or have you forgotten?"

It was too late. As Frances led Jean out of the captain's office, supported—or perhaps restrained—on the other side by the rating, she could just hear, over the noise of Jean's sobbing, the woman officer: "I can't say it surprises me," she was saying, her voice querulous, self-justifying. "I was told before we set out. Warned, I should say. Those Aussie girls are all the same."

14

If you receive the personal kit of a relative or friend in the Forces, it does not mean that he is either killed or missing . . . Thousands of men, before going overseas, packed up most of their personal belongings and asked for them to be sent home. The official advice to you is: "Delivery of parcels is no cause for worry unless information is also sent by letter or telegram to next of kin from official sources."

DAILY MAIL, MONDAY, 12 JUNE 1944

TWENTY-THREE DAYS

Jean was taken off the ship during a brief, unscheduled stop at Cochin. No one else was allowed to disembark, but several brides watched as she climbed into the little boat, and, refusing to look at them, was motored toward the shore, an officer of the Red Cross beside her, her bag and trunk balanced at the other end. She didn't wave.

Frances, who had held her that first evening through tears and hysteria, then sat with her as her mood gave way to something darker, had tried and failed to think of a way to right the situation. Margaret had gone as far as asking to see the captain. He had been very nice, she said afterward, but if the husband didn't want her anymore, there wasn't a lot he could do. He hadn't actually said, "Orders are orders," but that was what he had meant. She had wanted to wring that bloody WSO's neck, she said.

"We could write to her husband," said Frances. But there was an awful lot to explain, not all of which they could do with any degree of accuracy. And how much to tell?

As Jean lay sleeping, the two women had composed a letter they felt was both truthful and diplomatic. They would send it at the next postal stop. Both knew, although neither said, that it was unlikely to make any difference. They could just, if they shielded their eyes from the sun, make out the boat as it came to a halt by the jetty. There were two figures waiting under what looked like an umbrella, one of whom took Jean's cases, the other of whom helped her on to dry land. It was impossible, at this distance, to see any more than that.

"It wasn't my fault," said Avice, when the silence became oppressive. "You don't need to look at me like that."

Margaret wiped her eyes and made her way heavily inside. "It's just bloody sad," she said.

Frances said nothing.

———

She had not been a beautiful girl, or even a particularly pleasant one. But Captain Highfield found that in the days that followed he could not get Jean Castleforth's face out of his mind. It had been uncomfortably like dealing with a POW, the putting ashore, the handing over into safe custody. The look of impotent fury, despair, and, finally, sullen resignation on her face.

Several times he had asked himself whether he had done the right thing. The brides had been so adamant, and the nurse's tones of quiet outrage haunted him still: "You have done her a great disservice." But what else could he have done? The WSO had been certain of what she'd seen. He had to trust his company—the same company he had warned that he would tolerate no such misbehavior. And, as the officer had said, if the husband no longer wanted her, what business was it of theirs?

And yet those two faces—the tall thin girl with her vehement accusation, and the raw grief on the face of the little one—made him wonder how much they were asking of these women, to travel so far on a promise based on so little. To put them in the face of such temptation. That was if it had been temptation at all . . .

The removal of the girl—the second to be taken off in such circumstances—had cast a pall over the ship. He could tell the brides felt more insecure than ever. They cast sidelong glances at him as he moved along the decks on his rounds, huddled into doorways as if fearful he might consign them to the same fate. The chaplain had attempted to address the women's fears with a few carefully chosen words during devotions but that had only added to their heightened anxiety. The women's officers, meanwhile, were ostracized. The brides, having heard of Jean's treatment, had chosen to express their contempt in various ways, some more vocal than others, and now several of the women's officers had come to him in tears.

Several weeks ago he would have told them all to pull themselves together. Now he felt bleak sympathy. This was not misbehavior: the brides were not on some great adventure. They were essentially powerless. And such powerlessness could invoke unusual emotions both in those who experienced it and the onlookers.

Besides, he had other concerns. The ship, as if she had heard of her own planned fate, had suffered a series of breakdowns. The rudder had jammed, necessitating an emergency switch to steam steering, for the third time in the past ten days. The water shortage continued, with the engineers unable to work out why the desalination pumps kept breaking down. He was supposed to pick up a further fourteen civilian passengers at Aden, including the governor of Gibraltar and his wife who had been visiting the port, for passage back to their residence, and was not sure how he was going to cater for them all. And he was finding it increasingly hard to disguise his limp. Dobson had asked him pointedly if he was "quite all right" the previous day and he had been forced to put his full weight on it even though it throbbed so hard he had had to bite the inside of his cheek to contain himself. He had considered going to the infirmary and seeing if there was something he could take; he held the keys, after all. But he had no idea what medicine he should use, and the prospect of doing further damage to it made him wince. Three more weeks, he told himself. Three more weeks, if I can hang on that long.

And that, in the end, was why he decided to hold the dance. A good captain did everything in his power to ensure the happiness and well-being of his passengers. A bit of music and some carefully monitored mixing would do everyone good. And he, of all people, understood the need for a diversion.

————

Maude Gonne was not well. Perhaps it was the subdued mood of the little cabin, which seemed empty without Jean's effervescent presence, that had drawn her down. Perhaps it was simply the effect of several weeks of poor food and confinement in the heat. She had little appetite and was listless. She was barely interested in her trips to the bathroom or late-night flits around the deck, no longer sniffing the unfamiliar salt air from under whatever disguise they chose to carry her. She had lost weight and felt damningly light, her frame insubstantial.

Frances sat on her bunk, one hand gently stroking the little dog's head as she wheezed her way into sleep, milky eyes half closed. Occasionally, perhaps remembering Frances's presence, she would wag her tail as if politely affirming her gratitude. She was a sweet old dog.

Margaret blamed herself. She should never have brought her, she had told Frances. She should have thought about the heat, the perpetual confinement, and left her in the only home she knew, with her dad's dogs and endless green spaces where she was happy. Frances knew that Margaret's uncharacteristic neurosis echoed the silent undercurrent of her thoughts: If she couldn't even look after a little dog properly, then what hope . . . ?

"Let's take her for a walk upstairs," she said.

"What?" Margaret shifted on her bunk.

"We'll pop her in your basket and put a scarf over the top. There's a gun turret a bit further on from the bathroom where no one ever goes. Why don't we sit out there for a bit and Maudie can enjoy some proper daytime fresh air?"

She could tell that Margaret was nervous about the idea, but she had few other options.

"Look, do you want me to take her?" Frances said, seeing how exhausted Margaret was. Discomfort meant she hadn't slept properly for days.

"Would you? I could do with a nap."

"I'll keep her out as long as I can."

She walked swiftly down to C Deck, conscious that if she looked confident in what she was doing no one was likely to stop her. Several brides were now undertaking duties on the ship, clerical work, and cooking. Some had even joined the recently formed Brides' Painting Party, and the sight of a woman on a deck previously considered the domain of service personnel was not as irregular as it might have been two weeks previously.

She opened the little hatch, then ducked, stepped out and propped it open behind her. The day was bright, the heat balmy but not oppressive. A gentle breeze lifted the silk scarf on Frances's basket and swiftly a small black nose poked out, twitching.

"There you go, old girl," Frances murmured. "See if that helps."

Several minutes later, Maude Gonne had eaten a biscuit and a scrap of bacon, the first morsels in which she had shown interest for two days.

She sat there with the dog on her lap for almost an hour, watching the waves rush by beneath her, listening to snatches of conversation and occasional laughter from the flight deck above, punctuated by the odd summons from the Tannoy. Although her clothes, unwashed for several days, felt stale and, occasionally, the movement of her body sent up scents that made her long for a bath, she knew she would miss this ship. Its noises had become familiar enough to be comforting. She wasn't even sure whether, like everyone else, she wanted to disembark at Aden.

She had not seen the marine in two days.

Another marine had been on duty the previous evenings, and even though she had spent an unusual amount of time wandering the length of the ship, he had failed to materialize. She wondered, briefly, if he was ill and felt anxious about the prospect of him being treated by Dr. Duxbury. Then she told herself to stop being ridiculous: it was probably for the best that she hadn't seen him. She had felt disturbed enough by Jean's removal without an impossible schoolgirl crush.

But almost an hour later, as she prepared to step inside, she found herself leaping back. His face was pale where many of his colleagues now sported Pacific tans, his eyes still shadowed, betraying sleepless nights, but it was him. The easy movement of his shoulders, square in his khaki uniform, suggested a strength she had not seen when he was immobile outside the door. He was holding a kitbag on his shoulder and she was paralyzed by the thought that he might be preparing to disembark.

Not sure what she was doing, Frances slid back against the wall, her hand to her chest, listening for his steps as he moved past her down the gangway. He was several paces beyond her when they slowed. Frances, inexplicably holding her breath, realized that he was going to stop. The door opened a little, his head came round, a couple of feet from hers, and he smiled. It was a genuine smile, one which seemed to rub the angles from his face. "You all right?" he said.

She had no words to explain her hiding-place. She was aware that she had blushed and made as if to say something, then nodded.

He gave her a searching look, then glanced down at the basket. "That who I think it is?" he murmured. The sound of his voice made her skin prickle.

"She's not too well," she replied. "I thought she needed fresh air."

"Make sure you stay well away from D Deck. There's inspections going on and all sorts." He glanced behind him, as if to make sure no one else was around. "I'm sorry about your friend," he said. "It didn't seem right."

"It wasn't," she said. "None of it was her fault. She's only a child."

"Well, the Navy can be an unforgiving host." He reached out and touched her arm lightly. "You okay, though?" She blushed again, and he tried to correct himself. "I mean the rest of you? You're all right?"

"Oh, we're fine," she said.

"You don't need anything? Extra drinking water? More crackers?"

There were three lines at the corners of his eyes. When he spoke, they deepened, testament to years of salt air, perhaps, or of squinting at the sky.

"Are you going somewhere?" she asked, pointing to his bag. Anything to stop herself staring at him.

"Me? No . . . It's just my good uniform."

"Oh."

"I'm off again tonight," he said. He smiled at her, as if this were something good. "For the dance?"

"I'm sorry?"

"You haven't heard? There's a dance on the flight deck tonight. Captain's orders."

"Oh!" she exclaimed, more loudly than she'd intended. "Oh! Good!"

"I hope they turn the water on for a bit first." He grinned. "You girls will all run a mile faced with the scent of a thousand sweaty matelots."

She glanced down at her creased trousers, but his attention had switched to a distant figure.

"I'll see you up there," he said, his marine mask back in place. With a nod that could almost have been a salute, he was gone.

———

The Royal Marines Band sat on their makeshift pedestal outside the deck canteen, a little way distant of the ship's island, and struck up with "I've Got You Under My Skin." The *Victoria's* engines were shut down for repairs and she floated serene and immobile in the placid waters. On the deck, several hundred brides in their finest dresses— at least, the finest to which they had been allowed access—were whirling around, some with the men and others, giggling, with each other. Around the island, tables and chairs had been brought up from the dining area, and were occupied by those unable or unwilling to keep dancing. Above them, in the Indian sky, the stars glittered like ballroom lights, bathing the seas with silver.

It could have been—if one bent one's imagination a little and ig- nored the presence of the guns, the scarred deck, the rickety tables and chairs—any of the grand ballrooms of Europe. The captain had felt an unlikely joy in the spectacle, feeling it (sentimentally, he had to admit) no less than the old girl deserved in her final voyage. A bit of pomp and finery. A bit of a do.

The men, in their best drill uniform, were looking more cheerful than they had done for days, while the brides—mutinous after the temporary closure of the hair salon—had also perked up considerably, thanks to the introduction of emergency salt-water showers. It had been good for them all to have an excuse to dress up a bit, he thought. Even the men liked parading in their good tropical kit.

They sat in now well-established huddles or chatted in groups, the men temporarily unconcerned by the lack of defining rank structure. What the hell? Highfield had thought, when he was asked by one of the women's service officers if he wanted to enforce "proper" separation. This voyage was already something extraordinary.

"How long does the *Victoria* take to refuel, Captain Highfield?"

Beside him sat one of the passengers, a little Wren to whom Dobson had introduced him half an hour earlier. She was small, dark and intensely serious, and had quizzed him so lengthily about the specifications of his ship that he had been tempted to ask her if she was spying for the Japanese. But he hadn't. Somehow she hadn't looked the type to have a sense of humor.

"Do you know? I don't think I could tell you offhand," he lied.

"A little longer than your boys do," muttered Dr. Duxbury, and laughed.

In thanks for their fortitude over the water situation, Captain Highfield had promised everyone extra "sippers" of rum. Just to warm up the evening a little, he had announced, to cheers. He suspected, however, that Dr. Duxbury had somehow obtained more than his allotted share.

What the hell? he thought again. The man would be gone soon. His leg was painful enough tonight for him to consider taking extra sippers himself. If the water situation had been different he would have placed it in a bath of cold water—which seemed to ease it a little—but instead he was in for another near sleepless night.

"Did you serve alongside many of the U.S. carriers?" the little Wren asked. "We came up alongside the USS *Indiana* in the Persian Gulf, and I must say those American ships do seem far superior to ours."

"Know much about ships, do you?" said Dr. Duxbury.

"I should hope so," she said. "I've been a Wren for four years."

Dr. Duxbury didn't appear to have heard. "You have a look of Judy Garland about you. Has anyone ever told you that? Did you ever see her in *Me and My Girl?*"

"I'm afraid not."

Here we go, thought Captain Highfield. He had already endured several dinners with his proxy medic, at least half of which had culminated in the man singing his terrible ditties. He talked of music so much and medicine so little that Highfield wondered if the Navy should have checked his credentials more carefully before taking him on. Despite his misgivings, he had not requested a second doctor, as he might have on previous voyages. He realized, with a twinge of conscience, that Duxbury's distraction suited him: he did not want an efficient sort asking too many questions about his leg.

He took a last look at the merriment in front of him; the band had struck up a reel and the girls were whooping and spinning, faces flushed and feet light. Then he looked at Dobson and the marine captain, who were talking to a flight captain over by the lifeboats. His work was done. They could take over from here. He had never been a great one for parties anyway.

"Excuse me," he said, pushing himself upright painfully, "I've got to attend to a little matter," and with that he went back inside.

———

"Jean would have loved this," said Margaret. Seated in a comfortable chair that Dennis Tims had brought up from the officers' lounge, a light shawl round her shoulders, she was beaming. A good sleep and Maude Gonne's recovery had significantly lifted her mood.

"Poor Jean," said Frances. "I wonder what she's doing."

Avice, a short distance away, was dancing with one of the white-clad officers. Her hair, carefully set in the salon, gleamed honey under the arc-lights, while her neat waist and elaborate gathered skirt betrayed nothing of her condition.

"I don't think your woman there is worrying too much, do you?" Margaret nodded.

Not two hours after Jean had gone, Avice had appropriated her bunk for storage of the clothes and shoes she wanted brought up from her trunk.

Frances had been so enraged that she had had to fight the compulsion to dump them all on the floor. "What's the matter?" Avice had protested. "It's not like she needs it now."

She was still celebrating having won that afternoon's cleverest-use-of-craft-materials competition with her decorated evening bag. Not, she told the girls afterward, that she would have had it within six feet of her on a night out. The important thing had been beating Irene Carter. She was now two points ahead of her for the Queen of the *Victoria* title.

"I don't think she worries about anything—" Frances stopped herself.

"Let's not think about it tonight, eh? Nothing we can do now."

"No," said Frances.

She had never been particularly interested in clothes, had fallen with relief into her uniform for almost as long as she could remember. She had never wanted to draw attention to herself. Now she smoothed her skirt: in comparison with the peacock finery of the other women, the dress she had once considered smart now looked dowdy. On a whim, she had released her hair from its tight knot at the back of her head, staring at herself in the little mirror, seeing how, as it hung loose on her shoulders, it softened her face. Now, with all the carefully set styles around her, the product of hours spent with rollers and setting lotion, she felt unsophisticated, unfinished, and wished for the reassurance of her hairpins. She wondered if she could voice her fears to Margaret, seek reassurance. But the sight of her friend's perspiring face and swollen frame, squeezed into the same gingham dress she had worn for the last four days, stopped the question on her lips. "Can I get you a drink?" she said instead.

"You beauty! Thought you'd never ask," Margaret said companionably. "I'd fetch them myself, but it'd take a crane to hoist me out of this chair."

"I'll get you some soda."

"Bless you! Do you not want to dance?"

Frances stopped. "What?"

"You don't have to stay with me, you know. I'm a big girl. Go and enjoy yourself."

Frances wrinkled her nose. "I'm happier at the edge of things."

Margaret nodded, lifted a hand.

It wasn't strictly true. Tonight, protected by the semi-darkness, by the sweetened atmosphere and lack of attention afforded her by the music, Frances had felt a creeping longing to be one of those girls whirling around on the dance floor. No one would judge her for it. No one would pay her any attention. They all seemed to accept it for what it was: an innocent diversion, a simple pleasure stolen under the moonlight.

She collected two glasses of soda and returned to Margaret, who was watching the dancers.

"I never was one for dancing," said Margaret, "yet looking at that lot right now I'd give anything to be up there."

Frances nodded toward Margaret's belly. "Not long," she said. "Then you can foxtrot half-way across England."

She had told herself it didn't matter, not seeing him. That, looking like she did, she might even prefer it. He was probably lost in that dark crowd, dancing with some pretty girl in a brightly colored dress and satin shoes. Anyway, she had become so used to pushing men away that she wouldn't have known how to behave otherwise.

The only dances she had been to in her adult life had been in hospital wards; those had been easy. She had either danced with her colleagues, who were generally old friends and kept a respectful distance, or with patients, to whom she felt vaguely maternal, and who generally retained an air of deference for anyone "medical." She would often find herself murmuring to them to "watch that leg," or checking whether they were still comfortable as they crossed the floor. The matron, Audrey Marshall, had joked that it was as if she was taking them for a medicinal promenade. She wouldn't have known how to behave, faced with these laughing, cocky men, some so handsome in their dress uniforms that her breath caught in her throat. She wouldn't have known how to make small-talk, or flirt without intent. She would have felt too self-conscious in her dull pale blue dress beside everyone else's glorious gowns.

"Hello there," he said, seating himself beside her. "I wondered where I might find you."

She could barely speak. His dark eyes looked steadily out at her from a face softened by the night. She could detect the faint scent of carbolic on his skin, the characteristic smell of the fabric of his uniform. His hand lay on the table in front of her and she fought an irrational urge to touch it.

"I wondered if you'd like to dance," he said.

She stared at that hand, faced with the prospect of it resting on her waist, of his body close to hers, and felt a swell of panic. "No," she said abruptly. "Actually, I—I was just leaving."

There was a brief silence.

"It is late," he conceded. "I was hoping to get up here earlier, but we had a bit of an incident downstairs in the kitchens, and a few of us got called to sort it out."

"Thank you, anyway," she said. "I hope you enjoy the rest of your evening." There was a lump in her throat. She gathered up her things, and he stood up to let her pass.

"Don't go," said Margaret.

Frances spun round.

"Go on. For God's sake, woman, you've kept me company all bloody night and now the least you can do is have a turn round the dance floor. Let me see what I'm missing."

"Margaret, I'm sorry but I—"

"Sorry but what? Ah, go on, Frances. There's no point in both of us being wallflowers. Shake a leg, as our dear friend would have said. One for Jean."

She looked back at him, then at the crowded deck, the endless whirl of white and color, unsure whether she was fearful of entering the throng or of being so close to him.

"Get on with it, woman."

He was still beside her. "A quick one?" he said, holding out his arm. "It would be my pleasure."

Not trusting herself to speak, she took it.

———

She wouldn't think tonight about the impossibility of it all. About the fact that she was feeling something she had long told herself it was unsafe to feel. About the fact that there would inevitably be a painful consequence. She just closed her eyes, lay back on her bunk, and allowed herself to sink into those moments she had stored deep inside: the four dances in which he had held her, one hand clasping hers, the other resting on her waist; of how, during the last, even as he kept himself, correctly, several inches from her, she could feel his breath against her bare neck.

Of how he had looked at her when he let go. Had there been reluctance in the way his hand had separated slowly from hers? Did it hurt anyone for her to imagine there had been? Was there not a strange emphasis on the way he'd lowered his head to hers and said, so quietly, "Thank you"?

What she felt for him shocked and shamed her. Yet the discovery of her capacity to feel as she did made her want to sing. The chaotic, overpowering emotions she had experienced this evening made her wonder if she was in the grip of some seaborne virus. She had never felt so feverish, so incapable of efficiently gathering her thoughts. She bit down on her hand, trying to stop the bubble of hysteria rising in her chest and threatening to explode into God only knew what. She forced herself to breathe deeply, tried to restore the inner calm that had provided solace in the last six years.

It was just a dance. "A dance," she whispered to herself, pulling the sheet over her head. Why can't you be grateful for that?

She heard footsteps, then men's voices. Someone was talking to the marine outside the door, a young substitute with red hair and sleepy eyes. She lay, only half listening, wondering if it was time for the watch to change. Then she sat up.

It was him. She sat very still for a minute longer, checking that she was not mistaken, then slid out of her bunk, her heart hammering in her chest. She thought of Jean and grew cold. Perhaps she had been so blinded by her own attraction to him that she had not seen what was before her.

She placed her ear to the door.

"What do you think?" he was saying.

"It's been a good hour," the other marine replied, "but I don't suppose you've got a choice."

"I don't like it," he said. "I don't like doing it at all."

She stepped back from the door, and as she did, the handle turned and it opened quietly. His face slid round it, an echo of its earlier self, and he had caught her there, shocked and pale in the illuminated sliver of the passage lights.

"I heard voices," she said, conscious of her state of undress. She grappled behind her for her wrap, and flung it on, tying it tightly around her.

"I'm sorry to disturb you," his voice was low and urgent, "but there's been an accident downstairs. I was wondering— Look, we need your help."

The dance had ended in several unofficial gatherings in various parts of the ship. One had emigrated to the sweaty confines of the rear port-side engine room, where a stoker had been waltzing a bride along one of the walkways that flanked the main engine. The accounts he'd had so far were unclear, but they had fallen into the pit that contained the engine. The man was unconscious; the bride had a nasty cut on her face.

"We can't call the ship's doctor for obvious reasons. But we need to get them out of there before the watch changes." He hesitated. "We thought . . . I thought you might help."

She wrapped her arms round herself. "I'm sorry," she whispered. "I can't go down there. You'll have to get someone else."

"I'll be there. I'll stay with you."

"It's not that . . ."

"You don't need to worry, I promise. They know you're a nurse."

She had looked into his eyes, then, and understood what he thought he was saying.

"There's no one else who can help," he said, and glanced at his watch. "We've only got about twenty minutes. Please, Frances."

He had never used her name before. She hadn't been aware he knew it.

Margaret's voice cut quietly through the darkness. "I'll come with you. I'll stay with you. If you'd feel better with a few of us around you."

She was in an agony of indecision, thrown by his nearness.

"Just have a look at them, please. If it's really bad we'll wake the doctor."

"I'll get my kit," she said. She reached under her bunk for the tin box. Opposite, Margaret got up heavily and put on a dressing-gown that now barely stretched round her belly. She gave Frances's arm a discreet squeeze.

"Where are you going?" said Avice, and pulled the light cord. She sat up, blinking sleepily as they were thrown into the light.

"Just for a breath of fresh air," said Margaret.

"I wasn't born yesterday."

"We're going to help a couple of people who have been hurt downstairs," said Margaret. "Come with us, if you want."

Avice looked at them, as if weighing up whether to go.

"It's the least you could do," said Margaret.

She slid off her bunk and into her peach silk robe, walked past the marine, who held the door back, a finger to his lips, and followed them as they went silently down the passageway toward the stairs.

Behind them, the red-headed marine shuffled back into place, guarding a cabin that was now empty but for a sleeping dog.

———

They heard the voices before they saw them: from deep in the belly of the ship, down what seemed to Margaret endless flights of stairs and narrow corridors until they reached the rear port-side engine room. The heat was intense; struggling to keep up with the others, she found herself short of breath and frequently had to wipe her brow with her sleeve. Her mouth tasted of oil. And then they heard a shrill weeping, punctuated by a hushed commotion of voices, male and female, some arguing, some cajoling, all underlaid by a momentous thumping and clanging, the sound of the great heart of the beast. Perhaps in response to the noise, Frances's pace quickened and she half ran, with the marine, along the passageway.

Margaret reached the engine room several seconds after everyone else. When she finally opened the hatch, the heat was such that she had to stand still for a moment to acclimatize.

She stepped on to the walkway inside and looked down, following the sound. Some fifteen feet below them, in a huge pit in the floor a little like a sunken boxing ring, a young seaman was half lying on the ground, his back to the wall, supported on one side by a weeping bride and on the other by a friend. A game of cards had apparently been abandoned on a crate in the corner and several upturned beakers lay on the floor. In the center a huge engine—a labyrinthine organ of pipes and valves—pumped and ground a regular, deafening beat from its huge metal parts, its valves hissing steam periodically as if to some infernal tune. On the far side, tucked under the walkway, another bride held the side of her face and wept. "What's he going to say, though? What will he think of me?"

Ahead, Frances was running toward the ladder that led down into the bowels of the engine, her feet silent on the ribbed metal floor. She pushed her way through the drunken crowd, fell to her knees and examined what lay beneath the blood-soaked dirty cloth wrapped round the man's arm.

Margaret leaned on the metal cable that acted as a safety rail to watch as one of the other girls peeled the injured woman's hand off her head and dabbed a livid wound with a wet cloth. Several ratings hovered at the edge of the scene, still in their good uniforms, pulling away oversized oxygen canisters and bits of guard rail. Two smoked with the deep breaths of those in shock. Around the walls the engine's pipes glowed in the dim light.

"He went over and the canisters fell on him," one man was shouting. "I couldn't tell you where they hit him. We're lucky the whole lot didn't go up."

"How long has he been unconscious?" Frances's voice was raised to be heard over the engine. "Who else is hurt?" There was no caution in her demeanor now: she was galvanized.

Beside her, the marine, loosening his good bootneck collar, was following her instructions, searching out items in her medical kit. He called instructions to the remaining seamen, two of whom darted back up the ladder, apparently glad to be out of the way.

Avice was standing on the walkway with her back to the wall. The uneasy look on her face told Margaret that she had already decided this was not a place she wanted to be. She thought suddenly of Jean, and wondered, briefly, whether any of them was safe, given the punishment meted out to her. But then she glanced at Frances as she bent over the unconscious man, checking under his eyelids with one hand, rummaging in her medical kit with the other, and knew she couldn't leave.

"He's coming round. Someone hold his head to the side, please. What's his name? Kenneth? Kenneth," she called to him, "can you tell me where it hurts?" She listened to him, then lifted his hand and pulled each finger. "Open that for me, please." The marine reached down to where she was pointing, and took out what looked like a sewing kit. Margaret turned away. Under her feet the walkway vibrated in time with the engine.

"What time did they say the watch was changing?" asked Avice, nervously.

"Fourteen minutes," said Margaret. She wondered whether she should go down and remind them of the time, but it seemed pointless: their movements were filled with urgency.

It was as she turned away that a man drew her attention. He was seated on the floor in the corner, and Margaret realized that in several minutes he had not taken his eyes from Frances. The peculiar nature of his gaze made her wonder if perhaps Frances's robe was too revealing. Now she saw that his attention was not quite salacious, but neither was it kindly. He looked, she thought, oddly knowing. She moved closer to Avice, feeling uncomfortable.

"I think we should leave," Avice said.

"She won't be long," said Margaret. Secretly she agreed: it was a terrible place. A bit like one might imagine hell, if one were that way disposed. Yet Frances had never looked more at home.

―――

"Sorry to do this to you, Nicol. I couldn't leave him. Not in the state he was in."

Jones-the-Welsh pulled at his bootneck collar with a finger, then glanced down at the oil on his trousers. "Last time I let Duckworth talk me into a bit of after-hours entertainment. Bloody fool! My drill's ruined." He lit a cigarette, eyeing the no-smoking signs on the walls. "Anyway, matey, I owe you."

"I think it's someone else you owe," said Nicol. He looked down at his watch. "Christ! We've got eight minutes, Frances, before we have to get them out of here."

Beside him, on the floor, Frances had finished cleaning the cut on the bride's face. The girl had stopped weeping and was in a state of white-faced shock, exacerbated, Nicol suspected, by the amount of alcohol she appeared to have drunk. Frances's hair, wet with sweat, hung lank round her face; her pale cotton robe, now stuck to her skin, was smudged with oil and grease.

"Pass me the morphine, please," she said. He got the little brown bottle out of her box. She took it, and then his hand, which she placed on a pad of gauze on the girl's face. "Keep hold of that," she told him. "Tight as you can. Someone check Kenneth, please. Make sure he doesn't feel sick."

With the fluency born of long practice, she removed the top from the bottle and filled a syringe. "Soon feel better," she said to the injured girl, and as Nicol shifted to give her room, she placed the needle next to her skin. "I'll have to stitch it," she said, "but I promise I'll make them as tiny as I can. Most of them will be covered by your hair anyway."

The girl nodded mutely.

"Do you have to do it here?" said Nicol. "Couldn't we get her upstairs and do it there?"

"There's a WSO patrolling the hangar deck," said one of the men.

"Just let me get on with my job," said Frances, with the faintest hint of steel. "I'll be as quick as I can."

They were carrying Kenneth out, passing him between them up the ladder, shouting to each other to watch his leg, his head.

"Your friend here isn't going to say anything, right?" Watching them, Jones scratched his head. "I mean, can we trust her?"

Nicol nodded. It had taken her several attempts to thread the needle; he saw that her fingers were trembling.

He was struggling to find ways in which he might thank her, express his admiration. Holding her, upstairs, as they danced, he had seen this awkward girl relaxed and briefly illuminated. Now, in this environment, she was someone he no longer recognized. He had never seen a woman so confident in duty and he knew, with a pride he had not felt before, that he was in the presence of an equal.

"Time?" said Frances.

"Four minutes," he said.

She shook her head as if faced with a private impossibility. And then he couldn't think at all. At the first stitch, one of the girl's friends had passed out, and Frances's mates were told to take her outside and pinch her awake. The stitching was interrupted again when two of the men started to brawl. He and Jones waded in to separate them. Time inched forward, the hands of his watch moving relentlessly from one digit to the next.

Nicol found himself standing, glancing at the hatch, convinced even over the deafening sound of the engine that he could hear footsteps.

And then she turned to him, face dirty, and flushed from the heat. "We're all right," she said, with a brief smile. "We're done."

"A little over a minute and a half," said Nicol. "Come on, we've got to get out of here. Leave it," he called to the ratings, who had been trying to fix the guard rail. "There's no time. Just help me get her up."

Margaret and Avice were standing by the hatch on the walkway above them, and Frances motioned to them as if to say they could leave now. Margaret waved as if to say they'd wait.

He stood and offered his hand so that she could stand. She hesitated, then took it, smoothing her hair from her face. He tried not to let his eyes drop to her robe, which now clearly outlined the elegant contours of her chest. Sweat glistened on her skin, running down into the hollow in dirty rivulets. God help me, thought Nicol. There's an image I'm going to struggle to forget.

"You'll need to keep that dry," she murmured to the girl. "No washing your hair for a couple of days."

"Can't remember the last time I got to wash it anyway," the girl muttered.

"Hang on," said Jones-the-Welsh, from beside him. "Don't I know you?"

At first she seemed to assume that he was addressing the injured girl. Then she registered that he was talking to her and something hardened in her expression.

"You were never at Morotai," said Nicol.

"Morotai? Nah." Jones was shaking his head. "It wasn't there. But I never forget a face. I know you from somewhere."

Frances, Nicol saw, had lost her high color. "I don't think so," she said quietly. She began to gather up her medical kit.

"Yeeees . . . yes . . . I know it'll come to me." Jones shook his head. "I never forget a face."

She stood, one hand lifted to her brow, like someone suffering with a headache. "I'd better go," she said to Nicol. "They'll be fine." Her eyes met his only briefly.

"I'll come up with you," he said.

"No," she said sharply. "No, I'll be fine. Thank you."

Bits of bandage and kit had skittered under the walkway, but she seemed not to care. She gathered her robe tightly around her, and picked her way past the engine toward the stairs, her kit under her arm.

"Oh, no . . ."

Nicol tore his gaze from Frances to Jones-the-Welsh. The man was staring at her and shaking his head, bemused. Then a wicked smile flickered across his face.

"What?" said Nicol. He was following her toward the ladder and reached for the jacket he had slung over a tool case.

"No . . . can't be . . . never . . ." Jones glanced behind him and suddenly located the man he apparently wanted to speak to. "Hey, Duckworth, are you thinking what I'm thinking? Queensland? It isn't, is it?" Frances had climbed up the ladder and was now walking toward the other girls, head down.

"Saw it straight away," came the broad Cockney accent. "The old Rest Easy. You wouldn't credit it, would you?"

"What's going on?" said Avice, from above. "What's he talking about?"

"I don't believe it," said Jones-the-Welsh, and burst out laughing. "A nurse! Wait till we tell old Kenny! A nurse!"

"What the hell are you talking about, Jones?"

Jones's face, when it met Nicol's, held the same amused smile with which he greeted most of life's great surprises, whether they were extra sippers, victories at sea or successful cheating at cards. "Your little nurse there, Nicol," he said, "used to be a brass."

"What?"

"Duckworth knows—we came across her at a club in Queensland, must be four, five years ago now."

His laughter, like his voice, carried over the noise of the engine to the ears of the exhausted men and the brides heading wearily out on to the walkway. Some had stopped, in response to Jones's exclamation, and were listening.

"Don't be ridiculous, man." Nicol looked up at Frances, who was nearly at the hatch. She stared straight ahead, and then, perhaps at the end of some unseen internal struggle, allowed herself to glance down at him. In her eyes he saw resignation. He found he had gone cold.

"But she's married."

"What? To her bludger? Manager's prize girl, she was! And now look! Can you credit it? She's turned into Florence Nightingale!" His burst of incredulous laughter followed Frances's swift footsteps all the way out of the hatch and back out along the passageway.

15

There was one girl from England,
Susan Summers was her name,
For fourteen years transported was,
We all well knew the same.
Our planter bought her freedom
And he married her out of hand,
Good usage then she gave to us
Upon Van Diemen's Land.

FROM "VAN DIEMEN'S LAND,"
AUSTRALIAN FOLK SONG

AUSTRALIA, 1939

Frances had checked the Arnott's biscuit tin four times before Mr. Radcliffe came. She had also checked the back of the cutlery drawer, in the pot behind the screen door and under the mattress in what had once, many years previously, been her parents' room. She had asked her mother several times where the money was, and in her mother's snoring, alcohol-fumed reply the answer was obvious.

But not to Mr. Radcliffe. "So, where is it?" he had said, smiling. The same way that a shark smiles when it opens its mouth to bite.

"I'm real sorry. I don't know what she's done with it." Her ankle was hooked behind the door to restrict his view inside, but Mr. Radcliffe leaned to one side and gazed through the screen to where her mother lolled in the armchair. "No," he said. "Of course."

"She's not very well," she said, pulling at her skirt awkwardly. "Perhaps when she wakes up she'll be able to tell me."

Behind him, she could see two neighbors walking along the street.

They murmured something, their eyes trained on her. She didn't have to hear the words to know the tenor of their conversation. "If you want I could stop by later with it?"

"What? Like your mum did last week? And the week before that?" He brushed at a non-existent crease in the front of his trousers. "I don't suppose there's enough left in her purse to buy you a loaf of bread."

She said nothing. The way he kept hovering, he seemed to expect her to invite him in. But she didn't want Mr. Radcliffe, with his expensive clothes and polished shoes, to sit down in the squalor of their front room. Not before she'd had a chance to put it right.

They faced each other on the porch, locked in an uneasy waiting game.

"You've not been around here for a while." It wasn't quite a question.

"I've been staying with my aunt May."

"Oh, yes. She passed on, didn't she? Cancer, wasn't it?"

Frances could answer now without her eyes filling. "Yes," she said. "I was there . . . to help her for a bit."

"I'm sorry for your loss. You probably know your mother didn't do too good while you were gone." Mr. Radcliffe glanced past her through the door, and she fought the urge to close it a little more.

"She's . . . dropped behind on her payments. Not just with me. You'll get no tick at Green's now, or Mayhew's."

"I'll manage," said Frances.

He turned to the gleaming motor-car that stood in the road. Two boys were peering at themselves in the wing mirror. "Your mother was a pretty woman when she worked for me. That's what the drink does to you."

She held his gaze.

"I suppose there's not a lot I can tell you about her."

Still she said nothing.

Mr. Radcliffe shifted on his feet, then checked his watch. "How old are you, Frances?" he said.

"Fifteen."

He studied her, as if assessing her. Then he sighed, as if he were about to do something against his better judgment. "Look, I tell you what, I'll let you work at the hotel. You can wash dishes. Do a bit of cleaning. I don't suppose you can rely on your mother to keep you. Don't let me down, mind, or you and she will be out on your ears." He had been back there, shooing away the boys before she'd had a chance to thank him.

———

She had known Mr. Radcliffe for most of her life. Most people in Aynsville did: he was the owner of the only hotel, and landlord of several clapboard properties. She could still remember the days when her mother, before the booze tightened its grip, had disappeared in the evening to work at the hotel bar, and Aunt May had looked after her. Later Aunt May rued the day she had told Frances's mother to go work there—"But in a two-horse town like this, love, you got to take the jobs when they come, right?"

Frances's own experience of the hotel was rather better. For the first year, anyway. Every day, shortly after nine, she would report for work in the back kitchen, alongside a near-silent Chinese man who scowled and raised a huge knife at her if she didn't wash and slice the vegetables to his satisfaction. She would clean the kitchens, slapping at the floors with a black-tendrilled mop, help prepare food until four, then move on to washing up. Her hands chapped and split with the scalding water; her back and neck ached from stooping at the little sink. She learned to keep her eyes lowered from the women who sat around bad-temperedly in the mid-afternoon with little to do but drink and bitch at each other. But she had enjoyed earning money and having a little control over what had been a chaotic existence.

Mr. Radcliffe kept the rent and paid her a little over, just enough to cover food and household expenses. She had bought herself a new pair of shoes, and her mother a cream blouse with pale blue embroidery. The kind of blouse she could imagine a different sort of mother wearing. Her mother had wept with gratitude, promised that, given a little time, she would be back on her feet. Frances could go away to college, perhaps, like May had promised. Get away from this stinking hole.

But then, freed of the responsibility of earning and even of keeping house, her mother had begun to drink more heavily. Occasionally she would come to the hotel bar and lean over the counter in her low-cut dresses. Inevitably, late into the evening, she would harangue the men around her, and the girls who worked there; she would swat at non-existent flies and shriek for Frances in tones that were both critical and self-pitying. Finally she would clatter into the kitchens to attack her daughter verbally for her failures—to dress nicely, to earn her keep, for allowing herself to be born and ruining her mother's life—until Hun Li grabbed her in his huge arms and threw her out. Then he would scowl at Frances, as if her mother's failures were her own. She didn't attempt to defend her: she had worked out years before that there was little point.

In the face of their poverty, Frances could never work out how her mother acquired the money to get as drunk as she did.

———

And then, one night, she disappeared—with the evening's takings.

Frances had been taking a five-minute break, seated on a bucket in the broom cupboard, eating a couple of slices of bread and margarine that Hun Li had left for her, when she heard the commotion. She had already put down her plate and stood up when Mr. Radcliffe stormed in. "Where is she, the thieving whore?"

Frances froze, wide-eyed. She already knew, with a familiar sinking feeling in her stomach, whom he was talking about.

"She's gone! And so has my bloody cash! Where is she?"

"I—I don't know," Frances had stammered.

Mr. Radcliffe, normally so urbane and gentlemanly, had become an enraged, puce-faced creature, his body somehow threatening to burst out of his shirt, his huge fists balled as if in an effort to contain himself. He had stared at her for what seemed like an eternity, apparently weighing up the possibility that she was telling the truth.

She had thought, briefly, that she might wet herself with fear. Then he had gone, the door slamming behind him.

They had found her two days later, unconscious, at the back of the butcher's. There was no money, just a few empty bottles. Her shoes were missing. One evening that same week, Mr. Radcliffe went round "to have a word with her" then came back to the hotel to tell Frances that he and her mother had decided it might be best if she left town for a while. She was bad for business. Hardly anyone would give the Lukes credit. He had personally helped her out. "Just till she straightens herself out a bit," he said. "Though God only knows how long that'll take."

Frances had been too shocked to react. When she arrived home that evening, took in the heavy silence of the little house, the bills sitting on the kitchen table, the note that failed to explain exactly where her mother was going, she had laid her head on her arms and stayed like that until, exhausted, she slept.

―――――

It had been almost three months later that Mr. Radcliffe had called her in. Her mother's shadow had diminished; people in town had stopped murmuring to each other as she passed—some even said hello. Hun Li had been conciliatory—had made sure that there were scraps of beef and mutton in her dinner, that she had regular breaks. Once he had left her two oranges, although he later denied it and raised his cleaver in mock anger when she suggested it. The girls in the bar had asked if she was doing all right, had tweaked her plaits in a sisterly manner. One had offered her a drink when she finished her shift. She had refused, but was grateful. When another had popped her head round the kitchen door and asked her to nip up to his office, she had flinched, afraid that she was about to be accused of theft too. Like mother like daughter—that was what they said in the town. Blood would always out. But when she knocked and entered, Mr. Radcliffe's face was not angry.

"Sit down," he said. The way he looked at her seemed almost sympathetic. She sat. "I'm going to have to ask you to leave your house."

Before she could open her mouth to protest, he continued, "The war's going to change things in Queensland. We've got troops headed up here and the town's going to get busy. I'm told there are people coming in who can pay me a much better rent on it. Anyway, Frances, it doesn't make sense for a young girl like you to be rattling around in it alone."

"I've kept up to date with my rent," said Frances. "I haven't let you down once."

"I'm well aware of that, sweetheart, and I'm not the kind of man to turf you out on the street. You'll move in here. You can have one of the rooms at the top, where Mo Haskins used to sleep—you know the one. And I'll take a reduced rent for it, so you'll have more money in your pocket. How's that sound?"

His confidence that she would be pleased with this arrangement was so overwhelming that she found it hard to say what she felt: that the house on Ridley Street was her home. That since her mother's departure she had started to enjoy her independence, that she no longer felt as if she was teetering on the brink of disaster. And that she did not want to be indebted to him in the way this arrangement suggested.

"I'd really rather stay in the house, Mr. Radcliffe. I—I'll work extra shifts to make up the rent."

Mr. Radcliffe sighed. "I'd love to help you there, Frances, really I would. But when your mum took off with my takings she left a great big hole in my finances. A great—big—hole. A hole that I'm going to have to fill."

He stood up, and walked over to her. His hand on her shoulder felt immensely heavy.

"But that's what I like about you, Frances. You're a grafter, not like your old mum. So, you'll move in here. A girl like you shouldn't spend the prime of her life worrying about the rent. You should be out, dressed up a bit, having fun. Besides, it's not good for a young girl to be seen to be living on her own . . ." He squeezed her shoulder. She felt immobilized. "No. You move your stuff in Saturday week and I'll take care of everything else. I'll send one of the boys over to give you a hand."

———

Afterward, she realized that perhaps the girls had known something she couldn't. That their sympathy, their friendliness and, in one case, hostility stemmed not from the fact that they lived under one roof, all girls together, as she had assumed, but from what they understood about her position.

And that when Miriam, a short Jewish woman with hair that stretched to her waist, announced she would spend an afternoon helping her to smarten herself up a bit it had perhaps been the result not of girlish friendliness, but of someone else's instruction.

Either way Frances, unschooled in friendship, had found herself too intimidated by the unfamiliar attention to protest. At the end of the day, when Miriam had set her hair, pulled tight the waistband of the deep blue dress she had altered to fit her and presented her to Mr. Radcliffe, boasting about the transformation, Frances had assumed she should be grateful.

"Well, look at you," Mr. Radcliffe said, puffing at his cigarette. "Who'd have thought, eh, Miriam?"

"Doesn't scrub up too bad, does she?"

Frances felt her cheeks burn under their scrutiny and the makeup. She fought the urge to cover her chest with folded arms.

"Good enough to eat. In fact, I think our little Frances has been wasted on old Hun Li, don't you? I'm sure we can find her something more decorative to do than bottle-washing."

"I'm fine," said Frances. "Really. I'm very happy working with Mr. Hun."

"Sure you are, sweetheart, and very fine work you do too. But looking at how darn pretty you've got, I think you're more use to me out front. So, from now on you'll serve drinks. Miriam here will show you the ropes."

She felt, as she so often did, outmaneuvered. As if, despite her supposedly adult position in the world, there were too many people who could make decisions on her behalf. And if she had caught something in Miriam's glance that made her feel something else, something vaguely disconcerting, then even she wouldn't have been able to articulate what exactly that was.

———

She should be grateful. She should be grateful that Mr. Radcliffe had given her the pretty attic room at a price far cheaper than she could have afforded. She should be grateful that he was taking care of her, when neither of her parents had had the good sense to do it themselves. She should be grateful that he had paid her so much attention, that he had ordered those two good dresses for her when he discovered she hardly had an outfit to her name that wasn't threadbare, that he took her out to dinner once a week and didn't let anyone say anything bad about her mother in front of her, that he protected her from the attentions of the troops flooding into town. She should be grateful that someone found her as pretty as he did.

She should have paid no attention to Hun Li when he took her aside one night and hissed at her in pidgin English that she should leave. Now. She wasn't a stupid girl, no matter what the others were saying.

So that first night when, instead of waving her off to bed, Mr. Radcliffe invited her to come to his rooms after dinner, it was hard to say no. When she had pleaded tiredness, he had pulled such a sad face and said she couldn't possibly leave him alone when he had entertained her all evening, could she? He had seemed so proud of the specially imported wine that it had been vital that she drink some too. Especially that second glass. And when he had insisted she sit on the sofa beside him instead of on the little chair, where she had been comfortable, it would have been rude to refuse.

"You know, you're actually a very beautiful girl, Frances," he had said. There had been something almost hypnotic about the way he kept murmuring it into her ear. About his broad hand, which, without her noticing, had been stroking her back, as if she were a baby. About the way her dress had slipped from her bare skin. Afterward, when she had thought back, she knew she had hardly tried to stop him because she hadn't realized, until it was too late, what she should have been stopping. And it hadn't been so bad, had it? Because Mr. Radcliffe cared about her. Like no one else cared. Mr. Radcliffe would look after her.

She might not be sure what it was she actually felt about him. But she knew she should be grateful.

———

Frances stayed at the Rest Easy Hotel for three more months. For two of those months she and Mr. Radcliffe (he never invited her to use his first name) settled into a twice-weekly routine of his nocturnal "visits." Sometimes he would invite her to his rooms after he had taken her out to dinner. On a few occasions he arrived, unannounced, in hers. She didn't like those times: he was often drunk, and once he had said almost nothing to her, simply opened her door and come crashing down on her so that she had felt like some kind of receptacle and stood, for hours after, trying to wash the smell of him from her skin.

She realized pretty quickly that she did not love him, no matter what he said to her. She knew now why he employed so many female staff. She saw, with not a little curiosity, that none of them envied her position as his girlfriend, even though he favored her—in wages, dresses, and attention—best of all.

But on the day when he suggested she "entertain" his friend for a little while, she had understood everything. "I'm sorry," she said, smile wavering as she looked at the two men, "I don't think I heard you right."

He laid his hand on her shoulder. "Neville here has a proper soft spot for you, sweetheart. Do me a favor. Just make him feel better."

"I don't understand," she said.

His fingers tightened on her. It was a sweltering night and they slid on her skin as they gripped her. "I think you do, sweetheart. You're not a stupid girl."

She refused, flushed to the roots of her hair that he had considered her capable of such a thing. She refused again, and tried, in one outraged look, to convey her hurt at what he had suggested. She half ran toward the stairs, tears of humiliation pricking her eyes, desperate to escape to the safety of her own room, conscious of the eyes of the other girls upon her, the catcalling of the now ever-present troops. But then she heard his thunderous steps behind her. By the time she reached her room he was behind her.

"What do you think you're doing?" he yelled at her, whipping her round to face him. His face was the same color as it had been when he had accused her mother of stealing.

"Get off me!" she screamed. "I can't believe you're asking me to do such a thing!"

"How dare you embarrass me like that! After all I've done for you—looking after you, forgetting all that money your mum stole off me, buying you dresses, taking you out, when everyone else in this town said I shouldn't touch any of the Luke family with a ten-foot pole . . ."

She was seated now, her hands pressed to her face as if she could block him out. Downstairs she heard someone break into song, and an answering jeer.

"Neville's a good friend of mine, you understand, you silly little girl? A very good friend. And his son's off to war and he's blue as anything and I'm just trying to take his mind off it all—and so here we are, the three of us having a nice evening, all friends together, and you start behaving like some spoiled kid! How do you think that makes Neville feel?"

She tried to interrupt but he stopped her.

"I thought you were better than that, Frances." Here his voice dropped, became conciliatory. "One of the things I always liked about you was that you were a caring sort of a girl. You didn't like to see people unhappy. Well, it's not a lot to ask in the great scheme of things, is it? Just to help someone whose son's gone off to maybe lose his life in battle?"

"But I—" She didn't know how to answer him. She began to cry, lifted a hand to her face.

He took it in one of his. "I've never forced you to do anything, have I?"

"No."

"Look, sweetheart, Neville's a nice man, isn't he?"

A small, gray-haired mustachioed mouse of a man. He had grinned at her all night. She had thought he found her conversation entertaining.

"And you care about me, don't you?"

She nodded mutely.

"It would mean such a lot to him. And to me. Come on, sweetheart, it's not like I ask much of you, is it?" He lifted her face to his. Forced her to open her eyes.

"I don't want to," she whispered. "Not that."

"It's half an hour of your life. And it's not like you don't enjoy it, is it?"

She didn't know how to reply. She had never been sober enough to remember.

He seemed to take her silence as acquiescence. He led her to the mirror. "Tell you what," he said, "you go and straighten yourself up a bit. No one wants to see a face full of tears. I'll have a couple of drinks brought up to you—that nice brandy you like—and then I'll send Neville up. You two will get on fine." He hadn't looked at her as he'd left the room.

———

After that she lost count of the number of times she did it. She knew only that each time she had been progressively more drunk—once she had been ill and the man had asked for his money back. Mr. Radcliffe got crosser and crosser, and she spent as much time as she could hiding in the bathroom, scrubbing her skin until it came off in raw red patches so that the girls winced as she walked by.

Finally, on the last occasion, as the bar grew noisier and the stairs were heavy with footfall, Hun Li had caught her when she ducked into the cellar. She had secreted a bottle of rum there and, faced with two off-duty servicemen who had gleaned the impression from Mr. Radcliffe that they might get the chance to spend some time with her, she had stood in the corner between the Castlemaine and Mc-Cracken barrels, swigging from a bottle that was already half empty.

"Frances!"

She had whipped round. Drunk, it had taken her time to focus, and she recognized him only by his blue shirt and broad arms. "Don't say nothing," she slurred, putting down the bottle. "I'll put the money in the till."

He had stepped closer to her, under the bare lightbulb, and she wondered whether he wanted to paw at her too. "You must go," he said. He flicked at a moth near his face.

"What?"

"You must go from here. This place no good."

It was the most he had said to her in almost eighteen months. She had laughed then, bitter, angry laughter that turned into sobbing. Then she had bent over, clutching her sides, unable to catch her breath.

He had stood awkwardly in front of her, then stepped forward gingerly, as if fearful of touching her. "I got this for you," he said.

She had wondered, briefly, if he was going to give her a sandwich. And then she saw that his fist was full of money, a dirty great wad of it. "What's this?" she whispered.

"That man last week. The one—" He faltered, not knowing how best to describe Mr. Radcliffe's latest "friend." "The one with the flash suit. He got a gambling place. I stole this from his car." He thrust his fist at her. "You take it. Go tomorrow. You can pay Mr. Musgrove to take you to the station."

She didn't move, and he thrust his fist forward insistently. "Go on. You earned it."

She stared at the money, wondering if she was drunk enough to have imagined this scene. But when she put out a finger, it was solid. "You don't think he'll tell Mr. Radcliffe?"

"So what? You be gone then. There's a train leaves tomorrow. Go on. You go." When she said nothing, he made a mock-angry face. "This is no good for you, Frances. You're a good girl."

A good girl. She stared at this man, whom she had thought hardly capable of speech, let alone such kindness. She took the money and put it into her pocket. His sweat had softened the notes, and they crumpled as they slid between the fabric. Then she moved to take his hand to say thank you.

When his failed to meet hers she grasped that Hun Li's sympathy might be tinged with something she didn't want to think about. Something that in just three months her "profession" had bestowed on her.

He nodded at her, as if ashamed of his own reticence.

"What about you?" she said.

"What about me?"

"You don't need this for yourself?" She didn't want to ask him: she could already feel it glowing beneficently in her pocket.

His face was unreadable. "I never needed it like you," he said. Then he turned, and his broad back vanished into the darkness.

16

TWENTY-FIVE DAYS

"Poor old girl. It wasn't a fate you deserved, however you look at it." He laid his hand gently on her, sensing, he fancied, the years of struggle echoing through the cool metal. "Too good for them. Far too good."

He straightened up, then glanced behind him, conscious that he was talking aloud to his ship and keen to ensure that Dobson had not witnessed it. Dobson had been thoroughly discomfited by the captain's changes in normal routine, and while he had enjoyed unbalancing the younger man, he recognized that there was only so far he could go before he became answerable to someone else.

There had not been a square inch of *Indomitable* that Highfield hadn't known, no part of her history with which he wasn't familiar. He had seen her decks submerged in high seas in the Adriatic, her huge frame tossed around as if she were a rowing-boat in a storm. He had steered her through the Arctic in the winter of '41, when her decks had been six inches thick with snow, and her gun turrets had become so encrusted with ice that twenty ratings with picks and shovels had had to spend hours trying to keep her workable. He had held her steady as she fought off the suicide bombers of the Sakishima Gunto airfields, when the kamikaze aircraft had literally bounced off the flight deck, covering her with tidal waves of water and aviation fuel, and he had swept her through the Atlantic, listening in silence for the ominous echo that told of enemy submarines.

He had seen her flight deck a huge crater when, during the early part of the war, no less than three Barracudas had collided in mid-air and crashed on to it. He was not sure whether he could count the number of men they had lost, the funerals at sea that he had presided over, the bodies committed to the water. And he had seen her at her last. Watched her deck canting as she slid down, taking with her those few men they had told him were already gone, his beloved boy, his body somewhere in the inferno that belched foul smoke over what remained above the surface, his funeral pyre. When her bow had sunk and the waves closed over her, there had been no sign left that she had existed at all.

The *Victoria's* layout was identical to that of her twin; there had been something almost eerie about it when he had first stepped aboard. For a while he had been resentful. Now he felt a perverse obligation to her.

They had contacted him that morning. The commander-in-chief of the British Pacific Fleet had wired him personally. In joking terms he had told Highfield that he could lay off the painting parties for the remainder of the voyage: no need to exhaust the men with too much maintenance. The *Victoria* would be examined in dry dock at Plymouth before being modified and sold off to some merchant shipping company or broken up. "Nothing wrong with the old girl," he had wired back. "Suggest most strongly the former course."

He had not told the men: he suspected most would not notice what ship they were on, as long as the messes were of a decent size, the money regular and the food edible. With the war over, many would leave the Navy for good. He, and the old ship, would be no more than a dim memory when war stories were exchanged over dinner.

Highfield sighed, and placed his weight tentatively on his bad leg. They would dock at Bombay the following day. He would pay no attention to the C-in-C's instruction. For several days now he had had teams of dabbers and ratings buffing, painting, polishing. The Navy knew that sailors kept busy were sailors less likely to get into trouble—and with a cargo like this one that struggle was constant.

There would not be a brass bolt on the ship that he couldn't see his face in.

The men, he guessed, were speculating that something was wrong with him. It was possible too that the governor of Gibraltar would notice. He was not a stupid man. I'm buggered if I'm leaving you early, he told the ship silently, tightening his grip on the rail. I'll hang on to you till my damn leg falls off.

———

"What you do, ladies, is mix one level tablespoon of the powdered egg with two tablespoons of water. Allow it to stand for a few minutes until the powder has absorbed all the moisture, then work out any lumps with a wooden spoon. You may have to be a bit vigorous . . . a bit of elbow grease, you know." She took in the blank faces. "That's an English expression. It doesn't mean . . . grease as such."

Margaret sat with her notebook on her lap, her pen in her hand. She had given up writing several recipes ago, distracted by the murmur of conversation around her.

"A prostitute? I don't believe it. Surely the Navy wouldn't let one travel with all the men."

"Well, they didn't know, did they? They can't have."

"There are all sorts of things you can bake with powdered egg. Add a bit of parsley or watercress and you can make quite a good . . . approximation of scrambled egg. So don't feel limited just because you may not have the ingredients you've been used to at home. In fact, girls, you will not have the kind of ingredients you've been used to at home."

"But who on earth would have married her? Do you think it was one of her . . . customers?"

"And what if he doesn't know? Don't you think the Navy should tell him?"

It had been the same story all over the ship. For the last few days Frances Mackenzie, possibly the least conspicuous passenger the *Victoria* had ever transported, had become its most notorious. Those who had had any dealings with her were fascinated that this supposedly demure young woman had such a checkered past. Others found the story of her past career compelling, and felt obliged to embellish it with information that no one was yet in a position to disprove. That was if anyone had had the inclination to do so; the next shore leave was still a fair distance away and there was little doubt it was the most fascinating thing that had happened on the voyage so far.

"I heard she was on the train. You know, the one they used to send up to the troops. It was full of . . . those sorts."

"Do you think they had to check her for diseases? I know they did on the American transports. I mean, we might have been sharing a bathroom with her, for goodness' sake."

Margaret had fought the urge to interrupt, to inform these stupid, gossiping women that they didn't know what they were talking about. But it was difficult when she herself had no idea of the truth.

It wasn't as if Frances was saying anything. On the night of the accident, she had retired to her bed and lain there, pretending to be asleep until the others had gone out in the morning, often doing the same when they came back. She had barely spoken, keeping her conversation to an absolute practical minimum. She had given the dog some more water. Had propped the door ajar. If that was all right with them. She had avoided the main canteen. Margaret wasn't sure that she was eating anything at all.

Avice had asked, rather ostentatiously, to be moved to another cabin, and when the only other bunk on offer had proven not to her liking, she had announced loudly that she wanted as little to do with Frances as possible. Margaret had told her not to be so bloody ridiculous, and not to listen to a load of bloody gossip. There would be no truth in it.

But it was difficult to be as vehement as she would have liked when Frances was doing so little to defend herself.

And even Margaret, never usually lost for words, had difficulty in knowing what to say to her. She was, she suspected, a little naïve at the best of times, and was having trouble reconciling the severely dressed, rather prim young woman with "one of those." Margaret's only knowledge of such women came from the poster with a picture of one in Dennis Tims's mess, with the uncompromising message: "Venereal Disease—the Silent Killer"; and the Westerns she had seen with her brothers, where the women all sat together in the back of some saloon. Had Frances worn tight-bodiced dresses and a dollop of rouge on her face to welcome men in? Had she enticed them upstairs, spread her legs and invited them to do God only knew what to her? These thoughts haunted Margaret, coloring her every exchange with Frances, despite all the kindnesses the girl had shown her. She knew it and it made her ashamed. She suspected that Frances knew it too.

"Well, I think it's disgusting. Frankly, if my parents knew I was traveling with someone like that they would never have let me on board." The girl in front of her straightened her shoulders with a self-righteous shudder.

Margaret stared at the powdered-egg recipes in front of her, at her distracted scrawl.

"It makes you wonder," said the girl next to her.

Margaret stuffed her notebook into her basket, got up and left the room.

———

Dear Deanna,

I can't tell you what fun I'm having on board—quite a surprise, all things considered. I somehow find myself in the running for Queen of the Victoria, a prize they award to the bride who has proven themself a cut above in all matters feminine. It will be lovely to be able to show Ian that I can be such an asset to him and his career. I have so far won points in craft, dressmaking, musical ability (I sang "Shenandoah"—the audience were most appreciative) and—you'll never guess—Miss Lovely Legs! I wore my green swimsuit with the matching satin heels. I hope you didn't mind too much me taking them. You seemed to wear them so seldom, and it seemed silly you keeping them "for best" when there is so little social life left in Melbourne now the Allies are leaving.

How are you? Mummy's letter said you were no longer in correspondence with that nice young man from Waverley. She was rather vague about what had happened—I find it very hard to think anyone would so cruelly drop a girl like that. Unless he had found someone else, I suppose.

Men can be such an enigma, can't they? I thank goodness every day that Ian is such a devoted soul.

I must go, dearest sister. They are "piping the hands to bathe," and I am simply desperate for a swim. I will post this when we next dock, and be sure to tell you of any adventures I have there!

Your loving sister,

Avice

It was the first time the brides had been allowed to bathe, and there were few who, still feeling the effects of the water shortage, were not making the most of it. As Avice finished her letter and headed out on to the foredeck, she could see around her hundreds of women submerged in the clear waters, squealing as they floated around lifeboats, while the marines and officers not manning the boats leaned over the ship's side, smoking and watching them.

There was no sign of the baby yet. Avice had examined herself with some pride, the still-flat stomach but an attractive hint of fullness to her bosom. She wouldn't be one of these flabby whales, like Margaret, who sat puffing and sweating in corners, ankles and feet as grotesquely swollen as an elephant's. She would make sure she stayed trim and attractive until the end. When she was large she would retire into her home, make the nursery pretty and not reveal herself again until the baby came. That was a ladylike way to do it.

Now that she no longer felt nauseous, she was sure that pregnancy would positively agree with her: aided by the constant sunshine, her skin glowed, her blonde hair had new highlights. She drew attention wherever she went. She had wondered, now that her condition was public knowledge, whether she should cover up a little, whether it was advisable to be a little more modest. But there were so few days left before they entered European waters that it seemed a shame to waste them. Avice shed her sundress, and straightened up a little, just to make sure that she could be seen to her best advantage before she lay decoratively on the deck to sunbathe. Apart from that unfortunate business with Frances (and what a turn-up that had been for the books!), and what with her steady notching up of points for Queen of the *Victoria*, she thought she had probably made the voyage into rather a success.

————

A short distance away, on the forecastle, Nicol was propped against the wall. Normally he would not have smoked on deck, especially not on duty, but over the past days he had smoked steadily and with a kind of grim determination, as if the repetitive action could simplify his thoughts.

"Going in later?" One of the seamen, with whom he had often played Uckers, a kind of naval Ludo, appeared at his elbow. The men would be piped to bathe when the last of the women were out.

"No." Nicol stubbed out his cigarette.

"I am. Can't wait."

Nicol feigned polite interest.

The man jerked a thumb at the women. "That lot. Seeing them out having a good time. Reminds me of my girls at home."

"Oh."

"We got a river runs past the end of our garden. When my girls were small we'd take them in on sunny days—teach them to swim." He made a breaststroke motion, lost in his memories. "Living near water, see, they got to know how to stay afloat. Only safe, like."

Nicol nodded in a way that might suggest assent.

"Times I thought I'd not see them again. Many a time, if I'm honest. Not that you let yourself think like that too often, eh, boy?"

Despite himself Nicol smiled at the older man's description of him.

"Still . . . still. Better times ahead." He drew hard on his cigarette, then dropped it into the water. "I'm surprised old Highfield let 'em in. Would have thought the sight of all that female flesh'd be too much for him."

The afternoon was set fair, as it had been for days. Below them, in the glassy waters, two women writhed and squealed their way on to one of the lifeboats, while others leaned over the ship's rail shouting encouragement. Another shrieked hysterically as her friend splashed her.

The man gazed at them in benign appreciation. "Cold fish, that Highfield. Always thought it. You got to wonder about a man always wants to be by himself."

Nicol said nothing.

"Time was, I would have argued the toss with anyone said he was a bad skipper. Got to admit, when we was on the convoys he did us proud. But you can tell he's lost it now. Confidence shot, isn't it, since *Indomitable?*"

The older man was breaking an unspoken convention among the men not to talk about what had happened on that night, let alone who might be to blame. Nicol did not respond, except to shake his head.

"Couldn't hand down orders. Not when it counted. I've seen it before—them that want to do everything their bloody selves. I reckon if he'd had his head screwed on proper that night he could have handed down orders and we would have saved a lot of men. He just got stuck in his bloody self. Didn't look at the big picture. That's what you need in a skipper—an ability to see the bigger picture."

If he had had a shilling for every armchair strategist he'd met in his years of service, Nicol observed, he'd have been a rich man.

"I allus thought it was a bit of a joke on the top brass's part, giving him her sister ship to bring home . . . No . . . I don't think you know a man till you seen him around his nearest and dearest. I've served under him five year and I've not heard a single person speak up for him."

They stood in silence for some time. Finally, perhaps recognizing that their exchange had been rather one-sided, the man asked, "You'll be glad to see your family again, eh?"

Nicol lit another cigarette.

She was not there. He hadn't thought she would be.

He had lain awake for the rest of that night, Jones's words haunting him almost as much as his own sense of betrayal. Slowly, as the night gave way to day, his own disbelief had evaporated, steadily replaced by the putting together of odd clues, inconsistencies in her behavior. Standing in the bowels of the ship, he had wanted her to deny it indignantly; wanted to hear her outrage at the slur. None had been forthcoming. Now he wanted her to explain herself—as if, in some way, she had tricked him.

He hadn't needed to ask any further questions to clarify what he had been told; not of her, anyway. When he returned to the mess she had still been the talk of the men. Wide-eyed little thing she had been, Jones-the-Welsh said, leaning out of his hammock for a cigarette. A ton of makeup on her, almost like the others had done it to her for a joke.

Nicol had paused in the hatch, wondering whether he should turn round. He wasn't sure what made him stay.

Jones himself had apparently been presented with her but declined. She stuck out because of her shape: "Thin as a whippet," he said, "with no tits to speak of." And because she was drunk, he said. He curled his lip, as if he had been offered something distasteful.

The manager had sent her upstairs with one of his mates and she'd fallen up the steps. They had all laughed: there was something comical about the skinny girl with all the makeup, drunk as a skunk, her legs all over the place. Actually, he said, more seriously, "I thought she was under age, you know what I'm saying? Didn't fancy having my collar felt."

Duckworth, an apparent connoisseur of such things, had agreed.

"Bloody hell, though. You'd never know now, would you? Looks like butter wouldn't melt."

No, Duckworth had observed. But for them recognizing her, no one would have known.

Nicol had begun to pull down his hammock. He had thought he might try for some sleep before his next watch.

"Now now, Nicol," came Jones's voice from behind him. "Hope you're not thinking about slipping in there for a quickie later. Need to save your money for that missus of yours." He had guffawed. "Besides, she's a bit better-looking now. Bit more polish. She'd probably charge you a fortune."

He had thought he might hit him. Some irrational part of him had wanted to do the same to her. Instead he had pasted a wry smile on his face, feeling even as he did that he was engaged in some sort of betrayal, and disappeared into the wash cubicle.

———

Night had fallen. *Victoria* pushed forward in the black waters, oblivious to the time or season, to the moods and vagaries of her inhabitants, her vast engines powering obediently beneath her. Frances lay in her bunk, listening for the now familiar sounds, the last pipes, muttered conversations and faltering footsteps that spoke of the steady settling of the ship's passengers to sleep, the sniffs and grunts, the slowing of breath that told the same story of the two other women in her cabin. The sounds of silence, of solitude, the sounds that told her she was free once again to breathe. The sounds she seemed to have spent a good portion of her life waiting for.

And outside, just audible to the trained ear, the sound of two feet shifting on the corridor floor.

He arrived at four a.m. She heard him murmuring something to the other marine as they changed guard, the muffled echo of the other man's steps as he went to some mess, or to sleep. She listened to the man outside as she had for what felt like hundreds of nights before.

Finally, when she could bear it no longer, she rose from her bunk. Unseen by the two sleeping women on each side of her, she tiptoed toward the steel door, her footsteps sure and silent in the dark. Just before she reached it, she stood still, eyes closed as if she were in pain.

Then she stepped forward, and quietly, carefully, laid her face against it. Slowly she rested her entire length, her thighs, her stomach, her chest against it, palms pressed flat on each side of her head, feeling the cool metal through her thin nightgown, its immovable solidity.

If she turned her head, kept her ear pressed against the door, she could almost hear him breathing.

She stood there, in the dark, for some time. A tear rolled down her face and plopped on to her bare foot. It was followed by another.

Outside, apart from the low rumble of the engines, there was silence.

17

Among the 300 different items the Red Cross has put aboard for the use of brides are bed linen, towels, stationery, medical and beauty preparations, and tons of tinned fruit, cream, biscuits, meat and boxes of chocolates. It has also provided 500 canvas folding deck-chairs and a special book on midwifery.

SYDNEY MORNING HERALD, 3 JULY 1946

TWENTY-SIX DAYS

A major port, especially one that had formed an important staging-post for most of the war years, can safely be assumed to have seen most things pass through its gates. Guns, armory, foodstuffs, silks, spices, troops, traders, holy texts and foul waste had all passed through, eliciting little comment.

Old hands could remember the nightmare roaring of the six white tigers confined to crates en route to the home of an American movie mogul; others the glowing gold dome of a temple for some vainglorious European head of state. More recently, for several weeks the harbor had hummed with a rare fragrance after a crane carrying five thousand bottles of sickly perfume had dropped its cargo on to the dockside.

But the sight of some six hundred women waiting to go ashore at Bombay brought the traffic at Alexandra Lock to a standstill. The women, lining the decks in their brightly colored summer dresses, waved down with hats and handbags, their voices filled with the energy of three and a half weeks spent at sea. Hundreds of children ran along either side of the dock, their arms stretched upward, calling to the women to toss down more coins, more coins. Small tugboats, hovering beneath the great bow like satellites, noisily dragged *Victoria* round, pulling her into position alongside the quay. As the ship glided gracefully into place, many of the women exclaimed loudly at how such a huge ship could fit through the lock; others exclaimed rather more vigorously at the smell, pressing white handkerchiefs to their glowing faces. And all along the quay eyes lifted to the great aircraft-carrier that no longer carried aircraft. Men and women standing in brightly colored robes and saris, troops, dockyard workers, traders, all paused to watch the Ship of Brides maneuver her way in.

"You must stick together and stay in the main thoroughfares." The WSO was struggling to be heard over the clamor of those desperate to disembark. "And you must return by twenty-two hundred hours at the latest. Captain Highfield has made it clear he will not tolerate lateness. Do you all understand?"

It was only a matter of months since the Indian sailors' mutiny at the harbor; they had gone on strike in protest against their living conditions. How this had escalated was still a matter of some debate, but it was indisputable that it had erupted into a fierce gun battle between English troops and the mutineers that had lasted several days. There had been several heated discussions about the wisdom of letting the women ashore but given that they had remained aboard at Colombo and Cochin, it did not seem fair to keep them any longer. The officer held up a clipboard, wiping her face with her free hand. "The duty officer will be taking names as each woman returns aboard. Make sure yours is among them."

The heat was fierce and Margaret clung to the side of the ship, wishing, as the crowd pressed and writhed around her, that she could find somewhere to sit down. Avice, beside her, kept standing on tip-toe, shouting back what she could see, one hand shielding her eyes against the bright sunlight.

"We must do the Gateway of India. Apparently everyone does the Gateway of India. And the Willingdon Club is meant to be lovely, but it's a few miles out of the city. They've got tennis courts and a swimming-pool. Do you think we should get a taxi?"

"I want to find a nice hotel, and put my feet up for half an hour," said Margaret. They had stood watching for almost the two hours it had taken *Victoria* to drop anchor, and the oppressive temperature had caused Margaret's ankles to swell.

"Plenty of time for that, Margaret. Us ladies in the family way must do our best to keep active. Ooh, look! They're about to let us off."

There was a queue for the gharries, the little horse-drawn carriages that would take the women to the Red Gate at the entrance to the dock. Those who had already made it down the gangplank were clustered around them, chattering away, checking and rechecking handbags and sunhats, pointing out the distant views of the city.

Through the gate, Margaret could see wide, tree-lined avenues, flanked by large hotels, houses and shops, the pavements and roads thick with movement. The solidity and space made her feel almost giddy after so long at sea, and several times she had found herself swaying, unsure whether it was due to heat or sea-legs.

Two women walked past, balancing oversized baskets of fruit on their heads with the same nonchalant ease as the brides wore their hats. They whispered to each other, covering their mouths and giggling through bejeweled fingers. As Margaret watched, one spied something on the ground. Her back ramrod straight, she stretched out a bare foot, picked up the object with her toes, took it in her hand and pocketed it.

"Strewth," said Margaret, who had not seen her own feet for several weeks now.

"There's a dinner-dance at Green's Hotel, apparently." Avice was checking notes in her pocket book. "Some of the girls from 8D are heading there later. I said we might meet them for tea. But I'm desperate to go shopping. I feel I've bought everything it's possible to buy from the PX."

"I just want a bloody seat," Margaret muttered. "I don't care about sightseeing or shopping. I just want dry land and a bloody seat."

"Do you really think you should use so much bad language?" Avice murmured. "It's really not becoming to hear it from someone in . . . your . . ."

It was then, as Avice's voice tailed away, that Margaret became aware of a shushing. She wondered what had caused it. Following the others' gaze, she turned to see Frances walking down the gang-plank behind them. She was dressed in a pale blue blouse, buttoned to the neck, and khaki trousers. She wore her wide-brimmed sunhat and glasses, but her red-gold hair and long limbs confirmed her identity.

She hesitated at the bottom, conscious perhaps of the quiet. Then, seeing Margaret's hand held aloft, she made her way through the women to where Margaret and Avice stood. As she moved, girls stepped back from her like parting seas.

"Changed your mind, then?" Margaret was conscious of her voice booming into the silence.

"Yes," said Frances.

"It'd drive you nuts to stay aboard too long, eh?" Margaret looked at Avice. "Especially in heat like this."

Frances stood very still, her eyes fixed on Margaret. "It is pretty close," she said.

"Well, I vote we find some bar or hotel where we can—"

"She's not walking around with us."

"Avice!"

"People will talk. And goodness knows what might happen—for all we know her former customers are walking the streets. They might think we're one of those . . ."

"Don't be so bloody ridiculous. Frances is perfectly welcome to walk with us."

Margaret was aware that all the women around them were listening. Bunch of chattering harpies, that was what her dad would have called them. Surely nothing Frances had done, whatever her past, warranted such treatment?

"You, perhaps," said Avice. "I'll find someone else to walk with."

"Frances," Margaret said, daring any of the women to speak again, "you're welcome to walk with me. I'd be glad of the company."

It was hard to tell from behind her sunglasses, but Frances appeared to glance sideways at the sea of closed faces.

"You can help me find somewhere nice to sit down."

"Just watch out she doesn't find somewhere to lie down."

Frances's head shot round and her fingers tightened on her handbag.

"Come on," Margaret said, holding out her hand. "Let's hit the old Gateway of India."

"Actually, I've changed my mind."

"Ah, come on! You might never get another chance to see India."

"No. Thank you. I—I'll see you later." Before Margaret had a chance to say any more she had disappeared back through the crowd.

The women closed ranks, murmuring in righteous indignation. Margaret watched the distant gangplank, just able to make out the tall thin figure walking slowly up it. She waited until it had vanished inside. "That was mean, Avice."

"I'm not horrid, Margaret, so you needn't look at me like that. I'm just honest. I'm not having my one trip ashore ruined by that girl." She straightened her hair, then placed a sunhat carefully on her head. "Besides, in our condition, I think it's best if we keep our worries to a minimum. It can't be good for us."

The queue had moved on. Avice linked her arm with Margaret's and walked her swiftly toward a gharry.

Margaret knew she should go to Frances: by even participating in this outing she had condoned Frances's treatment. But she was desperate to feel land under her feet. And it was so difficult to know what to say.

———

With only a handful of brides left aboard, the ship had become a maelstrom of focused activity: teams of ratings prowled decks normally closed to men, scrubbing, painting and polishing. Several were on their knees on the flight deck, fighting with foam and wooden brushes to rid the gray concrete of its lingering rainbow puddles of aviation fuel. Small tugs unloaded huge crates of fresh fruit and vegetables, feeding them through hatches into the hold, while on the other side the tankers began to refuel the ship.

In other circumstances, Frances might have enjoyed the sight of the ship at work, fully engaged in its normal course of duties. Now she took in the smirk of the duty officer at the top of the gangplank, the knowing glance he exchanged with his mate as she re-embarked, showing him her station card. She saw the lingering glances of the painting parties, the lowered eyes and muttered greeting of the officer who had previously wished her a cheerful good morning.

Over the last few days she had wondered at how it was possible to feel so lonely in a ship so full of people.

She was a few steps away from the little dormitory when she saw him. She had told herself that her previous outings around the ship had been to give herself some fresh air; to make herself leave the sweaty confines of the cabin. Now, as she recognized the man walking toward her, she knew she had not been honest with herself.

She glanced down at her clothes, unconsciously checking herself as she had once done while on duty, feeling her skin prickle with a mixture of anxiety and anticipation. She was unsure of what she could possibly say to him. She knew he would have to say something now: they were too close for him not to.

They stopped. Looked at each other for just the briefest moment, then stared at their feet.

"Going ashore?" He indicated the harbor.

She could see nothing on his face, no clue. Should I be grateful for the mere fact that he has spoken to me at all? she wondered. "No . . . I—I decided to stay here."

"Enjoy the peace and quiet."

"Something like that."

Perhaps he hadn't wanted to talk to her but was too gentlemanly to hurt her feelings.

"Well . . . as much peace as you can find with . . . with this . . ." He gestured to where a party of engineers were repairing some piece of equipment high up, joking noisily with each other as they worked.

"Yes," she said. She could think of nothing else to say.

"You should make the most of it," he said. "It's . . . hard to find a bit of space to yourself on board. I mean real space . . ."

Perhaps he might understand more than he was saying, she thought. "Yes," she said. "Yes, it is."

"I—"

"Hey, Marine."

The rating walked toward them, holding out a note, his cap pulled at a jaunty angle over one eye. "They want you in the control room before your watch. Briefing for the governor's visit." As he came closer she could see he had recognized her. The look the younger man gave her as he handed over the note made her wince. "Excuse me," she said, cheeks reddening.

As she turned away, she half hoped he might ask her to wait a moment. That he might say something, that told her he didn't see her as the rest of them did. Say something, she willed him. Anything.

Moments later she wrenched open the door to the dormitory and let it shut heavily behind her. She leaned against it, her back sticking through her blouse to its unforgiving surface. Her jaw was clenched so tightly that it ached. She had never thought until now about life's fairness, at least not in relation to herself. Her patients had suffered, and she had occasionally questioned why God could take one or leave another in such pain. She had never wondered about the fairness of her own experiences: she had long ago discovered that it was better not to think about those years. But now, with all the other emotions swirling around inside her in some infernal cocktail, she felt the pendulum swing from bleak despair to blind fury at the way her life had turned out. Had she not suffered enough? Was this, and not what she had seen in the war, the real test of her resolve? How much more was she expected to pay for?

Maude Gonne, perhaps understanding that Margaret had gone ashore, scratched restlessly at the door. Frances stooped, picked her up and sat down with her on her lap.

The dog took no comfort from this. In fact she paid Frances no attention. Frances sat there stroking, gazing at the milky, unseeing eyes, the quivering body desperate for only one person.

Frances held the dog close to her, pitying her plight. "I know," she whispered, laying her cheek against the soft head. "Believe me, I know."

———

Accustomed to the intense heat of Bombay, and oblivious to the huge fans that whirred overhead, the waiters in the cocktail bar of

Green's Hotel were visibly perspiring. The sweat glistened on their burnished faces and seeped into the collars of their immaculate white uniforms. But their discomfort was less to do with the heat—it was a relatively mild evening—than the endless demands of the hundred or so brides who had chosen that bar to end their day's shore leave.

"If I have to wait one more minute for my drink I swear I'll have words with that man," said Avice, wafting the fan she had bought that afternoon and eyeing the unfortunate waiter as he ducked through the crowd, tray held aloft. "I'm wilting," she said, to his departing back.

"He's doing his best," said Margaret. She had been careful to sip her drink slowly, having guessed from the packed bar that service was likely to be slow. She was feeling restored: she had been able to elevate her feet for half an hour, and now let her head rest on the back of the chair, enjoying the light breeze created by the overhead fan.

It was the same everywhere: in Greens, the Bristol Grill, the grand Taj Mahal hotel; a combination of the *Victoria* and several troopships landing at once had swamped the harbor area with would-be revelers, men made gay and reckless by the end of the war and their increasing proximity to home. They had looked in at several places before deciding that at Green's they might get a seat. Now, from their vantage-point on the veranda, they could look back through the archway at the dance area, which was now populated by men and women casting hopeful—and sometimes covetous—looks in the direction of the tables. Some of the brides had begun drinking John Collins and rum punches at lunchtime and were now feeling the effects of their encroaching hangovers. They seemed listless and vaguely discontented, their makeup sliding down their faces and their hair limp.

Margaret felt no guilt at hogging her seat. Heedless of the heat and dust, and of her own oft-stated "delicate condition," Avice had dragged her everywhere that afternoon. They had walked around all the European shops, spent at least an hour in the Army and Navy Stores and another bartering with the men and small boys who besieged them with apparently unmissable bargains. Margaret had swiftly grown tired of haggling; it felt wrong to hold out for the odd rupee faced with the abject poverty of the salesmen. Avice, however, had leapt into it with astonishing enthusiasm, and spent much of the evening holding aloft her various purchases and exclaiming at the prices.

Margaret had been overwhelmed by the little they had seen of Bombay. She had been shocked at the sight of Indians bedding down in the street, at their seeming indifference to their conditions. At their thin limbs next to her own milk-fed plumpness, at their physical disabilities and barely dressed children. It made her feel ashamed for the nights she had moaned about the discomfort of her bunk.

Her drink appeared, and she made a point of tipping the waiter in front of Avice. Then, as he departed, she stared out at *Victoria*, floating serenely in the harbor, and wondered guiltily if Frances was asleep. All its lights were on, giving it a festive appearance, but without either aircraft or people the flight deck looked empty, like a vast, unpopulated plain.

"Ah! A seat! Mind if we join you?" Margaret looked round to see Irene Carter, flanked by one of her friends, pulling out the chair opposite. She gave a wide, lipsticked smile that did not stretch to her eyes. Despite the heat she looked cool and brought with her a vague scent of lilies.

"Irene," said Avice, her own smile something of a snarl. "How lovely."

"We're exhausted," said Irene, throwing her bags under the table and lifting a hand to summon a waiter. He arrived at her side immediately. "All those natives following you around. I had to get one of the officers to tell them to leave me alone. I don't think they know how upsetting they can be."

"We saw a man without legs," confided her companion, a plump girl with a mournful air.

"Just sitting out on a rug! Can you imagine?"

"I think he might have been stuck there," the girl said. "Perhaps someone put him down and left him."

"We've hardly noticed. We've been so busy shopping, haven't we, Margaret?" Avice gestured at her own bags.

"We have," said Margaret.

"Bought anything nice?" said Irene. Margaret fancied there was a steely glint in her eye.

"Oh, nothing you'd be interested in," said Avice, her own smile glued in place.

"Really? I heard you'd bought something for the Queen of the *Victoria* final."

"Natty Johnson saw you in the Army and Navy," said the plump girl.

"That? I don't suppose I'll wear it. To be honest, I haven't given a thought to what I'll wear."

Margaret snorted quietly into her drink. Avice had spent the best part of an hour parading in front of the mirror in a variety of outfits. "I wish I knew what Irene Carter was wearing," she had muttered. "I'm going to make sure I knock her into a cocked hat." She had spent on three new dresses more money than Margaret's father would spend on cattle feed in a year.

"Oh, I dare say I'll dig something out of my trunk," said Irene. "It's only a bit of fun after all, isn't it?"

"It certainly is."

Bloody hell, thought Margaret, gazing at Avice's butter-wouldn't-melt smile.

"Couldn't agree more," said Irene. "You know what, Avice? I shall tell all those girls who've been whispering that you're taking it too seriously that they're quite wrong. There." She paused. "And that I've heard that direct from the horse's mouth." She lifted her drink as if in a toast.

Margaret had to bite her lip hard to stop herself laughing at Avice's face.

The four women, forced together through lack of spare tables rather than camaraderie, spent the best part of an hour and a half seated together. They ordered a fish curry; Margaret found it delicious but regretted it when indigestion struck. The other brides, however, made a show of fanning their mouths and pronouncing it inedible.

"I hope it hasn't done any harm to the baby," said Avice, laying a hand on her non-existent bump.

"I heard your news. Congratulations," said Irene. "Does your husband know? I'm assuming it *is* your husband's," she added, then laughed, a tinkling sound, to show she was joking.

"I believe we're getting post tomorrow," said Avice, whose own graceful smile had gone a little rigid. "I imagine he'll have told everyone by now. We're having a party when we get to London," she said. "We felt we rather missed out, with the war, so we're going to have a do. Probably at the Savoy. And now, of course, it will be a double celebration."

The Savoy was a good one, Margaret thought. Irene had looked briefly furious.

"In fact, Irene, perhaps you'd like to come. Mummy and Daddy will be flying from Australia—the new Qantas service?—and I'm sure they'd love to see you. What with you being so new in London, I'm sure you'll be glad of all the friends you can get." Avice leaned forward conspiratorially. "Always makes you feel better to have at least one date in the social diary, doesn't it?"

Ka-*pow*! thought Margaret, who was enjoying herself now. This was far dirtier than anything her brothers had ever done to each other.

"I shall be delighted to come to your little gathering, if I can," said Irene, wiping the corners of her mouth. "I'll have to check what our plans are, of course."

"Of course." Avice sipped her iced water, a little smile dancing on her lips.

"But I do think it's lovely that you'll have something to take your mind off things."

Avice raised an eyebrow.

"Oh, this horrid business with you having befriended a prostitute. I mean, who on earth could have known? And so soon after your other little friend was caught fraternizing with those grubby engineers."

"With her knickers down," said the plump girl.

"Well, yes, that's one way of putting it," said Irene.

"I hardly—" Avice began.

Irene's voice was concerned: "It must have been so worrying for you, not knowing if you were going to be tarred with the same brush . . . you know, with what everyone's been saying about your dormitory and what goes on there. We've all so admired your stoicism. No, your little social do is a very good idea. It will quite take your mind off things."

———

The afternoon had stretched into evening, and with the fading of the light her thoughts had grown darker. Unable to face the confines of the cabin any longer, she had toyed with the idea of leaving the ship. But she had no one to accompany her, and Bombay seemed to require a certain robustness of spirit that she did not own. She had stepped out and headed for the boat deck, close to where she had sat with Maude Gonne just a week earlier.

Now she stood, while the harbor lights glinted steadily on the inky water, interrupted occasionally by the noisy passage of tugs and barges. A strange conjunction of scents, spices, fuel oil, perfume, rotten meat, expanded in the stilled air so that she was both entranced and repelled by the mere act of breathing. Her thoughts had calmed a little now; she would do what she had always done, she told herself. She would get through. It was only a couple more weeks until she reached England and she had learned long ago that anything could be endured if you tried hard enough. She would not think of what might have been. The men who had best survived the war, she had long ago observed, had been those able to live one day at a time, those able to count even the smallest of blessings. She had bought herself a packet of cigarettes at the PX. Now she lit one, conscious that it was a self-destructive gesture but savoring the acrid taste. Across the water, voices called to each other and from somewhere further distant Indian music drifted, one long, mournful filigree note.

"You want to watch out. You're not meant to be here."

She jumped. "Oh," she said. "It's you."

"It's me," he said, stubbing out his own cigarette. "Maggie not with you?"

"She's ashore."

"With all the others."

She wondered if there was a polite way of asking him to leave her.

He was wearing his engineer's overalls; it was too dark to see the oil on them but she could smell it under the scent of the smoke. She hated the smell of oil: she had treated too many burned men who had been saturated with it, could still feel the tacky density of the fabric she had had to peel off their flesh.

I shall start nursing again in England, she told herself. Audrey Marshall had sent her off with a personal letter of recommendation. With her service record there would be no shortage of opportunities.

"Ever been to India before?"

She was annoyed at the interruption of her thoughts. "No."

"Seen a lot of countries, have you?"

"A few," she said. "Mainly bases."

"You're a well-traveled woman, then."

It's because Margaret isn't here, she thought. He's one of those men who needs an audience. She did her best to smile. "No more than anyone else who's seen service, I imagine."

He lit himself another cigarette and blew the smoke meditatively into the sky. "But I bet you could answer me a question," he said.

She looked at him.

"Is there a difference?"

She frowned. On the shore, two vehicles were locked in an impasse, horns blaring. The sound echoed across the dockyard, drowning the music.

"I'm sorry?" She had to lean forward temporarily to hear him.

"In the men." He smiled, revealing white teeth in the darkness. "I mean, is there a nationality you prefer?"

From his expression she knew she had heard what she suspected. "Excuse me," she said. She moved past him, her cheeks burning, but as she reached for the handle of the hatch, he stepped in front of her.

"No need to have an attack of modesty on my account," he said.

"Will you excuse me?"

"We all know what you are. No need to skirt round it." He spoke in a sing-song voice so that it was a second before she had gauged the menace in what he was saying.

"Please would you let me pass?"

"You know, I had you all wrong." Dennis Tims shook his head. "We called you Miss Frigidaire in the mess. Miss Frigidaire. We couldn't believe you'd even married. Had you down as wedded to one of those Bible-bashers, a virgin for life. How wrong we were, eh?"

Her heart was racing as she tried to assess whether she would be able to push past him for the door. One of his hands rested lightly on the handle. She could feel the confidence behind his strength, the sureness of a man who always, physically, got his own way.

"So prim and proper, with your blouses buttoned up to your neck. And really you're just some whore who no doubt persuaded some fool pollywog sailor to stick a ring on your finger. How'd you do it, eh? Promise him you'd save it all for him, did you? Tell him he was the only one who meant anything?"

He put out a hand toward her breast and she batted it away.

"Let me out," she said.

"What's the matter, Miss Priss? Not like anyone's around to know." He gripped her arms then, pushed her backward toward the guard rail. She stumbled as his weight met her like a solid wall. In the distance, from the hotel near the harbor, she could hear laughter.

"I've seen girls like you in a million ports. Shouldn't allow your sort on board," he muttered wetly into her ear.

"Get off me!"

"Oh, come on! You can't expect me to believe you're not making a bit on the side while you're here—"

"Please—"

"Step away, Tims."

The voice came from her right. Tims's head lifted, and she glanced across his shoulder. He was standing there, his eyes burning black in the dim light.

"Step away, Tims." His tone was icy.

Tims checked the other man's identity, smiled and abandoned it, as if unsure how chummy he should be. "A little dispute over payment," he said, backing away from her and ostentatiously checking his trousers. "Nothing you need to concern yourself about. You know what these girls are like."

She closed her eyes, not wanting to see the marine's face. She was shaking violently.

"Get inside." The marine spoke slowly.

Tims seemed remarkably cool. "Like I said, Marine, just a disagreement about price. She wants to charge twice the going rate. Considers us sailors a captive market, know what I mean?"

"Get inside," said Nicol.

She stepped closer to the wall, unwilling even to be in Tims's line of vision.

"We'll keep this to ourselves, eh? Don't suppose you want the captain to know he's carrying a brass. Or who her friends are."

"If I see you so much as look in Mrs. Mackenzie's direction for the remainder of the voyage, I'll have you."

"You?"

"It might not be on board. It might not even be on this voyage. But I'll have you."

"You don't want to make an enemy of me, Marine." Tims was at the hatch. His eyes glittered in the darkness.

"You aren't listening to me."

There was a moment of exquisite stillness. Then, with a final, hard look at the two of them, Tims backed through the hatch. She was about to breathe out when his huge, shorn head reappeared. "Offered you half price, has she?" He laughed. "I'll tell your missus . . ."

They listened as Tims's footsteps faded in the direction of the stokers' mess.

"Are you all right?" he said, quietly.

She smoothed her hair off her face and swallowed hard. "I'm fine."

"I'm sorry," he said. "You shouldn't have to . . ." His voice tailed off, as if he were unsure of what he wanted to say.

She was unable to determine if she was brave enough to look at him. Finally, "Thank you," she whispered, and fled.

———

When he returned there was only one other marine in the mess: the young bugler, Emmett, was fast asleep, arms stretched behind his head with the relaxed abandon of a small child. The little room smelled stale; the heat was heavy in the air, on the discarded ashtrays and unfilled shoes. Nicol removed his uniform, washed, and then, his towel round his neck and the water already evaporating from his skin, pulled his writing-paper from his locker and took a seat.

He was not a letter-writer. Many years ago, when he had tried, he had found that his pen stumbled over the words, that the sentiments on the page rarely mirrored what he felt inside. Now, however, the words came easily. He was letting her go. "There is a passenger on board," he wrote, "a girl with a bad past. Seeing what she has suffered has made me realize that everyone deserves a second chance, especially if someone out there is willing to give them one, in spite of what they carry with them."

Here he lit a cigarette, his gaze fixed ahead on nothing. He stayed like that for some time, oblivious to the men arguing down the corridor, the sound of the trumpet practice going on in the bathroom, the men who were now climbing into their hammocks around him.

Finally he put the nib of his pen back onto the paper. He would take it ashore tomorrow and wire it. No matter the cost. "I suppose what I am trying to say is that I'm sorry. And that I'm glad you've found someone to love you, despite everything. I hope he will be good to you, Fay. That you have the chance of the happiness you deserve."

He reread it twice before he saw that he had written Frances's name.

18

Now you understand why British soldiers respect the women in uniform.
They have won the right to the utmost respect. When you see a girl in khaki
or air-force blue with a bit of ribbon on her tunic—remember she didn't get
it for knitting more socks than anyone else in Ipswich.

A SHORT GUIDE TO GREAT BRITAIN, WAR AND NAVY
DEPARTMENTS, *WASHINGTON, DC*

THIRTY-THREE DAYS

The governor of Gibraltar was known not only throughout the Navy
but the British civil service as an unusually intelligent man. He had
built a reputation as a major strategist during the First World War,
and his diplomatic career had seen him rewarded for his hawk-like
tactical and observational skills. But even he had stared at the forward liftwell for several moments before he could acknowledge what
he was seeing.

Captain Highfield, in the process of taking him up on to the flight
deck ready for the welcoming performance by the Royal Marines
Band, cursed himself for not checking the route beforehand. A liftwell was a liftwell. He had never thought they'd be bold enough to
string their underwear along it. White, flesh-colored, gray with overuse or cobweb-delicate and edged with French lace; the brassières
and foundation garments waved merrily all the way up the cavernous
space, mimicking the pennant that had welcomed the great man
aboard. And now, here he was, the cream of the British diplomatic
service, on Highfield's great warship, surrounded by an orderly parade of immaculately dressed seamen, transfixed by lines of bloomers.

Dobson. The man would have known about this, yet had chosen
not to warn him. Captain Highfield cursed his leg for confining him

to his office that morning and allowing the younger man the opportunity. He had felt unwell, had decided to rest, knowing that today would be long and difficult, and had trusted Dobson to make sure that everything was A1. He might have known he'd find a way to undermine him.

"I . . . You'll find this is something of an unconventional crossing," Captain Highfield ventured, when he had composed himself enough to speak. "I'm afraid we've had to be a little . . . pragmatic about procedure."

The governor's mouth had dropped open, his cheeks betraying the faintest flush of color. Dobson's face, serene under his cap, gave away nothing.

"I would add, Your Excellency, that this is by no means any indication of the level of our respect." He tried to inject a note of humor into his voice, but it fell flat.

The governor's wife, handbag held in front of her, nudged her husband surreptitiously. She inclined her head. "Nothing we haven't seen before, Captain," she said graciously, her mouth twitching with what might have been amusement. "I think the war has exposed us all to far more frightening scenes than this one."

"Quite," said the governor. "Quite." The tenor of his voice suggested that this was unlikely.

"In fact, it's admirable that you're going to such lengths to keep your passengers comfortable." She laid a hand on his sleeve, a glimmer of understanding in her face. "Shall we move on?"

Things improved on the flight deck. Having embarked the governor and the other passengers at Aden, the *Victoria* had begun to make her way slowly north along the Suez Canal, a silver vein of water, lined by sand dunes, that shimmered so brightly in the intense heat that those gazing from the sides of the ship felt obliged to shade themselves. Despite the heat, the brides were gay under parasols and sunhats, the band gamely keeping up despite the discomfort of even tropical rig in such temperatures.

The men having resumed their duties, the governor and his wife had agreed to judge the Tap Dancing competition, the latest in the series of the Queen of the *Victoria* contests devised to keep the women occupied. Shielded by a large umbrella from the worst of the sun, armed with iced gin and tonic and faced with a line of giggling girls, even the governor had warmed. His wife, who had taken the time to chat to each contestant, eventually awarded the prize to a pretty blonde girl, a popular choice given the hearty congratulations of the other brides. She had confided to Highfield afterward that she thought the Australians were "rather a nice lot. Terribly brave to leave their loved ones and come all this way." Infected with a little of the merriment of the afternoon, he had found it hard to disagree.

And then it had all gone wrong again.

Captain Highfield had been about to announce that the event was over, and suggest that he and his new passengers depart below decks to where the cook had prepared a late lunch, when he had noticed a flurry of activity on the starboard side. The *Victoria* was moving sedately past a military camp and the brides, spotting large numbers of Caucasian men, had flocked to the edge of the flight deck. Their brightly colored dresses fluttering in the breeze, they waved gaily at the bronzed young men who had stopped work to watch them pass, calling down greetings. As he leaned over to see, he could hear the women's squeals, could just make out the enthusiastic waving from the bare-chested men below, now jammed up against the wire perimeter fence, squinting into the sun.

Highfield stared at the scene, making sure his suspicions were correct. Then it was with a heavy heart that he reached for the Tannoy. "I am gratified that you have given our guests, the governor and his wife, such a rousing welcome," he had said, watching the governor's back stiffen in his tropical whites as he too took in the scene below. "There will be extra refreshments in the forward hangar for those who would like tea. In the meantime, you might be interested to know that the young men you are waving to are German prisoners."

———

Irene Carter had approached her after the contest to tell her she was glad Avice had won—"Best to make the most of those legs before the old varicose veins set in, eh?"—and to show off her latest delivery of post. She had received seven letters, no less than four from her husband.

"You must read us yours," she said, sunglasses masking her eyes. "My mother says she's been inviting yours round for tea since they discovered we were shipmates. They'll be desperate to know what we've been doing."

And I bet you've told her everything, thought Avice.

"Hey-ho. I'm off to tea and to read Harold's letters. Did you get many?"

"Oh, heaps," said Avice, brandishing hers in the air. There had been only one from Ian. She had tucked it under her mother's so that Irene couldn't tell. "Good luck with the next contest, anyway," she said. "It's fancy dress, I believe, so I'm sure you'll do much better. You're getting so tanned you could wear a scarf round your waist and go as a native." And clutching her "certificate," Avice walked, with as little conceit as she could muster, away.

Frances wasn't in the dormitory. She rarely was anymore. Avice thought she was probably hiding somewhere. Margaret was attending a lecture on places to visit in England. She kicked off her shoes and lay down, preparing to read Ian's latest communication in an atmosphere of rare privacy.

She scooted through the letters from her father (business, money, golf), mother (travel details, dresses) and sister ("quite happy by myself, thank you, blah-blah-blah"), then came to Ian's envelope. She gazed at his handwriting, wondering at how one could sense authority even in ink and paper. Her mother had always said there was something immature about men with bad handwriting. It suggested that their character was somehow unformed.

She glanced at her wristwatch: there was ten minutes before the first lunch shift. She had just time to read it. She peeled it open and gave a little sigh of pleasure.

A quarter of an hour later, she was still staring at it.

———

Frances and Margaret were seated in the deck canteen when the rating found them. They had been eating ices. Frances was now accustomed to the relative hush that descended whenever she dared show herself in public. Margaret had chattered away with grim determination. Once or twice she had asked the most persistent starers whether it was a bite of her ice-cream they were after and sworn at them under her breath as they blushed.

"Mrs. Frances Mackenzie?" the rating had asked. He looked painfully young: his neck hardly filled the collar of his uniform.

She nodded. She had been half expecting him for days.

"Captain would like to see you in his offices, ma'am. I'm to bring you."

The canteen had gone quiet.

Margaret blanched. "Do you think it's the dog?" she whispered.

"No," said Frances, dully. "I'm pretty sure it's not that."

She could see from the expressions on the faces around her that the other women were pretty sure too. Not Wanted Don't Come, the whisper started. Only this time the brides evinced no anxiety.

"Don't be long," said a voice, as she left the canteen. "You wouldn't want people to start talking."

———

Avice lay on the bed. From somewhere nearby there was a strange sound, a low, guttural moan, and it was with distant surprise that she realized it was emanating from her own throat.

She stared at the hand holding the letter, then at the wedding ring on her slim finger. The room receded around her. Suddenly, she threw herself off her bunk, fell on to her knees, and vomited violently into the bowl that had never been removed after her early days of sickness. She retched until her ribs hurt and her throat burned, arms wrapped round her torso as if they were the only thing stopping her whole self turning inside-out. Through coughing, she could hear her own voice, spluttering, "No! No! No!" as if she were refusing to accept that this monstrosity could be real.

Finally, spent, she pushed herself back against the bunk, her hair plastered in sweaty tendrils round her face, limbs awkward and ungainly on the hard floor, her dress, her makeup unheeded. She wondered if the whole thing had been a dream. Perhaps the letter didn't exist. The sea could get you like that—she had heard plenty of sailors say so. But there it was on her pillow. In Ian's handwriting. His beautiful handwriting. His beautiful, horrific, diabolic handwriting.

Outside, she could hear the clicking heels of a group of women who were chattering as they passed. Maude Gonne, positioned just behind the door, raised her head, as if waiting to hear a familiar voice among them, and then, disappointed, laid it between her paws.

Avice followed the sound, head swaying like a drunk's. She felt detached from everything. There was nothing she wanted more than to lie down. Her head felt as if a great weight were pressing down on her. She could do nothing except stare at the ribbed metal floor.

She shoved the bowl back under her bed. Despite the smell, the unforgiving metal beneath her, her wet hair, she lay down, eyes on the other letter open beside her. Her mother had written:

> *I've told everyone that the celebration will be at the Savoy. Daddy got a very advantageous rate because of one of his contacts in the hotel business. And, Avice darling—you'll never guess—the Darley-Hendersons are going to make it part of their round-the-world trip, and if that wasn't exciting enough the Governor and his wife have said they're coming too. People seem so much happier to travel now the war is over. And they will ensure we get your picture into* Tatler. *Darling, I might have had my doubts about this wedding, but I have to tell you I'm pleased as punch about this trip. We'll put on a do that will have not just Melbourne but half of England talking for months!*
>
> *Your loving Mother*
>
> *PS Pay no attention to your sister. She's a little bit sour at the moment. Case of the green-eyed monster, I suspect.*
>
> *PPS We've not heard yet from Ian's parents, which is a pity. Could you ask him to send us their address so we can contact them ourselves? I want to know if there is anyone special they'd like to invite.*

———

It had been a long, rather wearing afternoon, and it was something of an effort to stand when the girl entered the room, so Captain Highfield stayed behind his desk to allow himself the chance to lean on it. The governor's arrival, and its attendant difficulties, had taken it out of him, and it was for that reason—and perhaps to save the girl's blushes—that he had chosen to hold this meeting without the aid of either the chaplain or WSO.

She stood in the doorway when the rating announced her and stayed there after he had left, clutching a small bag. He had seen her at close quarters twice now and she was physically striking. Only her demeanor stopped her being a compelling figure. She had seemingly developed the trick of receding into the background; now that he had briefed himself through her notes, he understood why.

Captain Highfield gestured to her to sit down. He stared at the floor for some minutes, trying to work out how to address the issue, wishing that, just this once, he could have handed over the captaincy to someone else. Disciplinary matters with his men were straightforward: one followed procedure, gave them a bawling-out if necessary. But women were different, he thought, exasperated, conscious of the woman opposite, of the women who had been in before her. They brought all their problems on board along with their tons of baggage, created new ones for good measure—and then made you feel guilty, wrong, for simply following the rules.

Outside the stand-easy was being sounded over the Tannoy, signaling the men's canteen break. He waited until there was silence. "Do you know why I have summoned you to see me?" he asked.

She did not reply. She blinked slowly at him, as if the onus was on him to explain himself.

Come on, man, he told himself. Get it over and done with. Then you can pour yourself a stiff drink.

"It has come to my attention that several days ago you were involved in something of an incident downstairs. In the course of looking into the matter, I've heard things that . . . have left me a little concerned."

It was Rennick who had told him, the previous evening. One of the stokers had approached him, muttered that there was all sorts of trouble being stirred up, and then what was being said about the girl. Rennick had not hesitated to tell Highfield: no one would have mentioned something like that to the Captain's steward without believing it would go straight to the head man.

"It's about your—your life before you came aboard. I'm afraid I have to bring this up, uncomfortable as it may be for you. For the welfare of my men and for the good conduct of everyone on board, I have to know whether these—these rumors are true."

She said nothing.

"Can I assume from your silence that they are not . . . untrue?"

When she failed to answer him a third time, he felt ill-at-ease. This, allied with his physical discomfort, caused him to become impatient. He stood, perhaps better to impress her with his authority, and moved round the desk.

"I'm not trying to deliberately persecute you, Miss—"

"Mrs.," she said. "Mrs. Mackenzie."

"But rules are rules, and as it stands I cannot allow women of—your sort to travel on a ship full of men."

"My sort."

"You know what I'm saying. It's difficult enough carrying so many women at close quarters. I've looked into your—your circumstances, and I can't allow your presence to destabilize my ship." God only knew what the governor of Gibraltar would say if he knew of the presence of this particular passenger. Let alone his wife. They had only just stopped shuddering at the thought of those gamboling German prisoners.

She stared at her shoes for some time. Then she raised her head. "Captain Highfield, are you putting me off the ship?" Her voice was low and calm.

He was half relieved that she had said it. "I'm sorry," he said. "I feel I have no choice."

She appeared to be considering something. Her demeanor

suggested that there was almost nothing surprising in what he had said to her. But in the faintest narrowing of her eyes there was contempt for it too.

This was not what he had expected. Anger, perhaps. Histrionics, like the other two unfortunates. He had posted the rating outside in anticipation.

"You are free to say something," he said, when the silence became oppressive. "In your defense, I mean."

There was a lengthy pause. Then she placed her hands in her lap. "In my defense . . . I am a nurse. A nursing sister, to be more precise. I have been a nurse for four and a half years. In that time I've treated several thousand men, some of whose lives I saved."

"It's a very good thing—that you managed to—"

"Become a worthwhile human being?" Her tone was sharp.

"That's not what—"

"But I can't, can I? Because I am never to be allowed to forget my so-called past. Not even several thousand miles distant from it."

"I wasn't suggesting that—"

She looked at him directly. He thought she might have squared her shoulders.

"I know quite well what you were suggesting, Captain. That my service record is the least important thing about me. Like most of the occupants of this ship, you choose to determine my character by the first thing you heard. And then act upon it."

She smoothed her dress over her knees and took a deep breath, as if she were having some trouble containing herself. "What I was going to say, Captain Highfield, before you interrupted me, is that I have treated in my career probably several thousand men, some of whom had been terrorized and physically brutalized. Some of whom were my enemies. Many of whom were only half alive. And not one," she paused for breath. "Not one of them treated me with the lack of consideration you have just shown."

He had not expected her to be so composed. So articulate.

He had not expected to find himself the accused.

"Look," his tone was conciliatory, "I can't pretend I don't know about you."

"No, and neither can I, apparently. I can only try to lead a useful life. And not think too hard about things that may have been out of my control."

They remained in an uneasy silence. His mind raced as he tried to work out how to deal with this extraordinary situation. Outside, he could hear muffled conversation and lowered his voice, sensing a way to salvage their dignity. "Look—are you saying that what happened wasn't your doing? That you might have been . . . more sinned against than sinning?"

If she would plead for herself, make a promise about her future conduct, then perhaps . . .

"I'm saying that it's none of your concern either way." Her knuckles were white with some contained emotion. "The only things that are your business, Captain, are my profession, which, as you'll know from your passenger lists and my service record, should you have cared to look at it, is nurse, my marital status and my behavior on board your ship, which, I think you'll find, has met all your requirements for decorum."

Her voice had gained strength. The tips of her pale ears had gone pink, the only sign of any underlying lack of composure.

He realized, with some bewilderment, that he felt as if he were the one in the wrong.

He glanced down at the papers that detailed the procedures for putting off brides. "Put her off at Port Said," the Australian Red Cross supervisor had said. "She might have to wait a bit for a boat back. Then again, a lot of them disappear in Egypt." Her "them" had contained an unmistakable note of contempt.

God, it was a mess. A bloody mess. He wished he'd never embarked on the conversation and opened this can of worms. But she had entered the system now. His hands were tied.

Perhaps recognizing something in his expression, she got to her feet. Her hair, scraped back from her forehead, emphasized the high, almost Slavic bones of her face, the shadows under her eyes. He wondered briefly whether before she left, she would try to hit him, as the little one had, and then felt guilty for having thought it. "Look, Mrs. Mackenzie, I—"

"I know. You'd like me to leave."

He was struggling for something to say, something that might appropriately convey the right mixture of authority and regret.

She was half-way toward the door, when she said, "Do you want me to look at your leg?"

His final words stalled on his lips. He blinked.

"I've seen you limping. When you thought you were alone. You might as well know that I used to sit out on the flight deck at night."

Highfield was now completely wrongfooted. He found he had moved his leg behind him. "I don't think that's—"

"I won't touch you, if that will make you more comfortable."

"There's nothing wrong with my leg."

"Then I won't trouble you."

They stood across the office from each other. Neither moved. There was nothing in her gaze that spoke of invitation.

"I've not . . . I've not mentioned it to anyone," he found himself saying.

"I'm fairly good at keeping secrets," she said, her eyes on his face.

He sat down heavily on his chair and drew up his trouser leg. He hadn't liked to look too closely at it for some days.

She was briefly disarmed. Stood back, then stepped forward and examined it closely. "It's clearly infected." She gestured to his leg, as if asking him whether he minded, then placed her hands upon it, tracing the wound's length, the swollen red skin round it. "Is your temperature raised?"

"I've felt better," he conceded.

She studied it for several minutes. He realized—with something approaching shame—that he had not flinched when she touched his skin. "I think you may have osteomyelitis, an infection that has spread into the bone. This should be drained, and you need penicillin."

"Do you have some?"

"No, but Dr. Duxbury should."

"I don't want him involved."

She expressed no surprise. He wondered if something in all this smacked of madness. He could not rid his mind of her startled expression when she had first seen his leg. And how she had immediately concealed it.

"You need medical help," she said.

"I don't want Duxbury told," he repeated.

"Then I've given you my professional opinion, Captain, and I respect your right to ignore it."

She got up and wiped her hands on her trousers. He asked her to wait, then moved past her and opened the door. He summoned the rating from the corridor.

The boy stepped in, his gaze flickering between the captain and the woman before him. "Take Mrs. Mackenzie here to the dispensary," Highfield said. "She is to fetch some items."

She hesitated, apparently waiting for some proviso, some warning. None came.

He held out his hand with the key. When she took it from him, she made sure her fingers did not touch his.

———

The needle went into his leg, the fine slither of metal sliding mechanically in and out of his flesh as it drew out the foul liquid within. Despite the pain of the procedure, Highfield felt the anxiety that had plagued him start to dissipate.

"You need another dose of penicillin in about six hours. Then one a day. A double dose to start with to push your system into fighting the infection. And when you get to England you must go straight to your doctor. It's possible he'll want you in hospital." She returned to the wound. "But you're lucky. I don't think it's gangrenous."

She said this in a quiet, unemotional tone, declining to look at his face for most of it. Finally, she placed the last of the gamgee tissue dressing on his leg, and sat back on her heels so that he could pull down his trouser leg. She wore the same khaki slacks and white shirt that he had seen her in on the day she had accompanied the younger bride to his office.

He sighed with relief at the prospect of a pain-free night. She was gathering together the medical equipment she had brought from the dispensary. "You should keep some of this here," she said, eyes still on the floor. "You'll need to change that dressing tomorrow." She scribbled some instructions on a piece of paper. "Keep your leg elevated whenever you're alone. And try to keep it dry. Especially in the humidity. You can take the painkilling tablets two at a time." She put the dressing and tape on his desk, then replaced the lid on his pen.

"If it starts to worsen you'll have to see a surgeon. And this time you can't afford to delay."

"I'm going to say there has been a misunderstanding." Her head lifted. "A case of mistaken identity. If you could spare some time during the rest of the voyage to administer those penicillin injections I would be grateful."

She stared at him, raised herself to her feet. She looked, perhaps for the first time that day, startled. She swallowed hard. "I didn't do it for that," she said.

He nodded. "I know."

He stood up, testing his weight gingerly on the injured leg. Then he held out his hand. "Thank you," he said, "Mrs. Mackenzie . . . Sister Mackenzie."

She stared at it for a minute. Given the astonishing composure she had shown so far, when she took it and looked up, he was surprised to see tears in her eyes.

19

THIRTY-FIVE DAYS (ONE WEEK TO PLYMOUTH)

In the anonymous space at the back of the lecture room, Joe Junior shifted restlessly, perhaps feeling unfairly confined by the limitations of his environment. Margaret, looking down on the dome of her stomach, watching her tattered notebook ride the seismic wave of his movement, like a little craft on water, thought she knew how he felt. For weeks, time on this ship had seemed to stall. She had felt a desperate need to see Joe, and a deepening frustration with the way the days crawled by. Now that they were in European waters, time was speeding past, leaving her in turmoil.

She was grotesque, she thought. Her belly was hugely swollen, the pale skin traversed by purple tributaries. She could squeeze her feet into only a stretched, gritty pair of sandals. Her face, never slender, now peered back at her from the mirror in the communal bathroom as a perfect moon. How could Joe still want me? she asked herself. He married a lithe, active girl who could run as fast as him, who could race him on horseback across the endless green acres of the station. A girl whose firm, taut body, unclothed, had moved him to a point beyond speech.

Now he would find himself tethered to a fat, lumpen, heavy-footed sow, who sat down breathless after the shortest flight of stairs. Whose breasts, pale and veiny, flopped and leaked milk. A sow who disgusted even herself. She was no longer reassured by the easy affection of their conversation a few weeks ago—how could she be? He hadn't seen her new appearance.

She shifted on the little wooden seat and breathed out a silent "oh" of discomfort. Today's lecture had been entitled "Things Your Men May Have Seen." Despite the title, it contained only repeated references to "unmentionable horrors," which the speaker had evidently considered too unmentionable to describe. What was important, the welfare officer said, was not to press your husband on what had happened to him. Most men, history had shown, were better off not dwelling on things but simply Getting On With It. They didn't want some woman haranguing them to tell her everything. What men needed was someone to distract them with gaiety, who could remind them of the joys of what they had been fighting for.

The way this man talked made Margaret feel for the first time that she and Joe were not partners, as she had assumed, but that there was, by dint of her sex and his experiences, a huge abyss between them. Joe had only once hinted at his personal canon of horrors: his friend Adie had been killed in the Pacific while he was standing just feet away from Joe on deck, and she had seen him blink furiously at the fine tide that rose in his eyes. She had not pushed him for details, not because she had felt this was something he should endure in private but because she was Australian. Of good farming stock. And the sight of a man's eyes filled with tears, even an Irishman's (and they all knew how emotional they could get), made her feel a little peculiar.

There would be added strains, the welfare officer had said, with them having come from very different continents. There was little doubt that that would be an extra pressure on them, no matter how warm the welcome they received from their British in-laws. He suggested the girls find themselves a friend within the family. Or perhaps exchange addresses with some of their new friends on board so that they had someone to talk to if they were particularly concerned.

But they might find, for a few months, that their husband became a little short-tempered, snappy, at times. "Before you censure him, perhaps take a moment to consider that there may be other reasons for his outburst. That he may have remembered something he doesn't want to burden you with. And perhaps before you loose your tongue in response, you might consider what your husband has done in the service of his country, and of yourselves. We have an expression in England." Here the welfare officer paused, and let his gaze span the little room. " 'Stiff upper lip.' It's what has kept our Empire strong these last years. I'd advocate that you use it often."

———

The marine officer's attendant had motioned to him twice now to help clear the wardroom. It took Jones's urgent "C'mon, man, shake a leg," to rouse Nicol from his reverie.

Around him the officers had finished their meal and were retiring to smoke pipes and read letters or old newspapers. There had been a long-running joke throughout lunch about the state of *Victoria*'s engines, and an open book on whether they were going to last until Plymouth. Another parallel joke, the subject of much ribald discussion, concerned three ratings who had been informed that they were to appear before the Admiralty Interview Board to try to become officers, and the possible answers that one would give, a young man widely considered to have the intelligence and demeanor of a mule.

"You half asleep, man?" Jones virtually shoved him through into the wardroom annex. "The XO had his eye on you through the toasts—you were standing there like a sack of spuds. At one stage I thought you were going to stick your hands in your bloody pockets."

Nicol was unable to answer. Standing to attention during the toasts would normally have been reflexive to him. Like polishing his boots, or offering to go extra rounds. But strange things had happened to his sense of responsibility.

He had been imagining her put off, and him following. During lunch he had allowed himself the daydream that her husband might send her a Not Wanted Don't Come, then cursed himself for wishing that shame upon her.

But he couldn't help it. When he closed his eyes, he saw her watchful face. The brief, bright smile she had bestowed on him when they had danced. The feel of her waist, her hands resting lightly on him.

Who had she married? Had she told him of her past? Worse, had the man been part of it? There seemed no way to ask her without implying that he, like the rest of them, was entitled to some sort of opinion on her life. What right had he to ask any of it?

These thoughts made his eyes screw shut against images he didn't want to own. In his mess the men, familiar with temporary visitations from war demons, allowed him a wide berth. They came back to haunt a man occasionally, buzzing low, divebombing his mind and scorching it black. Perhaps I could tell her, he thought. I could explain a little of what I feel. Saying it might act like a pressure valve. She wouldn't have to do anything about it.

But even as the words formed in his mind, he knew he could not speak out. She had created a future for herself, found some stability. He had no right to say or do anything that might interfere with it.

Last night he had stared up at the constellations that had once intrigued him, now cursing the conjunction of planets that had caused their paths to veer past each other at a point that might have redeemed them both. I could have made her happy, he thought. How could the unknown husband say the same? Or perhaps some selfish part of him just wanted to atone and diminish his own sense of guilt by being her savior.

It was this uncomfortable revelation that forced him to his conclusion, which prompted him to swap his shifts with Emmett and kept him, for the next few days, well away from her.

It was no longer her past that troubled him. It was that she had escaped it.

"Leading hand was still in his pit at ten to bloody eleven in the morning. You should have heard the captain: 'You're no more fit to be a leading hand than one of those bloody girls downstairs.' You know where he was, don't you? Master-at-arms reckons he was in the infirmary with the American. Investigating the . . . curative properties of alcohol."

There was a burst of laughter. He stared up at the picture of the King, which took pride of place on the wall, then took his place next to Jones, preparing to file out of the wardroom. He had received a wire four days after he had sent his own. It said simply, 'Thank you!' The exclamation mark, with all it conveyed, had made him wince.

———

Unexpectedly, the dog began to howl when Margaret opened the door. She placed her hands frantically round Maude Gonne's muzzle and stumbled for the bed, hissing, "Shush! Shush, Maudie! Shush now!" The dog had barked twice, and Margaret had come as close as she ever had to smacking her. "Shut up now!" she scolded, her eyes fixed on the door. "Come on, now, settle down," she murmured, and the dog turned tight circles on her bunk. Margaret looked guiltily at her watch, wondering when she could next take her out. Maude Gonne had tried to escape several times now. Like Joe Junior, she thought, the confinement was starting to tell. "Come on now," she said, her tone soothing. "Not much longer, I promise."

Only then did she realize she was not alone in the dormitory.

Avice was lying motionless on her bunk, facing the wall, her knees drawn up to her stomach.

Margaret stared at her as the dog leapt down and scratched half-heartedly at the door. It was, she calculated, the fourth day that Avice had lain like this. On the few occasions that she had risen for food she had picked at whatever was on her plate, then excused herself. Seasickness, she had said, to enquiries. But the water hadn't been choppy.

Margaret stepped forward and bent over the prostrate figure, as if she could glean some clue from her face. Once she had done this believing Avice to be asleep, and had felt a mixture of shock and embarrassment when her eyes were wide open. She had wondered whether to talk to Frances: perhaps Avice was suffering from some medical complaint. But given the bad blood between the two women, she didn't feel it fair on either of them.

Besides, Frances was rarely here now. For reasons no one could explain, she had been helping out in the infirmary, Dr. Duxbury having gleefully accepted the responsibility of organizing the final of the Queen of the *Victoria* contest. Otherwise she disappeared for several hours every day, and offered no explanation as to where she had been. Margaret supposed she should be glad to see her so much happier, but she missed her company. Alone, she had had altogether far too much time to think. And, as her dad was fond of saying, that was never a good thing.

"Avice?" she whispered. "Are you awake?"

She did not reply until the second prompt. "Yes," she said.

Margaret stood awkwardly in the center of the little dormitory, her distended body briefly forgotten as she tried to work out what to do for the best. "Can I . . . can I get you anything?"

"No."

The silence expanded round her. Her mother would have known what to do, she thought. She would have marched up to Avice, taken her in her arms in that confident maternal way of hers, and said, "C'mon, now, what's up?" And faced with her degree of certainty, Avice would have confessed her anxieties, or her medical problems, or her homesickness or whatever was troubling her.

Except her mother wasn't there. And Margaret was no more capable of taking Avice in her arms unprompted than she was of rowing this ship all the way to bloody England. "I could get you a cup of tea," she ventured.

Avice said nothing.

———

Margaret lay on her bed reading for almost an hour, not feeling able to leave either Avice or the dog, whom she did not trust to keep quiet.

Outside, the faint increase in movement of the ship told of the shift into cooler, rougher waters. Now, after weeks aboard, they were finely attuned to the vibrations of the *Victoria*, used to the ever-present hum of her engines, able to ignore the incessant piped commands that punctuated every quarter-hour.

She had begun a letter to her father, then discovered she had nothing to say about life on board that she had not already told him. The real events that had taken place she could not conceive of putting on paper, and the rest of it was just waiting. Like living in a corridor, waiting for her new life to begin.

She had written to Daniel instead: a series of questions about the mare, an urgent demand that he should skin as many darn rabbits as he could so that he could get over to England to see her. Daniel had written once, a letter she had received at Bombay. It comprised just a few lines and told her little, other than the state of the cows, the weather, and the plot of a movie he had seen in town, but her heart had eased. She had been forgiven, those few lines told her. If her father had threatened him with the belt to do it he would have put a blank sheet in an envelope rather than comply. There was a sharp rap on the door, and she leapt on her dog, cutting short her bark. Holding her, she broke into a fake coughing fit, trying to emulate the noise. "Hold on," she said, her broad hand clamped gently but firmly round Maude Gonne's muzzle. "Just coming."

"Is Mrs. A. Radley there?"

Margaret faced Avice's bunk. Avice, blinking, sat. Her clothes were crumpled, her face pale and blank. She slid slowly to the floor, lifting a hand to her hair. "Avice Radley," she said, opening the door a little way.

A young rating stood before her.

"You've had a wire. Come through the radio room this afternoon."

Margaret dropped the dog behind her and stepped forward to take Avice's arm. "Oh, my God," she said involuntarily.

The rating registered the two wide-eyed faces. Then he thrust the piece of paper into Avice's hand. "Don't look like that, missus—it's good news."

"What?" said Margaret.

He ignored her. He waited for Avice's eyes to drop to the paper before he spoke again, his voice thick with mirth. "It's family. Your folks are going to be in Plymouth to meet you off the ship."

———

Avice had sobbed for almost twenty minutes, which had initially seemed excessive and had now become alarming. Margaret, her previous reticence forgotten, had climbed on to Avice's bunk and now sat beside her, trying not to think about the way it creaked ominously under her weight. "It's okay, Avice," she kept saying. "He's all right. Ian's all right. That bloody wire just gave you a bit of a fright."

The captain wasn't best pleased, the rating had said gleefully. Said he'd be using the radio room for taking down shopping lists next. But he'd allowed the message through.

Margaret tutted. "They shouldn't have sent someone down here like that. They must have known it would scare you half to death. Specially someone in our condition, eh?" She tried to get the girl to smile.

Avice failed to answer her. But eventually the sobbing subsided, until it was just a stuttering echo of itself, a breath that caught periodically in the back of her throat. Finally, when Margaret felt the worst was over, she stepped down.

"There now," she said uselessly. "You get some rest. Calm yourself down a bit." She lay on her own bunk and began to chat about their plans for the last few days—the best lectures to attend, Avice's preparations for the Queen of the *Victoria* final, anything to shake her out of her depression. "You've got to wear those green satin shoes again," she rattled on gamely. "You don't know how many girls would give their eye teeth for them, Avice. That girl from 11F said she'd seen some just like them in *Australian Women's Weekly*."

———

Avice's eyes were raw and red-rimmed. You don't understand, she thought, as she stared at the blank wall, not registering the endless stream of words that floated up from below. Just for a moment, I thought everything was going to be okay, that there was going to be a way out of this for me.

She lay very still, as if somehow she could turn herself to stone.

Just for a moment, I thought they had come to tell me he was dead.

———

"So, anyway, there I was, dirty water up to my ears, pans sloshing up and down the galley, ship listing forty-five degrees to port, and the old boy wades in, looks me up and down, empties several pints of bilge water out of his cap and says, 'I hope those aren't odd socks you're wearing, Highfield. I won't have standards slipping on my ship.'"

The captain stretched out his leg. "Best bit about it was he was right. God only knows how he could tell under four foot of water, but he was right."

Frances straightened up and smiled. "I've had matrons like that," she said. "I reckon they could tell you the number of pills in every bottle."

She began to place the instruments back in the carrying case.

"Ah," said Highfield. He cleared his throat. "Well, then. Forty-one torpedo heads, separated from cases, two empty cases, thirty-two bombs, most dismantled, four cases ammunition for 4.5 inch magazine, one case 4.5 inch HA/LA twin mounting, nine cases assorted armaments, small-arms magazine and pom-poms. Oh, and twenty-two rounds for several assorted handguns. Those currently locked in my personal stores."

"Something tells me," said Frances, "you're not entirely ready for retirement."

Outside, behind his left shoulder, the sun was setting. It sank toward the horizon at a gentler pace than it had in previous waters. The ocean stretched around them, its grayish hue the only clue to the cooler temperature. Now they were often pursued by gulls, scavenging after the gash, or rubbish, the ship's cook threw overboard, or bits of biscuit the girls hurled at them for the fun of watching them catch scraps in mid-air.

Highfield leaned forward: the scar tissue on his leg was like melted candlewax. "How's it . . . ?"

"Fine," she said. "You must be able to feel it."

"I feel better," he said. Then, catching her eye, "It's still a little sore, but much improved."

"Your temperature's normal."

"I thought I'd got a touch of the tropical sweats."

"Probably had those too." She knew he felt better. It was in his demeanor; something in him was no longer quite so grimly contained. Now his eyes held a glint of something else, and his smile came readily. When he stood straight, it was with pride rather than the desperation to prove he still could.

He had embarked on another story; one about a missing torpedo case. She had finished, and allowed herself to sit neatly in the chair opposite him and listen. He had told her this story some days previously but she didn't mind: she sensed that he was not a man who talked easily. A lonely man, she had concluded. She had often found those in charge to be the loneliest.

Besides, she had to admit, faced with the cold reception she still received from most of the brides, with Avice's strange melancholy and the marine's absence, she enjoyed his company.

". . . and the ruddy man was only using it to cook fish. 'Couldn't find anything else that looked like a fish kettle,' he said. I tell you, when we thought about it, we were only grateful he hadn't used the warhead."

Highfield's laugh emerged from him like a bark, as if it surprised him, and she smiled again, keen not to reveal her familiarity with what he had said. He would glance at her after each joke, an infinitesimal movement, but one in which she recognized his awkwardness with women. He would not want to bore her. She would not allow him to think he had.

"Sister Mackenzie . . . can I offer you a drink? I often have a little tot at this time of day."

"Thank you, but I don't drink."

"Sensible girl." She watched as he maneuvered himself round his desk. It was beautiful, a deep walnut color embossed with dark green leather. The captain's private room could have sat happily in any well-off house, with its carpet, paintings and comfortable upholstered chairs. She thought of the sparse conditions of the men below, their hammocks, lockers and bleached tabletops. Nowhere but in the British Navy had she seen the blatant difference in the men's living conditions, and it made her wonder about the country she was heading to. "How did you do it?" she asked, as he poured his drink.

"What?"

"Your leg. You never said."

He was standing with his back to her and for a moment it went still enough for her to understand that her question had not been as inconsequential as she had intended. "You don't have to tell me," she said. "I'm sorry. I didn't mean to pry."

It was as if he had not heard her. He stoppered the decanter, then sat down again. He took a long slug of the amber liquid, and then he spoke. The *Victoria*, he said, was not his ship. "I served on her sister, *Indomitable*. From 'thirty-nine. Then shortly before VJ Day we came under attack. We had six Albacores, four Swordfish and God knows what else up there trying to cover us, men on all the guns, but nothing hit them. I knew from the start we were done.

"My nephew was a pilot. Robert Hart. Twenty-six years old. My younger sister Molly's boy . . . He was a . . . We were close. He was a good chap."

They were briefly interrupted by a knock on the door. A flash of irritation briefly illuminated Highfield's features. He rose and walked heavily across the floor. He opened the door, glanced at the papers that were handed to him and nodded at the young telegraphist. "Very good," he muttered.

Frances, still lost in the captain's previous words, barely noticed.

The captain sat down again, dropping the papers beside him on the desk. There was a long silence.

"Was he . . . shot down?" she said.

"No," he said, after another slug of his drink. "No. I think he would have preferred that. One of the bombs dropped into number-two hold and blew out several decks, from the officers' berths to the center engine room. I lost sixteen men in that first explosion."

Frances could imagine the scene on board, her nose scenting the smoke and oil, the screams of trapped and burning men in her ears. "Including your nephew."

"No . . . no, that's the problem. I was too late getting them out, you see? I'd been blown off my feet, and I was a bit dazed. I didn't realize how close the explosion had been to the ammunition stores.

"The fire cracked several of the internal pipes. It ran along the tiller flat, the steering-gear store and the admiral's store and came up again under the ammunition conveyor. Fifteen minutes after the first, they caught and blew out half the innards of the ship." He shook his head. "It was deafening . . . deafening. I thought the heavens themselves had cracked open. I should have had more men down there, checking the hatches were closed, stopping the fire."

"You might have lost more."

"Fifty-eight, all told. My nephew had been on the control platform." He hesitated. "I couldn't get to him."

Frances sat very still. "I'm sorry," she said.

"They made me get off," he said, his words coming thick and fast now as if they had waited too long. "She was going down, and I had my men—those who could still stand—in the boats. The seas were eerily calm, and I could see the boats all sitting there below me, almost still, like lily-pads on a pond, all smeared with blood and oil as the men hauled in the injured from the water. It was so hot. Those of us still aboard were spraying ourselves with the hoses, just to try to stay on the ship. And while we were trying to reach our injured men, while bits of the ship were cracking open and burning, the bloody Japanese kept circling. Not firing anymore, just circling above us, like vultures, as if they were enjoying watching us suffer."

He took a gulp of his drink.

"I was still trying to find him when they ordered me off." He dropped his head. "Two destroyers came alongside to help us. Finally saw off the Japanese. I was ordered off. And all my men sat there and watched as I let the ship go down, knowing that there were probably men alive down there, injured men. Perhaps even Hart."

He paused. "None of them said a word to me. They just . . . stared."

Frances closed her eyes. She had heard similar stories, knew the scars they caused. There was nothing she could say to comfort him.

They listened to the Tannoy calling the ladies to a display of felt-work in the forward lounge. Frances noted, with surprise, that at some point it had become completely dark outside.

"Not much of a way to end a career, is it?"

She heard the break in his voice. "Captain," she said, "the only people who still have all the answers are those who have never been faced with the questions."

Outside his rooms the deck light stuttered into life, throwing a cold neon glow through the window. There was a brief burst of conversation as several men left the squadron office and a pipe called repetitively "stand by to receive gash barge alongside."

Captain Highfield stared at his feet, then at her, digesting the truth of what she had said. He had a long slug of his drink, his eyes not leaving hers as he finished it. "Sister Mackenzie," he said, as he put his glass on the table, "tell me about your husband."

———

Nicol had stood outside the cinema projection room for almost three-quarters of an hour. Had he been allowed in to view the film, he would have been unwilling to watch *The Best Years of Our Lives*, even with its happy endings for those servicemen returning home. His attention was focused on the other end of the corridor.

"I can't believe this," Jones-the-Welsh had said, as he dried himself in the mess. "I heard she was being put off. The next thing captain's saying it's all a bloody misunderstanding. It was not, I can tell you. You saw her, didn't you, Duckworth? We both recognized her. Don't understand it." He rubbed briskly under his arms.

"I know why," said another marine. "She's in there having a drink with the skipper."

"What?"

"In his rooms. The old weather-guesser just took him in the long-range reports, and there she is, curled up with him on the settee having a drink."

"The sly old dog," Jones said.

"She's not silly, eh?"

"Highfield? He couldn't get a bag-off in a brothel with a fiver sticking out of his ear."

"It's one rule for us and another for them, that's for sure," said Duckworth, bitterly. "Can you imagine them letting us bring a brass back to the mess?"

"You must be mistaken." Nicol had spoken before he realized what he was saying. The words hung heavy in the ensuing silence. "She wouldn't be in the captain's rooms." He lowered his voice. "I mean, there's no reason for her to be there."

"Taylor knows what he saw. I can tell you something else. It's not the first time, either. He reckons it's the third time this week he's seen her in there."

"Third time, eh? C'mon, Nicol, old boy. You know the reason as well as I do." Jones's braying voice had exploded into laughter. "How'd you like that, boys? Sixty years old and our skipper's finally discovered the joys of the flesh!"

Finally, he heard voices. As he stood back against the pipes, the captain's lobby door opened. The air was punched silently from his lungs as he saw the slim figure step out lightly and turn to face the captain. He didn't have to look long to confirm who it was: her image, every last detail, was now as deeply imprinted on his soul as if it had been etched there.

"Thank you," Highfield was saying. "I don't really know what else to say. I'm not usually given to . . ."

She shook her head, as if whatever she had bestowed upon him was nothing. Then she smoothed her hair. He found himself stepping back into the shadows. I'm not given to . . . to what? Nicol's breath lodged in his chest and his mind went blank. This was not how he had felt when his wife had revealed her affair. This was worse.

They muttered something he couldn't catch, and then her voice rose again. "Oh, Captain," she called, "I forgot to say . . . Sixteen."

Nicol could just make out Highfield staring at her, his expression quizzical.

She began to make her way toward the main hangar. "Sixteen penicillin left in the big bottle. Seven in the smaller one. And ten sealed dressings in the white bag. At least, there should be."

He could hear the captain's laughter the whole way down the gangway.

20

The boredom of weeks at sea has to be experienced to be fully understood and the frustrations of such an existence were to many, in the long run, in-finitely more damaging to the mind than the potential hazards of being blown up by the enemy... when we were not fighting the enemy, we were fighting amongst ourselves.

L. TROMAN, WINE, WOMEN AND WAR

TWO DAYS TO PLYMOUTH

In the absence of horses and a track, or of trainee pilots who could be guaranteed to end up in the soup occasionally, it should perhaps have been of little surprise that such fierce betting lay on the immaculately coiffed heads of the Queen of the *Victoria* contestants. It was possible that Mrs. Ivy Tuttle and Mrs. Jeanette Latham might have been a little demoralized to know that they were jointly forty to one against or, indeed, that knowing she was five to two on might have put a swagger into Irene Carter's already undulating step. But for days now it had been common knowledge that the real favorite, with a good proportion of the ship's company putting a shilling or more on her blonde tresses, was Avice Radley.

"Foster says there's some fair-sized punts on her," yelled Plummer, the junior stoker.

"There's some fair-sized somethings," roared the departing watch.

"He reckons if she comes in first he's going to have to pay out half the money he won on the gee-gees at Bombay."

Within hours they would have entered the cool, choppy waters of the Bay of Biscay, but more than a hundred feet below the flight deck, down in the engine pit, the temperatures were still at a shirt-drenching hundred or so degrees. Tims, naked to the waist, swung the polished wheels that sent the steam into the engine's turbines while Plummer, who had been oiling the main engine, felt round the bearings for overheating, occasionally swearing as his skin met scalding metal.

Between them, the bridge telegraph dial relayed the orders from above to put the engines over to "make smoke" or "full speed" in an effort to get through the rough as soon as possible, and around them, above the incessant grinding and roaring of the engine, the tired old ship creaked and groaned in protest. Steam persisted in escaping through valves in little belches of effort; the rags that tried to quell them were damp and sodden with scalding water. In these emissions, the *Victoria* insisted on showing her age; her many dials and gauges looked out at them with the blank insouciance of a bloody-minded old woman.

Plummer finished tightening a bolt, secured his spanner in its wall-mounting, then turned to Tims. "You not had a few bob on one of them, then?"

"What?" Tims glowered.

He was a mean-looking man in a bad mood, but Plummer, who was used to him, rattled on: "The contest tonight." The noise of the engine was such that he used gesture to convey added meaning to his words. "There's a lot of money riding on it."

"Load of rubbish," said Tims, dismissively.

"Like to see them all lined up in their little swimsuits, though, eh?" He drew curves in the air, and pulled a lascivious face. It sat almost comically on his adolescent features. "Get you in the mood for the missus."

This seemed to make Tims more bad-tempered. He wiped his shining forehead with a filthy rag, then reached down for a wrench. The choppier waters sent tools thumping and clanging across the floor, a hazard to shins and toes. "Don't know what you're getting so excited about," he growled. "You're on duty all night."

"Two pounds I've got on that Radley girl," Plummer said. "Two pounds! I got my bet on when she was still three to one against so if she wins I'm bloody quids in. If not, I'm in the drink. I promised my old ma I'd pay for us all to go to Scarborough. But I'm an optimist by nature, see? I reckon I can't lose."

He was lost in appreciation of some imagined scene upstairs. "Looked bloody fantastic in her swimsuit for the Miss Lovely Legs, that girl. Great pair of pins on her. D'you think it's something they give them in Australia? I've heard half the girls back home have got rickets."

Tims, apparently oblivious, was staring at his watch.

Plummer rambled on: "All the officers get to see it, you know. How's that fair, eh? Two more nights on board, and all the officers get to see the girls in their swimsuits and we're stuck down here in bloody center engine. You know the marines are switching shifts at nine so even they'll catch some of it. One rule for one lot, another rule for us. Hardly fair, is it? Now the war's over, they should take a look at all the injustices of the bloody Navy."

Plummer checked a dial, swore, then glanced at Tims, who was staring at the wall. "Here, you all right, Tims? Something got on your wick, has it?"

"Cover me for half an hour," Tims said, turning toward the exit hatch. "Something I need to do."

———

Had he been able to see the opening stages of the Queen of the *Victoria* contest, young Plummer might have felt less confident about his trip to Scarborough. For Avice Radley, despite being widely considered a shoo-in for winner, was looking curiously lackluster. Or in racing terms, as one of the seamen put it, not dissimilar to a three-legged donkey.

Perched on the makeshift stage alongside her fellow contestants, faced by the heaving tables that made up the women's last formal supper, she looked pale and preoccupied, despite the glowing scarlet of the silk dress she wore, and the glossy wheat sheen of her blonde hair. As the other girls giggled and clutched each other, trying to keep their balance in high heels as the ship dipped under them, she stood alone and aside, smile fading, eyes shadowed with some distant concern.

Twice Dr. Duxbury, the host for the evening's proceedings, had taken her hand, tried to get her to elaborate on her plans for her new life, to recall her favorite moments of the voyage. She had seemed not to notice him, even when he broke into his third rendition of "Waltzing Matilda."

That'll be the morning sickness kicking in, at least one bride had observed. All mothers-to-be looked rotten for the first few months. It was only a matter of time. A few, less generous types suggested that perhaps without foundation garments and cosmetics Avice Radley had never been the beauty everyone had taken her for. And when you compared her to the glowing Irene Carter, resplendent in pale peach and blue, apparently heedless of the heaving waters, it was hard to disagree.

Dr. Duxbury tailed off to polite, scattered applause. There were only so many times one could applaud the same song, and it was possible the surgeon was too well lubricated to be aware of his audience anyway.

At last he registered the frantically signaling lieutenant commander at the end of the stage and, after several attempts, pointed theatrically at the captain, raising his palms as if to suggest that no one had told him.

"Ladies," said Highfield, standing quickly, perhaps before Duxbury could start singing again. He waited as the hangar gradually fell silent. "Ladies . . . As you know, this is our last night's entertainment on *Victoria*. Tomorrow night we will dock at Plymouth, and you will spend the evening organizing your belongings and double checking with the women's service officers that you have someone to meet you and somewhere to go. Tomorrow morning I will discuss the arrangements more fully on the flight deck, but for now I just wanted to say a few words."

The women, many of whom were fizzing with nervous anticipation, watched, nudging and whispering to each other. Around the edges, the men stood, their arms behind them, backs to the walls. Ratings, officers, marines, engineers: all in dress uniform in honor of the occasion. For some, Highfield realized, it would be the last time they wore it. He glanced down at his own, knowing it would not be long before he would say the same.

"I can't—I can't pretend this has been the easiest cargo I have ever had to transport," he said. "I can't pretend I even relished the prospect of it—although I know some of the men did. But I can tell you this, as a 'lifer,' as some of us naval folk are known, it has been the most . . . educational.

"Now, I won't bore you with a lengthy speech about the difficulties of the course you have chosen. I'm sure you've had quite enough of that." He nodded toward the welfare officer and heard a polite ripple of laughter. "But I will say that you, like all of us, will probably find the next twelve months the most challenging—and hopefully rewarding—of your lives. So what I wanted to tell you is this: you are not alone."

He looked around at the hushed, expectant faces. Under the harsh lights of the hangar deck the gilt buttons of his uniform shone.

"Those of us who have always served are going to have to find new ways of living. Those of us who have found ourselves profoundly changed by the experience of war will have to find new ways of dealing with those around us. Those who have suffered are going to have to find ways of forgiving. We are returning to a country that is likely to be unfamiliar to us. We, too, may find ourselves strangers in that land. So yes, brides, you face a great challenge. But I want to tell you that it has been both a pleasure and a privilege to be part of your journey. We are proud to claim you as our own. And I hope that when you look back, in happiness, to the early years of your time in Britain, you think of this as not simply the journey to your new life but the start of it."

Few would have noticed that during some of this speech he seemed to be speaking to one woman in particular, that when he had said, "You are not alone," his gaze might have rested on her a little longer than on anyone else. But it was irrelevant. There was a brief silence, and then the women clapped, a few calling out until gradually the applause and cheering had ignited the entire room.

Captain Highfield took his seat, having nodded gratefully at the blur of faces. It had not come solely from the women below him, he observed, trying not to smile as much as he wanted. It had come from the men. "What did you think?" he murmured to the woman beside him, his chest still puffed with pride.

"Very nice, Captain."

"Not a great one for speeches, generally," he said, "but in this case I thought it appropriate."

"I don't think anyone here would disagree. Your words were . . . beautifully chosen."

"Have the girls stopped staring at you yet?" He spoke without looking at her, so that from the other tables it might appear that he was simply thanking the steward for his plate of food.

"No," said Frances, taking a forkful of fish. "But it's quite all right, Captain." She didn't need to add: I'm used to it.

Captain Highfield glanced at Dobson, two seats down, who was evidently not yet used to it. Having squinted at sea for almost forty years, Highfield's sight was not as good as it had been. But even he could discern the words emanating from the XO's downturned mouth, the expression of disapproval on his face. "Making a mockery of the ship, he is," he was muttering furiously into his damask napkin. "It's as if he's set out to turn us all into a laughing-stock."

The lieutenant beside him noticed Highfield staring at them, and colored.

Highfield felt the ship lift under him as it broke another wave.

"Glass of cordial, Sister Mackenzie? You sure you wouldn't like anything stronger?" He waited until it had ridden out, then lifted his glass in salute.

———

It would only be for twenty minutes. The engine was running much better, or at least as well as she was ever going to. It was two whole pounds. And Davy Plummer was buggered if he was going to sit down there by himself in the engine room while every matelot from here to the Radio Direction Finder office watched girls parade in their swimsuits.

Besides, he was leaving the Navy once they got back to Blighty. What were they going to make him do if they found him off duty for once? Make him swim home?

Davy Plummer checked the temperature gauges that needed to be checked, ran a cloth over the more problematic pipes, stubbed out his cigarette underfoot and, with a swift glance behind him, ran two at a time up the steps on to the gangway and toward the exit hatch.

———

The votes were in and Avice Radley had lost. The judging panel, which comprised Dr. Duxbury, two of the women's service officers and the chaplain, all agreed that they had wanted to give the prize to Mrs. Radley (Dr. Duxbury had been particularly impressed by her rendition a week earlier of "Shenandoah") but felt that, given her extremely lackluster performance on the final night, her marked disinclination to smile and her frankly perplexing answer to the question, "What do you most want to do when you finally get to England?" (Irene Carter, "Make the acquaintance of my mother-in-law"; Ivy Tuttle, "Raise money for the war orphans"; Avice Radley, "I don't know") and her immediate disappearance after it, there was only one choice for overall winner.

Irene Carter wore her hand-sewn sash with the cooing, tearful delight of a new mother. It had been, she announced, the finest trip she had ever undertaken. She felt, frankly, as if she had made at least six hundred new friends. And she hoped they would all find the happiness in England she was sure they deserved. She couldn't begin to thank the crew enough for their kindness, their efficiency. She was sure the whole room would agree that the captain's words had been a real inspiration. It was when she started thanking her former neighbors in Sydney by name that Captain Highfield intervened and announced that if the officers and men would like to clear the tables to the sides of the room, the Royal Marines Band would provide music for a little dancing. ("Dancing!" chirruped Dr. Duxbury, and several women moved swiftly away from him.)

Davy Plummer, standing near the back of the bandstand, glanced in disgust at the handwritten betting slip Foster had given him not two days earlier, screwed it up and thrust it deep into the pocket of his overall. Bloody women. For all those fancy odds, that one couldn't have looked any worse with a paper bag over her head. He was about to return to the engine room when he saw two brides standing in the corner. They whispered something behind their hands.

"Never seen a working man before?" he said, holding out the sides of his overalls.

"We were wondering if you were going to dance," said the smaller, blonder girl, "but whether you could do it without getting us all oily."

"Ladies, you have no idea what a stoker can do with his hands." Davy Plummer stepped forward, his betting slip forgotten.

He was, after all, an optimist by nature.

The crowning ceremony was due at a quarter to ten. That gave Frances almost fifteen minutes to nip along the passageway and pick up the photographs of the Australian General Hospital that Captain Highfield had asked to view. Her photograph album was in her trunk down in the hold but she always kept a few of her favorite snaps—the first ward tent, the dance in Port Moresby, Alfred, in a book by her bed. She ran lightly along the corridor that led from the hangar to the dormitories, occasionally touching the wall to keep her balance.

Then she stopped.

He was standing outside the dormitory, removing a cigarette from a soft packet. He put it into his mouth, glanced sideways at her. The way in which he did this told her that her appearance was no surprise to him.

She had not seen him since he had arrived on the gun turret with Tims. She had had to fight the suspicion that he had avoided her since then, had several times considered asking the younger marine why he had taken over the night watch.

She had pictured him so many times, had taken one side in so many silent conversations, that to see him in the flesh was overwhelming. Even as her feet took her toward him she felt her own reticence return and brushed vaguely at her skirt.

She paused at the door, unsure whether to step inside. He was in his dress uniform, and she was overcome by a flash memory of the night they had danced, in which she had been held against that dark cloth. "Want one?" he said, holding the packet toward her.

She took one. He held the flame toward her so that she didn't have to bend to him as it lit. She found, as she ducked, that she could not take her eyes off his hands.

"I saw you at the captain's table," he said eventually.

"I didn't see you." She had looked. Several times.

"Wasn't meant to be there."

His voice sounded strange. She drew on her cigarette, conscious that however she stood she felt awkward.

"Quite unusual for him to invite one of the women to join him."

The temperature of her blood dropped a couple of degrees. "I wouldn't know," she said carefully.

"I don't believe he's done it once this trip."

"Is there something you want to say?"

He looked blank.

She forgot her previous awkwardness. "Surely what you're asking is why I, of all people, was seated at the captain's table?"

He set his jaw. For the briefest moment, she could see how he might have looked as a child. "I was just . . . curious. I came to see you the other afternoon. And then I saw you . . . outside the captain's—"

"Ah. Now I see. You weren't asking, just implying."

"I didn't mean—"

"So you've come to question me over the standard of my conduct?"

"No, I—"

"Oh, what will you do, Marine? Report the captain? Or just the whore?"

The word silenced them both. She chewed her lip. He stood alongside her, his shoulders still squared as if he were on duty.

"Why are you talking like this?" he asked quietly.

"Because I'm tired, Marine. I'm tired of having every single one of my actions judged by ignorant people who then find me wanting."

"I didn't judge you."

"The hell you didn't." She was suddenly furious. "I can't be bothered to explain myself anymore. I can't be bothered to try to improve anyone's opinion of me if they can't be bothered to see—"

"Frances—"

"You're as bad as the rest of them. I thought you were different. I thought you understood something about me, understood what I was made of. God knows why! God knows why I chose to invest you with feelings you were never capable of—"

"Frances—"

"What?"

"I'm sorry about what I said. I just saw you . . . and . . . I'm sorry. Really. Things have happened that have made me . . ." He tailed off. "Look, I came to see you because I wanted you to know something. I did things in the war . . . that I'm not proud of. I haven't always behaved in a way that people—people who don't know the full circumstances—might consider to be admirable. There's none of us—not even your husband probably—who can say they did."

She stared at him.

"That's all I wanted to tell you," he said.

Her head hurt. She put out a hand to the wall, feeling the floor rise and fall under her feet. "I think you'd better go," she said quietly. She could not look at him. But she could feel his eyes on her. "Goodnight, Marine," she said, emphatically.

She waited until she heard his footsteps walking smartly toward the hangar area. The rocking of the ship's floor made no difference to their rhythm and she listened to them, metronomic, until the sound of a hatch door closing told her he had gone.

Then she closed her eyes, very tightly.

————

In the center engine room, somewhere below the hangar deck, the number-two oil spray, the high-pressure feed pump that transferred fuel to the boiler, succumbed to what might have been age, stress, or perhaps the bloodymindedness of a ship that knows she is about to be decommissioned and, split. A tiny fault line, perhaps less than two centimeters long, which allowed the pressurized fuel to bubble out, dark and seething, like spittle in the corner of a drunk's mouth. And then to atomize.

It is impossible to see the hot spots in a ship's engine, the places where small areas of metal, weakened by fractures or the strain on its joints, reach terrible internal temperatures. If they cannot be detected by the many gauges around the engine room, or by the treacherous act of feeling for them through rags, one discovers them by chance— conclusively when fuel leaks on to them.

Unseen and unheard by the humans who relied upon it, the *Victoria*'s center engine hammered energetically forward, unseen, too red, too hot. The fuel hung briefly in the air in tiny, unseen droplets. Then the exhaust duct, inches from the cracked fuel pipe, glinted, like malice in a devilish eye, ignited and, with a sudden *whumph!* took its chance.

———

Fool. Bloody fool. Nicol slowed outside the oilskin store. One more night until she left for good, one more in which he could have told her a little of what she meant to him, and instead he had acted like a pompous fool. A jealous adolescent. And in doing so he had shown himself to be no better than any of the other judgmental fools on this leaking old ship. He could have said a thousand things to her, smiled at her, shown her a little understanding. She would have known then. If nothing else, she would have known. As bad as the rest of them, she had told him. The worst of what he had always suspected of himself.

"Blast it," he said, and slammed his fist into the wall.

"Something bothering you, Marine?"

Tims was blocking the passageway, overalls thick with oil and grease, something more inflammatory illuminating his expression. "What's the matter?" he said softly. "Run out of people to discipline?"

Nicol glanced at his bleeding knuckles. "Get on with your work, Tims." Bile rose in him.

"Get on with your work? Who d'you think you are? Commander?"

Nicol glanced behind him at the empty corridor. No one was visible on G Deck; those not on duty were all in the hangar area, enjoying the dance. He wondered, briefly, how long Tims had been standing there.

"Your ladyfriend bothering you, is she? Not giving it up, like you thought?"

Nicol took a deep breath. He lit a cigarette, extinguished the match between finger and thumb and thrust it into his pocket.

"Got an itch you can't scratch?"

"You might think you're a big man on this ship, Tims, but in a couple of days' time you'll just be another unemployed matelot like the rest of them. A nothing." He tried to keep his voice calm, but he could still hear in it the vibration of barely suppressed rage.

Tims stood back on his heels, crossed his huge forearms across his chest. "Perhaps you're not her type." He lifted his chin, as if a thought had occurred to him. "Oh, sorry, I forgot. Everyone's her type, provided they've got two bob . . ."

The first punch Tims seemed to expect and ducked away. The second was blocked by the stoker's own blinding upper cut. It caught Nicol unawares, exploding under his chin so that he crashed backward into the wall.

"Think your little whore will still find you pretty now, Marine?" The words came at him like another blow, cutting through the sound of the engines, the distant hum of the band, the disconsolate clank of the lashings swinging against the side. The blood in his ears. "Perhaps she just didn't think you were man enough for her, with your prissy uniforms, always following orders."

He felt the stoker's breath on his skin, could smell the oil on him. "Did she tell you how she likes it, did she? Did she tell you she liked to feel my hands on them titties, liked to—"

With a roar, Nicol threw himself at Tims and brought them both crashing down. He pummeled blindly at the flesh before him, not even sure what his fists were connecting with. He felt the man wrench his body underneath him, saw the great fist come round as it caught him again. But he could not stop now, even if he felt himself in danger. He hardly felt the blows that rained down upon him. A blood mist had descended, and all the anger of the past six weeks, of the past six years, forced their way out of him through his fists and his strength, and curses flew through his clenched teeth. Something similar—perhaps his humiliation in front of a woman, perhaps the inequities of twenty years' service—seemed to provide the motor for Tims's own assault, so that in their welter of blood and blows and punches neither man registered the siren, despite the proximity of the Tannoy above their heads.

"Fire! Fire! Fire!" came the urgent, piped instruction. "Standing Sea Emergency Party, close up at Section Base Two. All marines to the boat deck."

————

The Queen of the *Victoria* contestants were being led from the stage, their polished smiles vanished from their faces, Irene Carter clutching her winner's sash round her like a lifejacket. Margaret glimpsed them briefly as, wedged in the sea of bodies, she found herself moving toward the door. Behind them, the tables stood abandoned, apple charlotte and fruit salad on the plates, glasses half empty. Around her, the women's voices had risen in nervous excitement, swelling to a little crescendo of fear with every new piped instruction. She held one hand protectively across her belly and made her way toward the starboard side exit. It was like fighting against a particularly strong current.

A voice shouted from somewhere ahead, "Quickly, ladies, please. Those with surnames N to Z gather at Muster Station B, all others to Muster Station A. Just keep moving now."

Margaret had made her way to the edge of the crowd when the women's service officer caught her arm.

"This way, madam." She held out her arms, pointing forward, a physical barrier to the starboard exit.

"I have to pop downstairs." Margaret cursed under her breath as someone elbowed her in the back.

"Nobody is allowed downstairs. Muster stations only."

Margaret felt the crush of bodies pushing past her, smelled the mingling of several hundred brands of scent and setting lotion. "Look, it's very important. I have to fetch something."

The woman looked at her as if she was a fool. "There is a fire on board," she said. "There is absolutely no going downstairs. Captain's orders."

Margaret's voice rose, a mixture of anxiety and frustration. "You don't understand! I have to go there! I have to make sure—I have to look after my—my—"

Perhaps the WSO was more anxious than she wanted to let on. Her temper flared right back. She blew her whistle, trying to steer someone to the right, then pulled it from her pursed lips and hissed, "Don't you think everyone has something they want to keep by them? Can you imagine the chaos if we let everyone start digging around for photograph albums or pieces of jewelry? It's a fire. For all we know it could have started in the women's cabins. Now, please move on or I'll have to get someone to move you."

Two marines were already locking the exit hatch. Margaret gazed around her, trying to locate another way down, and then, her chest tight, moved forward in the crush.

———

"Avice." Frances stood in the doorway of the silent dormitory, staring at the motionless form on the bunk in front of her. "Avice? Can you hear me?"

There was no response. For a minute, Frances had thought this was because Avice, like most of the brides, now declined to speak to her. She would not normally have persisted. But something, perhaps in the pale set of the other woman's face, the dazed look in her eyes, made her ask again.

"Just go away," came the reply. It sounded reduced, at odds with the aggression of the words.

Then the siren had started. Outside, in the gangway, a fire alarm rang, shrill and insistent, followed by the sound of rapid footfalls outside the door.

"Attack party close up at fire in center engine. Location center engine. All passengers to the muster stations."

Frances glanced behind her, all else forgotten. "Avice, that's the alarm. We've got to go." At first she thought perhaps Avice had not understood what the siren meant. "Avice," she said irritably, "that means there's a fire on board. We've got to go."

"No."

"What?"

"I'm not going."

"You can't stay here. I don't think it's a drill this time." The sound of the alarm sent adrenaline coursing through Frances. She realized she was waiting for the sound of an explosion. The war's over, she told herself, and forced herself to breathe deeply. It's over. But that didn't explain the panicked sounds outside. What was it? A stray mine? There had been no thump of ammunition, no jarring vibration in the air that told of a direct hit. "Avice, we've got to—"

"No."

Frances stood in the middle of the dormitory, unable to make sense of the girl's behavior. Avice had never been in battle: her body would not thrill with fear at the mere sound of a siren. But she must understand. "Will you go with Margaret, for Pete's sake?" Perhaps it was because it was Frances asking her to leave.

Avice lifted her head. It was as if she hadn't heard a thing. "You're okay," she said, her voice hard. "You've got your husband, in spite of everything. Once you get off this ship you're free, you're respectable. I've got nothing but disgrace and humiliation ahead of me."

The alarm had been joined by a distant Tannoy. "Fire! Fire! Fire!" Frances was having trouble keeping her thoughts straight.

"Avice, I—"

"Look!" Avice was holding out a letter. It was as if she were deaf to the anxious voices, feet running outside. "Look at it!"

Fear meant that initially Frances could not make sense of the words on the paper in front of her. It had sucked the moisture from her mouth, sent her thoughts tumbling against each other. Every cell was screaming at her to move toward the door, to safety. With Avice's eyes on her, she ran her gaze distractedly over the letter again, this time picking out "sorry" and grasped that she might be in the presence of some personal catastrophe. "Sort it out later," she said, gesturing toward the door. "Come on, Avice, let's get to the muster station. Think of the baby."

"Baby? The baby?" Avice stared at Frances as if she were an imbecile, then sank down on her pillow in weary resignation.

"Oh, just go," she said. She buried her face in her pillow, leaving Frances to stand dumbly by the door.

———

It took Nicol several seconds to realize that the arms hauling at him were not Tims's. He had been flailing around, fists flying, head moving dully backward and forward with each impact, but he was dimly conscious that the last time they had landed on flesh the wail of protest had not been the stoker's. He reeled back, eyes stinging as he tried to focus, and gradually, became aware of Tims several feet away, two seamen bent over him.

Emmett was pulling at his jacket with one hand, while the other rubbed his temple. "What the hell are you doing, Nicol? You've got to get upstairs," he was saying. "To the muster stations. Got to get the brides into the boats. Jesus Christ, man! Look at the state of you."

It was then that he became aware of the alarm, and was surprised he had not noticed it before. Perhaps the ringing in his ears had drowned it.

"It's center engine, Tims," the young stoker was shouting. "Shit, we're in trouble."

The fight was forgotten.

"What happened?" Tims was on his feet now, leaning over the younger man. A long cut ran down his cheek. Nicol, struggling to his feet, wondered whether he had bestowed it.

"I don't know."

"What have you done?" Tims's huge, bloodied hand shot out and gripped the boy's shoulder.

"I—I don't know. I took five minutes to go and see the girls. Then I went back down and the whole bloody passage was filled with smoke."

"Did you shut it off? Did you close the hatch?"

"I don't know—there was too much smoke. I couldn't even get past the bomb room."

"Shit!" Tims looked at Nicol. "I'll head down there."

"Anyone else in center engine?"

Tims shook his head, wincing. "No. The Artificer had gone off. It was just the damn fool boy." The first wisp of smoke found its way into the men's nostrils, prompting a short, loaded silence.

"It's the captain," said Tims. "He's jinxed, that Highfield. He'll do for us all."

21

A is for ARMY of which we are fond,
B is for BRIDES both brunette and blonde,
C is for COURAGE they had lots,
D is for DISTANCE we covered by knots,
E is for ENDEAVOR to give of our best,
F is for FORTITUDE put to the test . . .
        IDA FAULKNER, WAR BRIDE, QUOTED IN FORCES SWEETHEARTS,
            WARTIME ROMANCE FROM THE FIRST WORLD WAR
                    TO THE GULF, JOANNA LUMLEY

The stoker firefighter emerged from the black smoke with the faltering steps of a blind man, one hand still clutching his hose, the other outstretched, waiting for the grasp that would pull him to safety. His smoke helmet was blackened, and the hands that reached forward to pull it off his head discovered, with burned fingers, how hot it was.

Green coughed and wiped soot from his eyes, then straightened and faced his captain. "Beaten back, sir. We've closed all the hatches we can, but it's spread to the starboard engine room. Drenching system hasn't worked." He coughed black phlegm on to the floor, then looked up again, eyes white in his sooty face. "I don't think it's reached the main feed tank, because it would have blown out the machine control room."

"Foamite?" said the captain.

"Too late for that, sir. It's no longer just a fuel fire."

Around him the team of marines and stokers, the naval firefighters, stood ready, clutching hoses and fire extinguishers, waiting for the orders that would send them in.

It had often been said of Highfield, on *Indomitable*, that he knew the location of every room, every compartment, every hold in his floating city without ever having to examine a map. Now he mentally traced the possible route of the fire through her sister ship. "Do we know which way it's headed?"

"We can only hope it spreads to starboard. That way we might lose the starboard engine, sir, but it will hit the air space. Above it we've got the lub oil tank and turbo-generator."

"So the worst that could happen is we're immobilized." Around him, the fire siren continued to wail in the cramped passageway. In the distance, he could hear the women being mustered.

"Sir."

"But?"

"But I can't guarantee it's spreading in that direction, sir."

Caught early enough, an engine-room fire could have been put out with extinguishers and, at worst, a hose. Even caught late, it could usually be contained with boundary hosing—spraying water on the outside walls to keep the temperature of the room down. But this fire—God only knew how—had already gone too far. Where were the men? he wanted to shout. Where the extinguishers? The bloody drenchers? But it was too late for any of that. "You think it might be heading toward the machine control room?"

The man nodded.

"If it blows out the machine control room, it will reach the warhead and bomb rooms."

"Sir."

That plane. That face. Highfield forced himself to push away the image.

"Get the women off the ship."

"What?"

"Lower the lifeboats."

Dobson glanced out of the bridge at the rough seas. "Sir, I—"

"I'm not taking any chances. Lower the lifeboats. Take a bloody order, man. Green, grab your men and equipment. Dobson, I need at least ten men. We're going to empty the bomb rooms as far as possible, then flood the bloody thing. Tennant, I want you and a couple of others to see if you can get to the passage below the mast pump room. Get the hatches open on the lub oil store and flood it. Flood as many of the compartments around both engine rooms as you can."

"But it's above water level, sir."

"Look at the waves, man. We'll make the bloody seas work for us for a change."

———

On the boat deck, Nicol was trying to persuade a weeping girl, her arms wrapped round her lifejacket, to climb into the lifeboat. "I can't," she shrieked, pointing at the churning black seas below. "Look at it! Just look at it!"

Around them, the marines struggled to keep order and calm, despite the sirens and piped instructions emanating from other parts of the ship. Occasionally a woman would cry out that she could see or smell smoke, and a ripple of fear would travel through the others. Despite this, the weeping girl was not the only one unwilling to climb into the boats, which, after the solidity of *Victoria*, bobbed precariously like corks in the foaming waters below.

"You've got to get in," he yelled, his tone becoming firmer.

"But all my things! What will happen to them?"

"They'll be fine. Fire will be out in no time and then you can re-embark. Come on, now. There's a queue building up behind you."

With a sob of reluctance, the girl allowed herself to be handed into the boat and the queue shuffled forward a few inches. Behind him the crowd of several hundred women waited, having been marshaled out of the hangar deck toward the lifeboats, most still in their evening dresses. The wind whistled around them, goosepimpling the girls' arms; they clutched themselves and shivered. Some wept, others wore bright, nervous smiles as if trying to persuade themselves that this was all some jolly adventure. One in three refused point-blank to get in and had to be ordered or even manhandled. He didn't blame them—he didn't want to get into a lifeboat either.

In the floodlit dark, he could see men who remembered *Indomitable*; they eyed each other while trying not to reveal it in their expressions, kept their attention focused on getting the women down into the relative safety of the waters below.

The next female hand was in his. It was Margaret, her moon face pale. "I can't leave Maudie," she said.

It took him several seconds to understand what she was saying. "Frances is down there," he said. "She'll bring her. Come on, you can't wait."

"But how do you know?"

"Margaret, you have to get into the boat." He could see the anxious faces of those swaying in the suspended cutter. "C'mon, now. Don't make everyone else wait."

Her grip was surprisingly strong. "You've got to tell her to get Maudie."

Nicol peered back through the smoke and chaos below the bridge. His own fears were not for the dog.

"You get into that one, Nicol." His marine captain appeared behind him, pointing to the one alongside. "Make sure they've all got their jackets on."

"Sir, I'd rather wait on deck, if that's—"

"I want you in the boat."

"Sir, if it's all the same I'll—"

"Nicol, in the boat. That's an order." The marine captain nodded him toward the little vessel, as Margaret's lifeboat disappeared down the side of the ship, then did a double-take. "What the bloody hell has happened to your face?"

Several minutes later, Nicol's boat hit the waters with a flat wet thud that made several girls shriek. Fumbling with safety straps and the problem of getting a lifejacket round a particularly hysterical bride, Nicol scanned the boats already on the water until he spotted Emmett. The young marine was gesturing at his single oar. "There's no bloody ropes," he was shouting, "and half the oars are missing. Bloody ship's a floating scrapyard."

"They were half-way through replacing them. Denholm ordered it after the last drill," said another voice.

Nicol searched for and found his own oars—he was lucky. They were safe. They could float all night for all it mattered. Around them, the sea churned dark gray, the waves not high enough to induce real fear, but sizable enough to keep the women's hold firm on the sides of the little boats. Above, through the whistling in his ears, he could hear the increasingly rapid piped instructions, now joined by the siren. He stared at the creaking ship; the faint but distinct plume of smoke that had emerged from the space below the women's cabins.

Get out, he told her silently. Get to somewhere I can see you.

"I can't keep close to you," shouted Emmett. "How are we going to keep the boats together?"

"Get out. Get out now," he said aloud.

"Here," said a woman behind him, "I know what we can do. Come on, girls . . ."

———

"I'm not going."

Frances had hold of Avice now, no longer caring what the girl thought of her, no longer caring how any physical contact would be received. She could hear the sound of the lifeboats hitting the water, the shouts of those leaving the ship, and was filled by the blind fear that they would not get out.

She tried to convey none of this to Avice who, she suspected, was beyond sensible thought. She hated the stupid girl, too shallow even to recognize the threat to their lives.

"I know it's hard but you've got to go now." She had kept her voice sing-song light for the past ten minutes. Sweet, reassuring, detached, the way she used to talk to the worst-injured men.

"There's nothing for me now," said Avice, and her voice rasped like sandpaper. "You hear me? Everything's ruined. I'm ruined."

"I'm sure it can be sorted out—"

"Sorted out? What do I do? Unmarry myself? Row myself back to Australia?"

"Avice, this is not the time—" She could smell smoke now. It made all the hairs on the back of her neck stand on end.

"Oh, how could you possibly understand? You, with the morals of an alleycat."

"We've got to get out."

"I don't care. My life is over. I may as well stay here—" She broke off as, above them, something crashed on to the deck. The shudder it sent through the little room seemed to knock Avice out of her trance.

A man's face appeared round their door. "You shouldn't still be in here," he said. "Leave your things and go." It seemed as if he were about to come in, but he was distracted by a shout from the other end of the passageway. "Now!" he said, and vanished.

Frances stared in horror at the door, just long enough to see the back legs of the little dog disappear through it. She toyed with the idea of going after her, but a glance at Avice's wild expression told her where her priorities lay.

There was another crash and a man's voice at the end of the hangar deck yelling, "Secure hatches! Secure hatches now!"

"Oh, for God's sake." Frances's grip was strong. She grabbed an arm and a handful of Avice's dress and pulled her out of the cabin, conscious that she was at last movable. The corridor was full of smoke. Frances tried to duck below it, a hand over her mouth and nose. "Gun turret," she yelled, pointing, and they stumbled, half blinded, their lungs scorched and protesting, toward it.

They fumbled with the hatch door, and fell outside, gasping and retching. Frances made her way to the edge and leaned over, so relishing the clearer air that it took her a minute to register the scene below: a web of boats spanning beneath them, linked by knotty brown lengths. She glanced up at the empty gantries and saw that all the boats were in the water. She knew there must still be men on deck—she could hear their voices filtering downward. But she could not work out how to get to them.

Someone saw them and shouted. Arms gesticulated from below. "Get out!" someone was shouting. "Get out now!"

Frances stared at the water, then at the girl beside her, still in her best dress. Frances was a strong swimmer: she could dive down, emerge among the lifeboats. She owed Avice nothing. Less than nothing. "We can't head up to the flight deck. There's too much smoke in the corridor," she said. "We're going to have to jump."

"I can't," said Avice.

"It's not that far. Look—I'll hold on to you."

"I can't swim."

Frances heard the crack of something giving outside, the hint of an inferno she did not want to face. She grabbed Avice and they struggled, Frances trying desperately to drag her toward the edge.

"Get off me!" Avice screamed. "Don't touch me!" She was wild, scratching and pounding at Frances's arms, her shoulders. Smoke was seeping under the hatch. From somewhere far below, Frances could hear women's voices calling up to them. She smelled something acrid and her heart was filled with fear. She grabbed a handful of Avice's silk dress and dragged her on to the gun turret. Her foot slipped, the rubber sole of her shoe sliding off metal, and she thought suddenly: What if no one rescues me? Then she heard a scream and, entangled, they were falling, arms and legs flailing, toward the inky black below.

———

The captain had the wrench in his hands, and was struggling to get the bomb off its clamp on the wall. "Get out!" he shouted at the men who, three strong, were carrying the penultimate bomb from the magazine. "Get the hose! Flood the compartment! Flood it now!" He had removed his mask to be better heard, and his voice was hoarse as he tried to speak and breathe.

"Captain!" yelled Green, though his mask. "Got to get out now."

"She's not going up. Got to be safe."

"You can't get them all off, sir. You don't have time. We can flood it now."

Afterward, Green thought Highfield might not have heard him. He did not want to leave his skipper there, but he knew there was only so much a man could do before the need to keep the other men safe overrode his concern.

"Start the flooding," Highfield was shouting. "Just go."

He turned, and as he did so, he heard something fall. He threw his smoke helmet blindly toward the captain, hoping it would reach him, that somehow he would see it through the smoke. His heart heavy with foreboding, he was out, pushing his men before him.

———

Frances broke through the surface, her mouth a great O, her hair plastered over her face. She could hear voices, feel hands pulling at her, trying to heave her out of water so cold it had knocked the breath hard from her chest. At first the sea had not wanted to relinquish her: she felt its icy grasp on her clothes. And then she was flopping, gasping, on the floor of the little boat like a landed fish, retching as voices tried to reassure her, and a blanket swiftly wrapped round her shoulders.

Avice, she mouthed. And then as the salt sting in her eyes eased, she saw her being hauled like a catch over the other end of the cutter, her beauty-pageant dress slick with oil, her eyes closed tight against her future.

Is she all right? she wanted to ask. But an arm slid round her, pulled her in tightly. It did not release her, as she expected, but held on, so that she felt the closeness of this solid body, the intensity of its protection, and suddenly she had no words. *Frances*, a voice said, close by her ear, and it was dark with relief.

———

Captain Highfield was laid out on the flight deck by the two stokers who had carried him there. The men stood around him, hands thrust in pockets, some wiping sweat or soot from their faces, spitting noisily behind them. In the distance, under the dark skies, there were shouts of confirmation as different parts of the ship were deemed to have stopped burning.

It's out, Captain, they told him. It's under control. We did it. They half whispered these words as if unsure whether he could still hear them. There would be other conversations later, about how ill-judged it was for a man of his standing, of his age, to throw himself into the firefighting efforts in such a reckless manner. There would be nodded observations of how bad he was at delegating, how another captain might have stood back and seen the bigger picture. But many of his men would approve. They would think of Hart, and their lost mates, and wonder whether they wouldn't have done the same.

But this was hours, days ahead. For now, Highfield lay there, oblivious to their words and reassurances. There was silence for a whole minute, as the men watched his slumped figure, still in his good dress uniform, wet and smoke-stained, eyes still fixed on some distant drama.

The men looked at him, and then, surreptitiously at each other. One wondered whether to summon the ship's doctor, who was organizing a sing-song among the occupants of the lifeboats below. Then Highfield raised himself on his elbow, his eyes bloodshot. He coughed once, twice more, and there was black phlegm on the deck. He moved his neck as if in pain. "Well, what are you waiting for?" he asked, voice gravelly, eyes full of fury. "Check every last bloody compartment. Then get the bloody women out of the bloody boats and back on bloody board."

———

It took two hours to make the ship safe. The Spanish fishing vessels that passed by shortly before dawn, checking that those still waiting on the water did not need rescuing, would speak for years after of the lifeboats, full of women in brightly colored evening dresses, their limbs arranged chaotically, singing "The Wild Rover No More." They were linked, like some giant cobweb, by taut brown stockings, knotted together in lengths.

There were two marines to each lifeboat. The water slopped against the side of the cutters, buoying the discarded or torn hosiery, which floated like brown seaweed on the surface of the water. The women's voices were low with relief and exhaustion as word spread that they would not have to spend much longer in the little vessels. That they, and their belongings, were safe.

He stared at her, and now, as Avice's sleeping body rested limply against her own, still wrapped in the blanket, she stared back, past the stooped bodies of the other women, silent and unblinking, as if their eyes were connected by an invisible thread.

———

The captain was alive. The fires were out.

They were to re-embark.

22

Remember, the army will not send you to a destination unless it has been verified that "that man" is there waiting. In short, consider yourself parcel-post delivery.

ADVICE CONTAINED IN A BOOKLET GIVEN TO WAR BRIDES
TRAVELING ABOARD THE ARGENTINA, IMPERIAL WAR MUSEUM

TWENTY-FOUR HOURS TO PLYMOUTH

It was several hours before the temperature had cooled enough to check it, but it was pretty clear once the working party got down there that the center engine room was beyond repair; the heat had melted pipework and welded rivets to the floor. The walls and hatches had buckled, and above it half of the seamen's messes were gone, the decks above them warping so far with the heat that several gantries had toppled over. Other ratings had donated blankets and pillows so that those who had lost bunks and belongings could sleep in relative comfort in the forward hangar space. Nobody complained. Those who had lost treasured photographs and letters comforted themselves with the thought that within twenty-four hours they were likely to see in person the subjects of those precious keepsakes. Those who remembered *Indomitable* were simply relieved that no lives had been lost. If the war had taught them nothing else, it had taught them that.

"Think you can limp into harbor?"

Highfield sat in the bridge, watching the gray skies clear to reveal patches of pure blue, as if in apology for the evening before. "We're less than a day away. We've got one working engine. I don't see why not."

"Sounds like the old girl suffered a bit." McManus's voice was low. "And a little bird tells me you were a little too stuck in for comfort."

Highfield dismissed thoughts of armament clamps and his raw

throat. He took another swig of the honey and lemon that his steward had prepared for him. "Fine, sir. Nothing to worry about. The men . . . looked after me."

"Good man. I'll take a look at your report. Glad you were able to bring it all under control—without frightening the ladies too much, I mean." His laugh echoed tinnily down the wire.

Highfield stepped out of the bridge, and stood on the flight deck. At the aft end, a row of men were making their way slowly along it, scrubbing off traces of the smoke that had filtered upward, their buckets of gray, foaming water slopping as they went. They worked around the areas that had buckled, which were not safe to walk on. Several marines had been busy constructing barriers around them. The damage was visible, but it was all orderly. When they sailed into Plymouth, Highfield's ship would be under control.

He had not lost a single one.

No one was close enough to hear the shaking breath that Highfield slowly let out as he turned to go back into the bridge. But that didn't mean it hadn't happened.

———

At least a hundred women had queued patiently by the main hatch since breakfast, waiting to be allowed back to their cabins. There had been hushed conversations about the state of their belongings, fears for cherished and carefully chosen arrival outfits now perhaps wrecked by water and smoke. Although there was no obvious damage on this deck, a brush against a wall or bunk left one with a shadow that revealed everything was veiled with a fine layer of soot. As they stood and talked, quieting for every piped instruction in case it heralded their being allowed in, more women drifted toward the queue.

Margaret, heavily pregnant and cumbersome as she was, tore through the hatch the minute it was opened, and was already in her cabin by the time the other brides had made it to the bottom of the stairwell. "Maudie! Maudie!"

The door had been open. She knelt down and peered under the two bottom bunks. "Maudie!" she cried.

"Have you tried the canteen? There's a lot of them still up there." A

WSO had stuck her head briefly round the door. Margaret turned and stared at her perplexed, until she realized the woman thought she was looking for another bride.

"Maudie!" She checked under every blanket, lifting bedrolls and tearing the sheets from the bunks in her desperation. Nothing. She was not in the beds, in any of the bags. She was not even in Margaret's hat, traditionally her place of comfort.

Margaret was hit with the scale of the search ahead at the exact moment she heard the scream. She stood very still for a minute, and then, as someone else cried, "What on earth is it?" she threw herself out of the door and lumbered down the passageway to the bathrooms.

Afterward she thought she had probably known even before she got there. It was the only other place Maudie knew on the ship, the only other place she must have thought she might find Margaret. She stood in the doorway, staring at the girls gathered by the sinks. She followed their eyes to the little dog lying pressed against the back of the door, several dark streaks on the tiled wall where she must have tried to scrabble her way out.

Margaret stepped forward and fell to her knees on the damp floor. A great sob escaped her. The dog's limbs were stiff, the body cold. "Oh, no. Oh, no."

Margaret's face crumpled like a child's. She gathered the little dog's body into her arms. "Oh, Maudie, I'm so sorry. I'm so, so sorry."

She stayed there for some minutes, kissing the wet hair, trying to will the body into life, knowing that it was hopeless.

She did not actually cry, those watching reported, just sat, holding the dog, as if absorbing some great pain.

Eventually, at the point where the anxious glances around her became whispers, she peeled off her cardigan and folded the dog into it. Then, with a grunt, one hand on the smudged wall, she got to her feet. She held the bundle close to her, as one would hold a baby.

"Would you . . . would you like me to fetch someone?" A woman laid a hand on her arm.

She didn't seem to hear.

Crying bitterly, Margaret walked back along the passageway, clasping her swaddled burden. Those who were not preoccupied with their own smoked belongings peered into it, curious about this baby's identity.

An uneasy hush had descended on the ship. Those women returning to their cabins did not chatter with relief, even though the worst damage to anyone's belongings had been a coating of soot. The night had shown them the precariousness of their position, and it had shaken them. The voyage was no longer an adventure. There was not one who wasn't suddenly overwhelmed by an ache to be home. Whatever that turned out to be.

The WSO placed a hand under her arm as Frances lifted herself on to the bed, surprised by how tired that small act made her feel. The woman pulled a blanket over her, then made to adjust the other round her shoulders. The marine removed his own supporting arm, and let go of her hand with a hint of reluctance. She caught his eye and her exhaustion briefly disappeared.

"I'm fine," she said, to the WSO. "Thank you, but really I am. I'd be just as good in my own bunk."

"Dr. Duxbury says anyone who's been in the water needs to spend a few hours under observation. You might have hypothermia."

"I can assure you I haven't."

"Orders are orders. You'll probably be out by teatime." The WSO moved to Avice's bed, tucking in her blankets in a brisk, maternal gesture that reminded Frances suddenly of the hospital at Morotai. But they were in a side room off the infirmary, some kind of detergent store, Frances guessed, from the boxes around them and the pervasive smell of bleach. There were charts on the walls, with lists of supplies, and locked cabinets containing items that might be flammable. Frances shivered.

"Sorry about the room," the WSO was saying. "We need the infirmary for the men who inhaled smoke, and we couldn't have you mixing. This was the only place we could put you two. Only for a few hours, though, eh?"

The marine, inches from her bed, was staring at her. Frances felt the warmth of his eyes and savored it. She could still feel the imprint of his arm round her as he half walked, half carried her back on board, his head so close to hers that, if she had inclined her neck a little further, she could have felt his skin against hers.

"Now, Mrs. Radley, are you comfortable?"

"Fine," Avice said, into her pillow.

"Good. I've got to pop next door and get the men comfortable, but I'll be back as soon as I can. When you're feeling up to it, I've brought you some nice clean clothes to change into. I'll put them just here." She placed the carefully folded pile on a small cabinet. "Now, I'm sure you ladies could do with a cup of tea. Marine, would you do the honors? It's chaos downstairs and I don't want to have to fight my way to the galley."

"I'd be delighted."

She felt his hand, the brief squeeze, and for a second she forgot about this room, about Avice, the fire. She was on a lifeboat, her eyes locked on to this man's, saying everything she had ever wanted to say, everything she had never believed she would want to say, without uttering a word.

"I'll take a look at those cuts later," she murmured to him, and fought the urge to touch his face. She imagined how his skin would feel under her fingertips, the tenderness with which she would care for the bruised flesh.

He glanced behind him as he walked toward the door. Smiled when he saw she was still watching him, one hand raised unconsciously to her hair.

"I don't suppose you particularly want to be stuck with me, do you?" As he closed the door, Avice's voice cut into the silence.

Reluctantly, Frances brought her thoughts to the woman in front of her. "I don't mind who I'm with," she replied coolly.

It was as if their hours in the lifeboat had never happened, as if

Avice, uncomfortable at having been rescued by this woman, was now determined to restore the distance between them.

"I've got a stomach-ache. This bodice is too tight. Will you help me out of it?"

Avice slid slowly out of her bed, her hair separated into pale, salted fronds. Frances helped her out of the ruined party dress, the stiff girdle and brassière, with impersonal care. It was only as she helped Avice back on to the bed that she saw the mark spreading slowly across the back of the peach silk robe. She stooped to pick up the soiled dress and saw further evidence. She waited until Avice had lain down, then stood stiffly beside her. "I have to tell you something," she said. "You're bleeding."

In the little room, piled high with boxes, they examined the robe in silence. Avice took it off and stared at the ruby stain, which was even now making its way on to the sheet. She saw in Frances's face what it meant. There was no visible change in her demeanor. She accepted the clean towel that Frances fetched without comment.

"I'm so sorry," said Frances, a pebble of discomfort lodged inside her. "It—it may have been the shock of the water." She had been prepared for Avice to scream at her, that she might relish the chance to add this lost child to Frances's list of supposed sins. But she said nothing, just acceded to Frances's quiet requests to lie still, put this towel there, take a painkiller or two.

Finally she spoke. "Just as well, really," she said. "Poor little bastard."

There was a brief, shocked silence, as if even she was surprised by her choice of words.

Frances's eyes widened.

Avice shook her head. Then suddenly, lurching up and forward like somebody choking, she began to wail. Racking sobs filled the little room and she sank back on to the narrow bed, her face buried in the sheet, the muffled noise passing through her as if with seismic tremors.

Frances dropped the dress, clambered quietly on to Avice's bed and sat beside her, stunned. She stayed there for some time until, unable to bear the terrible sound any longer, she put her arms round the girl and held her. Avice neither pushed her away nor leaned in to her. It was as if she was so locked into her own private unhappiness that she did not know Frances was there.

"It will be all right," Frances said, not knowing if she could justify her words. "It will be all right."

It was some time before the sobbing subsided. Frances fetched more painkillers from the dispensary and a sedative, in case it proved necessary. When she returned, Avice was lying back against the wall, a pillow propped under her. She wiped her eyes, then gestured to Frances to pass her her dress, from which she pulled a piece of tattered, damp paper. "Here, you can read this properly now," she said.

"Not Wanted Don't Come?"

"No. Oh, he wants me, all right . . ."

Avice thrust it toward her and, conscious that they had traversed some barrier, Frances took it and this time read properly the bits that had not run in the waters of the Atlantic.

> *I should have told you this a long time ago. But I love you, darling, and I couldn't bear the thought of your sad face when I told you, or the slightest possibility of losing you . . . Please don't misunderstand me—I'm not asking you not to come. You need to know that the relationship between me and my wife is far more like brother and sister than anything. You, my darling, mean far more to me than she ever could . . .*
>
> *I want you to know I meant every word I said in Australia. But you must understand—the children are so young, and I am not the type to take my responsibilities lightly. Perhaps when they are a little older we can think again?*
>
> *So, I know I'm asking a lot of you, but just think about this in your days left on board. I've got a fair bit put away, and I could set you up in a lovely little place in London. And I can be with you a couple of nights a week, which, when you think of it, is more than most wives see their men in the Navy . . .*
>
> *Avice, you always said that us being together was all that mattered. Prove to me, darling, that this was the truth . . .*

As Frances digested the final words, she didn't know whether she should look Avice full in the face. She did not want her to think she was gloating. "What will you do?" she said carefully.

"Go home, I suppose. I couldn't while there was . . . but now, I suppose, it can be like nothing happened. None of it happened. My parents didn't want me to come anyway." Her voice was thin and cold.

"You will be all right, you know."

In her reaction to this, there was just a hint then of the old Avice: the superciliousness that told Frances that what she had said, what she was, were worthless. Avice dropped the letter on to the bedcover. The way she looked at Frances now was naked, unembarrassed. "How do you carry on living," she asked, "with all that hanging over you? All that disgrace?"

Frances understood that, for once, the words were not as harsh as they sounded. Beneath Avice's pallid complexion, there was genuine curiosity in her eyes. She chose her words carefully. "I suppose I've discovered . . . we all carry something. Some burden of shame."

Frances reached under the girl, pulled out the towel and checked the size of the stain. She hid it discreetly, then handed her another.

Avice shifted on the bed. "And yours has been lifted. Because you found someone prepared to take you on. Despite your—your history."

"I'm not ashamed of who I am, Avice."

Frances picked up the soiled items for the WSO to take to the laundry. Then she sat down on the bed. "You might as well know. I've done one thing in my life that I'm ashamed of. And that wasn't it."

The Australian Army Nursing Service had set up a recruiting depot in Wayville, near the camp hospital. She had been a trainee nurse for some time at the Sydney Showground Hospital, had worked for a good family in Brisbane to finance her training, and now, single, medically fit, without dependants and with a glowing reference from her matron, the newly formed Australian General Hospital was keen to take her. She had had to lie about her age, but the knowing look the CO had given her when she calculated her new date of birth told her she wasn't the first. There was a war on, after all.

Joining the AGH, she said, had been like coming home. The sisters were stoic, capable, cheerful, compassionate and, above all, professional. They were the first people she had ever met who accepted her as she was, appreciated her effort and dedication. They came from all over Australia and had no interest in her history. Most had a reason for their lack of a husband, of dependents, and it was rarely one they wanted to dwell on. Besides, the necessities of their job meant they lived from day to day, in the present.

She had never tried to contact her mother. She thought it probably betrayed a rather ruthless streak in her personality, but even that hard knowledge about herself did not tempt her to change her mind.

Over several years they had served together in Northfield, Port Moresby and, lastly, in Morotai, where she had met Chalkie. During that time she had learned that what had happened to her was not the worst thing that could happen to a person, not when you considered the cruelties inflicted in the name of war. She had held dying men, dressed wounds that had made her want to retch, cleaned out stinking latrines, washed foul sheets, and helped erect tents that were threadbare from overuse and mold. She thought she had never been as happy in her life.

Men had fallen for her. It was almost par for the course in the hospital—many of them had not seen a girl for some time. A few kind words, a smile, and they bestowed on you all sorts of qualities you might or might not have. She had assumed Chalkie was one of those. She thought, in his delirium, that it was possible he could not see past her smile. He asked her to marry him at least once a day and, as with the others, she had paid him little attention. She would never marry.

Until the day the gunner arrived.

"Was he the man you fell in love with?"

"No. The one who recognized me." Here she swallowed. "He came from the same unit that had been stationed by the hotel where I had lived all those years ago. And I knew there would be a time when I had to leave Australia, that it would be the only way I could ever get away from . . ." She paused. "So I decided to say yes."

"Did he know? Your husband?"

Frances's hands had rested quietly in her lap. Now her fingers linked, separated, linked again. "The first few weeks when I knew him he was delirious half the time. He knew my face. Some days he thought we were already married. He occasionally called me Violet. Someone told me that was the name of his late sister. Sometimes, late at night, he would ask me to hold his hand and sing to him. When the pain got very bad, I did, even though I have a terrible voice." She allowed herself a small smile. "I never knew a man as gentle. The night I told him I would marry him, he cried with happiness."

Avice's eyes closed with pain, and Frances waited until the cramp had passed. Then she continued, her voice clear in the darkening room. "He had this CO, Captain Baillie, who knew Chalkie had no family. He knew, too, that I had nothing much to gain from the marriage, and that in simple terms it would make him happy. So he said yes where, I suppose, plenty wouldn't. It wasn't very honorable on my part, I suppose, but I did care for him."

"And you knew you would get your passage out."

"Yes." A half smile played across her lips. "Ironic, really, isn't it? A girl with my history marrying the only man who never laid a finger on me."

"But at least you kept your reputation intact."

"No. That didn't happen." Frances fingered her skirt, the same grubby, salt-hardened one she had worn on the lifeboat. "A few days before Chalkie and I were married I was sitting outside the mess camp, washing bandages, when that gunner came up and—" she choked "—tried to put his hand up my skirt. I screamed, and hit his face quite hard. It was the only way I could get him off. But the other nurses ran out and he told them it was all I was good for. That he had known me in Aynsville. That was the decider, see? It was such a small town, and I had told them where I came from. They knew it had to be true." She paused. "I think it would have been easier for them if he had told them I'd killed someone."

"Did anyone tell Chalkie?"

"No. But I think that was out of sympathy for him. Oh, some chose to ignore it. I suppose when you've been so near death people's reputations cease to matter. But they all knew how he felt about me, and he was fragile. The men are loyal to each other . . . It comes out in strange ways sometimes."

"But the nurses did what I did in judging you?"

"Most of them, yes. I think the matron took a different view. We'd worked together for a long time. She knew me—she knew me as something else. She just told me I should make the most of what he had given me. Not many people get a second chance in life."

Avice lay down and stared at the ceiling. "I suppose she was right. No one has to know. No one has to know . . . anything."

Frances raised an eyebrow, unconvinced. "Even after all this?"

Avice shrugged. "England's a big place. There are a lot of people. And Chalkie will look after you now."

As Frances failed to reply, Avice asked, "No one told him in the end, did they? Not after all that?"

"No," Frances said. "No one told him."

———

On the other side of the door, where he had been listening, still holding two stone-cold tin mugs of tea, the marine moved his head gently away from the hard surface, and closed his eyes.

23

There were romances and several weddings took place and, as it was Dutch Territory, many pieces of paper had to be signed ... The dentist usually made the wedding ring with his drill, and wedding frocks ranged from creations out of white mosquito nets to AANS ward uniform ... According to army policy, the bride returned to Australia soon after.

A SPECIAL KIND OF SERVICE, *JOAN CROUCH*

MOROTAI, HALMAHERAS ISLANDS, 1946

"I know it's irregular," said Audrey Marshall, "but you saw them. You saw what it's done to her."

"I find it all rather hard to believe."

"She was a child, Charles. Fifteen, from what she told me."

"He's very fond of her, I'll grant you."

"So what harm would it do?"

The matron pulled open a drawer and took out a bottle of pale brown liquid. She held it up and he nodded, declining the addition of chlorinated water that sat in a jug on her desk. They had meant to talk earlier, but there had been an accident on the road to the American radar unit: a jeep had collided with a Dutch supplies lorry and overturned, killing one man and injuring two others. Captain Baillie had spent more than an hour with the Dutch authorities, filling in forms and discussing the incident with the Dutch CO. One of the men had been his batman; he was shaken and exhausted.

He took a sip, plainly not wanting to have to consider this new problem on top of everything else. "It could cause all sorts of trouble. The man doesn't know his own mind."

"He knows he loves her. It would make him happy. And, besides, what can she do? She can't stay in nursing now everyone knows. She can't stay in Australia."

"Oh, come on, it's a big place."

"Someone found her here, didn't they?"

"I don't know . . ."

Matron leaned over the desk. "She's a good nurse, Charles. A good girl. Think what she's done for your men. Think of Petersen and Mills. Think of O'Halloran and those wretched sores."

"I know."

"What harm? The boy's got no money, has he? You said he had no family to speak of." Her voice dropped a little. "You know as well as I do how ill he is."

"And you know I've tried jolly hard to discourage this kind of thing. All that bloody paperwork for a start."

"You're on good terms with the Dutch. You've told me yourself. They'll sign whatever you hand them."

"You're convinced that this is a sensible idea?"

"It would bring him some happiness and give her a lifeline. She'd be entitled to go to England. She'll make a superb nurse over there. What harm can that do?"

Charles Baillie sighed deeply. He put down his glass on the desk and turned to the woman opposite. "It's hard to refuse you anything, Audrey."

She smiled with the satisfaction of someone who knows the battle is won. "I'll do what I have to do," she said.

The chaplain was a pragmatic man. Weary of the pain and suffering he had seen, he had been easily persuaded to help. The young nurse, a favorite of his, was a perfect illustration of the redemptive powers of marriage, he told himself. And if it enabled the poor soul beside her to be even partly lifted from the horrors of his last weeks, he felt pretty sure his God would understand. When the matron had thanked him, he had replied that he thought the Almighty was more of a pragmatist than any of them knew.

Congratulating themselves on their solution, and with perhaps the faintest curiosity as to how their plan would be received by its subjects, the three sat in the matron's office long enough to celebrate their good sense with another drink. For medicinal purposes, of course, the matron said with a grin, remarking on the pallor of Captain Baillie's face. She couldn't stand to see a man with a pale face: she always wanted to check them for blood disorders.

"Only problem with my blood is there's not enough whisky in it," he muttered.

They toasted Sister Luke, her future husband, the end of the war and Churchill for good measure. Shortly after ten o'clock they walked out into the tented ward, a little more erect, a little less relaxed, as they stood before their charges.

"She's in B Ward," said the sister, who was reading a letter at the night desk.

"With Corporal Mackenzie," said the matron, turning to Captain Baillie not a little triumphantly. It would work out well for everyone. "There, you see?"

They walked through the sandy pathway between the beds, careful not to wake those men already sleeping, then pushed back the curtain to enter the next ward, Captain Baillie pausing to slap, with a curse, the mosquito that had landed on the back of his neck. Then they stopped.

Sister Luke glanced up as she heard them enter. She looked at them with wide, unreadable eyes. She was leaning over Alfred "Chalkie" Mackenzie's bed, three-quarters of which was still covered by a mosquito net. She was pulling a white Navy-issue sheet over his face.

Avice was sleeping when the marine returned with two new, still-hot cups of tea. He knocked twice and entered, watching his feet as he crossed the little room. He placed the two mugs on the table between the beds. He had been half hoping that the WSO would be with them.

Frances had been standing over Avice and jumped, evidently having not expected to see him. A little color rose to her cheeks. He thought she looked exhausted. A few hours ago he might have given in to the urge to touch her. Now, having heard her words, he knew he would not. He moved back toward the door and stood, legs apart, shoulders square, as if to reaffirm something to himself.

"I—I wasn't expecting you," she said. "I thought you'd been called off to do something else."

"I'm sorry I took so long."

"Dr. Duxbury's given me the all-clear. I'm just getting my things together so I can go back. Avice will probably spend tonight in here. I may come back to make sure she's okay. They're a bit overstretched."

"She all right?"

"She'll get there," Frances said. "I was going to find Maggie. How is she?"

"Not too good. The dog . . ."

"Oh." Her face fell. "Oh, no. And she's all by herself?"

"I'm sure she'd be glad of your company." She still hadn't changed her clothes and he ached to wipe the dark smudge from her cheek. His hand tightened behind him.

She stepped forward, glanced back at the sleeping Avice. "I thought about what you said," she said, her voice low and conspiratorial, "that the war has made us all do things we're not proud of. Until you said that, I had always thought I was the only one . . ."

He had not anticipated this. He took a step backward, not trusting himself to speak, half wanting to cry to her not to go on. Half desperate to hear her words.

"I know we haven't always been able to speak . . . honestly. That it's . . . complicated, and that other loyalties might not always . . ." She tailed off, and her eyes flashed up at him. "But I wanted to thank you for that. You've . . . I'll always be glad you told me. I'll always be so grateful that we met each other." The last words were rushed, as if she had had to force them out while she still had the courage to say them.

He felt suddenly small, wretched. "Yes. Well," he said, when he could form words, "it's always nice to have made a friend." He felt mean even opening his mouth as he added, "Ma'am."

There was a little pause.

"Ma'am?" she repeated.

The shy smile had disappeared; a movement so delicate he thought only he could have detected it. I have no choice, he wanted to shout at her. It is for you I'm doing this.

She searched his face. What she found there made her look down and away from him.

"I'm sorry," he said. "I've got to go now. Things to do. But . . . you'll like England."

"Thank you. I've heard a lot about it from the lectures."

The rebuke in her words felt like a blow. "Look . . . I hope you'll always think of me . . ." his hands were rigid at his sides ". . . as your friend." That word had never sounded so unwelcome.

She blinked a little too swiftly, and in shame he made himself look away.

"That's very kind, but I don't think so, Marine," she said. She let out a small breath, then turned, and began to refold the clothes in the little pile on her bed. Her voice, when it shot back, was sharp with hurt: "After all, I don't even know your name."

———

Margaret stood toward the aft end of the flight deck by the lashings, a cardigan stretched round her thickened waist, a headscarf trying and failing to stop her hair whipping too hard round her face. Her back was to the bridge and her head was dipped over the bundle in her arms.

The skies were gray now, rain-laden clouds hanging heavy and sullen in the sky. Huge, wheeling albatross tailed the boat, riding the therms as if they were attached by invisible wires. From time to time she looked down at the little bundle and more tears plopped on to the woolen fabric, darkening it in small, irregular spots. She wiped them gently with a thumb and uttered another silent apology to the stiff little body.

The wind and her headscarf meant that she didn't hear Frances arrive beside her. When she saw her she could not be sure how long she'd been there. "Burial at sea," she said. "Just trying to pluck up the courage to actually do it, you know?"

"I'm so sorry, Maggie." Frances's eyes were bleak. The hand she reached out to Margaret was tentative.

Margaret wiped her eyes with her palm. She shook her head and let out a little "Gah!" of despair at her inability to control herself.

There seemed to be no clear distinction between the sea and the sky; the dark, unwelcoming seas lightened at the far horizon, grayed, then disappeared into the rolling clouds. It was as if they were sailing toward nothing; as if navigation itself could only be an act of blind faith.

Some time later, long before she felt ready, Margaret stepped forward. She hesitated for a moment, holding the little body tight to her, tighter than she would have dared if there had still been life in it.

Then she stooped, a little noise escaped her throat, and she dropped the little bundle into the sea. There was no sound.

She held the rail with white-knuckled fingers, even now shocked at how far above the waves she stood, fighting the urge to stop the ship, to retrieve what she had lost. The sea seemed suddenly too huge, a cold betrayal rather than a peaceful end. Her arms felt unbearably empty.

Beside her, Frances pointed silently.

The beige cardigan was just visible, far below them on the surface, a tiny scrap of pale color. Then it dipped under the foamy wake. They did not see it again. They stood in silence, letting the breeze mold their clothes to their backs, watching *Victoria*'s wake foam, then rise, separate and disappear.

"Have we been mad, Frances?" she said, at last.

"What?"

"What the bloody hell have we done?"

"I'm not sure what—"

"We've left everything, all the people we love, our homes, our security. And for what? To be assaulted and then branded a trollop, like Jean? To be quizzed over your past by the bloody Navy, like some kind of criminal? To go through all this and then be told you're not wanted? Because there's no guarantee, right? There's nothing says these men and their families are going to want us, right?"

Her voice caught on the wind.

"What the hell do I know about England? What do I really know about Joe or his family? About babies? I couldn't even look after my own bloody dog . . ." Her head dipped.

They were oblivious to the damp deck beneath them, the stares of the dabbers painting on the other side of the island.

"You know . . . I have to tell you . . . I think I've made a terrible mistake. I got carried away with the idea of something, maybe escaping from cooking and cleaning for Dad and the boys. And now I'm here, all I want is my family. I want my family back, Frances. I want my mum." She was crying bitterly. "I want my dog."

Eyes blinded by tears, she felt Frances put her thin, strong arms round her. "No, Maggie, no. It's going to be fine. You have a man who loves you. Really loves you. It will be fine."

Margaret wanted to be convinced. "How can you say that after everything that's happened here?"

"Joe is one in a million, Maggie. Even I know that. And you have a wonderful life ahead of you because it's impossible for them not to love you. And you're going to have a beautiful baby and you will love him or her more than you ever imagined. Oh, if you only knew how much I . . ."

Frances's face contorted and volcanic hiccups exploded from her chest, with an unstoppable, messy torrent of tears, and the hug she gave Margaret in comfort became an attempt to comfort herself. She tried to apologize, to pull herself together, waved her hand in mute apology, but she could not stop.

Margaret, shocked into togetherness, held her. "Hey now," she said weakly. "Hey now, Frances, c'mon . . . c'mon, this isn't like you . . ." She stroked the hair, still pinned back from the night before. It must be the shock, she thought, remembering the sight of the two girls dropping into that churning sea. She felt sick with guilt that she hadn't checked that Frances was all right. She held her, in mute apology, waiting for the storm to subside.

"You're right. We'll be okay," she murmured, stroking Frances's hair. "We might end up living near each other, right? And you write me, Frances. I haven't got anyone else over here, and Avice is going to be as much use as a chocolate teapot. You're all I've got . . ."

"I'm not what you think." Frances was crying hard enough to draw attention now. A small group of sailors stood at the far end of the flight deck, watching and smoking. "I can't begin to tell you . . ."

"Ah, c'mon, it's time to leave all that behind." She wiped her own eyes. "Look, as far as I'm concerned, you're a great girl. I know what I need to know, and a little bit that I didn't. And you know what? I still think you're a great girl. And you'd better bloody keep in touch with me."

"You're . . . very . . . kind."

"You were going to say round, right?"

Despite herself, Frances smiled.

"Hey! You two! Come away from there!"

They turned to see an officer standing by the island, waving them in. Margaret turned back to Frances. "Ah, c'mon, girl. Don't get sappy on me now. Not you of all people."

"Oh, Maggie . . . I'm so . . ."

"No," she said. "This is our new start, Frances. New everything. Like you said, it will be all right. We'll make it all right."

She hugged Frances close to her as they began to walk across the huge deck. "Because it can't be for bloody nothing, can it? We've got to make it all right."

––––––

The men were still working as they went down to the dormitory after dinner; scrubbing, polishing, painting, grumbling, their conversations audible in the passageways despite the excited chatter of brides collecting their belongings. Couldn't see the point, the men muttered to each other. Ship was going to scrap anyway. Didn't see why bloody Highfield couldn't have given them one day's bloody rest. Didn't he know the war was over? Frances was comforted, in spite of it all: she had not seen him since the fire and the ratings' words told her everything she needed to know about how he was.

As they came through the hatch into the dormitory area, a small part of her hoped the marine would be standing there. That even though there were to be none on duty tonight he might be outside, his feet locked in their habitual position, his eyes sliding to hers in silent complicity.

But the corridor was empty, as was the one above it, but for women wheeling backward and forward, reclaiming borrowed cosmetics, offering up disembarkation outfits for each other's opinion. Perhaps it was for the best. She felt as if her emotions were running too close to the surface, as if the hysteria and fearful anticipation that ran through the ship had infected her too.

"Good evening, Mrs. Mackenzie." It was Vincent Duxbury, in a cream linen suit. "I understand we may be seeing you in the infirmary later. Nice to have you on duty." He tipped his hat to them, and walked jauntily on, whistling, she thought, "Frankie and Johnny."

Mrs. Mackenzie. Sister Mackenzie. And there was no point wishing things were different, she told herself, as she helped Margaret into the little room. There never had been. She, more than anyone, knew that.

———

She had left Margaret in the dormitory some time after nine thirty, grief and the exhaustions of pregnancy conspiring to produce sweet narcolepsy. Most nights Margaret had to get up, two or three times lately, to pad sleepily to the women's lavatories down the corridor, nodding a greeting to those marines still on duty. Tonight she had failed to wake, and Frances, making her way back to Avice in the infirmary, was glad of it.

She walked along the silent passageway, her soft shoes making almost no noise as she passed the closed doors. In other cabins tonight the air was thick with the scent of face cream liberally applied, the walls bright with carefully laundered dresses, sleep disturbed by the prickle of rollers, hairpins and excited dreams. Not in our little cabin, Frances thought. Margaret had attempted to pin her hair and then, swearing, given up. If he didn't want her now, looking like this, she had reasoned, there was little chance that having hair like Shirley bloody Temple was going to make a difference.

And Frances walked, her hair unrollered, her thoughts dark as the seas outside, her mind trying to close hatches against what must not be considered, like a seaman trying to stop a flood. She tripped up the steps toward the infirmary, nodding to a solitary rating hurrying by with a package under his arm.

She heard the singing before she reached the infirmary. She listened, working out its provenance. From the hoarse sound of the voices and the words of the songs, she deduced that Dr. Duxbury had the men singing show tunes. From the loose quality of the harmonies, she thought perhaps the infirmary might be a little lighter on sterile alcohol than it had been the previous day. In another time, she might have reported him—or gone in and addressed the matter herself. Now she stayed mute. There were just a few hours left on board. Just a few hours left of this ship. Who was she to judge whether the men should sing or not?

The song collapsed in a melancholy trail. Frances let herself in silently, eyeing in the dim light the girl who lay pale and motionless on the bed.

The worst, for Avice, was over. She was asleep now, pale and somehow diminished, the coverlet and rough Navy-issue blanket pulled high round her neck. She frowned in her sleep, as if even now anticipating the trials of the weeks ahead.

She left the light off, but instead of climbing into the spare bed, Frances walked over to the little chair beside it and sat down. Here she stayed for some time, staring at the cardboard boxes around them, listening to the sounds of the singing, which had begun again, punctuated by coughing, or by Dr. Duxbury interrupting to offer some alternative version. Beneath the noise in the adjoining room she listened to the remaining engine, weaker and less dynamic than it had been, imagining the curses of the stokers who sweated away in their efforts to bully the unwilling ship into harbor. She thought of the navigator, the radio operator, the duty watch, all the others still awake across this vast ship, contemplating their return to their families, the changes that lay ahead. She thought of Captain Highfield, in his palatial quarters above them, knowing that tonight might be the last he spent at sea. We all have to find new ways of living, he had told them. New ways of forgiving.

I have to try to feel as I did when I first stepped aboard, she told herself. That sense of relief and anticipation. I have to forget that this, and he, ever happened. Instead, she would thank Chalkie every day for what he had given her.

It was the least she could do in the circumstances.

She thought she might have drifted off to sleep when she heard the sound. A cough so discreet, so far on the periphery of her consciousness that she was never quite sure afterward why it had woken her. She opened an eye, gazed across at Avice's dim shape, half expecting her to sit up and demand a glass of water. But Avice didn't move.

She sat upright, and listened.

Another cough. The kind of cough that denotes the desire to draw attention. She slid out of the chair and made her way across the floor. "Frances," a voice said, so quietly that only she could have heard it. And then again. "Frances."

She wondered briefly if she was still asleep. Next door Dr. Duxbury was singing "Danny Boy." He broke off to weep noisily, and was consoled by those around him.

"You shouldn't be here," she murmured, stepping forward. She did not open the door. They were all under the strictest instructions: there was to be no mixing this evening, the XO had warned, as if the fact of it being the last night might induce a kind of sexually charged madness.

For a moment he said nothing. Then, "I wanted to make sure you were all right."

She shook her head in incomprehension and exhaled slowly. "I'm . . . fine."

"What I said . . . I didn't mean . . ."

"Please don't worry." She didn't want to have this conversation again.

"I wanted to tell you . . . I'm glad. I'm glad to have met you. And I wish . . . I wish . . ." There was a long silence. Her heart was pounding.

The singing had stopped. Somewhere, out in the Channel, a fog-horn sounded. She stood there in the dark, waiting for him to speak again, then realized the conversation was ended. He had said all he was going to say.

Barely knowing what she was doing, Frances moved closer to the door. She laid her cheek against it, waiting in silence until she heard what she was waiting for. Then she stepped back and opened it.

In the dim light outside the infirmary, his eyes were shadowed, unreadable. She stared up at him, knowing that this was the last time she would see this man, trying to make herself accept a fate that for the first time she wanted to smash into little pieces. He was not hers to want. She had to keep telling herself that, even if every atom of her screamed the opposite.

"Well." Her wavering, brilliant smile would have broken his heart. "Thank you. Thank you for looking after me. Us, I mean."

Frances allowed herself a last look, and then, not sure why, she held out a slim hand to him. After a moment's hesitation, he took it, and they shook solemnly, their eyes not leaving each other's face.

"Time to get to bed, boys. Got to be fresh for the morning!"

They stared at each other. Vincent Duxbury's voice increased in volume as the infirmary door opened, throwing out a rectangular flood of light. "Home, boys! You're going home tomorrow! 'Home, home on the range . . .'"

She tugged him into the little room, and closed the door silently behind them. They stood inches apart, listening as the men fell out of the infirmary into the passageway. There was much slapping of backs and a brief, painful interlude of coughing.

"I have to inform you," said Dr. Duxbury, "that you are quite the finest band of men I have ever had the privilege . . . 'My merry band of brothers . . .'" His voice floated along the passageway, was briefly joined in tuneless discord by the others.

———

She was so close he could feel her breath upon him. Her body was rigid, listening, her hand still unwittingly in his. Her cool skin was blistering.

"'My merry band' . . . la la la *la*." If it hadn't been that she had chosen that moment to look up at him he might never have done it. But she had raised her face, lips parted, as if in a question, and put her hand to the cut above his brow, tracing it with her fingertips. Instead of stepping away from her, as he had intended, he raised his hand to hers, touching it, and then, more firmly, enclosing it within his own.

The singers outside increased in volume, then broke into conversation. Someone fell over and from a distance there was a muffled "You there!," the brisk steps of someone in authority.

Nicol hardly heard them. He heard instead her faint exhalation, felt the answering tremble in her fingertips. His skin burning, he brought her hand down, let it slide across his face, feeling no pain even as it touched those places that were sore and bruised. And then he pressed it, hard, to his mouth.

She hesitated, and then, with a sound that was like a little gasp of despair, she pulled back her hand and her mouth lifted to his, her hands gripping his now as if she would make them stay on her forever.

It was sweet, so sweet as to be indecent. Nicol wanted to absorb her into him, to fill her, enclose her, take her in to his very being. I knew this! some part of him rejoiced. I know her! Fleetingly, as he became aware of the heat of his own desperate need, he felt a hint of danger, something condemnatory, and was unsure whether it was directed at her or himself. But then his eyes opened and locked with hers, and in their infinite pain and longing there was something so shocking, so honest that he found he could not breathe. And as he lowered his face to hers again it was she who pulled back, one hand raised to her lips, her eyes still on his. "I'm sorry," she whispered. "I'm so, so sorry." She glanced briefly at Avice, still asleep on the bed, then lifted a hand fleetingly to his cheek, as if imprinting the sight and feel of him on some hidden part of her.

Then she was gone, the men outside exclaiming as they tried to grasp what they had seen. The storeroom door closed gently but firmly between them, the dull metallic clang like that of a prison gate.

———

The ceremony was carried out at nearly half past eleven on Tuesday night. In different circumstances, it would have been a beautiful night for a wedding: the moon hung low and magnified in a tropical sky, bathing the camp in a strange blue light, while the whispering breeze barely disturbed the palm trees, but offered discreet relief from the heat.

Aside from the bride and groom, there were just three people in attendance: the chaplain, the matron and Captain Baillie. The bride, her voice barely audible, sat by the groom for the entire service. The chaplain crossed himself several times after the ceremony, and prayed that he had done the right thing. The matron shushed the captain's own thoughts that he might not be, and reminded him that, given the state of the world around them, this one small act should not play on his conscience.

The bride sat, head bowed, and held the hand of the man beside her, as if in apology. At the end of the service she placed her pale face in her hands and sat still for some time, until her face emerged again, gasping slightly, like a swimmer breaking through water.

"Are we done?" said the matron, who seemed the most composed of them all.

The chaplain nodded, his brow still furrowed, eyes cast down.

"Sister?" The girl opened her eyes. She seemed unable, or unwilling, to look at the people around her.

"Right," said Audrey Marshall, looking at her watch and reaching for her notes. "Time of death, eleven forty-four."

24

When the aircraft carrier Victorious *reached Plymouth last night . . . some of the girls were so eager to get a glimpse of Britain that they crowded against a stanchion till it collapsed and twenty of them fell eight feet to the deck below. They were unhurt. One bride could not share the general excitement. She learned at the end of her 13,000-mile journey that her husband who was to have met her had been posted missing after a flying accident.*

DAILY MIRROR, WEDNESDAY, 7 AUGUST 1946

EIGHT HOURS TO PLYMOUTH

A naval uniform, unsupported by the human frame, is a curious thing. With its thick dark material, its braid and brass buttons, it speaks of whole other realms of being, of parades, of the effort—pressing, mending, polishing—involved in its upkeep. It speaks of propriety, routines and orderly habits, of those who inhabit it and those whose uniforms match it. Depending on its stripes, or badges, it also speaks of a history of conflict. It tells a story: of battles fought and won, of sacrifices made. Of bravery and fear.

But it tells you nothing about a life. Highfield stared at his uniform, carefully pressed by his steward, now hanging under little epaulettes of tissue paper, ready for its last outing when *Victoria* docked the following day. What does that uniform say about me? he thought, running his hand down the sleeve. Does it tell of a man who only knew who he was when he was at war? Or of a man who realizes now that the thing he thought he was escaping from, intimacy, humanity, was what he had lacked all along?

Highfield turned to the chart that lay folded upon his table with a pair of dividers. Beside it stood his half-packed trunk. He knew where his steward would have placed it, did not have to slide his hands too far under the carefully packed clothes before he found the frame that had spent the last six months face down in his drawer. Now he took it out, unwrapped the tissue paper in which Rennick had thoughtfully placed it. It was a silver-framed photograph of a young man, his arm round a smiling woman who tried, with one hand, to stop the wind blowing her hair in dark ribbons across her face.

It would make a man of the lad, he had told his sister. The Navy turned boys into men. He would take care of him.

He stared at the image of the young man grinning back at him, one arm resting on his wife's shoulders. Then he moved the chart a little and placed it upright on the table. It would be the last thing he would take from this ship.

They were a matter of hours from Plymouth. By the time the women woke, the ship would be preparing to disgorge them into their new lives. Tomorrow, from the earliest pipes, the ship would be a vortex of activity: endless lists crossed and checked, women and men queuing for their trunks, the procedural and ceremonial duties involved in the bringing of a great ship into harbor. He had seen it before, the excitement, the nervous anticipation of the men waiting to disembark. Except this time the war was over. This time they knew their leave was safe, their return permanent.

They would pour off the ship, straight into those tearful embraces, eyes shut tight in gratitude, the pawing excitement of their children. They would walk or drive off in noisy cars to homes that might or might not be as they remembered them. If they were lucky, there would be a sense of a hole filled.

Not everyone would be so lucky. He had seen some relatives turn up even after they had received the dreaded telegram, unable or unwilling to accept that their John or Robert or Michael was never coming home. You could spot them even in the teeming crowds, their eyes fixed on the gangplank, hands tight on handbags or newspapers, hoping to be proved wrong.

And then, on board, there were those like Highfield. Those whose return was not marked by joyous or clamorous thanks, but who made their way inconspicuously through the crowds of jostling, reunited families, perhaps to be met miles away by the muted pleasure of relatives who tolerated them through familial pity. Through duty.

Highfield stared again at the uniform he would wear for the last time tomorrow. Then he pulled out a chair, sat down at his desk and began to write.

> *Dear Iris,*
>
> *I have some news for you. I am not coming to Tiverton. Please send Lord Hamworth my apologies and tell him I will be happy to make up any financial disadvantage my decision might cause on his part.*
>
> *I have decided, upon reflection, that a life on land is probably not for me . . .*

———

Nicol could think of nowhere else to go. Even at a quarter to one at night the mess was a seething mass of noisy men, high on anticipation and extra sippers, pulling their photographs from their lockers and packing them into overstuffed kitbags, exchanging stories about where they would be, what they wanted to do first. If the missus could find someone to mind the kids . . . He had not wanted to sit among them, had not thought himself capable of deflecting their good-natured joshing. He needed to be alone, to digest what had happened to him.

He could still taste her. His body was charged, shot through with painful urgency. Did she hate him? Did she consider him no better than Tims, or any of them? Why had he done that to her, when she had spent weeks, years even, despising men who thought of her only in that way?

He had gone up to the flight deck.

He had not expected to find himself in company.

The captain was standing on the foredeck, in front of the bridge. He was in his shirtsleeves, head bare to the wind. Nicol, emerging on to the deck, halted in the doorway and prepared to retreat but

Highfield had spotted him and Nicol realized he would have to acknowledge him.

"Finished your watch?"

Nicol stepped forward so that he was standing beside the captain. It was cold out here, the first time he had felt properly cold since they left Australia. "Yes, sir. We're not posted outside the brides' area tonight."

"You were outside Sister Mackenzie's lot, weren't you?"

Nicol looked up sharply. But the captain's look was benign, lost in thought. "That's the one, sir." He couldn't believe that she had been disgusted. Her cool hands had been pulling him in, not pushing him away. Nicol felt almost dizzy with uncertainty. How could I have done it after what Fay has done to me?

The captain's hands were thrust deep into his pockets. "They all all right, are they? I heard two of them were in the sick bay."

"All fine, sir."

"Good. Good. Where's Duxbury?"

"He's—er—I believe he's probably taking a nap, sir."

The captain gave him a sideways look, registered something in Nicol's face and let out a faint but definite "hmph." "You married, Nicol? Not sure I can remember if Dobson told me."

Nicol paused. He stared at the point where the black sea met the sky and a patch of stars were revealed as the clouds parted, the moon briefly illuminating the endlessly moving landscape. "No, sir," he said. "Not anymore." He noted the captain's inquiring look.

"Don't become too enamored of your freedom, Nicol. A lack of responsibility, of ties . . . can be a two-edged sword."

"I'm starting to understand that, sir."

They stood there for some time in companionable silence. Nicol's thoughts churned like the seas, his skin prickling when he thought of the woman below. What should I have done? he asked himself, over and over. What should I do?

Highfield stepped a little closer to him. He pulled a cigar box from his pocket and offered one to Nicol. "Here. Celebration," he said.

"My last night as a captain. My last night after forty-three years in the Navy."

Nicol took the cigar and allowed the older man to light it, his hand braced against the sea breeze. "You'll miss it. Out here."

"No, I won't."

Perplexed, Nicol turned to him.

"I'm going to go straight back out," Highfield said. "See if I can crew merchant ships, that kind of thing. I'm told there's plenty of demand. I don't know, Nicol. These girls have made me think. If they can do it . . ." He shrugged.

"You don't feel . . . like you've earned your time on land, sir?"

The captain exhaled. "I'm not sure, Nicol, that I'd know how to be on land. Not for any length of time."

Somewhere beneath their feet, the riveted metal plates that made up *Victoria's* flight deck groaned, signaling some distant tectonic shift. The two men gazed across the repainted surface, the sectioned-off areas where her innards lay exposed to the night sky. Their thoughts drifted to the engine, whose labored efforts were apparent in the juddering, the broken trails of foam that should have been a continuous, sweeping line in the water. The ship knew. They both felt it.

Captain Highfield drew on his cigar. He was in his shirt, but he didn't seem to feel the cold. "Did you know she served in the Pacific?"

"*Victoria?*"

"Your charge. Sister Mackenzie."

"Sir." What was she doing now? Was she thinking of him? Unconsciously he raised his hand to his face where she had touched it. He had hardly heard what the captain was saying.

"Brave woman. Brave the lot of them, really. Think about it. This time tomorrow they'll know which way their future lies . . ."

With that man, the man Nicol wanted to hate, wanted to disparage for the mere fact that he had a claim to her. But the way she had described him—how could he hate the gentle, affectionate soldier? How could he despise a man who had managed, from a sickbed, to be more of a husband than he himself had ever been . . . ?

Nicol's head felt feverish, despite the chill night air. He thought he might have to leave, to be alone somewhere. Anywhere.

"Sir, I—"

"Poor girl. She's the second one on board, you know."

His skin was burning. He had a sudden urge to dive into that cool water.

"Second what, sir?"

"Widow. Had a telegram yesterday for one of the girls on B Deck. Husband's plane went down in Suffolk. Training flight, would you believe?"

"Mrs. Mackenzie's husband was killed?" Nicol froze. He felt a stab of guilt, as if he had willed this to happen.

"Mackenzie? No, no, he . . . he died some time ago. Back in the Pacific. Odd decision, really, to leave Australia with nothing to come to. Still, that's the war for you." He sniffed the air, as if he could detect the proximity of land.

Widowed?

"Look at that. Hardly worth going to sleep now. Here, Nicol, come and have a drink with me."

Widowed? The word held a glorious resonance. He wanted to shout, "She's a widow!" Why hadn't she told him? Why hadn't she told anyone? "Nicol? What do you fancy? Glass of Scotch?"

"Sir?" He glanced toward the hatch, desperate suddenly to get back to her cabin, to tell her what he knew. Why didn't I tell her the truth? he thought. She might have confided in me. He understood suddenly that she had probably believed her status as a married woman offered her the only protection she had ever had.

"Your devotion to duty is admirable, man, but just this once I'm ordering you. Let your hair down a little."

Nicol felt himself lean toward the hatch. "Sir, I really—"

"Come on, Marine, indulge me." He waited, until he was sure Nicol was heading toward his cabin. Then he glanced at him, a rare, sly conspiracy in his smile. "Besides, how will that little dog get any rest if it's always listening to you shuffling around outside the door?"

As he turned in, Highfield wagged an admonishing finger. "Not a lot gets past me, Nicol. I might be about to be pensioned off, but I'll tell you this—there's not much goes on on this ship that I don't know about."

———

By the time he leaves the captain's rooms it is too late to wake her. He does not mind now: he knows he has time. His stomach full of whisky, and his mind still ringing with that word, he has all the time in the world. He squints against the too-bright blue of the skies as he heads across the flight deck, slows along the hangar deck, and then, as he reaches the women's area, he stops, savoring the dawn silence, the sound of the gulls crying from Plymouth Sound, the sound of home.

He stares at the door, loving that rectangular slab of metal as he has never loved anything. Then, after a moment's hesitation, he turns, places his hands behind his back, and stands outside, his feet planted on the smoke-damaged floor, blinking slowly, head a little muzzy from the drink and cigars.

He is the only marine who will, tomorrow morning, be wearing an unpressed, unpolished uniform. He is the only marine to be disobeying orders by being in close, illegal proximity to the brides.

He is the only marine on duty the entire length of the hangar deck, and there is a look of something proud and proprietorial, mixed with unutterable relief on his face.

25

Australian brides—655 of them—of British sailors stepped into England last night when the 23,000-ton aircraft carrier Victorious *anchored at Plymouth. They brought with them these stories:*

ADVENTURE—*Mrs. Irene Skinner, aged 23, descendant of the Rev. Samuel Marsden, who settled in Australia in 1794, said: "We may settle in Newfoundland, in England or in Australia, or in fact anywhere where we will find adventure and contentment."*

ROMANCE—*Mrs. Gwen Clinton, aged 24, whose husband lives in Wembley, spoke of her marriage: "He was billeted with me in Sydney. I was fascinated by him, and that was the end of it."*

PESSIMISM—*Mrs. Norma Clifford, 23-year-old wife of a naval engineer: "They tell me you cannot get any shoes at all in England." She brought 19 pairs with her.*

DAILY MAIL, 7 AUGUST 1946

PLYMOUTH

"I'm not coming out. I tell you—I've changed my mind."

"Come on, Miriam. Don't be daft."

"I tell you, I've changed my mind. I've had another look at my photographs and I've decided I don't like the look of him."

Margaret sat on the edge of her bunk, listening to the urgent exchange coming from the next cabin. The women had been shouting at each other for almost half an hour now; the unfortunate Miriam appeared to have bolted herself in, and none of the others who shared the room, all of whom had been queuing for the bathroom at the time, could get dressed.

As some of the WSOs had predicted, it was chaos. Around the unfortunate inhabitants of 3F, brides ran up and down the corridors, shrieking over mislaid belongings or missing friends. There had been an endless stream of piped instructions to the men, all in preparation for disembarkation, while the air was filled with the sound of seamen calling to each other as they performed last-minute tasks. The WSOs were already congregating at the gangplank, ready for their final duties: to confirm that each bride had been checked off, was in possession of all her cases, that she would be passed into safe hands.

"Brides' second sitting, last call for the canteen, last call for the canteen." The Tannoy hissed and clicked off.

Insulated from all the activity, and without Avice and Frances, the dormitory was silent. Margaret glanced down at her outfit; she could only squeeze into one of her dresses now, and it was straining at the seams. She rubbed at a little oil mark, knowing it would do no good.

"Just pass me my slip, then, Miriam, will you? We can't stand out here all morning."

"I'm not opening the door." The girl's voice was hysterical.

"It's a bit late for that. What are you planning to do? Flap your arms and fly home?"

Her small suitcase, neatly packed, stood at the end of her bunk. Margaret smoothed the blanket beside it where Maudie had lain and took a deep, wavering breath. This was the first morning she had not been able to eat even a piece of dry toast. She felt sick with nerves.

"I don't care! I'm not coming out."

"Oh, for goodness' sake. Look, get that marine there. He'll help. Hey! You!"

Margaret sat still, conscious of a shuffling against her door. Puzzled, she opened it and stepped back as the marine fell into the cabin, in a heavy tumble of limbs.

"Hello," said Margaret, as he tried to push himself upright.

"Excuse me." A woman padded up to Margaret's door, her hair in a toweling turban. She addressed Nicol: "Miriam Arbiter's locked herself in our cabin. We can't get at our clothes."

The marine rubbed his head. It was obvious to Margaret that he was barely awake. She sniffed, noting with some surprise the faint whiff of alcohol that emanated from him, then bent down a little, to make sure he was who she thought he was.

"We're meant to be ready to go ashore in less than an hour, and we can't even get at our things. You'll have to fetch someone."

Suddenly he seemed to register where he was. "I need to speak to Frances." He scrambled to his feet.

"She's not here."

He looked startled. "What?"

"She's not here."

"How have I missed her?"

"Look, Marine, please can you sort this out? I need to set my hair or it'll never be dry in time." The girl in the doorway pointed at her watch.

"She came back last night and then she went again."

"Where is she?" He grasped Margaret's wrist. His face was alive with anxiety, as if he had only just worked out how close they all were to dispersing. "You've got to tell me, Maggie."

"I don't know." Then she understood something that had been nagging at her for weeks. "I guess I thought she might be with you."

―――――

Avice stood in the infirmary bathroom, applying a final coat of lipstick. Her eyelashes, under two layers of block mascara, widened her marble-blue eyes. Her skin, which had been ghostly pale, was now apparently glowing with health. It was always important to look one's best, especially at an occasion, and that was the marvelous thing about cosmetics. No one would know what awful things were going on inside one, given some pressed powder, rouge and a good lipstick. No one would know that one still felt a little shaky, even if there were mauve shadows under one's eyes. Underneath the dark red two-piece, firmly enclosed by a quality girdle, there was no clue that one's waist had been even an inch wider than it was now, or if what remained of one's dreams was still bleeding away into unmentionable wads of cotton padding. No one would need to know if secretly one felt like one had been literally turned inside-out.

There, she thought, as she stared at her reflection. I look—I look . . .

He would not be there to meet her. She knew this as surely as she believed that now, finally, she knew him. He would wait until he had heard from her, until he knew which way the land lay. If she said yes, he would fall on her with protestations of eternal love. He would probably spend years telling her how much he loved her, how he adored her, how anyone else (she could not bring herself to use the words "his wife") meant nothing to him. If she told him she didn't want him, she suspected he would grieve for a few days, then probably consider himself to have had a lucky escape. She pictured him now, at the kitchen table, his mind already on this ship, bad-tempered and distant with this uncomprehending Englishwoman. A woman who, if she knew Ian as well as Avice did, would choose not to ask too many questions as to the cause of his foul mood.

The WSO, for whom the word "brisk" might have been coined, stuck her head round the door. "You all right, Mrs. Radley? I've arranged for your small suitcase to be taken up to the boat deck for you so you won't have to carry anything." She smiled brightly. "There, now. Don't you look a hundred per cent better than yesterday? Everything all right?" She nodded toward Avice's stomach and lowered her voice discreetly, even though they were the only people in the room: "Did you have any more undergarments you wanted me to fetch from the laundry room?"

"No, thank you," said Avice. After everything else she had been forced to endure, she was not prepared to suffer the indignity of discussing her underwear with a stranger. "I'll be ready in two minutes," she said. "Thank you."

The WSO withdrew.

Avice placed her lipstick back in its case and dusted a last layer of fine powder over her face. She stood for a moment, turned a few degrees to each side, checking her reflection—a well-practiced movement—and then, just for a second, her face fell and she gazed baldly at herself, seeing beyond the carefully pinked cheeks, the disguised eyes. I look, she thought . . . wiser.

———

Highfield stood on the roof of the bridge, flanked by Dobson, the first lieutenant and the radio operator, and gave orders down the intercom to the coxswain as the great old warship negotiated her way by degrees into the narrower water, and the English coastline, at first a misty hint, grew into solid reality around them. Below him the sailors, dressed in their number-one uniforms, stood in perfect lines round the outside edge of the flight deck, while officers and senior ranks manned the island area—a "Procedure Alpha," or Prod A, as it was known to the men. They stood in near silence, feet apart, hands behind their backs, immaculate dress somehow disguising the tired, shabby vessel they traveled on. Coming alongside was traditionally one of the finest moments of a captain's journey: it was impossible not to be filled with pride, standing on a great warship with one's men below, the noise of the welcoming crowd already in their ears. Highfield knew that there wasn't a man among them for whom the last few months weren't briefly forgotten in the well-ordered pleasure of such a ceremony.

Not so *Victoria*. Engine hiccupping, rudder threatening intermittently to jam, the battered ship labored in, bullied by the engineers and tugs, oblivious to the beauty of the hills of Devon and Cornwall that swelled on each side of her. When he had visited the starboard engine room earlier that morning, the chief engineer reported that it was probably just as well they were finally home. He wasn't sure he would be able to get her going again. "She knows she's done her job," he observed cheerfully, wiping his hands on his overalls. "She's had enough. I got to say, sir, I know how she feels."

"Port bridge, alter course to zero six zero."

He turned to the radio operator and heard his command repeated back to him.

The light was peculiarly bright, the kind of light that heralds a fine, clear day. Plymouth Sound was beautiful, an appropriate send-off for the old ship, and a good welcome, he thought, for the brides. A few white clouds scudded across the blue sky, the sea, flecked with white horses, glinted around the ship, somehow reflecting her in a little of their glory. After Bombay and Suez, after the endless muddied blue of the ocean, everything looked an impossible green.

The docks had begun to fill almost at first light. First a few anxious-looking men, their collars turned up against the cold, smoking or disappearing briefly to refuel with tea and toast, then larger groups, families, standing in huddles on the dockside, occasionally pointing at the approaching ship. Waving at those brides who were already on the deck. The radio operator had had an exchange with the harbor-master and members of the British Red Cross. He had reported that some of the husbands had been forced to sleep in doorways; there was not a room to be had in the whole of Plymouth.

"Hands to harbor stations, hands to harbor stations, hands out of the rig of the day, clear off the upper deck, close all doors and hatches." The Tannoy closed off. It was the last command before they came into harbor.

The captain stood, his hands on the rail in front of him. They were coming home. Whatever that meant.

————

Nicol had checked the infirmary, the deck canteen and the brides' bathroom, prompting a shrieking near-riot in the process. Now he ran swiftly along the hangar deck toward the main brides' canteen, oblivious of the curious glances of the last women returning from breakfast. Arm in arm they walked, their hair set, their dresses and jackets pressed into razor-sharp creases, their shoulders hunched with excitement. Twice he had passed other marines as they headed for the flight deck; seeing him at speed, and knowing his reputation, they had assumed him to be on some urgent official duty. Only after-ward, as they registered the crumpled state of his uniform, his un-shaven face, might they have remarked that Nicol was looking a bit rough. Amazing how some men felt able to let themselves go once they knew they were headed home.

He skidded to a halt at the main doorway, and scanned the room. There were only thirty or so brides still seated: so close to disembar-kation, most were finishing their packing, waiting on the boat deck or in turrets, skirts billowing in the stiff sea breeze. He paused for a moment, waiting for this girl to turn, or that one to look up, making sure neither of them was her. Then he cursed his befuddled head.

Where would he start his search? There were people milling around everywhere. In half an hour, how was he meant to find one person in a ship, a rabbit warren of rooms and compartments, among sixteen hundred others?

———

"Trevor, Mrs. Annette." The WSO stood at the top of the gangway and waited for Mrs. Trevor to fight her way to the front of the group. There was a brief hush before a suitcase was held aloft by a blonde woman, hair set in huge ringlets, hat askew as a result of her struggle through the others. "That's me!" she squealed. "I'm getting off!"

"Your belongings have been cleared by Customs. Your trunks will be on the dockside, and you will need proof of identity when you collect them. You may disembark." The WSO moved her clipboard to her left hand. "Good luck," she said, and held out a hand.

Mrs. Trevor, her eyes already on the bottom of the gangplank, distractedly shook it and then, hoisting her case to her hip, made her way down, wobbling in her high heels.

The noise was deafening. On board the women's voices rose in a swell of anticipation, their heads bobbing as they fought to catch a glimpse of a loved one in the crowd. Around the bottom of the gangplank, several marines now stood firm, holding back the crowds pressing forward to meet them.

On the dockside, a brass band played "Colonel Bogey," and a loudhailer tried vainly to direct people away from the edge of the quay. Jostling groups cheered and waved, trying to attract attention, shouting messages that were carried away on the breeze, lost in the general cacophony.

Margaret stood in the queue, her heart thumping, hoping it wouldn't be too long before she could sit down. The woman in front of her kept jumping up and down in an attempt to see over the others' heads and had twice barged into her. Normally this would have been enough for Margaret to mutter a salty word or two in her ear, but now her mouth was dry, nervousness rooting her to the spot.

It all seemed so abrupt, so rushed. She had had no chance to say goodbye to anyone, not Tims, not the cook at the flight-deck canteen, not her cabin-mates, both of whom had vanished into thin air.

Was this it? she thought. My last links with home, just vanishing on the breeze?

As the first bride reached the bottom of the gangplank a cheer went up, and the air was lit with a battery of flashbulbs. The band struck up "Waltzing Matilda."

"I'm so nervous I think I'm going to wet myself," said the girl next to her.

"Please let him be there, please let him be there," another was muttering into a handkerchief.

"Wilson, Mrs. Carrie." The names reeled off, faster now. "Your belongings have been cleared by Customs . . ."

What have I done? Margaret thought, staring out at this strange new country. Where was Frances? Avice? For weeks this had been a distant dream, a holy grail to be grasped at in dreams, imagined and reimagined. Now it was here she felt unbalanced, unready. She thought she had never felt more alone in her life.

And suddenly there it was. Spoken twice before she heard it: "O'Brien, Mrs. Margaret . . . Mrs. O'Brien?"

"Come on, girl," said a neighbor, shoving her to the front. "Shake a leg. It's time to get off."

———

The captain had just begun to show the Lord Mayor round the bridge when an officer appeared at the door. "Bride to see you, sir."

The mayor, a pudding-shaped man whose chain of office hung from his sloping shoulders like a hammock, had shown an almost irresistible urge to touch everything. "Come to say their last goodbyes, eh?" he remarked.

"Show her in."

Highfield thought he had probably known even before he saw her who it would be. She stood in the doorway, flushing as she saw the company he was in. "I'm sorry," she said, faltering. "I didn't mean to interrupt."

The mayor's attention was on the dials in front of him, his fingers creeping toward them.

"XO, look after the mayor for a moment, would you?" Ignoring Dobson's glare, he walked over to the doorway. She was dressed in a pale blue short-sleeved blouse and khaki trousers, her hair pinned at the back of her head. She looked exhausted, and unutterably sad.

"I just wanted to say goodbye and check that there was nothing else you wanted me to do. I mean, that everything is okay."

"All fine," he said, glancing down at his leg. "I think we can say you're dismissed now, Sister Mackenzie."

She gazed down at the dockside below them, teeming with people. "Will you be all right?" he asked.

"I'll be fine, Captain."

"I don't doubt it." He realized he wanted to say more to this quiet, enigmatic woman. He wanted to talk to her again, to hear more about her time in service, to have her explain the circumstances of her marriage. He had friends in high places: he wanted to ensure that she would find a good job. That her skills would not be wasted. There was no guarantee, after all, that any of these girls would be appreciated.

But in front of his men, he could say nothing. Nothing that would be considered appropriate, anyway.

She stepped forward and they shook hands, the captain acutely conscious of the other men's curious glances. "Thank you . . . for everything," he said quietly.

"The pleasure was all mine, sir. Just glad to have been able to help."

"If there is ever . . . any way, in which I might help you, I'd be delighted if you would allow me . . ."

She smiled at him, the sadness briefly lifting from her eyes, and then, with a shake of her head, which told him he could not be the answer, she was gone.

————

Margaret stood in front of her husband, stunned briefly into muteness by the immutable fact of him. The sheer handsomeness of him in his civilian clothes. The redness of his hair. The broad, spatulate tips of his fingers. The way he was staring at her belly. She pushed back a strand of hair and wished suddenly that she had made the effort to set it. She tried to speak, then found she did not know what to say.

Joe looked at her for what seemed an eternity. She was shocked at how unfamiliar he appeared, here, in this strange place. As if this new environment had made him alien. Self-consciousness made her look down. Panicked and curiously ashamed, she felt paralyzed. Then he stepped forward with a huge grin. "Bloody hell, woman, you look like a whale." He threw his arms round her, saying her name over and over, hugging her so tightly that the baby kicked in protest, which made him jump back in surprise.

"Would you credit that, Mother? A kick like a mule, she said, and she wasn't wrong. How about that?" He rested his hand on her belly, then took hers. He gazed into her face. "Ah, Jesus, Maggie, it's good to see you."

He enclosed her in his arms again, then reluctantly released her, and Margaret found herself clinging to his hand, as if it were a lifeline in this new country. It was then that she saw the woman standing with him, a couple of steps back, a headscarf tied round her head, her handbag clutched under her bosom as if she did not want to interfere. As Margaret attempted self-consciously to straighten her too-tight dress, all fingers and thumbs, the woman stepped forward, a smile breaking over her face. "Margaret, dear. I'm so glad to meet you. Look at you—you must be exhausted."

There was the briefest pause and then, as Margaret struggled for words, Mrs. O'Brien stepped forward to fold her into her chest. "How brave you are," she said into her hair. "All this way . . . away from your family . . . Well, don't you worry. We'll look after you now. You hear me? We're all going to get along grand."

She felt those hands patting her back, smelled the faint, maternal smell of lavender, rosewater and baking. Margaret did not know who was more surprised, she or Joe, when she burst into tears.

———

The marine captain grabbed him as he was trying the door to the infirmary. Nicol pulled away from the tight grip on his shoulder. "Where the bloody hell have you been, Marine?" His face was furious.

"I've been—I've been looking for someone, sir." Nicol had exhausted most of the ship: the only conceivable place remaining was the flight deck.

"Look at the state of you! What the hell's happened to you, man? Prod A, that's what it was. All men on the flight deck. Not a bloody great hole where you should have been."

"I'm sorry, sir—"

"Sorry? *Sorry?* What the bloody hell would happen if everyone decided not to turn up, eh? Look at you! You smell like a bloody brewery."

From outside, he heard another dull cheer. Outside. He had to get outside on to the decks. There, he could check with one of the WSOs whether Frances had left the ship. For all he knew she might, at this very moment, be preparing to step off.

"I'm shocked at you, Nicol. You of all people—"

"I'm sorry, sir, I've got to go."

The marine captain's mouth dropped open. His eyes bulged. "Go? You've got to go?"

"Urgent business, sir." And then he ducked under the man's arm, the apoplectic voice still ringing in his ears as he took the steps three at a time.

————

Avice saw them before they saw her. She stood beneath the gun turret, her hat pinned tightly to her head so that it wouldn't blow away, and watched the little group below. Her mother was wearing the hat with the huge turquoise feather in it. It looked curiously ostentatious among all the tweeds, dull browns and grays. Her father, his own hat wedged low on his brow as he preferred it, kept glancing around him. She knew who he was looking for. In the mêlée of naval uniforms, he would be wondering how on earth they would ever find him. She barely noticed her surroundings, the scenery behind the dockyard. What was the point when she knew now that she would not be staying?

"Radley. Mrs. Avice Radley."

Avice took a deep breath, brushed the front of her jacket and made her way slowly to the bottom of the gangplank, her back as straight as that of a model, her chin held high as she tried to disguise the awkwardness in her walk.

"There she is! There she is!" She heard her mother's squawk of excitement. "Avice, darling! Look! Look! We're here!"

In front of her, where the gangplank met the dockside, a bride whom Avice recognized from the dressmaking lectures was ambushed at the bottom of the steps and swept into the arms of a soldier. She dropped her bag and the hat she had been holding in her left hand, and was locked to him for an interminable length of time, her hands clutching his hair, his face pressed to hers, as they occasionally broke off to touch noses and murmur each other's name. Unable to get past them, Avice had to stand there, trapped on the gangplank, trying to look away as the couple were passionately reacquainted.

"Avice!" Her mother was bobbing up and down on the other side of them like a brightly colored cork. "There she is, Wilf! Look at our girl!"

Finally, the soldier realized he was holding up the other brides, uttered a half-hearted apology, then swept his girl off to the side. You know how it is, he had grinned.

Oh, yes, Avice replied. I know how it is.

Her mother ran the last few steps to meet her, her face tearful with happiness. "Oh, darling, it's so good to see you! How about this, eh? Nice surprise?"

Her father moved forward and held her. "Your mother hasn't stopped fretting since you left. Couldn't bear the thought of you two on bad terms on opposite sides of the world. How's that for devotion, eh, Princess?"

There was such love and pride on both their faces. Avice realized, with horror, that if they carried on her face would crumple.

Deanna stepped forward. She was wearing a new cerise suit. "Which one was the prostitute? Mummy nearly came out in hives when she got Mrs. Carter's letter."

"Where's Ian?" Her mother was peering into the faces of the men in naval uniform. "Do you think he's brought his family?"

"You'd better not have lost my shoes," said Deanna, under her breath. "I want them out of your case before you disappear."

"He won't be here," Avice said.

"He's never been sent off already. I thought the men were going to be allowed to meet you!" Her mother's gloved hand pressed to her face. "Well, thank goodness we came, Wilf. Don't you think?"

"Is his family coming to meet you anyway? We've heard nothing from them." Her father took her arm. "I've brought them a wireless. Top of the range."

Avice stopped, set her face as straight as she could. "He's not coming, Dad. He's never coming. There's been . . . there's been a change of plan."

There was a short silence. Her father turned to her. Avice thought she might have heard a snort of delight from her sister. "What do you mean? You're not telling me I've just spent four hundred dollars on flights when there's no bloody celebration going to take place? Have you any idea how much this trip has cost—"

"Wilf!" Her mother turned back to her daughter. "Avice, darling—"

"I'm not going to talk about it here, on a dockside full of people."

Her parents exchanged a glance. Deanna was unable to disguise her pleasure at this unexpected turn of events. It was as if she were impressed by the scale of Avice's personal catastrophe.

As the four of them stood on the quay, the crowds milling around them, a distant loud-hailer called for someone, please, to come to the harbormaster's office to reclaim a small child. She was wearing a red coat and said her name was Molly. They had no further information.

Avice stared back at the ship. A bride was running recklessly down the gangplank in high heels. When she reached the bottom she launched herself into the arms of an officer, who lifted her off the ground, twirling her round and round in his arms. She could see he was an officer from his uniform. She had always been good on uniforms. Don't say anything else, Avice willed them, biting her lip. Don't say one more word. Or I'm going to stand here and howl so loudly that the whole of Plymouth will be brought to a halt.

Her mother adjusted her hat, pulled her fur a little closer round her shoulders, then took Avice's arm and tucked it into the crook of her own. Perhaps understanding, perhaps seeing something in her daughter's expression, she chose not to look her full in the face. When she spoke, there was a faint but definite break in her voice. "Well, dear, when you're ready we'll have a little chat at the hotel." She began to walk. "It's a very nice hotel, you know. Beautiful-sized rooms. We've got our own lounge area attached to the bedrooms and views all the way to Cornwall . . ."

———

Frances walked slowly down the gangplank, her suitcase in her right hand, the other trailing lightly down the handrail. She was, she thought, invisible in this crowd of cheering, embracing people. As she drew closer to the dockside, she saw faces she recognized from the past six weeks, wreathed in smiles, contorted in emotional tears, pressed in passion to their husbands and, just for a moment, she allowed herself to imagine what it would have been like to be one of those girls for whom there was an embrace at the end of the gangplank, for whom there was not one but several pairs of welcoming arms to claim her.

She kept walking. A new start, she told herself. That was what it was all about. I have made a new start.

"Frances!" She turned to see Margaret, her dress riding up over her plump knees as she waved wildly. Joe stood beside her, an arm round her shoulders. An older woman held her other arm. She had a kind face, not unlike Margaret's own, which was now beaming and tear-stained.

Frances went toward her. Her steps felt surprisingly unsteady on dry land and she struggled to walk without lurching. The two women dropped their bags and embraced.

"You weren't going to go without my address, were you?"

Frances shook her head, sneaking a glance at the two proud people who had claimed Margaret as their own. On the ship she and Margaret had felt like equals; now, alone in a sea of families, she felt diminished.

Margaret took a pen from her husband and accepted a scrap of paper from her mother-in-law. She put pen to paper, paused and laughed. "What is it?" she said.

He laughed too, then scribbled something on the paper, which Margaret placed in Frances's hand. "As soon as you get settled, you write me with your address, you hear? My good friend Frances," she explained to the two of them. "She helped look after me. She's a nurse."

"Pleased to meet you, Frances," said Joe, thrusting out a huge hand. "You come and see us. Whenever."

Frances tried to return some of his warmth in her own grasp. The older woman nodded and smiled, then glanced at her watch. "Joseph, train," she mouthed.

Frances knew it was time to leave.

"You take care now," Margaret said, squeezing her arm.

"I'll look forward to hearing how it all goes," said Frances, nodding at her belly.

"It'll be fine," Margaret said, with confidence.

Frances watched the three of them as they made their way to the dockyard gates, still chatting, arms linked, until people closed round her and she couldn't see anymore.

She took a deep breath, trying to dislodge the huge lump in her throat. It will be all right, she told herself. A fresh start.

At that point, she glanced back at the ship. There were men moving around, women still waving. She could see nothing, no one. I'm not ready, she thought. I don't want to go. She stood, a thin woman jostled by the crowds, tears streaming down her face.

———

Nicol pushed his way to the front of the queue and several of the waiting women protested loudly. "Frances Mackenzie," he shouted at the WSO. "Where is she?"

The woman bristled. "Do you mind? My job is to sign these ladies off the ship."

He grabbed her, his voice hoarse with urgency. "Where is she?"

They stared at each other. Then her eyes narrowed and she ran her pen down several pages. "Mackenzie, you say. Mackie . . . Mackenzie, B. . . . Mackenzie, F. That it?"

He grabbed the clipboard.

"She's gone," she said, snatching it back. "She's already disembarked. Now, if you'll excuse me."

Nicol ran to the side of the ship and leaned over the rail, trying to see her in the crowd, trying to make out the distinctive, strong, slim frame, the pale reddish hair. Below him thousands of people were still on the side, jostling, weaving past each other, disappearing and reappearing.

His heart lodged somewhere high in his throat, and, in despair, he began to shout, "Frances, Frances," already grasping the scale of his loss, his defeat.

His voice, roughened with emotion, hovered for a moment over the crowds, caught, and then sailed away on the wind, back out to sea.

———

Captain Highfield was almost the last man to leave the ship. He had undergone his ceremonial goodbye, flanked by his men, but at the gangplank, he stood, looking out, as if reluctant to disembark. When they realized he was in no hurry to move, a number of senior officers had filed past, wishing him well in his future life. Dobson made his goodbye as brief as possible, and talked ostentatiously of his next posting. Duxbury departed arm in arm with one of the brides. Rennick, who stayed longest, declined to look him in the eye, but enclosed his hand firmly within his own and told him in a tremulous voice "to take a little care after yourself."

The captain laid a hand on his shoulder and pressed something into his palm.

And then he was alone, standing at the top of the gangplank.

Those few who were watching from the dockside, the few who were minded to pay him any attention, given the more pressing matters they had to attend to, remarked afterward that it was strange to see a captain all by himself on such an occasion when there were so many crowds below. And that, strange as it might sound, they had rarely seen a grown man look more lost.

26

It was the last time I ever saw her. There were so many people, screaming and yelling and pushing to get to each other, and it was impossible to see. And I looked up, and someone was pulling at my arm and then a couple ran toward each other and just locked on to each other right in front of me and kissed and kissed, and I don't think they could even hear me when I asked them to get out of the way. I couldn't see. I couldn't see a thing.

And I think it was then that I realized it was a lost cause. It was all lost. Because I could have stood there for a day and a night and hung on forever but sometimes you just have to put one foot in front of the other and move on.

So that was what I did.

And that was the last I saw of her.

Part Three

27

It seems so sad that I left so many wonderful mates, and never heard about them from that day to this . . . one met so many people during the war in times of great comradeship. Most people who recall those days admit to making the same mistake of not keeping in touch.

L. TROMAN, WINE, WOMEN AND WAR

2002

The stewardess walked down the aisle, checking that all seatbelts were fastened for landing, with an immaculate, generalized smile. She did not notice the old woman who dabbed her eyes a few more times than might have been necessary. Beside her, her granddaughter fastened her belt. She placed the in-flight magazine in the pocket on the back of the seat in front of her.

"That's the saddest story I've ever heard."

The old woman shook her head. "Not that sad, darling. Not compared to some."

"I guess it explains why you had such a reaction to that ship. My God, what are the chances of that happening, after all those years?"

She shrugged, a delicate gesture. "Pretty small, I suppose. Although perhaps I shouldn't have been surprised. Lots of ships that leave the Navy are recycled, as it were."

She had recovered her old composure. Jennifer had watched it ease back over her, a clear shell, hardening with every mile that stretched between themselves and India. She had even managed to scold Jennifer several times, for mislaying her passport, for drinking beer before lunchtime. Jennifer had been amused and reassured. Because by the time they had got on to the flight she had said almost nothing in sixteen hours. She had been reduced somehow, more frail, despite the restorative comforts of the luxurious hotel and the first-class lounge in which the airline staff had allowed them to wait. Jennifer, holding her hand, touching the papery skin, had felt the guilt bear down on her with even more determination. You shouldn't have brought her, it said. She's too old. You dragged her across continents and kept her waiting in a hot car, like a dog.

Sanjay had whispered that they should call a doctor. Her grandmother had barked at him as if he had suggested something indecent.

And then, shortly after take-off, she had begun to talk.

Jennifer had ignored the stewardess offering drinks and peanuts. The old lady pushed herself a little upright and spoke as if they had spent the last hours not in terrible silence but deep in conversation.

"I hadn't thought of it as anything but a travel arrangement, you see?" she said suddenly. "A means of getting from A to B, a hop across the seas."

Jennifer had shifted uncomfortably, unsure how to respond. Or whether a response was even required. She let her thoughts drift briefly, wondered if she should have rung her parents. They would blame her, of course. They hadn't wanted Gran to go. It was she who insisted that they go together. She had wanted to show her, she supposed. Widen her horizons. Show her how things had changed.

Her grandmother's voice had dropped. She had turned to the window, as if she were speaking to the skies. "And there I was, feeling things I never expected to feel. And so exposed to all those people, knowing it was only a matter of time . . ." She gazed out of the window, at the heavenly landscape, the rippled carpet of white clouds sitting serenely in space.

"A matter of time . . . ?"

"Till they found out."

"About what?"

There was an abrupt silence.

"About what, Gran?"

Her grandmother's eyes landed on Jennifer and widened, as if she was surprised to find her there. She frowned a little. Lifted her hands an inch or two from the armrests, as if reassuring herself that she could.

Her voice, when it came, was polite, unemotional. A coffee-morning voice. "Would you be kind enough to get me a drink of water, Jennifer dear? I'm rather thirsty."

The girl waited a moment, then got up, found an obliging stewardess from whom she took a bottle of mineral water. She poured it into a glass, and her grandmother drank it in efficient gulps. Her hair had matted during the journey, and stood upright round her head like a dandelion halo. Its fragility made Jennifer want to weep.

"What did they find out?"

Nothing.

"You can tell me, Gran," she whispered, leaning forward. "What it was that upset you back there? Let it out. There's nothing you could say that would shock me."

The old woman smiled. Then she stared at her granddaughter with an intensity the young woman found almost unnerving. "You with your modern attitudes, Jenny. Your little arrangement with Sanjay and your therapeutic phrases and your 'letting it all out' . . . I wonder just how modern your views really are."

She didn't know what to say to that. There was something almost aggressive in her grandmother's tone. They had sat, watched the in-flight film and slept.

———

And then finally as she woke, her grandmother had told her the story of the marine.

———

He was waiting, as they had known he would be, by the arrivals barrier. Even in that crowd of people they would have recognized him anywhere: the erect bearing, the immaculately pressed suit. Despite his age, and failing eyesight, he saw them before they saw him and his hand was already signaling to them.

Jennifer stood back as her grandmother picked up speed, and then, dropping her cases on the floor, embraced him. They held on to each other for some time, her grandfather's arms wrapped tightly round his wife, as if fearful that she would absent herself again.

"I've missed you," he murmured into her gray hair. "Oh, my darling, I've missed you," so that Jennifer, kicking at the toes of her shoes, looked around at the other families, wondering if anyone had noticed. She felt somehow as if she was intruding. There was something pretty unsettling about passion in a pair of eighty-year-olds.

"Next time, you come with me," her grandmother said.

"You know I don't like to go far," he said. "I'm quite happy at home."

"Then I'll stay with you," she said.

In the car, their bags stowed behind them, her grandmother somehow rejuvenated, Jennifer had begun to tell her grandfather the story of the ship. She had just got to the part where they had discovered the broken vessel's name when he turned off the ignition. As she tried to express her grandmother's shock—in a way that did not reflect too badly on herself—she saw that he was staring at her with unexpected intensity. She broke off and he turned to his wife.

"The same ship?" he said. "It was really *Victoria*?"

The old lady nodded.

"I thought I'd never see her again," she said. "It was . . . It gave me quite a turn, I can tell you."

Her grandfather's eyes didn't leave his wife's face. "Oh, Frances," he said. "When I think of how close we came . . ."

"Hang on," Jennifer said. "Are you saying *you* were the marine?"

The two old people exchanged a glance.

"You?" She turned to her grandmother. "Grandpa? You never said! You never said Grandpa was the marine."

Frances Nicol smiled. "You never asked."

——————

He had run, he told Jennifer, as they drove out of the sprawling mass of Heathrow, the equivalent of a mile and a half by the time he had searched the ship and worked out she had already gone. All the time he had been shouting her name. Frances! Frances! Frances! And then he had done the same on land, pushing his way through the throng of people on the dockside, running in circles, physically pushing people out of the way, his uniform crumpled and dirty, the sweat beading on his skin. The pitch of emotion around him was such that nobody paid him the slightest heed.

He had shouted until he was hoarse. Until his chest hurt from running. Then, as he despaired, chest heaving, hands thrust on to his knees, the crowds at the jetty had thinned, and by chance he had seen her. A tall, thin figure, standing with her package and suitcase, her back to the sea, staring at her adopted homeland.

———

"What happened to the others?"

Frances smoothed her skirt. "Margaret and Joe went back to Australia after his mother died. They had four children. She still writes to me at Christmas."

"So no regrets?"

Frances shook her head. "I think they were very happy. Oh, don't get me wrong, Jenny dear, no marriage is without its hiccups. But I always had the impression that in Joe Margaret had found a good man."

"What about Avice?" She laid a heavy emphasis on the A, as if still amused by the anachronistic nature of her name.

"I don't really know." It had begun to rain, and Frances was watching the drops streaming diagonally across the glass. "She wrote once to say she'd gone back to Australia and to thank me for everything I'd done. Rather a formal letter, but I suppose that wasn't a surprise."

"I wonder what happened to him," said Jennifer. "I bet he divorced that woman in the end."

"Do you know? He didn't. We met him once, didn't we?" Her grandmother nudged her grandfather. "At a drinks do about twenty years ago. We were introduced to them and I remembered where I'd heard the name before."

Jennifer leaned forward, interested. "Did you say anything?"

"No. Well, not exactly. But in conversation I made sure I told him what ship I'd come over on, and gave him a bit of a look. Just so he knew. He went quite pale."

"Went home pretty early, if I remember," said her grandfather.

"That's right, he did." They beamed in joint satisfaction.

Jennifer sat back in the upholstered seat, wishing she could light a cigarette. She pulled her phone from her back pocket to see if Jay had texted her again, but her inbox was empty. She would text him when she got home. He would be back in two weeks and she wanted to see him again, but she didn't want him getting any ideas. He had the potential, she thought, to get clingy. "You know, I don't understand why you two didn't just get it together on the ship, if you liked each other so much," she said, putting her phone away. She was vaguely irritated by the way they looked at each other then, as if what they had shared had been something she could not possibly understand.

Her voice became more assertive. "It just strikes me that people of your generation often made things far more difficult for yourselves than they needed to be."

They said nothing. Then, from the back seat, she watched her grandfather's hand slide over to take her grandmother's and give it a squeeze. "I suppose that's possible," he said.

———

When he had told her the truth about his marriage, about what it meant for the two of them, she had been silent. She had sat down on the grass, her expression stilled, as if she were only just able to absorb what he was telling her.

"Frances?" He seated himself beside her on the grass. "Remember what you said to me, the night the planes went over the side? It's over, Frances. It's time to move on."

She had turned to him slowly, her expression almost fearful, as if she could not trust herself to believe what he was saying.

"This is the beauty in it, Frances. We're allowed this. No, we're entitled to it."

Underlying the determination, there was a faint note of panic in his voice, as if she might somehow disallow herself the chance to be happy, as if he, too, might be one of the things for which she felt the need to atone.

"We're entitled, you hear me? Both of us."

She had stared fiercely at her feet, and he had thought briefly that she was still closed to him. Unreachable. And then he had seen that she was hiccupping, as if her chest struggled to contain some huge, unbalancing emotion.

A faint sound escaped her, and he saw she was smiling and crying at the same time, her hand reaching clumsily across the ground for his.

They had stayed there for some unknown period of time, their hands entwined, pressed into the rough grass. Chattering families passed them on their way home, occasionally eyeing them knowingly but without curiosity, a marine and his sweetheart, reunited after a lifetime spent apart.

"You are Nicol," she had told him, as she traced the still bruised lines of his face with her fingers. "The captain told me. Nicol. Your name is Nicol." The way she said it was joyful. It made it sound like treasure.

"No," he said, with certainty, and as he spoke his voice sounded strange, unfamiliar even to himself, for it had been years since anyone had said this word. "I am Henry."

The Giver of Stars

A #1 *New York Times* Bestseller

When Alice Wright marries handsome American Bennett Van Cleve, she escapes her stifling life in England, but small-town Kentucky quickly proves equally claustrophobic. So when a call goes out for a team of women to deliver books on horseback as part of Eleanor Roosevelt's new traveling library, Alice signs on enthusiastically. This is a breathtaking story of five extraordinary women—and the men they love—and their remarkable journey through the mountains of Kentucky and beyond.

Me Before You

A #1 *New York Times* Bestseller
Now a Major Motion Picture

Louisa Clark is an ordinary girl living an exceedingly ordinary life when she takes a job working for the acerbic Will Traynor, now confined to a wheelchair after an accident. *Me Before You* brings to life two people who couldn't have less in common, and asks, "What do you do when making the person you love happy also means breaking your own heart?"

After You

A *New York Times* Bestseller

After the transformative six months spent with Will Traynor, Louisa Clark is struggling without him. Lou knows that she needs to be kick-started back to life. For her, that will mean learning to fall in love again, with all the risks that brings.

Still Me

A *New York Times* Bestseller

Louisa Clark arrives in New York confident that she can embrace this new adventure, working for the super-rich Gopnik family. Soon, she meets Joshua Ryan, who brings with him a whisper of her past. But Lou finds herself carrying secrets, and when matters come to a head, she has to ask herself, "How do you reconcile a heart that lives in two places?"

PAMELA DORMAN BOOKS/VIKING   PENGUIN BOOKS

Ready to find your next great read? Let us help. Visit prh.com/nextread

Paris for One and Other Stories

A *New York Times* Bestseller

After being stood up by her boyfriend on a romantic weekend trip to Paris, Nell discovers a version of herself she never knew existed: independent and intrepid. *Paris for One* is quintessential Jojo Moyes—as are the other stories that round out the collection.

One Plus One

A *New York Times* Bestseller

Your husband has vanished, your stepson is being bullied, and your math whiz daughter has a once-in-a-lifetime opportunity that you can't afford to pay for. That's Jess's life in a nutshell—until an unlikely knight offers a rescue.

The Girl You Left Behind

A *New York Times* Bestseller

Paris, 1916, Sophie Lefèvre must keep her family safe while her husband fights at the front. Almost a century later, Sophie's portrait hangs in the home of Liv Halston. After a chance encounter reveals the portrait's true worth, a battle begins over its troubled history in this breathtaking love story.

The Last Letter from Your Lover

Now a Major Motion Picture

In 1960, Jennifer Stirling wakes up in a hospital with no memory of who she is or how she got there. She finds an impassioned letter from a man for whom she seemed willing to risk everything. In 2003, journalist Ellie Haworth discovers an old letter containing a man's ardent plea to his married lover, and she is determined to learn their fate in this remarkable novel.

PAMELA DORMAN BOOKS/VIKING   PENGUIN BOOKS

The Horse Dancer

Sarah's grandfather gives her a beautiful horse named Boo, hoping Sarah will follow in his footsteps to join an elite French riding school. But then her grandfather falls ill. When Natasha, a young lawyer, meets Sarah, she impulsively decides to take the girl under her wing. But Sarah is keeping a secret that will change everything.

Night Music

Isabel Delancey, a violinist in London's orchestra, has always taken her privileged life for granted. But when her husband dies suddenly, leaving her with a mountain of debt, she and her two children are forced to abandon their home and move to a now-dilapidated manor Isabel inherited in the English countryside. As she fights to make her house a home, Isabel will discover an instinct for survival she never knew she had—and that a heart can play a new song.

Silver Bay

Liza McCullen will never fully escape her past, but the tight-knit community of Silver Bay offers the safety she needs. That is, until Mike Dormer shows up at her aunt's hotel.

The Ship of Brides

1946. World War II has ended and young women are fulfilling the promises made to the men they wed in wartime. For Frances Mackenzie, the journey aboard HMS *Victoria* will change her life forever.

The Peacock Emporium

In the sixties, Athene Forster was the most glamorous girl of her generation. Thirty-five years later, her daughter Suzanna Peacock is struggling with her notorious mother's legacy. The only place Suzanna finds comfort is in her coffee bar and shop, The Peacock Emporium. But only by reckoning with the past will she discover that the key to her history, and her happiness, may have been in front of her all along. . . .

PAMELA DORMAN BOOKS/VIKING   PENGUIN BOOKS

Ready to find your next great read? Let us help. Visit prh.com/nextread